WARRIOR of
LEGEND

ALSO BY KENDARE BLAKE

Three Dark Crowns
One Dark Throne
Two Dark Reigns
Five Dark Fates
Queens of Fennbirn

All These Bodies
Champion of Fate

Anna Dressed in Blood
Girl of Nightmares
Antigoddess
Mortal Gods
Ungodly
In Every Generation
One Girl in All the World
Against the Darkness

WARRIOR

of

LEGEND

KENDARE BLAKE

Quill Tree Books
An Imprint of HarperCollinsPublishers

Quill Tree Books is an imprint of HarperCollins Publishers.

Warrior of Legend

Copyright © 2024 by Kendare Blake LLC

Library of Congress Control Number: 2024940630
ISBN 978-0-06-297723-6 (hardcover) — ISBN 978-0-06-341696-3 (int.)

Typography by David Curtis
24 25 26 27 28 LBC 5 4 3 2 1
First Edition

WARRIOR of
LEGEND

ONE

WANDERER

1.

THE ARISTENE OF GLORIOUS DEATH

The hero was dead. His body lay still, his eyes open and sightless, the expression on his face less one of surprise than of wonder—one could almost believe he lay gazing up at the lightening sky after a night of good storytelling, were it not for the blood.

But the hero was dead, and no amount of tears or shouting to the gods would change that, though his people seemed inclined to try. His warriors wept and thumped their chests. They tore their clothes and struck the ground with their fists. He'd left them behind when he'd come on this quest, to spare them, but they'd followed anyway. They'd even brought his mother, dragged the poor woman out in the dark and the rain. She knelt over his body, grasping at every uninjured part of her son: his shoulders, grown so strong and broad; his arms that threw the deadliest spears. The hands she'd held since he was a boy. So perhaps she'd not needed to be dragged after all.

Reed watched them mourn from the cover of the trees. He fought brilliantly, she wanted to tell them. He came out of the darkness upon his enemies like a ghost. Five men to his one and he'd slain them all, an angry bear against their wolves. The village had thought they truly were wolves at first. Hungry wolves who raided their livestock and took meat hanging in the drying huts.

But what sort of wolves also stole young women? Only the sort of wolves who were men.

Reed had felt no remorse as she helped her hero kill them. His blade cleaved through arms and sank deep into bellies, and though one of his foes landed a mortal wound, he hadn't fallen until the last was pierced on the end of his dagger.

The hero's mother wiped rain and tears from her eyes. "Find her," she cried. "Find the Aristene!" *Find her and kill her* were words that didn't need to be spoken. That goal was plain to see from the hate upon the warriors' faces, and the flash of steel in the dawning light. Well, let them try. They would search all day, but they would find nothing. Not even a trail to follow after her clever black horse had doubled back in his own hoofprints and swum them upstream.

From her hiding place deep in the trees, Reed looked one last time at her hero. He seemed smaller now than he had been in life, and younger, his expression slack and the lines smoothed away. His glory had fed Kleia Gloria well, and his people would sing songs of him that would nourish the goddess and the order for years after. Reed had done her duty, and he had met his fate. There was no need for a long goodbye.

"Aristene!" his mother screamed.

Reed turned to look at Silco, and her black stallion's eyes glittered. Without a word, the Aristene and Areion sank back into the shadows.

Far away in Atropa, that silent city of the Aristene, the fresh infusion of glory was strong enough to pull Ferreh from sleep. She sat up and placed a hand to her chest. Her heart was pounding, the glory so great she could almost hear the cries of battle, the clash of steel. Almost taste the gold of it on her tongue in smooth spices and warmth. But beneath that was another taste: coppery and sinister, and under the triumphant heat, her limbs were tense.

The elder of the order got out of bed and reached for a wrap of linen, then changed her mind and pulled her armor through the aether. It settled on her shoulders and tightened about her waist; braided leather overlaid with engraved ovals of silver, a comforting weight to banish the last of her unease. Outside her window the white city was quiet. Only she and Tiern might have been senior enough within the order to feel the glory come, though a few might have smiled and stretched like cats. And because of her mentor bond to Reed, Aster was sure to have murmured in her sleep.

It was no mystery where the fresh infusion had come from. Glory like they'd just received came from only one source and meant only one thing: Reed's latest hero was dead.

Ferreh exhaled. Dawn was hours away, but she would get no more rest. She threw her coverlet up over her pillow.

Ferreh followed the rounded hall to the stairs that led up to the interior of the Citadel's golden dome. With traces of the nightmare still lingering, she sent her consciousness out to the edges of the Veil, to assure herself that the barrier still held. But it did. Of course it did. Thanks to Reed, the division between Atropa and the world of men was stronger than ever. This was the third hero Reed had sent to Kleia Gloria in less than a year, throwing herself into her new role of Glorious Death with a fervor none had expected. And that some feared would cost her too much.

"She'll burn herself out." That was what Aster had said when she had spoken with Ferreh and Tiern after the last hero's reaping. "She's not thinking clearly. Her heart was broken. She's in pain."

"You underestimate her," Tiern had replied. "The goddess chose her for this."

Aster had looked at Ferreh, and Ferreh had seen the question in her gray eyes. *Did Kleia Gloria choose her? Or did you?*

For it had been Ferreh who'd bestowed the gift, giving the initiate her blood to drink, and with it that terrible purpose: Glorious death, which ensured that every hero Reed was granted from the well was fated to meet their end at the point of a blade, at the end of a spear, in a hail of arrows. That all were fated to die.

"What if she gets hurt?" Aster had asked. "What if she dies? What will it all have been for?"

Ferreh mounted the stairs, pushing the memory aside. Aster was a good Aristene and a good soldier. A good mother. But she was no leader. She didn't carry the fates of the order upon her back. She didn't see the will of their goddess. Aster saw only Reed.

As she stepped up into the great space of the dome, Ferreh's skin prickled, not from the cold—nowhere in Atropa was ever truly cold—but from the quiet. The high, cut windows were open and allowed air and moonlight to bounce off the walls and the floor, but there was no sound. Once, long ago, the nights had been loud with Aristene. They had milled through the streets, had crowded out the darkness with their drinking and songs. But now . . .

Across the dome sat the sacred well, a haphazard shape crafted of multicolored stones; light-colored stone the shade of bright sand, and smooth, black veins of obsidian. Flat layers of dull gray shale. Each piece taken from a different place. The well had a peculiar beauty in the daylight, but tonight the dim turned it monstrous, tricks of the shadows making it appear to slant and crouch, making it seem small, and yet also larger than it should be.

Ferreh walked over to it. The elder of the order wasn't fooled by shadows any more than she was frightened by dreams. She passed the painted murals on the walls, their vibrant color muted in the dark. She cast a glance at the silver circle of the World's Gate sleeping within the floor.

"You felt it, too?"

Ferreh jumped like a poked cat. "Tiern. I didn't hear you."

Tiern stepped up from the last stair, her hair of many colors loose around her shoulders. She too was in her armor, the silver lighter and sharper than Ferreh's, the white cape shorter. But that was unremarkable. Tiern was always in her armor. It was whispered that she even slept in it, if indeed she ever slept. She joined Ferreh beside the well and took her hand, blowing on Ferreh's fingers as if to warm them, her thumb gently stroking Ferreh's deep brown skin in a rare show of physical affection. "So? Are you going to look or not?"

Ferreh placed her hand upon the heavy stone cap but found that she didn't want to remove it. "I don't need the well to show me what I already know. Glorious Death has sent us another hero."

"But something troubles you." Tiern reached out and removed the well covering herself, sliding it over to rest against the base. "Something serious enough to scare you into your armor in the middle of the night."

"You're not the only one who finds the silver and white a comfort."

"I don't find it a comfort." Tiern looked down at the silver that adorned her chest like a layer of gleaming dragon scales. "I just look good in it." She smiled, waiting.

"It's something about Reed," Ferreh said. "A sense of something wrong. It began not long after she sent her first hero to the goddess. And it is getting worse." At first it was nothing—a worry that was barely more than an itch between her shoulder blades. But the itch had grown to a sting, and from a sting to a burn. Now it was a seed stuck between Ferreh's armor and her skin, and the longer she left it there the deeper it cut and the more it embedded itself.

"Machianthe," said Tiern. "Her name is Machianthe now. And if you don't start using it, it's never going to stick."

It never will stick, Ferreh almost said. *Reed will always be Reed.* But the words wouldn't take shape. They suddenly felt untrue.

Ferreh laid her hand upon the cool stone. She leaned over the side of the well and looked down.

Despite the shadows, the waters within the sacred well shone brightly with reflected moonlight. For a moment, Ferreh thought that was how they would remain: gently rippling, a balm from the goddess for her troubled thoughts. And then the water began to swirl.

It moved slowly at first. Lazily, like it was annoyed by her seeking. But soon enough the water inside the sacred well was a whirlpool, and in the center, Ferreh saw Reed.

Only not the Reed she knew.

This Reed walked with a lowered brow, and the whole of her body was shrouded in darkness. Her hands dripped blood, and there was something wrong with the way she moved. Some change to her limbs and the slant of her shoulders. In the vision, she raised a blade to cleave a man in two—and didn't stop until he was hacked to pieces. Ferreh gasped, and Reed's eye shifted as if she could see her through the water.

Ferreh reeled away from the well so far that her back slammed against the wall of the dome.

"What?" Tiern cried. She gripped the sides of the well and looked into it, but Ferreh knew she would see nothing. The vision was already gone, the waters already still. All the same, Tiern slid the stone cap back into place, leaning hard upon it as if to seal something inside. She took Ferreh by the shoulders.

Ferreh let the other elder lead her from the dome and through the halls of the Citadel, to the half-circle room where they often took their ease. The same room of seats and cushions, tables and game boards where they had first set eyes on Reed, back when she was a skinny child with long, tan limbs and sharp teeth. Ferreh felt herself placed amid the cool pillows. She breathed deep of the breeze that moved between the pillars as Tiern used a torch to start a fire. She heard the creak of a pot being swung over the flames, and sometime later, a warm stone cup was placed between her hands.

"Drink."

Ferreh sipped. It was too sweet and too hot, but the burn in her throat felt good. It was also unstrained and dotted with floating, suspended leaves. Tiern hadn't called for an acolyte to brew it. She'd known that the elders required privacy.

"Is that better?" Tiern asked.

"Yes," Ferreh lied, even as the vision from the well draped her like damp cloth. She could still feel the mist of the water as it churned and struck her face. She could still smell the cloying mineral scent.

"What did you see?"

Ferreh gazed down into the dark liquid of her tea. "Only my own fears."

"But what did you see?"

When Ferreh didn't answer, Tiern looked away, staring into the fire.

"You saw a warrior who could cut down any enemy," she said. "With hands full of blood, and eyes—"

Ferreh looked up.

"You are not the only one who dreams."

"So what do we do?" Ferreh asked.

"Nothing."

"But what we saw—"

"What we saw was the weapon of the order," Tiern said. "The weapon we set out to create."

"No, Tiern. What we saw was a warning. The goddess's warning, given to us so that we may yet have time to avert it." She waited for Tiern to agree, as she always did. But she was surprised when the other elder chuckled.

"Gentle Ferreh." In the firelight Tiern's eyes were as jewels in the hilt of a dagger. "Your schemes have rebounded on you. You wanted the girl to love us so she would take on this duty willingly. You didn't imagine that you would come to love her back.

"I love her, too," Tiern went on. "In my way. And unlike you, I will love her no matter what."

"No matter if she becomes . . . This cannot be what you want," Ferreh said.

"The order safe? Our city secure? That is more than what I want; that is my task. That is our task, sister, and you knew—nothing comes without a cost."

But in Ferreh's mind, glorious death had been the cost. Reed's entire immortality spent guiding heroes to their dooms; how could Kleia Gloria ask for more than that? And if she could, then what sort of goddess had she, in her desperation, become?

"I will not let this happen," Ferreh said, and Tiern looked at her pityingly.

"There is nothing you can do."

"There is always something that can be done. And I swear to you, Tiern, that I will find a way to save her."

2.

TRAVELING WITH AREION

Reed and Silco stayed with the river, putting distance between themselves and the dead hero. Since Silco had no fondness for swimming, they kept to the shallows or cantered along the bank, heading north against the current where boats would be slow to follow. Only once had she thought she heard their pursuers and left the river to hide in the ferns. But it was only a family of small, striped jackals howling and barking a chorus.

By midmorning they'd traveled far enough to feel confident they weren't being followed. Reed dismounted and removed Silco's saddle and bridle, then started a small fire on the shore. She waded into the shallows to feel along the sandy bottom with her toes for the place where the bank dropped off and clams liked to make their beds, and when she found it, lowered herself in up to her chin. She searched the silt with her fingers. It wasn't long before she touched the edge of a shell, and smiled as she felt it pull closed. She dug it up: a nice large clam, dark and rippled, nearly the size of her palm. She threw it onto the bank and went back for another.

It was comforting work, where the current was slow and the world quiet, no voices but insects and birdsong. Reed had known how to fish and clam since she was a child. Her mother had taught her. She pulled up another oval shell and rinsed it clean of sand. It had been a long time since she'd thought of her mother. Her first mother, who had been killed by Ithernan raiders along with the rest of her family, in a settlement beside a river not unlike this one. Reed remembered how her mother's arms had thrust out straight when she'd charged the raiders who attacked them. But when she tried to recall the sound of her voice, the voice that rose in her memory was of another, more recent mother: the mother of her hero.

Ronja had been her name. And right then she would not have been speaking but screaming, wailing in pain over the fallen body of her son.

Reed threw another clam up onto the bank. He'd been a good hero, already a leader and blooded in battle, but young enough that he'd known little of betrayal. It had been easy to befriend him and earn his trust. Even easier to flatter him and convince him to hunt down his enemies all alone.

Well, not alone. She'd been there, to fight at his side. And to remain in his shadow when the time came, and let him charge ahead to meet his glorious fate.

That glory still danced at the edges of her vision in bits of gold. It had kept her and Silco warm as they splashed through the river. Reed turned around, wondering where the black colt had gone, and saw him, or rather, she saw his back, as his head and neck were submerged as he grazed on the eelgrass that swayed along the bottom. She watched for a long time as her headless horse wandered along the depths. A very long time, longer than a mortal horse could have possibly stayed under. But Silco was an Areion now. An immortal horse of the Aristene, and as such he could hold his breath longer and run farther than other horses, even with his bad hoof.

Still, he'd been under for a long time.

"Silco!"

The black horse's head popped up from the river, eyes squinted against the wet. Long grass trailed from either side of his mouth like a great green beard. Reed laughed and went over to tug the ends.

"Do you think you can catch me a fish while you're at it?" she asked, and he shook his head and sprayed her with water droplets.

Reed went to the shore and gathered her clams. She didn't have a pot to boil them so instead she cooked them on a hot stone, steaming the shells open with some wine from the wineskin that hung from Silco's saddle. After she'd eaten she called Silco out of the river to dry (he obeyed, but when he reached the shore he rolled in the sand) and lay back in the sun.

She wasn't sure how much time had passed when she awoke to movement in the trees. Not long—the shadows had only shrunk toward midday. She looked at Silco and the horse betrayed nothing, but his left ear had turned in the direction of the woods. Reed glanced at her boots lying in the grass along with the knives she kept tucked inside. *Let it be only a deer, or another family of jackals*, she thought. *Let it be the wind.* She had done her duty by the hero; her guidance of him hadn't been out of malice. She had no desire to fight his friends or cause his people more pain.

It was only for the glory, she thought, imagining what she would say to them. *For the greatness of his deeds, and the bravery that his memory will bring to the world.*

But their pain was too fresh. They wouldn't understand.

She and the Areion waited in the quiet, but no screaming warriors charged them from the trees. No arrows flew to sink into their sides.

Reed stood and put on her boots. She brushed the last of the dried sand from Silco's flanks and put his saddle back on, then kicked out the embers of her fire. "We should keep moving," she said. "It's most of the day yet before we can open the Veil and return home." Silco stomped his bad hoof in what might have been agreement, but he gazed longingly at the river and its rich stores of eelgrass.

Home, Reed thought. Atropa. Strange how much she ached to return to it, yet once she was there, found herself anxious to leave. Since she'd become an Aristene she'd spent no more than four days in the white city at a stretch. She rubbed her neck. She was weary, and not only because of a morning spent on the run. Three young heroes had gone to Kleia Gloria in the space of less than a year. She could almost hear Aster's words, whispered into her ear: *Reed, there is no racing through immortality.* She had plenty of time. Time was what she chose it to be.

But Reed was newly immortal, and that would take some getting used to. She heard a splash and turned to Silco. He'd backed up to the river and plopped both of his hind hooves in.

"No. You've had enough." Another splash. Another step. "Silco! You have your saddle on!" Splash, splash, his eyes widening as he went deeper, as if he had no idea how such a thing was happening. "Sil . . . co . . . ," she growled, and the horse turned tail and plunged back under, soaking his saddle and all Reed's scant belongings with it. She charged into the water, boots immediately soaked, to throw herself at him with a screech. He lifted his head. His mouth was again full of long grass and he happily slapped her with it.

"Is this truly the best the Aristene have to offer?"

Reed and Silco froze and looked at the shore. Veridian stood upon the bank. The apostate of the order, who along with Aster had rescued them from the Ithernan raiders so long ago. Her tall red horse, Everfall, stood beside her, also watching.

"Veridian!" Reed wiped water from her eyes, aware that she and Silco looked like a pair of drowned rats. "What are you doing here?"

"Looking for you," Veridian replied. "I smelled the glory last night like smoke upon the wind. 'That could only be Reed,' I said. 'I should seek her out, make sure that she hasn't been injured.'" A broad grin spread across Veridian's cheeks and Reed exhaled in relief.

Reed waded onto land and embraced the shorter woman. It was a soaking and soggy embrace, but Veridian was unlikely to mind; as usual, she was dressed like a vagabond, in a threadbare shirt and worn-thin leather leggings. Her long blond hair hung down her back, twisted with knots in some places.

"Don't tell Aster," Reed said.

"That you were frolicking in the river with your Areion like a pair of ducklings? Of course I'm going to tell her."

"She still thinks of me as her initiate."

Veridian gazed fondly up at Reed, searching out the changes that had come since Reed's Joining in the sacred cave. She'd gotten no taller, but there was a firmness to her muscle that hadn't been there before. "You will always be her initiate. But give her time. A hundred years, and she'll stop treating you like a child."

Reed rolled her eyes. But she would be lying if she said that part of her didn't relish that. She would never take having a mother for granted, having someone in whose eyes she was always young, always learning, always loved.

"Show me your armor," Veridian said.

Reed stepped back and called it up, drawing it from the aether to settle upon her shoulders and tighten about her waist. It flooded her blood with strength and magic, and her heart beat faster seeing its brightness reflected upon Veridian's face. The apostate walked around her in a circle and whistled.

The armor of a full Aristene was finer than that of an initiate, whose magic was only borrowed from their mentors. When Reed's true armor had come to her, it was fuller, with a thicker silver plate upon her chest and bands set upon her back like ornate bones. Upon each of her leather wrist guards, the goddess had stamped a portrait of Silco.

"It's not as grand as Lyonene's," Reed said, looking down at it. "Her wrist guards and greaves are etched in gold." Uncommon armor for an uncommon warrior, Lyonene liked to say. Her armor allowed for more movement as well. And more bared skin.

"Yours will be far grander, in time," said Veridian, though she didn't sound happy about it. "An Aristene's armor changes with her deeds. And your deeds are already becoming legend."

Reed traced her fingers around the portrait of Silco on her wrist. One day she might be completely covered with beautiful engravings. She might bear a shield as fine as Ferreh's. Reed stole a glance at Veridian. She'd become an apostate long ago, choosing to leave the order rather than become a Glorious Death. What became of an apostate's armor? Did it tarnish? Did the leather fastenings rot away to nothing? She knew that Veridian still fought with the strength of an Aristene. But she had never called her armor, and when they'd traveled through the Veil to Atropa, it hadn't appeared as the others' had.

"Did they give you a new name?" Veridian asked.

"Machianthe."

"Machianthe," Veridian repeated, trying it out on her tongue. "It's a fine name."

"A fine waste, more like," Reed smiled. "Everyone still just calls me Reed. And I'm still Reed in my own head."

"We all have many things we're called," the apostate said thoughtfully. "To me, for instance, you will always be Foundling. Where do you go from here?"

"I was returning to Atropa."

"So soon? Why not put it off? There's a port not far with a good inn. Stay a night and keep an immortal outcast company."

Reed turned back to the river as if the mouth of the Veil was already there, yawning black. She wanted to return. To bask in the elders' praise of her newest offering. And already she could feel the call of the sacred well, and the next hero inside it.

"Come now, Machianthe. It's only one night."

She turned back. "All right. One night."

3.

AN APOSTATE'S CHOICE OF INN

The road they walked was rutted and overgrown. Reed squirmed in the saddle, uncomfortably damp thanks to Silco's last dive for more eelgrass.

"Has he spoken yet?" Veridian asked with amusement, watching as the pair of them engaged in their usual war of wills: Reed shifting her weight and the horse giving a buck.

"That's only a story old Aristenes tell to initiates," Reed grumbled. None of the Areion in the order had ever spoken. Or at least not with their mouths. All were able to get their points across with well-placed teeth, hooves, or tails.

"It is no story," Veridian said. "Everfall talks. In his sleep."

Reed turned sharply to eye the tall red gelding, whose gaze remained fixed on the road. Reed cocked an eyebrow. "And what did he say?"

"He said, 'aimless.'" Veridian took a breath and imitated a horse groaning in his sleep. "Eeeemwissss." She laughed when Reed's lips drew into a thin line. "You look like Aster when you do that. But perhaps I was only hearing things. You'd think they'd all have spoken by now, if they were actually able. Especially considering what we've done for them." The apostate tugged at the collar of her threadbare shirt so the tip of her heart scar showed pink. It was the mark borne by every Aristene and the price of joining the order: a sword driven through your chest by your own hand. When Reed had pressed the blade to her heart inside the sacred cave, Silco had been a mortal horse. When she opened her eyes as an Aristene, he had been something else, and the sword lay once again in her hand, the wound in her chest already healed.

"Maybe we should try to teach them," Reed suggested. She prodded Silco's shoulder with her finger. "And maybe only curse words." The black colt twisted his neck around and bit her in the foot. She smiled, and then grimaced as he took a bad step into a rut. At least it was a short ride to the port city of Verrin, where according to Veridian they would find warm, soft beds of straw and good food.

They caught sight of it just before sunset, nestled along the shores of Basin Cove. To Reed it looked like a termite colony, mud built upon mud. But as the sun dipped toward the water it cast Verrin in pinks and purples, and oil lamps lit in windows, dots of orange and yellow flickering to life and giving away the shapes of buildings. From a distance, Verrin showed its share of pretty lights, but up close it was squalid. As they rode through the streets, the air reeked of unkempt gutters and even less-kempt rats, and of refuse left to rot in the streets downwind of the markets.

"This is the city with the cozy inn?" Reed asked.

Veridian shrugged. She called to one of the children chasing rats in the gutter. "Boy! Where is the finest stable?"

He paused in his rat-catching to peer up at them through one slitted eye. "The finest?" It was unclear whether he doubted the apostate's ability to pay or the quality of his city, but eventually he gestured vaguely up the street. "That way and past the candlemaker."

"Thank you." Reed tossed him a copper.

The boy's eyes brightened. He clutched the coin and ran to catch up.

"I can show you to the groom you want. If you're looking to cure that foot of his," the boy said, studying Silco's ambling, uneven stride.

"There is no curing that foot of his," Reed said, and she and Veridian urged the horses to a trot, Silco's jolting, his head bobbing— exaggerated, she thought, for the boy's benefit.

"Then why do you ride him?" the boy called as they left him behind.

"Because he is mine," Reed called back.

Up the street they passed the candlemaker, and a shabby marketplace, the canopies sagging and torn. They dismounted beneath a swinging sign—a wooden placard painted not with a horse but a goat and a cart.

"Not a good omen," Reed commented.

"Don't be so glum." Veridian took Everfall's reins from over his head. "This is life on the road. Gone are your days of endless summer spread out in the shadow of Storm King Mountain." That was true. The days when to fight meant to spar with blunt-edged practice swords and draw no blood, when hunting meant grabbing one of Aster's stupid Orillian noblebirds straight out of a bush, had passed. Life in the Summer Camp was only for initiates.

Reed thought of Lyonene, out in the world, guiding her own heroes. And she thought of Gretchen, the friend who had left them, who had chosen a mortal life with a boy she loved. She missed them. But at least she would never lose Lyonene. She and Lyonene would meet in Atropa until the order's days came to an end.

As Veridian haggled with the grooms, Reed wandered up the street to get a view of the harbor and feel the salt air touch her skin. The port of Verrin was nothing grand, no vast marketplace of brightly colored stalls and merchants with jewels in their belts. It was a long stretch of shore and wooden docks, where seabirds cried riding currents of air, webbed feet hanging in the wind like two tiny orange sails as they searched for smelt or the dropped pieces of some sailor's breakfast. Reed scanned the flags of the few larger vessels, noting the eagle and snake of Valostra and two flying the red stripes of Erleven. She always searched the flags in ports, and smiled whenever she saw the blue-and-gold shield of Cerille or the black-and-gold of Rhonassus. But in truth, she was always looking for one ship in particular: the salt-stained sails of Glaucia on the ships of Prince Hestion.

King Hestion now. For he was king there, or would be soon enough since his brother was dead. Since her Hero's Trial, Reed had stayed far from Glaucia's borders. Yet sometimes when she passed through a port, curiosity would get the better of her, and she would find herself in a tavern asking for news. The only tales she'd heard were from the War of Rhonassus, of Prince Belden's great and glorious sacrifice when he'd killed the monster king at the cost of his own life.

That tale was the legend the Aristene intended. So Belden's glory would spread across the world upon the waves.

"No vessels from ports you know?"

Reed startled as Veridian joined her. "You're worse than Aster. Sneaking up on me. Assuming you know what I'm thinking."

"Perhaps you're just no good at hiding it," Veridian said. "But keep yourself away from Glaucia. No matter how much you think you'd like to know—you wouldn't want to know."

"I owe it to him," Reed said. "To make sure that he's thriving."

"Why?"

"Because I killed his brother."

"You did no such thing," Veridian said, her tone sharp, as if she took the view as a personal affront. "But stay away all the same. The welcome you'd receive in Glaucia might be a sword to your throat, or an arrow through your back. And you can't go letting yourself get killed after Ferreh bled her gift for you, Glorious Death." She gestured back to the stable. "We should find another. These prices are too high."

"Just pay them," Reed said. She shoved her pouch of coins into Veridian's chest.

Veridian smiled and reached inside. "Now that's sorted, let's go and find ourselves some drink!"

Before she followed, Reed cast one more look toward the ships. But Veridian was right. For better or worse, all that had passed between her and Hestion was over.

Reed suspected that during the day the tavern would look like little more than a mud hovel, but at night, lit from within by lamps and candles, the place looked as inviting as any castle. The sign nailed to the wall was weathered with age, but the carved image of a cup, plate, and knife was still clear enough. She and Veridian made their way inside and fit themselves into a table in a shadowy corner.

"Do you have any food left?" she asked the tavernkeeper when the old woman came to set down two cups of ale.

"The bottom of a kettle of fish stew that's not much fish and mostly clams," the woman replied. "A loaf of bread for three coppers more." Veridian gestured with her fingers and Reed set a piece of silver on the table. The woman eyed her suspiciously before sliding it into her palm. "Best not be showing silvers in here, miss." She glanced at Veridian, scraggly-haired and looking like a beggar, dirty and thin. Then she looked at Reed, tall and broad-shouldered with a sword in its scabbard set beside her on the bench. "Not even such a large miss as you."

"Thank you for your advice," Reed replied.

"And for more ale!" Veridian called as the tavernkeeper wandered away. "Imagine, thinking us helpless. Calling you 'large miss.'"

"She was only being kind. We're two women, traveling alone. And you look"—Reed paused when the apostate's eyes fixed on her—"little."

"I am little." Veridian swallowed the last of her ale. "But all that means is that no one sees me coming. Besides, there's no one here fit to give us trouble. Most are half-asleep over their cups."

The tavernkeeper returned with the stew, along with a whole, small loaf of brown bread, and even a dish of butter. Instead of more ale she set down a clay carafe of wine.

"Even I know our ale's no good," the woman said. "There's rooms in the back as well, if you'd like one. That silver is more than enough to buy you a meal and a night's lodging."

"We sleep with our horses," Veridian replied, and the woman squinted curiously.

Reed tore off a chunk of bread and dragged it through the butter.

The wine had been sweetened with honey, probably to mask a lack of quality, but she drank it anyway. It made the stew more palatable. It truly was the bottom of the kettle, full of silt from the clams, and tasted like a muddy riverbed.

Reed's eyes wandered across the tavern. In the center, a table of three fishermen pushed away their emptied bowls and turned their attention to their pitcher. Others sat alone, scraping bits of bread across empty plates. No one glittered to her Aristene eyes. There were no heroes here tonight, not even a whisper of glory upon the air.

"Your last hero is not even ash on his funeral pyre," Veridian said. "And you're already hungry for more."

Reed recalled her magic like a hawk to its perch. "Of course I am. I am an Aristene now. That is the Aristene nature."

"Is it?" Veridian asked mildly. She lifted her bowl to her lips, and chewed through fish and clams. Reed could hear the silt grinding against her teeth. She shouldn't have spoken so, lecturing Veridian on Aristene nature, as if the apostate had not been of the order, and for much longer. It couldn't be easy for Veridian to watch Reed walk the same path that she had turned away from. The exact same path: for Tiern had offered the blood of glorious death to Veridian, too. But Veridian had said no.

"Well." Veridian refilled Reed's cup. "For this one night at least, can you not leave these farmers alone? Let them die old and in their beds."

"Of course." Reed sipped her wine. She didn't say that Verrin was a port city, and most of these men were sailors, not farmers. She didn't ask how many men Veridian had actually seen die old and quietly in their beds. In her experience, death was rarely merciful.

"This hero you sent to the goddess last night—how many does that make for you?"

"Three," Reed said.

"Three heroes dead in less than a year."

"Three glorious deaths," Reed amended, voice low.

"The elders must be pleased." And indeed they were. After the first they'd been relieved—after the second, Tiern had laughed with joy, and smacked Reed so hard on the back that it had left a brief bruise beneath her armor.

Veridian refilled her own cup and drained it. She was drinking too much; just watching her gulp and wipe away the drops that ran down her chin made the bad stew sit cold and heavy in Reed's belly.

She glanced at the three fishermen as they laughed, heads thrown back and teeth showing, and with slight surprise she realized that they looked like her father. They had the same wild black hair, worn in the same style. The same hawkish noses. The same brown eyes that wrinkled at the corners and danced when they laughed.

"Sailors from Sirta," Veridian said, following her gaze. "I could take you there, if you wish. It hasn't been so long since your family left it for your settlement in Orillia. We could find what family remains. Uncles. Cousins. Even the parents of your father, or mother."

Reed watched the sailors drink their ale and pick at their bread. Though the language they spoke was foreign to her ears, the tone and rhythm felt familiar, as if she understood the sentiment if not the words. But that was an illusion. By now she no longer remembered what her father really looked like, and of her mother all she remembered clearly was the shape of her body when she charged the raider. Her unblinking eyes, lit by fire, telling Reed to stay hidden. It was after that, that Reed's memories grew clearer. Because after that there was Aster, and Silco. The feeling of being carried away on the front of Rabbit's saddle. And there was Veridian.

"You've offered that before," Reed said. "After you saved me, when Aster wanted to bring me to the elders. You said I should come with you to Sirta instead. I said no then."

"And you're saying no now." Veridian raised her cup so Reed had to raise her own—she touched them together and both drank. "I just thought I'd ask, once more."

Veridian called for another carafe of wine and cajoled Reed into paying for it. They ate more bread and some crumbling cheese. They drank, and soon enough, were drunk, Reed's elbows resting heavily atop the table.

"Who would win in a fight between you and Aethiel?" Reed asked. Aethiel, the enormous Aristene with the band of black tattooed across her forehead. The Aristene who had once been a queen of the famed island of Fennbirn.

"Aethiel is my sister, and my friend," Veridian replied. "She is an admired ally. And I would lay her flat on her back before she knew what was happening."

Reed laughed. "That can't be true. Aethiel is strong and brutal and . . . so much larger than you."

"Larger does not mean better. Look at you and Lyonene—" She tapped her temple with a forefinger. "It is we small and clever ones you must look out for."

"Then what about . . . you and Aster? Have you ever sparred?"

"You are like a child." Veridian grinned, swaying. "Asking

questions and wishing for tales."

"But who?"

"Aster is the most balanced warrior I have ever known." She took a drink. "And I would beat her soundly."

Reed's mouth drew into her familiar thin line. "I'm starting to think wine gives you an inflated view of yourself."

"You were the one who asked. But it would never come to that. Aster and I would never fight. I would lay down my sword."

Reed rested her chin in her palm. "How did you fall in love?" she asked.

"Has she never told you?" Veridian glanced at her sidelong, but it was plain that the memory was fond. Then she scoffed. "For an ox, you have grown the eyes of a calf."

"Fine." Reed thought a moment. "Then what about Ferreh and Tiern?"

"Who would win in a fight?" Veridian leaned back. "Now that is an interesting question. Few Aristene now living can remember what Ferreh was like in battle. But she defended the white city when it came under attack. Some say she was among the ones who worked the spell that whisked Atropa away behind the Veil."

"I thought Kleia Gloria did that."

"But through who? The goddess works through the Aristene. She works through you; she would work through me, if I would let her. She doesn't come down into the worlds of men and smash them with her own fists . . . not anymore." Veridian sighed wistfully.

"Now back to the question—Tiern is the teeth of the order, and she has earned that title. When she fights she is more than warrior; she is a monster."

Reed had seen that. Tiern had battered down the Rhonassan defenses in the final battle of her Hero's Trial. She'd leaped atop the unbreachable wall and rent armored men to pieces. The apostate paused, and for a moment the game took on a serious glint. If the elders fought, the entire city of Atropa was like to collapse around them.

"I suppose it is anyone's guess," Veridian said. "But my coin would be on Tiern."

Reed leaned back. It was late and the tavern nearly empty. They'd best be making their way back to the stable and the horses. She gathered up the last of their bread as a snack for Everfall and Silco. But as she stood, the apostate's hand shot out and grabbed her by the wrist.

"And what of you?" Veridian asked. "One day Aristene will sit around tables like these and ask these same questions about Machianthe."

Reed smiled. "I can't even best Lyonene."

"That won't be true for much longer. Soon you'll be able to lay Lyonene in the dirt. Soon you'll be able to hurt Aster."

"I wouldn't do any of those things." Reed tried to pull free, but Veridian held her fast. The joviality had gone from her eyes, reddened from drink. They fixed upon Reed, the apostate's fingers digging in deep as she jerked her closer.

"Listen to me," Veridian said, her voice a harsh whisper. "I may be only an apostate, but I am also a warrior of centuries. You go too fast. You send heroes to their deaths like it is nothing."

"It's not nothing—"

"Be silent! Listen!" Veridian swallowed. Her eyes wobbled. "I know you do it because you are running from something. But if you keep on for much longer you will forget what you run from and only run toward. Toward and toward, to death and more death. You can't keep doing this and keep . . . yourself." Reed might have asked what she meant, but the apostate dropped abruptly asleep, her chin lowering to the table with a soft thud.

Reed smoothed the ragged blond hair out of Veridian's eyes. She looked innocent, and sad—a frown bent the edges of her mouth and tugged at her brow; her fingers curled and showed the dirt embedded beneath her short, uneven nails. It was hard to believe that this was the same fierce woman who had freed her from the Ithernan raiders with coin and combat, that this was one of the order's greatest, whose gift allowed her to see the beats of past battles and whose aim with a bow had never been matched.

"Why won't you just come home?" Reed whispered. "To be happy again, with Aster."

Veridian's eyes fluttered open. "Don't leave me, Reed," she said.

"Rest," Reed said. "I won't leave. Not tonight."

4.

MISSING MENTOR

Ferreh found Aster at the bottom of the slow slope of road that led to the site where the new library would be built. She was bent over a table, staring at drawn plans. Her gray Areion, Rabbit, stood beside her, her long face draped over Aster's shoulder. The mare saw the elder first, and nudged her rider upright.

"Elder," Aster said, and smiled.

Ferreh glanced at the plans, held down upon the table by four flat stones.

"We've added columns." Aster pointed to the etching of the portico, outlined in charcoal, the columns large and topped with the carved heads of horses. "They'll be roughly shaped by the laborers in the quarry before being transported through the Veil to be finished here."

"They will be beautiful," said Ferreh. Aristene artists and sculptors were among the finest in the world, their skills enhanced by the gifts of Kleia Gloria and fine-tuned through decades of practice. Immortal lives were so long. There was nothing but time to develop talents or discover new ones; in Aster's mortal life she had none of the skill required for building, and now she was placed in charge of the design of an entire library.

The elder watched her as she gazed down at the plans with pride, a grand vision sketched out in charcoal and ink. She looked well in a garment of lightweight brown cloth that reached her knees and folded over one shoulder, her hair tied back with a length of white cord. There were no lines around her eyes or across her forehead, no gray streaks at her temples, nor would there ever be. She didn't truly look that much older than Reed; it was only because she'd found Reed as a child that the two seemed now as mother and daughter. Such was the way with all the Aristene. It was only because she'd existed for centuries that anyone deigned to call Ferreh "elder."

Well, Ferreh thought, except perhaps for Aethiel. The former queen had lived a full life and had even borne triplet daughters. It was only Aethiel's exuberance that made her seem still young.

"It's hard to imagine how much stone will be needed," Aster said. "Harder to imagine the Aristene who will have to guide it back through the swallowing throat of the Veil." But it couldn't be mined here. Atropa must remain unspoiled.

Ferreh looked out over the familiar landscape: grass dotted with white clover and yellow buttercups leading up to green, forested hills, where even the wolves in the woods were small and shy, and rarely raided for sheep. It was a peaceful place. A lonely place.

"It will be beautiful," Ferreh said again. "But who will remain here to enjoy it?"

Aster set aside the sketches. In the stillness, the emptiness of the city was even more apparent. "I felt another hero rise," Aster said softly. "Another of Reed's."

"Yes. She is doing well," said Ferreh, though the tone of her voice suggested the opposite. "She will rise quickly within the order."

Reed had been a terrified, traumatized child, all legs and cuts and bruises the night that they'd first met, when Aster had brought her through the Veil. But when Ferreh had looked into Reed's eyes, it wasn't fear that she saw inside them. It was anger, the kind of anger born from having something stolen away, and Ferreh had known then that anger would grow into ambition, and a need to have again what was once taken. She'd known that such anger would never really go away.

Aster worried at the edge of the sketches with her fingers. The goddess had chosen well when she'd sent Aster to Reed. Aster was the perfect mentor, the perfect mother for a girl who had already lost one. It was through Aster that Reed was made theirs. Through Aster, and Lyonene, and even difficult Veridian. And yes, through the favor of Ferreh herself. They had joined their hands around that angry girl and her angry horse and forged a bond that was unbreakable. Or at least Ferreh hoped that it was.

"Aster. I have a task for you."

"Yes, elder?"

"Lyonene lingers in Cerille. It is time that she returned and took another hero from the sacred well. Reed will return soon, to find her next hero in the waters, and I would see them reunited. Initiates ought to be kept close in these early years."

"If she can be brought in time. I'm surprised that Reed isn't here already, and she'll stay just long enough to lean over the well and then be gone again."

Ferreh smiled. "She will settle. It is as you said: she runs through heroes to escape her own pain. She would settle sooner if her mentor and her dearest friend are near, to help her ease it." *Perhaps then we may halt the coming of the monster Kleia Gloria warned us of*, she thought.

"You are right, as always," Aster said. "But why does it fall to me to retrieve Lyonene? Where is Sabil?" Sabil, the small, dark Aristene who had been Lyonene's mentor.

"Sabil is in Valostra, meeting the family of a new initiate."

"Another initiate," Aster said thoughtfully. "Does it seem likely that she will join us?"

Ferreh kept her features steady. "The signs are favorable."

Aster nodded and smiled, for real this time. "Do you remember when the Summer Camp was full to bursting? Full of young women stringing bows, the air loud with the sound of swords clashing? When every mentor was tasked with three girls."

"Jana once had five."

"No wonder she's so mean," Aster said, and Ferreh chuckled. "I miss those times. I thought they might be returning, when Reed and Gretchen and Lyonene all came to us of a similar age. But . . ." But there had been none since. Three fine candidates, two of whom were some of the finest Ferreh had ever seen. She, too, had hoped it was a sign that the time of the Aristene was coming around again.

"I still believe those times will return," said Ferreh. "I believe in our Glorious Death. That there was meaning in her coming. So go, and bring her sister home, so she might help heal her broken heart."

5.

THE COURT OF CERILLE

Lyonene leaned against Alsander in a secluded alcove of the palace. They'd snuck away from his father's court after watching King Alectos argue with the Cerillian nobility, and it had taken no time for Alsander to find his way beneath Lyonene's gown.

"It shouldn't please me to see him under attack," Alsander whispered, sated after their hurried coupling. "But it does."

"He has been a tyrant your whole life," Lyonene replied. "Why shouldn't you take some satisfaction?" His father, the king, had been harried by nobles unhappy about the scarcity of goods within the city, and the lack of ships within the port. Scarcity that Lyonene and Alsander had orchestrated.

"It will not be long now," he said. "He's vulnerable."

"And already the nobles look to you," Lyonene added. "They know it was you who secured fresh trade from Rhonassus. Their hero. Their golden prince on his golden stallion." His eyes quickened when she spoke like that, and he turned to pin her again against the wall.

"Your hero," he said. "And you, my Aristene. Together we can do anything."

"Anything and everything." She kissed him teasingly, and pushed him away.

Tugging the folds of her gown back into place, she had to tug hard to cover the bright pink skin of her heart scar. All Aristene carried a similar mark, but sometimes looking at it made her sick to her stomach. She wasn't supposed to be there, in Cerille. It was long past the time when she should have looked into the sacred well and taken a new hero for herself. She should be somewhere far away, chasing glory. Serving the goddess she'd sworn to serve.

But that is what I'm doing, Lyonene thought. She ran her fingers lightly across Alsander's temple. "There is so much more you are capable of," she whispered. "I won't leave you until your destiny is complete."

He grinned. "Then I will never complete it. I will earn glory after glory, become a king of kings. I will conquer the world."

"I don't doubt that you can. But first we must get you the crown of Cerille. And we can't do that if we're always sneaking away to do this."

Alsander fixed his own clothing, fastening the belt around his light linen tunic. "You like sneaking away."

"I like it just as well when we are alone and relaxed in the dark."

"When are we ever 'relaxed' in the dark?" he asked. As they slipped out of their hidden alcove, he pushed his hand inside her gown again and laughed when she slapped it away. Then he bowed to her before rounding a corner to disappear.

Lyonene sighed. What was it about him? He was handsome, and an excellent lover, but Lyonene had bedded many of the same. Yet she craved Alsander more than any young man or woman who'd come before.

It's because he's mine, she thought. *And because he needs me.*

Her time at the court of Cerille had been spent orchestrating Alsander's ascent to the throne. And it hadn't been easy. The nobles there were like a nest of vipers tied together at the tails. Disentangling them without being bitten—and redirecting their fangs in more desirable directions—had taken all her wiles. For every knot she untangled, she wove herself a new one in the form of a favor owed or a bribe paid. Sometimes at night, after Alsander was satisfied, Lyonene lay awake envisioning the delicate web she'd woven around King Alectos and wondering if it would one day snap back around her like a net. It was dangerous to move against a sitting king. Dangerous even for an Aristene. But Alsander was right. She liked the secrets and the sneaking. She was suited for it.

Lyonene reached up and twisted her tawny hair into the style that King Alectos preferred. Since she had been his son's honored adviser during the War of Rhonassus, Alectos tolerated her presence. But he disliked women who spoke as loudly as she did, and when she lowered her eyes he seemed to sense she was doing it only to humor him. She'd tried to work her way into his good graces. After all, the task of stealing his throne would have been easier had the old goat actually liked and trusted her. So she'd worn the modest gowns, and she'd bitten her tongue when his advisers spouted nonsense. She'd tried to behave, even though doing so had made her fingernails cut bloody half-moons into her palms.

"Lady Lyonene."

A servant girl stood in the hall. Waiting. For who knew how long. Lyonene glanced in the direction that Alsander had gone and the girl flushed scarlet. But it wasn't important. Everyone in the city knew that she and Alsander were lovers. It was widely gossiped about behind their backs and politely ignored when facing them.

"Yes?"

"Lady Isadora wishes to see you."

Lyonene kept her expression carefully neutral. "Lady" Isadora was the king's newest mistress. A pretty creature with a long, pale neck and soft skin, long hair that shone in a shade of burnished copper. Alectos had found her in the house of Lord Vengia, one of the lesser nobles. She'd been a ward, an orphan or an unwanted daughter from some poorer relation.

Lyonene made her way to the rooms of the king's mistress, past the crescent garden and its fountains of leaping stone fish spitting water at each other in pleasant arcs. She went up the long mosaic staircase where tiles depicted the profile of Cerille's god haloed by the rays of the sun in shining yellow and orange. On her way she passed few people; the streets below were bustling and busy but the palace itself was sparse and quiet. Her heels crunched loudly on the paths of crushed seashells as she crossed through the courtyard, doing her best to keep to the shade. Isadora had summoned her during the heat of midday on purpose, so Lyonene would arrive with her gown clinging damply and the wisps of her golden hair stuck to her neck and forehead.

But Lyonene couldn't blame her. A mistress was never assured of her position; Isadora did these things not to be cruel but to preserve herself.

She knew that. Yet it didn't make it less tiresome.

"Lady Isadora," Lyonene said as she entered, only a slight emphasis on the first word. She didn't bow—an Aristene never bowed unless they were traveling in disguise, and all in Cerille knew what Lyonene was—but she inclined her head. Isadora rose from a nest of embroidered pillows, their silks so bright it seemed she'd been sitting upon a clutch of jeweled eggs.

"*Lady* Lyonene," she said, with the same slightly mocking tone. She came to Lyonene's side, and slipped her wrist through Lyonene's elbow so their arms were companionably linked. Both could feel Lyonene's sweat gathered where their skin touched and Isadora made a pitying face. The mistress's rooms were cool and airy. And if ever they weren't airy enough, two attendants stood ready with great fans woven from reeds.

"You wished to see me?" Lyonene asked.

"I have some news."

"News?" She couldn't imagine what it could be, or why it would be shared with her. For as much as she'd tried to ingratiate herself with the king, she'd not tried at all with Isadora. There was no point. The girl would be discarded within the year, her service to the Crown paid for with a far better marriage than Lord Vengia could ever have managed. Though, Lyonene thought, still not a sufficient payment for sharing the old goat king's bed. For that the girl deserved a bathtub filled with rubies. And soap. Lots and lots of soap.

"Of the most joyous kind," said Isadora. She'd led Lyonene near an arched doorway, where the sun could spill across them. "No doubt you've wondered about my absence these weeks past. I'm afraid I was unwell."

"I am sorry to hear it." Truthfully, Lyonene hadn't noticed that Isadora had been missing. Hadn't she just seen her leaning across the king's lap at the merchant's dinner? But perhaps not. Time passed quickly when one was plotting a coup.

"But that is all in the past," Isadora said brightly. "I can finally speak of it. Now that the physicians say it's safe."

"Physicians," Lyonene repeated, and noticed for the first time the way Isadora was shielding her belly with the flat of her hand. Lyonene's throat tightened. It wasn't possible. The old goat was simply . . . too old. . . .

"I am with child," Isadora declared. "The king is overjoyed. He feels certain that it will be a boy. Right now he is informing Prince Alsander of his new brother's coming!"

Lyonene struggled to smile. A pregnant mistress. A newborn son. Alectos was a cruel king, and an even crueler father. He would wield the existence of this child like a sword. He would point it at Alsander's throat. She could hear his voice of gravel, and see the sneer upon his face. *You thought your claim to the throne was a foregone conclusion, didn't you, boy? Well, perhaps not.*

"How wonderful for you, Isadora."

"How wonderful for all of us," Isadora corrected her. "It is known that the king has long wished for another prince, for the security of Cerille."

"I wish you many blessings," said Lyonene. Many blessings, she prayed to Kleia Gloria, and the birth of a girl. "Please excuse me; I should find the prince and congratulate him."

She departed quickly, not caring how it seemed or how ashen her face must have turned. Alsander would be furious at this news. And more than furious, he would be in danger. If the child was born a boy, it would throw the line of succession into question. And then everything they'd planned for might be lost.

6.

VERIDIAN'S KEEPER

The next day when Reed woke in the stable, she was surprised to find Veridian already up and gone. Though not gone for good—Everfall still stood in his stall, dozing with his chin resting on Silco's back. Reed sat up and stretched, rubbing her eyes against the sun breaking through the stable's open doors. She peered down the aisle and caught a glimpse of the stable boy's head rising in and out of view as he worked through straw with a pitchfork.

Reed stepped across the partition to greet her horse, and rubbed his nose absently as she looked at the hay bales where she'd laid Veridian down the night before. *Don't leave me, Reed.* She'd sounded like a lost child. It troubled her to think that Veridian suffered as she wandered the world alone.

"What would Aster want us to do?" Reed whispered, and Silco, sensing for once that the question was more important than his breakfast, looked quietly at the hay. Then he took Reed's shirt in his teeth and tugged her closer.

Stay, that tug meant. *Stay and help her.* But how? The sadness in Veridian's voice and the hopelessness in her eyes were of a kind that Reed had no grasp of.

"You're awake."

Veridian strode through the open doors, looking far better than

Reed felt, despite having been far drunker. She held up a palm of flat bread.

"I got breakfast. A man in the market was frying them and they're just the thing to settle your stomach after last night's horrible wine and silt stew."

At the mention of the muddy stew, Reed's belly gurgled. She took a piece of bread and bit into it, fried crisp to the edges and stuffed with bits of egg and ground meat. It would have been delicious had her stomach not felt like a ship tossed at sea. She ate slowly as Veridian tended to her saddlery, securing her bedroll and knives, checking her bow in preparation to be off. Before they'd come to Verrin, she'd sung its praises, but one night in it and she seemed eager to leave. Perhaps there was nowhere in the world she could stand to be for longer than that.

"What's your hurry?" Reed asked.

"What's your lack of hurry? I thought I'd wake and find you gone back to Atropa through the Veil."

"You asked me to stay," Reed said, brow furrowing.

"And you listened?" Veridian paused just long enough to look at Reed with a cock of her head. "How touching. But that ought to teach you not to pay attention to your old aunt Veridian when she's drunk."

Reed blinked. She was having a hard time keeping up with the apostate's changing moods. This Veridian was the other side of the coin to last night's pathetic creature whom Reed had to carry back to the stable.

Finished with her packs, Veridian slapped her palm down on the pommel of her saddle. "Well, as long as you're here another day, why not stay longer?"

"Veridian, we have to get back to Atropa."

"To Atropa, and the sacred well. You take so many heroes there will be none left over for anyone else!"

Reed smiled and rubbed her eyes, still groggy. "I guess I'm just not in the habit of looking after apostates."

Veridian stiffened, and Reed realized what she'd said as her mood shifted again.

"And I," Veridian said, "am not in the habit of adopting stray puppies. Do you think because I wander I have nothing to teach you? Or perhaps you already think you have nothing to learn."

"I—" Reed sputtered. "You—you said—!" She didn't know what to say. It was at Veridian's request that they had come with her to Verrin, Veridian's pleading that made them remain an extra night. "I am no stray puppy!" Reed stood, ready to argue, when she heard the unmistakable sound of horse teeth. Silco and Everfall were biting at each other: Everfall held his neck low and Silco swooped in to bite it only to have the red gelding swing out of reach at the last moment. Then Silco extended his neck for Everfall to try to bite.

"What are they doing?" Reed asked.

"They're being boys." Veridian walked to the horses and shoved them apart. Then she stood beside her gelding and patted his shoulder. "He has so few chances to play with other Areion." She gazed up at the tall red horse, whose eyes were bright, his ears pricked. "We would like it if you came with us. We would be grateful."

Reed scowled into her fried bread, though it was settling her stomach. She tore off a bit with no meat in it and gave it to Silco, who chewed it messily to make most of the egg drop to the dirt.

"We can't ride with you for long," she said finally, and Veridian grinned.

"Wonderful," she said, her tone light but her eyes curiously empty. "Now get yourself together. Verrin has heated baths; we'll visit them before we depart."

It was as they emerged from the baths that they sensed it: the odd sensation of the Veil opening and closing, as an eye in the center of their minds. Only this time, the feeling also came with the knowledge of what had stepped through it.

"Did you feel that?" Reed asked.

"Feel what?" Veridian asked, though it was clear that she had. Reed had seen her stiffen.

"Aster."

"Aster?" Veridian turned. "What about Aster?"

"She's just come through the Veil. Did you not sense her?"

"I feel it when the Veil opens if it is not too far away. I don't feel who it spits out."

"Then how do I?" Reed asked.

"It's the lingering tether of the bond between mentor and initiate. It will fade."

Reed frowned. She valued her independence but she didn't know if she wanted it to fade. She liked the idea of knowing when Aster was in the world of men. And she could even vaguely sense where she'd gone. "I think she's in Cerille. What could she be doing there?"

"You're asking the wrong apostate," Veridian said, and turned away.

Reed looked toward the harbor. Cerille was not far from Verrin, a one-day sail, if the winds were right. Most of the boats were local fishing vessels, but a few were large enough to be sailing there. Or at least close enough to drop them off with the offer of enough coin.

"Let's go to the docks and find a ship," Reed said.

Veridian scowled. "I thought you said you would ride with me? And now you want to run straight back to your mentor?" But Reed could see through that scowl. Veridian wanted to see Aster, no matter what she said. And once they were reunited, it would be all too easy for Reed to slip away back to Atropa.

She was about to walk toward the ships when suddenly her magic pulled at her bones.

"Veridian." She raised her chin and inhaled. "Do you smell that?"

Veridian raised her nose and sniffed. "Smoke," she said.

"And glory."

Reed moved quickly, following the pull through the streets toward the black plume billowing up into the sky.

The fire blazed just off the village square, lit like day as flames licked up the sides of an inn and erupted from the windows of the upper floor. Smoke poured from them like water and more seeped through the very walls. Reed stepped out of the way as people ran past rolling barrels and carrying buckets. Up and down the street, buildings were being emptied of goods and inhabitants.

Reed looked at the inferno. The building was lost, yet there was glory here. Her magic still pushed.

Across the square, a young woman bent above a horse trough, soaking herself with water from head to toe. Her breath came fast—she was afraid. But the air above her shoulders glittered gold as she considered whether to race into that dragon's throat. To save others.

Reed felt Veridian stumble to her side.

"Do you see her?" Reed asked. The pull of the glory was intoxicating. It coated the young woman and grew in brightness, there for the taking. "If she goes in," Reed heard herself say, "she won't come back out." But she would go, if Reed gave her the courage.

Before Reed could move, Veridian crossed the square and struck the woman across the face. She fell into an unconscious heap.

"What are you doing?" Reed ran to them. The gold was gone; the young woman's chance at glory had passed. "She would have saved someone!"

"At what cost?" Veridian looked at the fire. "That's a fool's errand if I ever saw one."

"You!" Reed shouted. "You just undermined the will of the goddess!"

"Oh—shut up, Reed!" With a glare, Veridian tore off their cloaks and dunked them into the water trough. She shoved one, sopping wet, into Reed's hands. "There are still people inside. Let's go!" Then she turned and ran toward the flames.

Reed scowled. She called up her armor and felt the cool silver slide over her chest and shoulders. They raced to the side of the tavern. Veridian pointed to the building across the alley.

"Up there and then we jump across!" They climbed until they perched in a cut-stone window. Then they turned back and dove into the building in flames.

Reed threw the soaked cloak over her shoulders as her lungs filled with smoke. The fire was loud, almost deafening as it cracked and consumed. She heard cries and leaped across a burning stair-case, her throat stinging with every breath. Through the smoke and orange glow, she saw a man kneeling protectively over a shape wrapped in a blanket.

A wooden beam creaked overhead. Reed dove and shoved it away before it landed upon them. The burns on her hands were instant.

"Is the child all right?" Reed asked. She pulled the blanket back and was greeted by two sets of eyes, one with a wet and only slightly singed black nose.

A little girl and her dog. Veridian landed on the wood beside them.

"Reed," the apostate said. "This is a dog."

"There's a child in there, too. Grab the man." She coughed and pointed, and Veridian threw him over her shoulder as Reed picked up the dog and child. They leaped through the burning building, back to the window where they'd come in. But the wall between them fell in a pile of sparks.

"Now what?" Reed coughed.

"I'm no pathfinder!"

Reed scanned the room and spotted a window. Too small to fit through, but too tempting not to try when just past it was cool air and freedom.

"Can we bash through that?"

They drew back their legs and kicked, and the face of the wall fell away, leaving them teetering on the edge. People below saw them and quickly maneuvered a cart filled with straw for them to jump into. Veridian looked down.

"You know that's not only straw. That's the cart they use to clean out the horse stalls and goat pens."

"We could jump past it," said Reed.

Veridian shrugged. "They've already gone to the trouble," she said, and jumped feetfirst.

Reed jumped not far behind and joined the apostate in the manure, careful to hold the child and her dog up high. After they were helped from the cart, she lowered them to the ground.

The girl was small, perhaps six or seven. She was unconscious, but roused when Reed gave her a gentle shake. The dog licked Reed's blistered fingers.

"You saved us," the man said, hugging his daughter to his chest. But they hadn't saved everyone. Across the square, the young woman who had once glittered with glory now wailed upon the ground, as the last of the building collapsed.

"Well." Veridian looked down at their soiled legs. "Back to the baths, then?"

Reed spun on her. "What did you think you were doing?" she demanded. "That girl was marked by Kleia Gloria; you saw it."

Veridian ignored her. She found a bucket of water and dunked her arms, washing away ash and soot. "We'll need to get some salve for those burns on your hands. Come here and let me clean them."

"Veridian!" Reed grabbed her by the elbow and felt blisters pop wetly on her palm. "An apostate may turn away from the order, but if you work against us—"

"Then what? You'll set the elders on me?" She shook water from her hands. "I can't just stand by and let these ordinary fools run into burning buildings."

"She wasn't an ordinary fool. She was mine!"

"And there it is." Veridian's eyes narrowed to slits. "It's not my interference that troubles you. It's that I cost you another glorious death. Haven't you had enough? The girl would have died!"

"But how many more would she have saved?" Reed clenched her fists. "You declined to become a Glorious Death, but I did not. I am one, and if you ride with me I won't have your judgment."

The tone of Reed's voice made Veridian step back.

"Now let's go get the horses and find passage to Cerille. We're going to see Aster."

"You should never have gone with Aster that night," Veridian said.

"But I did, and there's no changing it. Let's go. And if you try to resist, I will knock you out and take you aboard tossed over Everfall's back."

7.

A BORROWED MENTOR

The sensation of the Veil opening made the back of Lyonene's neck tighten into gooseflesh. It was strong and it was close. And if it was close, that meant it was for her.

Sabil, she thought. Her old mentor, come to find her and drag her back to the order by her ear, not that Sabil had ever before done such a thing. Her small, dark-haired mentor had always been patient and kind, quietly proud of her initiate's achievements and how easily she seemed to achieve them. Personally, Lyonene thought she should have crowed louder about it.

At once, Lyonene banished her modest gown in exchange for her full regalia—white cape, silver and leather, sandals that wrapped up her ankles, and light leather greaves. She would be a spectacle in the palace, the bared skin of her legs judged by every male eye she passed, but it didn't feel right to welcome her mentor in anything else.

She walked through the garden and up the steps to a balcony that gave a good view of the city below. Where was Sabil's shining armor of scales? When would she see it, blinding her with reflected light?

I won't be pulled away, she thought. *And she won't arrive to find me panicked.*

She would lay out the plans she'd devised for Alsander. She would show her mentor that Kleia Gloria was being served. She and

Alsander would host Sabil at a fine feast, as their personal guest. And then her mentor would go, and leave her alone.

But even Lyonene had to admit, that sounded like a fairy story.

When evening came, softly as it always did in Cerille, Sabil had still not arrived, and Lyonene had begun to relax. Perhaps she'd been wrong about the nearness of the Veil. Or perhaps she'd simply been mistaken about the purpose of it, and one of her Aristene sisters had business with a hero somewhere close by. Lyonene sipped from a gold cup of wine, sweetened with honey. She was reclined on a couch beside the window of her chamber, enjoying the view of the riverbank, where torches and lamps burned like jewels, and threw orange ripples onto the water.

She was safe. She'd been mistaken. She could probably send her armor away, so Alectos could stop grinding his teeth.

"Lady Lyonene, a guest has arrived. She said she was a member of . . . your order."

The girl delivering the message spoke hesitantly. To her, and to most others in Cerille, the Aristene were a mystery. They'd heard the tales from those who came back from the war, and saw that Lyonene was treated as a valued adviser, but they'd never seen her strength or her magic for themselves. King Alectos didn't like for Lyonene to show it.

"She awaits you in the sunset courtyard, beside the fountain."

Lyonene thanked the girl and made her way through the palace on soft, slippered feet. When she stepped into the warmer air of the courtyard, she looked around. The space was lit nightly by lanterns covered in orange cloth, and the birdsong had given way to the chirping of insects. Someone moved behind the fountain and Lyonene summoned a forbearing smile to her lips. But the smile fell away to a soft O as the person who stepped out was not Sabil but Aster.

"Aster?"

The tall, brown-haired Aristene wasn't in her armor but a finely woven gown of sea blue, knotted at the shoulders, and a braided belt that trailed a chain of gold.

"Gloria Thea Matris, sister."

"Gloria Thea Matris," Lyonene said, giving a quick duck of her chin. "What's wrong? Is it Reed?"

Aster chuckled and came to take Lyonene by the hands. "Reed is fine."

Lyonene sighed. Because when it came to Reed, one never knew. She looked at Reed's mentor. *Sister*, Aster had called her just now. How strange to hear that word added to that greeting, and even stranger to hear it from Aster's mouth, when for so long she had been a mentor and Lyonene an initiate. Lyonene had thought that when she joined the order, its magic would change her somehow—add weight to her very bones. But Lyonene was still herself. Just with a few new tricks. And enough strength in her arm to break a shield.

"But if Reed is fine," Lyonene said, "then why have you come?"

"To bring you back to Atropa, of course. The elders call."

So it was as Lyonene had expected, only with an unexpected face. Lyonene regretted that. Sabil she knew. Sabil she could have persuaded. Aster was different. Lyonene often downplayed Aster's virtues and rank within the order to Reed, but in truth Lyonene had always been slightly dazzled by her.

"Where is Sabil?"

"Away, seeking another initiate."

"Another initiate," Lyonene mused. "A replacement for me, so soon?"

"Not a replacement," Aster replied. "A sister. Our numbers dwindle, Lyonene, and you know well that Sabil makes for a fine mentor."

She supposed she did. And Sabil would be the one to go, as Aster was unlikely to take another initiate anytime soon. Or perhaps ever. Reed had been a special case.

"Come and sit." Lyonene gestured to a round stone table ringed by a bench. She snapped her fingers at the attendants, hiding ever-ready in the shadowed interior of the hall. "Bring wine for our guest. The evening meal is past, but I can send for fruits and bread from the kitchens."

"That is ample enough." Aster sat down. "I trust the palace is still well stocked. Whose idea was it to starve out the ports?"

Lyonene stiffened. But she shouldn't have been surprised. Aster knew the Aristene ways. It must have been obvious to her as she'd come through the capital. The lack of ships. The bare market.

"It's not a poor strategy," Aster said. "Making things harder to get. When people are used to ease, even a little hardship may spark revolt."

Lyonene eyed Aster cautiously, but it was no use denying it; her game was up. "Last week one of the nobles' wives wept at the lack of imported fruits."

Aster smiled. "And meanwhile Alsander keeps the goods flowing from Rhonassus and plays the savior. Ah, there he is now."

Alsander swept into the courtyard in a flurry of trailing robes. He'd readied for bed and his clothing was silken and shimmering, deep blue and green, embroidered with lions in gold thread. Lyonene's expression tightened. With the robes flaring behind him and his blue eyes flashing he was reminiscent of an insulted peacock.

"What are you doing here?" he demanded of Aster. "You will not take her against her will." He held up his fist as if ready to give an order, and Lyonene looked hurriedly inside the palace. Good goddess, if he had brought guards . . .

"Prince Alsander." Aster didn't bow, but she at least stood, a more polite greeting than he'd earned. "I have heard much of you from my initiate, Reed."

"Reed? Then you are—" He looked to Lyonene and back again. "Aster." He dropped a short bow. "Forgive my rudeness. It is an honor to meet you. But why have you come?"

Aster glanced at Lyonene, giving her a chance to explain for herself—Aristene didn't like to interfere in the business of another's hero—but Lyonene's mind had become a blank. "It's just as you say," Aster replied. "I've come to collect."

"But you see," Lyonene said, recovering her voice before Alsander could levy any threats. She spoke carefully; ears of the servants were open in the dark. "That I'm needed here."

"I do. And you will still be needed when your duty to the order is finished. This summons isn't forever, and it isn't instant. You may have three days to settle your affairs. If I may remain as your guest."

8.

AN INITIATE, A MENTOR, AND AN APOSTATE WALK INTO CERILLE. . . .

In the day that it took to reach Cerille—on a merchant vessel named the *Saltmaid*—the blisters on Reed's hands had healed, hardening to scabs that fell off to show soft new skin underneath.

"Almost time to disembark," Veridian said as they stood beside their horses. She glanced at Silco's trembling black nose. Even as an Areion, he didn't like to sail. "Does he need to be blindfolded again?"

"No. Getting *off* the ship is never the problem."

Silco squealed and stomped; in the stall beside him, Everfall tossed his head and made a noise that sounded suspiciously like "silly colt."

"Did he just speak?" Reed asked. "Is that what passes for an Areion's voice?"

"It sounded like a normal snort to me." Veridian leaned on her horse's shoulder. "I didn't imagine one so brave as Silver and Combat to be such a pain. At least his rider doesn't get seasick—but then, you wouldn't. Your people were seafaring."

"My people are the Aristene," said Reed, still cross with her for her interference at the Verrin fire. "Aster and Aethiel, Ferreh and Lyonene—they are my family now. Even you."

"Even me?" Veridian smirked. "A girl who once lost a mother

now has two. Kleia Gloria does have her plans."

The goddess did have her plans. The voyage had been fast and smooth; the crew so mellow that Reed wondered if they were under some kind of dull, unremarkable curse. As the ship dropped anchor, Reed looked out at the coastline.

She'd never been there before. She knew of it, of course, from her studies and Lyonene's tales. But it was one thing to be told of a place and another to arrive in it. It had its own smell, for a start—of greenery but not of flowers, and also slightly of smoke. Not the unpleasant smoke of a burning building but the good wood smell of fires of purpose; for cooking and clay firming, drying and pre-serving meat. On either side of the harbor rose short white cliffs, and the beach was pale sand—soft-looking and dotted with large boulders. Gray-and-brown seabirds circled in the sky and made their homes in cracks and crevices of the cliffside.

Reed was eager to get ashore, but when she saw the small boat that would ferry them through the bay, she stiffened.

"What about the horses?"

Veridian shrugged. "They will swim behind."

The water was clear and calm. But the thought of Silco swim-ming made her go cold. She turned on the captain.

"Get the horses in the boat."

"They won't jump into the boat," he objected.

"These will."

"They'll capsize us—"

"I'll swim with them." Veridian removed her sword.

"No—" Reed grasped the apostate's elbow. "It was in the sea, in a bay just like this one, that Silco's hoof was injured."

"It will not happen again, Reed. I will not let it. Trust me."

Veridian dove off the bow. When she surfaced, she whistled to the horses, and Everfall leaped in like he was half sea lion, but Silco wouldn't budge. When the crew tried to urge him he kicked and twisted to bite like an angry horse-shaped snake.

It seemed that Reed would have to swim as well. She removed the sword from her back, and her belt of knives, and the blades from her boot, then shoved the items into the captain's chest. "I should take back some of those silvers I gave you," she said before she turned and dove.

The water was pleasant. Cool but not cold. She called to Silco, and Everfall tried to show him it was safe, paddling circles, happy as a duck. Silco snorted and shook his head, but finally he stomped his foot, backed up, and vaulted into the water. He made a horse-size splash and shrieked when he surfaced, his eye rolling angrily at Reed as he swam with his black nose pointed skyward in distaste.

"Keep ahead of us," Reed said to the captain as he and two crewmen rowed beside them. "Watch for coral and rocks."

"The swim is longer than you think, lady," the captain cautioned. "We'll bring you aboard when you tire."

But of course Reed and Veridian didn't tire. They ran with the horses out of the surf, and the horses and Veridian shook like dogs, flinging water from their manes and hair.

When the boat beached, Reed collected their things and paid the captain the balance that was owed. Then she shoved the prow hard and launched them back into the sea.

"You've the strength of lions in your arms," the captain called. "I do not know who you are. But it has been an honor to ferry you."

Veridian chuckled as the men rowed away. "Your effort to shock them has gone unrewarded."

They dried and saddled the horses, then rode into the city. As they passed the marketplace Reed noted the empty spaces in the merchant stalls. Extra straw had been placed between goods to make the displays appear fuller. And the taverns they passed teemed with young men: dockworkers who were not working.

"Does something trouble you?" Veridian asked. "You're an Aristene now—sometimes feelings are more than feelings. Sometimes they are omens from Kleia Gloria."

"Is this one of your lessons, apostate?" Reed asked, and Veridian scowled.

"Well, what, then? How do you mean to find Aster? You don't even know why she's here." When Reed had no answer, Veridian scoffed. "Why don't we go to the palace and ask Lyonene?"

"Lyonene? What is she still doing in Cerille?"

"We can ask her that, too." Veridian nudged Everfall onward, and Reed and Silco followed with renewed interest. It had been long months since they'd seen their friend. And Prince Alsander, who wasn't really so bad, or at least he hadn't been by the time the war was over.

"How do you know Lyonene is here?" Reed asked.

"Did you not speak at all with the crew? Did you not ask a single question about the state of affairs at our destination?"

Reed made no reply, only grumbled to herself. She gazed up at the palace as they crossed a wide, arched bridge. The palace of King Alectos was built not from white stone but pale yellow, and gave the impression of gold. The columns were nearly as high as those that

adorned the Citadel of Atropa, the chapiters at the tops sculpted
with ornate bursts of leaves. Vines grew up the sides, flowering
white and pink and pale purple. Butterflies and insects with wings
that looked like gemstones swooped lazily from bloom to bloom.

"We are here to see Lady Lyonene," Reed said to the guards
at the gate.

"Who seeks her?"

"Machianthe," Veridian replied before Reed could answer. "She
will know. And she'll be cross if you don't hurry."

The guards traded another look, and Reed resisted the urge to
kick Veridian in the shin. They didn't know what game Lyonene was
playing in the court of Cerille. Wrong words could ruin whatever
the Aristene had planned. But of course, Veridian would know this.

"Are you trying to ruin things for her as well?" Reed asked
quietly as they dismounted and were led onto the palace grounds.

"I don't know what you mean." Veridian gave Everfall's reins
over to an attendant. They'd been brought to a courtyard bordered
by ornamental grass that moved in the warm wind. It was topped
by sprigs of white and gold that waved back and forth like fans in
a maiden's hand.

"Send someone with wine," Veridian said as she sat at a stone
table. "That is what this country is known for, is it not?" Then she
lay back and shielded her eyes with her forearm.

It wasn't long before attendants arrived with a silver carafe of
wine and two silver goblets. The wine they poured was a perfect pale gold, the same as the stone that composed the palace.
Veridian took up her goblet, drained it, and held it out for them
to pour again.

"Aster is here," Reed said. "Do you mean to be drunk when you see her?"

"I mean to be drunk all the time," said Veridian. "But this pale vintage is not going to do it."

"Ox!"

Reed turned. "Lyonene!"

The two friends laughed and ran to wrap their arms around each other in what was half an embrace and half a contest of wills. A contest that Reed eventually won, using her advantage of size to lift Lyonene straight off her feet.

"I have missed you, Ox," Lyonene said when Reed had put her down.

"Don't you mean 'Machianthe'?" Veridian asked.

"She will always be 'Ox' to me." Lyonene raised her brows. "A mentor and an apostate arrive at my gate. Whatever have I done to deserve the honor? And oh—Gloria Thea Matris, sisters."

"Gloria Thea Matris," Reed said while Veridian made a crude gesture. "A mentor, you said—then Aster is here?"

"Yes. She didn't tell me you were coming."

"That's because she didn't know." Veridian waved at Reed. "It was her idea."

"Are we not welcome?" Reed asked discreetly. There was no warrior about Lyonene. She carried no sword and wore no armor. Her lion's mane of hair had been tamed by a knotted bun, and her gown was a soft pink, the same shade as the blossoms on the vine. On her arms she wore several gold bands.

"Of course you're welcome," Lyonene said. "Come inside. You will have baths, and dine with the king."

"We just had baths," Veridian muttered as she took up her goblet and the rest of the carafe to follow.

Though it was warm outside, the interior of the palace was cool and comfortable. It caught a breeze off the sea that passed through a thousand striped flowers before it reached their noses. Lyonene led them down a curving colonnade to a room with a balcony that faced a garden. It was large and airy, the bed draped with thin linen.

"Aster's chamber is that way. Though I don't know if you'll find her in it."

"I'll find her," said Veridian. "Don't worry about that. Are you coming, foundling?"

Reed would have, but Lyonene grasped her wrist. "Reed, will you come with me to the stable? I would see Silco, and make sure he is placed close to my Strawberry. She misses the company of her fellow Areion. Is that all right, Veridian?"

"As you will, children," Veridian said, and wandered away.

The stable was downwind of the palace near the river, where the horses could easily be watered, and the pastureland stretched out into a valley bordered by trees. As they walked past the stalls of fine horses, mostly white or black, Reed caught sight of a tall stallion with a coat of gold: Phaeton, Alsander's horse, taken from the legendary herd of Lacos. He stretched his neck above the door and Lyonene stroked his nose.

"Strawberry!" Reed exclaimed when she saw the horse's red-and-white mottled head. "How are you, little mother?" She took the mare's face in her hands and scratched hard behind her ears.

"She seems to like you better than she does her own rider," Lyonene noted.

"Well. I was her rider, in Rhonassus." It was Strawberry who had carried Reed into the hills to hunt, after Silco had been injured, and though Reed had great admiration for the horse, she was still surprised that Lyonene had chosen her as her Areion. Strawberry was strong and smart, but she was also small, and the least impressive of all the horses in Lacos's legendary herd.

Lyonene reached into the next stall to pat Silco's shoulder. "What are you doing here, Ox? Have you come to convince Aster to let me stay?"

"I didn't even know you were here. Why are you still here, Lyonene?"

Lyonene looked away. Her eyes grew distant as she absently stroked Silco's glossy black coat. "What I've started here I can't undo," she murmured. "If I leave him now, he's in danger."

"Oh, Lyonene." Reed stopped scratching the horse. "What have you done?"

"I'm making him a king," Lyonene replied. "My first hero would be a king. Isn't that what I've always said?"

"Alsander is the sole heir. He will be king, in time."

But Lyonene shook her head fiercely. "King Alectos's new mistress is with child."

"With child?" Reed blinked. "King Alectos must be near sixty!"

"Yes." Lyonene frowned. "He's understandably thrilled that it still works."

"That may be, but a baby is only a baby, and months from being born. There is no guarantee it will be a son, and what kind of king would place the security of his line upon a child when he already has a healthy, grown prince?"

"A cruel one, and a fool." Lyonene exhaled ruefully. "If Alectos is alive when the child is born and the child is born a boy, we will have problems."

"You're going to kill him."

"Better him than the child."

"Lyonene!"

"Don't pity the old goat, Reed. He may look harmless, but he is not. Many here at court whisper that Alsander's mother didn't die of illness but of poison from the king's own hand. He married her for the foreign alliance and then came to hate her foreign blood. And everything that came forth from it."

Reed frowned. Poor Alsander. She remembered how he'd seemed when they'd first met in Lacos: how he'd masked his insecurity with his sword, how he'd tried to assert himself above Hestion and Belden. And she remembered the look on his face when Belden had given him the smallest amount of praise: a look that said he'd scarcely heard such words before.

"I'm surprised you dared this," Reed said quietly. "When we met in Lacos you described this place as a pit of vipers. As if they'd cut off your head if they got a glimpse of your magic."

"And they would. Does it look like I'm wearing my armor? Their view of me changed when Alsander returned from Rhonassus and the Aristene had earned the respect of the soldier class. Truly it is weakness that will cost you your head here, Reed. And every member of the nobility is sniffing the air, waiting for me to show it." She looked down. "We are so close to finishing what we started. But if I leave Alsander now I will return to find his head on a pike."

"You're caught in a storm of your own making," said Reed, and

Lyonene did not deny it. But her green eyes sparkled; she thrived in this—reveled in moving pieces about on the game board.

"You judge me for this foolishness, Ox. I know you do."

But Reed did not. She more than anyone knew what it was to be caught between her hero and her duty to the order. But they weren't initiates anymore; they were Aristene. And the Aristene answered when the goddess called.

9.

DINNER AT COURT

The evening meal was held in a great banquet room, the wall facing the sea open and supported by thick pillars. Reed, Aster, and Veridian arrived through a tall archway adorned with a mosaic of blue and yellow tiles. Tables were set in a large half circle, and they were led to one of the last of them. Not a place of honor near the king but rather the farthest away, as if the nobility of Cerille couldn't wait to bid them goodbye, or was trying to lure them back outside. The king's seat was at the apex like the keystone of an arch, the open space in the center reserved for dancers and musicians, and the distance from one wing of the circle to the other was too far away to speak to those seated on the other side. It was pleasing to look upon, but cold. Reed preferred the raucous, close gatherings of Glaucia, where as many stories were passed around the table as ale, and those tables were scattered with spilled food and crumbs, not set with so many gold candlesticks that people feared to reach for their wine.

She looked to the royal table, where Lyonene sat beside Alsander. The crown prince sat stiffly, his shoulders rigid and his face so drawn that Reed wondered if he was ill. On his other side was his father, King Alectos, in a gold crown. An old man, yet some might still think him handsome, with a graying nest of wavy hair brushed back from quick blue eyes. In his youth he must have looked much like Alsander, though the resemblance seemed to be the only link between them. Father and son didn't acknowledge one another. They ate. They drank. They spoke to other people.

"These little birds are good," Veridian said to Reed's right.

Reed looked down the table at the line of golden birds on plates. They were probably raised on the palace grounds and spoiled like pets, and today instead of a hand-feeding received a wrung neck. But there were worse ways to die. Veridian snatched Reed's bird from her plate.

"First my purse and now my dinner? I am as a bank to you and also a kitchen?"

Veridian grinned around a mouthful of meat. "You are a most useful traveling companion. I can see why Aster kept you for so long."

On the apostate's other side, Aster laughed softly, and Reed's irritation with Veridian softened. They were together now, and Veridian's unhappiness would ease.

"She's going to get herself into trouble," Veridian said quietly, referring to Lyonene. "An Aristene is made to serve. To shepherd what glory the goddess gives. Not to curate her own."

"We all curate our own," said Aster. "We all serve glory where we find it."

"You make it sound like she happened across him like a shiny stone in a field. There are reasons the heroes of the trial are left behind. The ties that bind them to the initiates will become too strong otherwise."

Reed lowered her eyes. Those words were too true. During all of those nights with Hestion, stealing away for moments alone, one touch of his hand could have blotted out the rest of the world. But Lyonene had always seemed immune to that kind of infatuation.

Veridian tossed a wing bone onto her plate. "Can no one stop that old beast from touching that girl?" At the royal table, King Alectos continued to ignore everyone except the young woman to his right, who he could not stop speaking to and could not keep his hands off.

"It is vulgar," Aster noted. "But kings will be kings."

Veridian spat another bone. "I hate that excuse. As if a king is not a man, as if a man is not a person who should be held to account like any other." The young woman beside Alectos appeared to be about Reed's age. Her cheeks were rosy and round, her hair the same bright gold as the candlesticks and wound through with delicate pink flowers. Would he be cruel to her as he was to Alsander's mother? Would he come to hate her, too, in time, and drop some poison into her cup?

If Kleia Gloria had willed his death, then I wouldn't blink at killing him, Reed thought. But the goddess had not willed it. Lyonene was not acting at the direction of the sacred well. She was making her own glory where she saw fit. And she was doing it for love.

To one side of the king, Alsander and Lyonene had begun to whisper together. Alsander seemed angry and the jut of his chin in the direction of the Aristene left little question as to why. He met Reed's eyes a moment, his blue ones like ice to her brown, and abruptly stood. When he left the room, Lyonene hurried after him.

Reed glanced at Aster. An Aristene shouldn't be seen scurrying after her hero. Perhaps Alsander had forgotten who Lyonene was. And perhaps she had forgotten, too, after spending too much time in gowns with her head bent, deferring to the king, playing her part so well that it had ceased to be an act.

Reed got up from the table and followed them. Her movements didn't go unnoticed; she felt the eye of every noble upon her like the pricks of pins on her skin—but what did it matter? The Aristene were beholden to no one here. She left the banquet hall and trailed Lyonene and Alsander through the palace until they disappeared into a chamber. She didn't wait a moment before bursting inside.

"Reed!" Lyonene exclaimed, but seemed relieved that it was her and not Aster. She sat down on the bed and put her hand to her forehead. The chamber they'd entered was the prince's own bedchamber. It faced to the east, and the light from the sunset was gentle inside, turning the white stone a soft orange. The wall above the bed had been adorned with decorative sabers, jewels winking in their gold hilts, and a fine woven tapestry of the battle against King Oreas hung over the prince's table. In it Alsander was depicted on horseback, charging the monstrous king with his sword arm aloft, moments from cutting off Oreas's head.

When he saw Reed looking at it, Alsander gave a sideways smile. They both knew that wasn't quite the way it had happened.

"It is good to see you, Reed," he said. "Or do you prefer Machianthe?"

"The crown prince of Cerille may call me whatever he likes at his court," Reed replied. "But I think a friend would use the name I was known to him by."

"Reed, then. For all of us who faced that monster"—he glanced at the image of King Oreas—"will be friends whenever we meet." He sounded like a king. He looked like a king, just the way he had at the end of the war, when he'd grown up enough to win his glory, and in doing so earned Lyonene her place within the order.

"I came to scold you for keeping her," Reed said. "But I think we all know she does nothing that she doesn't want to."

"Instead of scolding us, will you help us, then?" He held out his hand and Lyonene took it and rose from the bed. "I know that as an Aristene she must go, but I don't wish for her to leave my side."

"Especially not now," Lyonene whispered. "We have enough noble support to make a play for the throne. But we can't act so close to the announcement of the pregnancy. Not even the nobles loyal to us would be able to pretend it wasn't murder."

"There would be civil war," Alsander agreed. "We need time to navigate this new . . . complication."

"Complication," Reed echoed. "Whatever the circumstances of its birth, the baby will be your brother or sister."

"I know that. But I'm finding it hard to endear myself to it when its mere existence puts my life at risk. After the crown is on my head, he—or she—will be safe. But until then, none of us are."

Lyonene laid her hand upon his chest. "I'm sorry. I don't want to go." Her voice lowered. "Sometimes I wish I had made a different choice. That I should have done what Gretchen did and walked away."

"You can't mean that," Reed said.

"I don't know what I mean."

Reed's heart began to pound a beat against her ribs. She thought of Gretchen, who had left them the night before their Hero's Trials. Gretchen who had worked so hard, who they had loved, and who they might never see again. It couldn't be like that with Lyonene.

Reed breathed a gulp of air into lungs that felt small.

"I'll take Lyonene's new hero for her," she said.

"What?" Lyonene asked, eyes wide.

"Can that be done?" Alsander asked.

"Of course it can't." Lyonene shook her head. "The order demands—the sacred well—"

"The order will allow me this," Reed said. They had to. The elders couldn't risk the loss of as fine an Aristene as Lyonene was. She was too valuable. Reed felt herself begin to smile. The more she thought of it, the surer she became. If the elders knew of this plan, they would understand. Of course, they could never be allowed to find out. "I am a Glorious Death," she said. "They need me."

She looked determinedly into Lyonene's doubtful face.

"You'll come to Atropa and look into the sacred well. And then I will go wherever it leads, in your place. *I will guide your hero for you and no one will ever know.*"

For a moment Lyonene just blinked. Then her lips softened into a frown. "You can't be saying this, Reed. You used to be such a good soldier."

"Except I'm not just a soldier anymore," Reed said. "I'm the savior. And I would save you, Lyonene. I would save you both."

Alsander nudged Lyonene hopefully.

"No. Thank you, Reed, but we can't," Lyonene replied. "We can't just—swap a hero." But Reed and Alsander continued to stare at her, and eventually her eyes took on a familiar, devious light. "Can we?"

Veridian and Aster lay on the large, soft bed in Aster's chamber. It was comfortable and cool, the air scented with the warm perfume of pink and yellow honeysuckle. The king of Cerille might be an old lech, but he knew how to treat his guests.

"I'll take the girls tomorrow night," Aster said. "Though part of me wishes to stay." Her fingers trailed soft sparks down the skin of Veridian's inner arm.

"So stay," Veridian whispered. "Let those girls find their own way home, and run away with me. We'll find some crumbling castle beside some long-forgotten sea and make it ours."

"Why must it be crumbling?" Aster giggled. "Can we not find a decent castle and roust the inhabitants instead?"

"If that is what you wish." Veridian smiled. She rolled over to gaze at Aster in the dark. There was just enough light to make out her profile and the curve of her grin. *Peace*, Veridian thought. *That is what I feel when I look at you. And it is the only time that I feel it.*

"Veridian? What's wrong?"

"Nothing." Veridian pulled Aster closer. Would that they could stay there, caught in this moment for eternity. But that was not how eternity worked. It was the moments she dreaded that seemed to linger. Times like these disappeared in a dawn come too soon. "Nothing, dearest." She kissed Aster's neck. "Nothing at all."

10.

AETHIEL'S SEA MONSTER

Day had just broken in Atropa as Aethiel's horse leaped from the black throat of the Veil and galloped down the hills toward the city. Foam and sweat stood out on the poor creature's neck and withers, but the big Aristene couldn't let it slow. They'd ridden hard from the port and straight through the endless darkness, and the bay mare had done it well, though Aethiel was too large for her and she carried another body besides. Aethiel kicked the mare again and heard her grunt. It was not much farther to the Citadel, and the elders. Then she could rest.

She raced past early-risen acolytes in the streets, their heads turning in curiosity as they jumped out of her path. When she reached the square she slid from her horse and pulled the reeking corpse down to lay over her shoulder. The acolyte who collected the mare cried out and held his hand to his mouth at the sight of it, and she wished she'd arrived under cover of dark.

Dead flesh pressed against her cheek as she bounded up the endless steps. But where to go once she was inside? She couldn't bring such filth into the sacred space of the dome. Perhaps she should have left the corpse in the meadow and brought the elders to it. But it was too late for that now.

At the top of the stairs, an acolyte she didn't recognize ran up with wide eyes, hand to her nose against the smell. "Aristene, what . . ."

Aethiel paused. Even with her Aristene strength, and the lingering strength of the war gift of Fennbirn Island, she'd begun to sag under the weight. It was all those steps. She'd always thought there were too many.

Rooms lined the hall in sets of dark wood doors and Aethiel headed for the largest. She burst inside, and heaved the corpse down onto a table. It had been set with tea and flowers; the corpse's bulk smashed the plates and pottery. Dark tea and water ran from broken pots and vases to drip to the floor, to mix with flung slime and congealed blood.

"Go and fetch the elders," Aethiel panted. She touched the wound below her neck that still leaked red. "And we will need new tea."

As the acolyte's footsteps faded down the hallway, Aethiel pulled out the bench and sat, placing her elbows beside the corpse. The body before her made little sense even to her, who had witnessed its changing. Below the waist, the flesh was a whale's shade of gray, and what had once been legs had fused together to end in a muscular tail. Above, the skin was still tanned and golden, the torso and head still that of a man. Or nearly so. Most men didn't have jaws that unhinged or mouths full of translucent teeth, sharp as daggers.

Had she found it in a net, Aethiel would have called it a sea monster. Had she not seen her hero become it before her very eyes.

I failed you, she thought as she looked at what remained of him. *I'm sorry*. But she didn't say so out loud. Queens did not apologize to men on her island, and though she'd been away from that place for a lifetime, the habit still held. The elders arrived in the doorway, and instead of rising to acknowledge them, Aethiel stayed where she was. Queens didn't bow on her island either. Or at least, not unless they felt like it.

"What is this?" Tiern approached and used her knife to lift one of the arms, unchanged save the growth of webbing between the fingers.

"It was a man," Aethiel replied. "It was my hero." And a fine one he had been, a seafarer with glories less at the point of a sword than at the prow of his vessel. The men he sailed with had whispered that with him at the helm, a ship was unsinkable.

Ferreh walked around the table, staring gravely at the corpse. When she came to Aethiel she gently moved her head aside to look at her wound.

"It will heal," Aethiel said gruffly.

"Could you not have set him on the floor?" Tiern gestured to the broken pottery, the spilled tea and water. She waved her hand before her face against the scent of rot and wiped her blade clean on her cape. "How did you kill it?"

"I threw him against a stone and broke his neck." Aethiel swallowed. She'd never killed one of her own heroes before. Nor had she often gotten them killed. But this one had not been himself when he'd slithered and slapped his way across the docks, his bones popping into new positions, his eyes devoid of all traces of the man he'd been only moments before. "I did it with my old magic. The power of the Aristene was subdued." She hadn't realized it until afterward, when the monster lay dead. She'd used the brute strength of her mind, the magic she'd been born with. She touched the wound in her neck. Had it been a small bit deeper, even she, who had once been the legendary war queen of Fennbirn Island, would have bled out and perished.

"I know this magic." Tiern sniffed at the corpse; her lips curled and she snarled like a wolf. "The smell of it. It is like Oreas of Rhonassus."

Ferreh inhaled sharply. King Oreas was a man who had become a monstrosity. Who they had fought and who would have bested them were it not for the actions of two initiates and their mortal heroes.

Tiern prodded the creature's reeking tail. "Like, but not the same. Oreas was far larger, and he didn't sprout a tail." She looked again at the webbing between the fingers, the translucent fangs that protruded from between thin, stretched lips.

"What could have caused this?" Ferreh's tone was calm and her touch gentle, but the muscles of her neck stood out like cords. "Who was near him, in the days before?"

"There was a fight in the port—he argued with a band of priests. But they were barely more than beggars." Aethiel stared at the twisted shape of her dead hero. "He took a small wound, but we killed them." The elders traded a look, and Tiern lifted the corpse, searching until she found the tiny, puckered cut above the rear right ribs. The skin around it had scabbed closed. But even dead it looked reddened. She reopened it with a small slice and stuck her fingers inside. Her eyes widened.

Her fingers emerged holding a fragment of bone. "This bone is not his." Tiern dropped it to the table with a hiss.

"A piece of the Scylloi Prophet?" Ferreh drew closer. Even the elder winced to look upon it, and having it near made Aethiel feel her blood loss anew.

"Look at that," Tiern whispered, and Aethiel leaned in as the gray of the tail turned back to golden flesh, and the webbing between the fingers slightly receded. "Interesting." But it was no miracle; the hero was still dead. "I wonder if the blight of the bone would disappear completely if given enough time."

"Does that mean I could have saved him?" Aethiel asked. "If I'd have removed it?"

"You could not have known," said Ferreh. "You did for him all that any of us could have done."

"But what must we do now?" Tiern asked. She waved her hand over the desecrated body. "Who are these priests? How do they have the bones of the prophet?"

"And why do they come for our heroes?" Ferreh murmured. She looked at the gore-streaked bit of bone.

"We need Machianthe," said Tiern. "Glorious death must strengthen the order before it is too late."

"What can Reed do?" Aethiel asked. "When not I, nor you"—she looked at Tiern—"could stand against the skull in Rhonassus?"

"You stood against it here," Tiern said. "With the magic of your island."

"The gift," Aethiel corrected her. "My war gift. But it was barely enough."

Ferreh took a deep breath. She sounded tired, though she looked the same as she had the first time Aethiel had seen her. One look and Aethiel had known immediately that Ferreh was a woman whom even a queen could serve.

"Perhaps we're too late," the elder said. "Perhaps there is no glory great enough. Perhaps we already failed when we could not convince Veridian to be the one to save us."

"But, Machianthe—"

"No, Tiern!"

"Do not tell me no!" Tiern reached down and curled her fist around the bone. "The skull of the Scylloi Prophet was not destroyed. And in shattering it we may have vanquished one enemy only to create an army of them instead!"

"We don't need Machianthe. These beasts can be slain. And these priests can be killed. I will find the priests. And I will send riders to the new king of Rhonassus, to collect what remains of the prophet's bones."

"You are being soft," Tiern said as Aethiel shifted uncomfortably. The elders seemed to have forgotten she was there and watching them. What was left of Aethiel's war gift rose and licked its teeth.

"Perhaps," said Ferreh. "But this is the way."

"This is your way," Tiern said. "But it is not mine." She looked at the corpse of the corrupted hero with disgust. Then turned on her heel and left. Aethiel waited for Ferreh to act, but the elder did nothing. The mind of the order might decide one thing. But if the teeth of the order still wished to bite, none had the authority to stop her.

11.

THE NEW HERO

Crossing through the Veil was easier as a full member of the order, but it still felt like being turned inside out. Reed and Silco raised their faces to the warm sunlight, taking a moment to recover. It was nicer coming home to Atropa than it was to leave; coming home was to be reinvigorated, and bathed in Kleia Gloria's magic. Though this time, she and Silco seemed to be the only ones who enjoyed it. Below them, Aster and Rabbit were already riding away down the hill, and behind them, Lyonene squinted against the bright light reflecting off the Citadel's gold dome.

Reed nudged Silco into a few strides of a jolting canter to catch up to Rabbit. "Aster," she said. "Is everything all right?"

"Of course." Aster glanced back. "Don't worry about Lyonene. The first gaze into the sacred well after the trial is the hardest. Not everyone leaves their first hero behind as successfully as you."

Reed looked down. The way she had left Hestion could be called many things but never a success. "I don't mean Lyonene. I meant—" She paused. "I know it can't be easy, parting from Veridian. Are you worried about her?"

Beneath Aster, Rabbit's dark gray ears flickered back and forth.

"Should I be?" Aster asked.

"I don't know. I wasn't traveling with her long, but . . . she seemed sad."

"I imagine she is often sad. I don't like to think of her out there, on her own."

"But you would know if she was in danger," Reed said. "You always say so."

Aster's expression grew clouded. "Not all dangers are the same," she whispered, and nudged Rabbit to a trot.

"Everyone is so troubled," Reed said, swaying atop Silco's odd, limping gait.

"It's easy to be chipper when you're returning home still sparkling with glory," Lyonene muttered as Strawberry ambled past. "The elders will be so pleased they'll probably throw you a parade."

"That would be nice," Reed said. "And I'm counting on their goodwill to be lasting . . . in case you and I get caught."

They rode down the hill, the white city of Atropa stretched out below like a trove of pearls. Sheep and goats speckled the hillsides and milled in lines throughout the valley, the mountain casting a short midday shadow. Near the eastern end, the ground had been cleared for the construction of the library.

"Look," Reed said, and pointed. "They've begun work on the foundation." Silco hopped a few paces until they'd caught up. "It will house books and scrolls, records of the deeds of every known Aristene and every hero they've guided." At her current pace, Reed realized it would not be long before she would require a shelf all her own. "We will watch its progress from these hills every time we come home."

"Strange to think that," Lyonene said. "The building of that library will take a hundred years and we'll still be alive when it's finished."

"We are Aristene now," Reed said. "Time no longer exists for us."

"No," Lyonene agreed. "Only for those we love. Alsander. Gretchen." *Hestion*, Reed thought, but wouldn't allow herself to say. "Someday all of those people will be gone," Lyonene said quietly. "And what will we be then?"

She nudged Strawberry ahead as they rode into the city behind Aster, passing shepherds and vendors, laborers and shopkeepers. The Aristene Ellora trotted by with a stag slung across her saddle. "Gloria Thea Matris, Aster! Little sisters!" she shouted. Mol, the tall, blond Aristene who rode beside her on a large white Areion, only glared. And she wasn't the only one. Sometimes when she returned to Atropa, Reed sensed questions in the eyes of her sisters. Questions about the circumstances surrounding her Joining. About why she'd been allowed to join them at all.

But that would fade, once they reaped the benefits of the glory she brought them.

"What was that about?" Lyonene asked when Mol had passed.

"Mol was there when I brought Hestion into the city," Reed replied. "I think she's disappointed I wasn't killed by the elders."

"As if they would have killed you, Glorious Death."

"Enough, children," Aster said, finally acknowledging them over her shoulder. "No one wants you dead."

"*Yet*," Reed mouthed, and Lyonene chuckled faintly.

They reached the square and dismounted to stand before the foot of the stairs. Aster started up without a word as Reed and Lyonene gazed at the gold-capped dome. Climbing those long stairs now was easy, but even though their legs didn't tire, the Citadel still loomed, and the ground still fell away until it felt like floating untethered from the earth.

"Are those the elders up there, waiting?" Lyonene asked.

"They must have felt us come through the Veil."

"We shouldn't have joked about them killing us," Lyonene muttered. "I feel as a cat ready to puff out her fur. You don't have to do this for me, Reed," she whispered. "You can still change your mind."

"It's not only for you. Think how nice it will be for me to guide a hero who for once isn't fated to die. Now go. Gaze into the well, and tell me what you see."

Lyonene took a deep breath and they took the stairs together, and reached the top to face the elders. Tiern gripped Reed by the shoulders and gave her a smacking kiss on both cheeks.

"Machianthe," she said.

"Gloria Thea Matris, elder."

"Gloria Thea Matris indeed," Tiern said, "for we felt your most recent hero pass through to the goddess. Ferreh," she called over her shoulder, "we should hold a great feast, so her sisters might honor all that Machianthe has done."

Reed looked at her hopefully, thinking of roast meats and ripe berries, the little pies stuffed with boiled egg and spices that the Atropan taverns served piping hot. But Ferreh frowned. "All Aristene serve glory. None are recognized above the others." The elder's tone was cool, and she looked at Reed without a trace of her usual affection. Reed glanced at Aster, who caught her eye with an accusatory look. *What have you done to displease her?* that look asked. But she had done nothing. She had been perfect. Better than perfect, she had been excellent; it was through her acts that the sun in Atropa shone so brightly, that the goddess was so richly satiated.

"You return quickly," Ferreh said, and Reed noticed that though the elder spoke to her, she hadn't used her name. Not Reed, not Machianthe, not even "initiate," as she sometimes still referred to her. "And though we are pleased by your bounty, it falls to me to say that you must ensure that all heroes are given the honor that is their due. A hero is sacred. Each must be guided with care."

"Yes, elder." Reed lowered her eyes, if only to keep Ferreh from seeing the fire in them. She'd expected praise, not a lecture. And to be scolded in front of Lyonene and Aster—she'd done nothing to deserve it. Reed stole a glance at Tiern, who stared at Ferreh angrily. Tiern's jaw clenched and unclenched as if she thought that heroes were not so much sacred as they were food.

But if Ferreh didn't like her pace, then she would slow it, and see if the elder liked that better. And if no Aristene were to be recognized above the others, what was the point in pushing herself so hard anyway?

"I will rest, then," Reed said. She looked pointedly at Ferreh, but if the elder caught her meaning, she gave no indication.

"Reed?" Lyonene asked.

"Go. I'll wait for you after."

Reed waited for Lyonene in the hall of the Aristene. She usually enjoyed wandering among the statues, looking into the blank eyes of stone and imagining what glories they'd seen. But today the statues were stone blurs. She couldn't stop thinking of Ferreh and wondering what she had done to make her unhappy.

She paced back and forth until she found herself before the statue of ancient Emaleth, who had been mentor to Aster. Perhaps she could offer some insight or advice. Reed reached up to touch the edge of the bone knife held in one of the statue's hands. Even in stone, Emaleth looked fierce. One side of the warrior's head was shorn to the scalp and on the other side her hair was short and blowing in the wind. The corner of her mouth carried the beginnings of a scowl, or a battle cry. A mentor like that wouldn't have let the elders insult her initiate.

Reed drew her hand back. That wasn't fair. It wasn't Aster's responsibility to defend her against the elders' judgments. But what, Reed wondered, did Ferreh want?

She had chosen Reed to be a Glorious Death. She was the one who had set that task within her as a bit placed into the mouth of a horse. To strengthen the order, she said. To win unparalleled glory. And Reed had delivered it, not once but three times. Yet now Ferreh seemed to think that she hadn't done it well enough.

The heroes are dead, Reed thought, *and the glory rose. What more do you wish of me?*

Returning to Atropa to trade heroes with Lyonene, she'd been worried about how she would explain not looking into the sacred well, but it turned out she hadn't needed to bother. Ferreh hadn't even blinked.

She crossed her arms, thinking of what Lyonene might see when she bent over the murky water of the well.

Aster said that visions from the well were varied. Faces seen in profile, shapes viewed in battle or in battles to come. Once, a vision came to her with a song, and she had no idea what it meant, like a riddle. She said that all heroes were riddles, puzzles to be worked out.

Reed had looked into the well four times. And each time what she'd seen had been much the same: a hero in some faraway place. One had been clothed in the skin of a bear. Another she'd seen through the winds of a blizzard, his shape so obscured by the weather and wrapped in furs that his features were barely visible. And the last, most recent one . . .

She paused. She couldn't remember what the vision was. She still remembered him—it had been little more than a week since their last battle. But the vision of him, the first time she'd seen him, had already faded from her mind. She was sad to realize that, because when the moment of glory came, when his blood stained the ground and she felt his glory carried to the goddess like gold, her time with him had felt eternal.

They all felt that way. Yet after it was over she was running through the Veil to seek the next.

There was only one vision that would never fade. Reed closed her eyes and saw Hestion.

Hestion as a young boy, his eyes like a storm and his hair wild. Hestion as a young prince, his shoulders broadened and his eyes searching. They had been joined by the well and by Kleia Gloria for nearly their entire lives. He was the only one who remained embedded in her memory.

A shadow fell across her and she opened her eyes.

"Well," Reed said as Lyonene approached. "What did you see? Where am I going?"

12.

OUTFITTED FOR MATCHMAKING

Lyonene's hero was a princess of Cassor, a small, landlocked country that was rich in gold but poor in army. The Cassan king looked to remedy that situation by using his daughter's marriage to secure an alliance that would further secure his borders. The Aristene assigned to her was to facilitate this match, allowing the princess to achieve a marriage far beyond her station. In short, Reed was going to be a matchmaker.

There was just one more thing they had to do in order for their plan to succeed. They needed to visit the Outfitter.

"This is crazy," Lyonene muttered as she and Reed made their way through the hall of the Aristene to the door that led down the steep, dark incline to the Outfitter's chambers. "Even if I tell you everything I saw in the well, the princess won't truly be yours. Only I can carry the thread of her destiny and see the possibilities of her actions. If you go, you'll have no more advantage of magic than you had during the Hero's Trial."

"Then it's a good thing I nearly passed my Hero's Trial," said Reed.

"This is crazy," Lyonene said again, grumbling. "I can't describe all of what I saw, the king, her family—her own face—all that knowledge and more imprinted on my mind."

"Lyonene, this was a lucky vision. It's only a marriage! How badly can I do?"

Lyonene's shoulders hunched as they walked and she flinched from the gazes of the statues as though they were spies. "We're going to get caught."

"Only if you don't stop looking so shifty," Reed hissed. They reached the door at the end of the hall. This was Lyonene's first hero as a full Aristene, and Reed realized that Lyonene had never actually met the ageless acolyte who readied Aristene warriors for the realms of their heroes. When the Outfitter had prepared them for their Heroes' Trials, the initiates had been told to wait outside while their mentors received her gifts. On that occasion she gave them only trinkets and supplies: a few fancy tunics, belts of silver cord, a small purse of coin, and for Lyonene the finery of royalty. But for a full member of the order, the Outfitter could do much more. She could imbue them with physical features, placing tattoos of unearned honor upon their skin that would vanish when the mission was complete. She could even enchant the tongue to speak a language it did not know how to speak.

Lyonene stepped back from the door. "I can't let you do this."

"Do you want to go back to Alsander or not?" Reed asked.

"You're absolutely mad, Ox," Lyonene said, eyes wide. "We won't even make it out of the Citadel. The Outfitter will know what we're up to, and then Tiern will drape her bed with our newly tanned hides."

"She won't if you follow my lead," Reed said, and pulled Lyonene through the door.

The Outfitter's quarters were far belowground, where the walls seemed damp and the air smelled of minerals and the straw that lined the floor. Reed led the way with a torch, one hand out upon the wall to steady herself.

"Would you call this rule breaking," Lyonene asked—Reed could hear the toes of her sandals shushing carefully against the stone steps—"or rule bending?"

"Neither," Reed replied. "For this is not a rule." Of true rules, there was really only one: wear no crowns, make no marriages, no oaths, and no vows, save those of the order.

"We'll still be punished if we're found out."

"So they'll make us spend time in service to the city. Maybe we'll have to perform some of the construction on the new library."

"Maybe they'll cut off our fingers," Lyonene muttered.

Or maybe they would be banished. When Reed was just a young initiate, Aster had once told her of such an Aristene.

They called her the Wolf. Shunned by her sisters, she had slowly gone mad, hunting the hills of Atropa, capturing and killing wolves and wearing their pelts. Stealing their pups to raise as her own. The Wolf hadn't been seen for many years, and of course for all Reed knew, Aster had made the whole thing up. But she had noticed that few of the Aristene rode through the eastern woods unaccompanied.

After what seemed like an age, they finally reached the bottom of the stairs, and the broad door of iron-banded wood.

"I've never been inside before," Lyonene whispered.

"It's not much," Reed said. "It reminds me of our huts in the Summer Camp." Reed reached out and lifted the latch.

"Wait—what has she given you for your other heroes?"

Reed shrugged. "Coin, mostly. Though when I traveled to the snow lands of Arden she turned my hair red so I would be taken for a mystic. And she gave me a fur blanket to throw on Silco that made him grow a thick winter coat and feathered feet to go through the snowdrifts."

"She can alter our Areion?" Lyonene's eyes widened. "Can she make Strawberry taller?"

"Lyonene, you chose her—"

"I know, Ox. I'm only joking."

With a deep breath, Reed shouldered through the door, and she and Lyonene spilled through into the small, warm room. The floor beneath their feet was softened by woven rugs, and a finely carved table sat in the center, surrounded by wooden chairs and a stone bench. Wildflowers from the hills burst from several vases and the air was fresher inside than out, a breeze coming through where the high ceiling curved up and back into the dark. Reed set her torch into a sconce near the entrance as they heard the sound of footsteps.

"She comes."

Lyonene grabbed Reed's elbow. "This was a mistake. We should go."

"Since when are you so unadventurous?" Reed asked. "Do you think it's a dragon who comes? Or a shambling corpse?"

"An Aristene doesn't fear a shambling corpse," Lyonene whispered. "But the Outfitter is a servant of the order like any other acolyte. She won't agree to this."

"She's not like any other acolyte. The Outfitter serves Kleia Gloria. Why should she care who does the harvesting so long as the crop comes in? But you're right." Reed tensed as the Outfitter's shadow came into view. "She won't help us, so follow my lead, as I said."

The Outfitter stepped out of the darkness. At first she seemed a huddled old woman wrapped in a blanket, but as the ceiling and walls widened to allow her full height, the shadows fell away to reveal folded arms draped in a long, woven veil, and strong legs moving beneath a pale blue skirt.

Reed and Lyonene bowed their heads.

"Welcome, Aristenes," the Outfitter said. "I've been expecting you."

"You have?" Lyonene asked, and she and Reed traded a worried glance.

"No. That's just what I always say. Makes me seem—" She waved her hand. "Magical."

"But you are magical," said Lyonene. "Aren't you?"

"I am. That's why I like to seem so." The Outfitter removed her veil. Beneath it her face was ageless—plain of feature and unwrinkled, though the hair atop her head was bright white. She went to her cupboard and took down three cups, then retrieved a pitcher. She brought them all back to the large, circular table in the center of the room and poured as they sat. Reed and Lyonene each took a cup, and the Outfitter raised hers and drank.

"Such good wine," Lyonene said.

"Atropan food is very good," the Outfitter said. "But Atropan wine? It's bland. Grapes grown in soil never enriched by fire and ash. Sweetened by honey made by bees who've never known a swatting." She took another swallow and studied Reed over the rim of her cup. "Back again so soon, Machianthe? Decades sometimes pass between glimpses of faces, but yours I have already seen thrice. Is it too much to hope that you are simply an accompaniment to your friend?" The Outfitter's eyes settled on Lyonene. "My, how the goddess does like them pretty. What is your name, child?"

"Lyonene."

The Outfitter nodded. "Lee-oh-neen. Lie-oh-ness. With a wild mane and sharp teeth."

"Do you have a name besides 'Outfitter'?" Lyonene asked. The Outfitter glanced at Reed and Reed felt heat rise to her cheeks. Three visits to her and she'd never thought to ask that.

"Of course I do," the Outfitter said. "Even the horses have names; they are not just called 'Areion.' My name is Gria."

"An interesting name," said Reed.

"It is not so interesting where I come from. I was not even the only Gria in my village. But that was a long time ago. And even farther away." She waved her hand again. "This Gria or that Gria doesn't matter. My story ended when I became this—" She opened her palms. "And now I am only this thing that I do, this aid that I give to those who will give aid to heroes." There was no bitterness in her voice, and none in her colorless eyes. The Outfitter was as an emptied bowl, whoever she had been before leached slowly out to make room for the magic.

She reached beneath the table and pulled up a large, shallow dish, heavy and made of gold not pounded thin but molded and rough, like a pot that had been shaped by hand.

"Blood," she said, and slapped a small, sharp knife down beside it. "Blood and gold to show the vision from the deep well." She regarded Lyonene. "One small splash, lioness. Won't kill you."

"Indeed it won't," Reed said, "but it will be mine again today."

"Yours again." Gria sighed, and in a stroke of luck for their scheme she stood and tottered away for another jug of wine. Quickly, Reed took up the knife and sliced into Lyonene's wrist, letting the blood stream down into the bowl in a thin, dark line. Then she collected some in her palm and shoved Lyonene's arm away to be hidden in her cape. When Gria turned back to them, Reed was squeezing the last of Lyonene's blood from between her fingers into the bowl. Gria gave her a length of bandage and Lyonene tore it for her, discreetly taking some to bind the cut on her arm, hidden beneath the table.

Gria leaned over the dish and peered in. She murmured to herself, and plunged all ten fingertips in to smear blood across the dense, glittering surface. To Reed and Lyonene it looked like nothing but blood, and Gria a toddler, playing in it. But after a few moments, the Outfitter sat upright.

"Not much," she said.

She wiped her fingertips clean, and used the same cloth to sop up the blood. Then she placed the dish back beneath the table and stood. "Come with me, big tree, and we will see you prepared for Cassor."

The Outfitter led them through an arched doorway into a room full of deep wooden chests and boxes, large and small, jeweled and plain. Some were covered in leather, others carved from stone. Reed fought a smile at the wideness of Lyonene's eyes—it was rare to see the worldly girl so full of wonder.

Gria moved between the chests, opening one and then another.

Inside could be glimpsed interiors of silver and gold, shining embroidered linings and vibrant painted murals.

"So many chests," Lyonene said. "So many treasures."

"Given only when needed. And only by me. Without my hands, you wouldn't be able to open the smallest drawer or jeweled case— not even with your Aristene strength."

Lyonene made a face. "That cannot be."

Reed shrugged. She had never thought to try, and it irritated her that she hadn't. Lyonene had often said she was incurious.

Gria extended a hand toward the chests and boxes: an invitation.

Reed and Lyonene approached a chest, large enough to crawl inside and secured with brass latches and buckles. Lyonene unfastened the buckles and flipped up the latch. She tried to open the lid and it wouldn't budge. It didn't move at all, not even when she bent and put her shoulder into it. Both the chest and the lid remained still, as if it was carved of one piece from the same stone of the floor.

"Try a small one," Lyonene said. Reed picked up a little gold box that had no latch or lock. But she couldn't lift the lid. She gripped the top and tucked it in the crook of her arm and pulled, arms flexing. She may as well have been trying to lift the entire Citadel. Lyonene came to help, and for a moment both Aristenes yanked on the box with all their might.

Nothing. Reed drew her sword.

"Maybe if we jam a blade between the edges." She raised her arm and took aim, and Gria laughed.

"Enough. Don't go breaking a perfectly good sword. You two are quite hardheaded; most take my word for it after they fail to open whatever thing they first choose." She walked over on soft-slippered feet and reached between them—the lid of the box opened without a creak and Lyonene scoffed and threw up her hands. Inside, the box held a needle and a spindle of fat gold thread.

"What is that?" Reed asked.

"That is what you need."

"Odd that we would choose that box of all the others to try," said Lyonene.

"Is it?" Gria asked as she took out the items. "Or was it empty until the moment I decided to put my hand upon it? Here." She pulled the needle loose with its tail of gold and held out her hand. Reed laid her own hand over the Outfitter's, palm up, and Gria drove the needle deep into Reed's skin.

She jerked back. But Gria's grip was as strong as the seal on the boxes as she slowly sewed Reed's fingers together.

"Be done in a moment." Gria sank the needle and pulled the thread. Prick and burn, prick and burn, until she knotted the ends and left Reed's hand throbbing and wetted with blood. Then she held her hand out for the other. When both were finished, the Outfitter bit through the thread with a quick snap of her jaw and replaced the needle and thread inside the box.

Reed held up her hands, monstrously bound and useless.

"This is no Cassor custom that I have ever heard of," said Lyonene. "How is she supposed to ride? To fight?"

"She is a matchmaker; she will not need to fight. But she must know how to sew." The Outfitter stared at Reed's hands with interest as the burning in them changed to an itch, and the itch to a tingle as the thread worked its way into the skin. "Gowns, and veils, and ornaments . . . She must know how to braid in coils. She must know which Cassor flowers can be tucked behind an ear and which will cause a facial rash. . . ." The gold thread disappeared into Reed's skin as if it never was. "And now her hands know all of that."

Reed flexed her fingers and marveled at her palms, turning them back and forth. She didn't really have a wish to know how to sew anything besides an arrow wound. But she sensed that were she to pick up that gold needle and thread, she would be able to stitch in nine patterns.

"Now to the dress," said Gria. "And the hat."

"The hat?" Reed squawked. The Outfitter walked to a wooden trunk and returned with a dress of red fabric. "Put this on," she said, and gestured behind an ivory curtain.

Reed took the clothes and went. With her height, the curtain wasn't much of a barrier, which made her change of clothes even more awkward: she hunched and bent, struggling with the straps of her sword. The red matchmaker's dress was plain except for twinkling bells that hung at the waist of the under-tunic and at the ends of the sleeves. They jangled as she forced her long arms through them. She couldn't imagine any matchmaker in the history of Cassor having the muscle and the shoulders that she did, yet the dress fit her perfectly.

"Don't forget the slippers," Gria called, and tossed them over the curtain. They were the same red and embroidered with roses. Reed scowled. But she put them on, and stepped out.

"That is not bad. Let us see the hat." The Outfitter produced it from beneath her arm. It was tall and round, the same red as the dress. It had small silver bells that tinkled like annoying and upbeat blowflies. Reed put it on, and Lyonene, who had been standing grave and composed, bent over laughing.

"You look horrible!"

"She looks like a matchmaker." Gria whacked her shoulder. "They all look horrible."

Reed glowered as she walked to Lyonene's side. But this had been her idea. "Is there anything else?"

"Only the coin." Gria reached into a deep pot of clay and pulled out a fat purse. Inside were coins of gold and silver, and what looked to be a few valuable trinkets: an emerald ring, a pin of silver in the shape of a bird, with red gems for eyes. "Always a good idea for a matchmaker to have bribery money.

"And with that, you are off to Cassor." The Outfitter ushered them out with a hand on each of their backs. The ruse had worked.

"Wait."

They looked back. Gria stood still, her ageless eyes unfocused, cheeks smooth and slack.

"There is something else." She cocked her head at a jeweled box and lifted the lid. Inside was a knife, its blade hidden in a sheath of dark brown leather. She removed it from the box and handed it to Reed, who took it out and studied it.

The blade was plain as the handle, no engravings, no daring curves. It could have been found in any Atropan kitchen, being used to cut carrots and hunks of meat.

"Mind the edge," Gria said. "It's coated in poison."

Reed held it to her nose and sniffed. There was something slightly acrid there. Something bitter. "What use does a matchmaker have for this?" she asked.

"I don't know. There was nothing in the blood to suggest it. Yet here it is."

Reed tucked it into her belt. "Gria, thank you," she said, but the

Outfitter was already returning to the shadows. Reed and Lyonene left the chamber, and made their way up the staircase and out of the Citadel.

"She seemed troubled by that," Lyonene said.

Reed touched the knife handle. "I don't mind it. It's the only part of this ridiculous costume that feels like it belongs to me."

"But none of it belongs to you." Lyonene stared at the matchmaker's garb warily, and Reed whisked it away into the aether in favor of her armor and cape.

"Don't worry about me, Lyonene. This is just a small thing. Now get back to Cerille, before Alsander's father cuts off his head."

13.

THE WORLD'S GATE

After Lyonene left through the Veil, Reed didn't immediately depart for Cassor. Instead she lingered into nightfall, listening to the ever-quiet city grow even more so, and watching the flickering of orange flames light the windows of taverns and homes from the top of the Citadel steps. As the moon rose, she tracked it across the sky, imagining it was the goddess's wide eye looking down.

When she'd been a child, Reed had thought of the goddess as another mother. She thought that when she became an Aristene the goddess would be even more so, the distance between them bridged by the tether of glory. Instead, Reed felt strangely severed. As if she'd moved somehow beyond Kleia Gloria's reach.

But that was a dangerous thought. More likely it was only a prayer, a hope that Kleia Gloria might look away for a time.

Just long enough for me to marry off this princess in Cassor, Reed thought. Cassor. In her mind the word had begun to sound like "ass sore" and she hoped that wasn't what the mission would become.

Without knowing what compelled her, she wound her way back through the Citadel, and up the steep, close steps that emerged into the dome. Silver moonlight flooded the vast space through the cut windows. The vibrant murals that stretched across the walls stood muted by the dark. But even in the shadows, the sacred well seemed to sparkle. Reed approached it, and ran her hand over its strange construction, haphazard and uneven, its shape molded from great chunks and thin slabs, slivers of shale and dashes of pebble. Stones from fallen cities, from fortresses that had long since crumbled. So many pieces of so many lands, holding back that dark, deep water.

And even though she'd promised to tend to Lyonene's hero, Reed's fingers itched to gaze down into it.

"Machianthe."

Reed turned. The silver overlay of Tiern's armor flashed in the moonlight.

"Elder."

"Have you looked again, into the well? What have you seen?"

"I haven't," Reed replied. She tried to think of a reason then for being inside the sacred space of the dome, but Tiern didn't seem to care.

Tiern walked across the floor, to the edge of the World's Gate, the vast silver disk set within the center of the floor. She carried something slung over her shoulder, and slid it to the ground. It looked like a dead animal. Long dead, were Reed to judge by the smell.

Reed walked closer as Tiern knelt above the World's Gate. The elder pressed her hand to it and Reed gasped; the great silver circle disappeared, and Tiern's face was bathed in pale light.

From the moment Reed had encountered the World's Gate as a child she had wondered about it. But in an offhand sort of way, the lazy way of a person who was certain that all mysteries would be revealed to them in time. She'd never truly considered what the World's Gate was, or even the nature of its name: it was a gate, and gates opened. They swung wide, and allowed things to pass through. But what those things might be it had never occurred to her to ask, until now, when she saw it lying open at Tiern's feet.

Tiern reached for the dead thing she'd carried. "Look," she said. Reed peered closer as the elder parted the cloth that shrouded the corpse. She'd seen death before—in her own small settlement, upon the battlefields of Rhonassus—but the sight of this made her recoil.

It was the body of a man, or it used to be. Below the waist his legs had fused together into a long and twisting tail. Sharp, dark claws tipped his fingers, and his eyes were flat and black and lidless.

"What is this?" Reed asked, breathing shallowly against the smell of rotting fish.

"Must I really tell you," Tiern replied gravely. It was not a question. Reed knew as well as the elder did, for she, too, had seen what had become of King Oreas. The abomination he had become, stretched and made into an unnatural monster by the influence of the skull of the Scylloi Prophet.

"This was a hero," Tiern went on. "One of Aethiel's." A sea monster for Aethiel, who loved to find her heroes upon ships.

"But the skull of the prophet was destroyed."

"It seems the pieces have a similar effect." Tiern reached into a pouch at her belt and opened her palm. A thin, sharp shard of blackened bone lay illuminated by the moon, but even had it been full dark Reed would have known what it was. She could feel it, a slight sickness in the pit of her stomach. It tugged on the edges of her Aristene magic, like a sucking mouth, and made her armor want to disappear back into the aether.

"How can you stand to be near it?" Reed asked.

"I am an elder. And the unpleasantness lessens, over time." Tiern rubbed her thumb across the smooth surface of the bone and tucked it back into her belt. "Something comes for us, Reed. We thought we put it down with the monstrous king, but we were wrong."

"What is it?" Reed asked.

"We do not know. Yet. Aethiel saw priests. . . ." Tiern's words drifted. She seemed lost in thought. "It would not be the first time that a god tried to come for Kleia Gloria."

"What, then, do we do?"

Tiern turned to her sharply. "*You* will do nothing. If you catch wind of any danger, you will return to Atropa immediately. You are far too precious to risk, Glorious Death. This creature"—Tiern curled her lip as she looked at it—"nearly killed Aethiel." Aethiel, who was among their strongest. She'd been a friend to Reed, had helped her escape after Oreas had imprisoned her. She'd helped them save Aster, and this *thing* had dared to hurt her, as some god dared to threaten Kleia Gloria and the order. Reed clenched her teeth angrily.

"That's why I have to help," Reed said. "I've faced this magic before—"

"That was different. You were less susceptible to it, you were an initiate—"

"I was mortal," Reed said. "And I faced it anyway."

"You are still mortal, Machianthe. All of the Aristene are mortal."

"So they are. And I won't stand by and let them remain in danger when I can fight these creatures and recognize their magic."

"I know why you would fight," Tiern said. "But you should not be going into the world of men at all."

"And yet I go," Reed replied fiercely. "I will go into the world.

I'll watch and listen. And if I see one of these—abominations—I will kill it."

Tiern paused. "Ferreh would not like that."

"So don't tell her."

The elder's eyes flashed, but it was as Veridian had said: Reed was becoming one of the strongest in the order. She was rising within the Aristene.

"Very well," Tiern said. She leaned down and grasped the tail of the corpse. A look of displeasure twisted her features as she heaved it into the gate. The thing was so stinking and foul that Reed thought the gate would vomit it back up. But it fell through the silver light until it disappeared.

"Where did it go?" Reed asked.

"None can say." Tiern passed her hand through the air and the gate closed, once again a broad disk of silver set into the floor. They stood. "Where do you go now?"

Reed couldn't tell her the truth. "I'm not sure."

"Well, wherever you go, keep your eyes sharp. These creatures have been seen most often in the company of priests in shabby gray robes. We don't know what god they worship, or what grudge they bear us, but if you discover one, send word and I will come to you. If you see one of these creatures"—she placed a hand upon Reed's shoulder—"then I pray that you can do as you say and kill it."

Reed nodded, and Tiern turned and disappeared from the dome.

Reed found Aster at the grounds of the new library. Her mentor was lying upon a large slab of stone, staring up into the night sky.

"What are you doing?" Reed asked.

But instead of replying, Aster reached out and pulled Reed down onto the stone with her. She placed her arm underneath Reed's head as a pillow. "I felt the Veil open again just now; I thought you might've gone without saying goodbye."

"I try not to do that," Reed said.

"Good." Aster rested her chin against the top of Reed's head. "I should have said more of a goodbye to Veridian. You said she seemed sad."

"I thought so," said Reed. "But she also seemed angry. She also seemed drunk."

Aster snorted. "Well, if she drinks too much she cries, and that is nothing to worry about." She took a breath. She seemed comforted, though it was a strange thing to be comforted by.

"I know you won't remain here for long," said Aster. "Where do you ride to?"

Reed frowned. She didn't want to lie to her mentor. "Aster, where does the World's Gate lead?"

"The World's Gate? It leads to many places, as the name would suggest."

"Like the Veil leads to many places?"

"The gate leads to more places than the Veil. And none of the same. If the Veil is a wrapping around this world, then the gate is a hole punched through this world," Aster said carefully, "to others."

"Others?" Reed glanced up at the stars. The idea was vast. Too big for her head, and the stone beneath her back felt like it had tilted. "How can that be?"

"Don't be troubled," Aster said, and squeezed her. "I felt the same when I came to understand the gate. But the world is almost always larger than you imagine, no matter in which one it is that you're currently standing. Nothing has changed from one moment ago."

That was true. And yet she'd just witnessed Tiern open the gate and throw a corpse into any number of worlds. Her mind turned to the sacred well, and its many different stones from many different places. How many came from soil she could never walk upon?

"Aster," she whispered, "have you felt anything wrong within the order? Or with the order's heroes?"

The fingers that had absently twined in Reed's hair stilled. "Of course not. Why would you ask that?"

"Because I worry. That we're weakening."

"Is that why you've been taking heroes like apples from a tree? You are a glorious death, but it's not your sole responsibility to strengthen the Aristene. We must all do our parts. It's long past time that I find a new hero of my own."

"No." Reed sat up.

"No?"

Aster didn't know what had happened to Aethiel's hero and the dangers of the prophet's skull, and Reed wanted to tell her. But if she did, Aster would try to stop her from leaving the safety of Atropa.

"I like knowing where you are," Reed said. "I like being able to return here and find you." She looked at her mentor sheepishly. Those words at least, were not a lie.

Aster cocked her head. Reed knew what she would say: that she must grow up, that Aster was a mentor, not a mother. But instead of speaking, Aster drew her down again upon her shoulder.

"Very well, foundling," she whispered. "I will wait a little longer. Now, where do you ride to?"

"To Cerille," Reed said, finally unable to avoid a falsehood. "I promised Lyonene I would keep an eye on Alsander until she returned."

Aster sighed, and Reed heard the frown in her voice. "You shouldn't have done that. It seems like a kindness, but it will only make things harder. She should already have bid him farewell."

Reed curled farther into her mentor's shoulder, as if she could make herself small and hide. If Aster was displeased by that little lie, she would be furious if she discovered the truth. *But she will never know the truth*, Reed thought. It was only one little hero. One little marriage. The deed would be done before any was the wiser, and by then the elders would be missing their infusion of glorious death. Reed would take a new hero, just as Lyonene was placing a crown on Alsander's head. Through the initiates, glory would come to the Aristene from all sides.

14.

OUTCAST AND SPY

Veridian departed from Cerille the morning after the Aristene. She rose when it was still dark from a bed that was no longer quite so comfortable without Aster in it beside her, and took advantage of the royal baths in preparation for long days upon the road. She also helped herself to the royal stores and stuffed sacks full with nuts and dried fruits, and stacks of the delicious strips of dried meat they made there, still tender and highly spiced. And then she met her horse near the stable. She'd sent a servant to saddle him, and he emerged tall and shining red, and carrying her saddlebags in his mouth.

"Good boy," she said, and rubbed his forehead. They were not like Aster and Reed. They didn't have the vast resources of Atropa to draw upon. Everfall knew never to leave their scant belongings behind.

Veridian swung up into the saddle without looking back. There was nothing to keep them in Cerille. Aster and Reed would not be returning. Yet somehow it still felt like she was leaving them.

She hadn't ridden far when she felt the Veil snap open and someone step through. Veridian stopped and looked at her horse.

"Who could that be?" she asked. In response, Everfall blinked his long red lashes. "Well, let's go and see."

* * *

Lyonene emerged from the Veil leading her little roan mare. As the blackness snapped shut behind them, both shook their tawny manes and shivered. Emerging on this side of the Veil was far less pleasant than emerging refreshed in the white city. Thank the goddess it was morning in Cerille. The day's growing warmth would quickly leech the chill from her and the Areion's bones.

Lyonene unbuckled Strawberry's saddle and removed her bridle, then dumped both into a nearby shrub.

"Find your way into your stall and get some rest," she said, and the horse ambled away. Lyonene took a breath. The air was perfumed by honeysuckle and jasmine, and it was still early enough for the city to be quiet, the silence broken only by the whistling songs of birds. It felt like home. But no matter how much time she spent there, Cerille was not her home. And no matter how she wished differently, Alsander wasn't either.

She moved through the courtyard and into the wide pathways of the palace, her sandaled feet slapping softly on the smooth stone floors. In her haste to find Alsander, she didn't bother to send away her armor, but at that hour the old goat king would still be asleep, laid out like a seal upon the sand with his mistress and her growing belly beside him. It wouldn't be long before both would lie like beached seals—but no, when Isadora's belly grew large enough to be unsightly, Alectos would banish her back to her own chambers.

It would surely be a small and welcomed mercy.

She reached the door of Alsander's bedchamber and whispered his name. Immediately she heard his footfalls; he must have already been awake. Perhaps he'd been unable to sleep last night without her, and the thought made her smile.

The door opened.

"Lyonene! Thank the bright god, you're back."

"You seem surprised. Did you have so little faith in Reed?"

Alsander's eyes traced every line of her face. "I feared they would try to keep you. Was it difficult to give Reed your hero?"

"There were a few tense moments," Lyonene said, thinking of the Outfitter. "But truthfully, it was quite simple." *Too simple*, her mind objected. Too easy. But some things were easy. It was only her devious personality that sought complications at every turn. She'd spent too long in the Cerillian court in the company of serpents and now trusted nothing.

Except that wasn't it. Something dug at her, like a burr caught in the folds of her gown.

The poisoned blade, she realized. Its presence had made no sense, even to Gria.

"Lyonene? What's wrong?"

But nothing was wrong. Reed was a Glorious Death. She was one of the finest warriors in the order. Whatever the blade signified, Reed could handle it. "I'm only thinking of how much we will owe Reed when this is over."

Alsander kissed her and his lips rumbled with a low laugh. "Were she to ask for half my kingdom I would give it." He took her hand. "Come with me now."

"Now? Where?"

But Alsander didn't reply. He turned back into his chamber and emerged with pale linen cloaks. He threw one over Lyonene and pulled the hood low to hide her face before donning one of his own.

He led her out of the palace and into the city, keeping to quiet side streets, streets she had never traveled before. They went so quickly that it wasn't long before Lyonene found herself lost. When Alsander finally stopped, it was before the steps of a temple.

"Alsander, what is this?"

He tugged her gently up the stairs. The temple was modest, white stone with a small wooden door. It was nothing like the great building in the center of the capital where royalty went to pray. That temple was massive, with broad archways and vaulted ceilings. It was hung with gold banners and flew flags embroidered with an image of the sun. The only thing that marked this building as a place of worship was a small mosaic orb in faded yellow tiles.

Inside the temple was not much finer. It could hold no more than twenty worshippers at a time, and there were none there. Perhaps there were none ever—the corners of the wooden pews were caked with dust, and the backs strung with cobwebs.

"Bagoas!" Alsander called. "Priest!"

At his hushed shout, a priest emerged from the vestry. He hurried toward them, adjusting the small gold medallion about his neck. The white of his robes was stained with soot at the bottom and the white cap he wore had a dent in it. Lyonene looked at Alsander questioningly. Who was this man?

"She has returned," Alsander said. "Will you do it?"

"Yes, yes, my prince," the priest replied. He was surprised, to be sure. But he was also afraid. "Now?" He glanced at Lyonene.

"Now what?" she asked.

Alsander turned and took both of her hands. "Lyonene, I want you to marry me."

She took a moment. Surely she'd misheard.

"I know it sounds like madness. But the moment you disappeared into that darkness I knew that I could never allow you to be taken from me again."

"My love—marriage or no, when the Aristene call, I must answer."

"I know that. But if we wed—" He slowed, and slipped his fingers into her hood to touch her hair. "If we are wed, it won't matter where you go. Part of you will always belong to me. We will never be divided."

"Alsander—"

"Please, Lyonene."

She looked into his eyes. It was unlike him to beg. Unlike him to look so desperate. Her absence, even for one night, had pained him. It had pained her, too.

"Members of my order are not permitted to marry."

"So we will not tell them. It will be our secret. My secret queen. Who rules beside me from the shadows of my throne." He smiled. "It was what you were going to do, anyway."

Lyonene's heart began to pound. She couldn't deny that she was tempted. Her life was devoted to Kleia Glora, but why couldn't she have this one small thing for herself?

"What about your heir?" she said. "You know I can't bear you one."

"I don't care about that. I don't care about anything but my country and you. I can't be without you, Lyonene." He searched her face. "Do you not feel the same? Do you not love me?"

"Of course I do, but . . ." She shook her head. Closed her eyes. She did love him. Impossible though it seemed. She, who had never wanted for admirers, who had never given up her heart, who had teased Reed and Gretchen when they fell in love themselves.

I want this, she thought. *I want him, and everything we can accomplish together.*

She opened her eyes.

"Yes."

When they exited the temple afterward, Lyonene was in a daze. She was a wife when she'd never thought to be one. She was loved by a man who would be a king. And she was happy.

"I will arrange something special at the feast tonight," Alsander said. "Dancers. Perfumed cherries. Roasted peacock presented with its feathers. And none but us will know the reason."

Lyonene leaned against him. Her lips still hummed from his kisses, and the words of his vows echoed inside her ears.

No oaths. No vows, save those made to the goddess.

Lyonene tensed. *Go away*, she thought. *You do not dictate everything.* She would cast the order from her mind. It was only one life that Alsander asked for. And her life would be so long. Surely she could give him this. Surely she could have it, this one secret.

They walked with their arms around each other, hoods drawn to conceal themselves as they returned to the palace through the winding side streets. When they reached the palace grounds Alsander pulled her close, and Lyonene was so distracted that she didn't see Veridian standing not far inside the gate of the walled garden.

"What are you doing here, Lyonene? Where is Reed?"

Lyonene twisted in Alsander's arms. "I—" she began. "I've returned to say goodbye." Not exactly a brilliant explanation, not that Veridian was likely to believe any that she came up with. "It's not what you think."

Veridian's eyes were dark, and the apostate gave her no time to protest before she'd grabbed Lyonene's hair and dragged her back toward the gate.

"I don't know what I think. I don't know what you've done. All I know is you're going back to Atropa."

"Veridian—" Lyonene reached behind her to try to pry Veridian's fingers loose. Just when she'd managed to grip them, Veridian shoved her free.

Alsander rushed to stand beside her. "Aristene, stop!"

"I am no Aristene, prince. And nor are you. So stay out of their business." Veridian's eyes blazed. "Where is Reed?"

At Veridian's shout, Alsander's hand went to his sword, and Lyonene jumped between them.

"We changed places," she cried. "I looked into the well and saw a hero in Cassor. And Reed went, to guide them."

Veridian stared at her, wide-eyed. Then she cursed under her breath. "What did you do to get her to go along with it?"

"It was her idea," Alsander said.

"Lies!" Veridian slid the sword from the scabbard on her back. The sound that it made was rough, as was the hand that gripped its worn handle. "You will go back through the Veil tonight. You will do your own duty."

Lyonene eyed the blade. Within the order, Veridian was a legend, but most of the stories were of her skill with a bow. Lyonene was better than Reed with a sword, and how many worthy adversaries could Veridian have encountered on her journeys? She would be rusty. Lyonene's fingers twitched.

Veridian lunged. It was fast, almost too fast to be tracked even though it had clearly been a testing blow. Lyonene's sword swung upright just as the apostate's met it, and the impact sent vibrations all the way to Lyonene's shoulder. Veridian was not rusty. She was angry, and a veteran of countless fights. It took only moments for Lyonene to be driven to the gates of the garden. She stumbled backward, and landed hard; her sword fell to the grass. Veridian raised her weapon, and Lyonene braced. A jolt of fear raced down her spine. Real fear, like she'd not felt since the first charge upon the beach of Rhonassus.

Veridian's sword froze, carefully controlled. "I'm not going to kill you. Only knock you out until nightfall, when I can drag you back to Atropa, where you belong."

"You cannot take her," Alsander said.

"Because your father has a knife to your back? Such is the way of royalty. You're clever enough; you may survive it. Now stand aside."

But Alsander didn't move.

"Stay out of the business of the Aristene!"

"This is not the business of the Aristene. It's mine. Lyonene is my wife! We were married in a secret ceremony just this morning."

The words hung heavy in the air, echoing though none would dare repeat them. *No oaths*, Lyonene heard whispered in her mind. *No crowns. No vows save those you make to the goddess.*

It was easy for Veridian to read the fear upon her face.

"You foolish initiate," Veridian said. Her sword lowered to her side. "You are so young. And beautiful. The kind of beautiful that trouble never seems to stick to. But you have no idea what this disobedience will cost."

Lyonene stood slowly, "I know what it costs," she said, ashamed of the tremor in her voice.

"Not even Aster and I have spoken vows to each other!" Veridian shouted. "Yet you think—in your youth, in your foolishness—that you can . . ." Her voice lowered. "The punishment for such a violation is death," she said, and Lyonene saw Alsander stiffen. "They will kill you, Lyonene, if they discover this."

Death. She'd known that, deep down. But it hadn't felt real. It still didn't, even after hearing it aloud. She was so dazed by the words that she barely heard Alsander draw his knife.

"Then they will never discover it," he growled, and lunged for Veridian. She caught him quickly and twisted the weapon out of his grasp. She looked at him, and then at Lyonene, and pushed past them to mount her waiting horse.

"You're leaving?" Lyonene asked. "Where?"

"It doesn't matter now, where you go, or I do," Veridian said.

Lyonene glanced at Alsander, who rubbed his wrist. "And you won't tell them?"

"Like I said," Veridian muttered, "I am no Aristene. I stay out of their business." The apostate looked down at them, at their nearness to one another, at their joined hands. For a moment it seemed she would give them another scolding.

Veridian turned her horse and rode away.

TWO

MARRIAGE BROKER

15.

THE DAUGHTERS OF THE CASSAN THRONE

Before Lyonene departed Atropa to return to Alsander and
Cerille, Reed bade her tell all she could remember of her vision
from the well.

*"The girl is meek and rarely smiles. Her eyes are brown, her hair is
brown, both browns as unremarkable as the backside of a mouse. You'll
know her by her folded hands, and yes, I suppose, by her name: Yngarue."*

"Yngarue?"

*"And if you think that's a mouthful, wait until you must speak with
her sister, Wyrnnigrid. This is never going to work, Reed."*

*"It's too late to change our minds. What would we do, go back to the
Outfitter and tell her we'd made a mistake and she needs to enchant
you instead?"*

*"I wouldn't need enchantments, Ox—I already know how to braid
hair."*

*"Lyonene, don't lose your nerve. Now, is there anything else I need
to know?"*

"Only one thing."

Lyonene's eyes had turned glassy.

*"The girl's first choice will be the wrong one. It will seem hard to
believe, but if Yngarue aims high enough, she may unseat a queen."*

"The girl's first choice will be the wrong one," Reed murmured to Silco as they ambled along the road that led to the castle of King Urdien, the ruler of Cassor. "What does that mean?"

Not even Lyonene had known the answer to that. It was a hint, a riddle given by the well. Silco turned his head to stare at his rider accusingly with one eye.

"Don't worry so much, Silco. It's only a marriage," Reed snapped. Except it wasn't. It was a glorious marriage, and that meant either a match of military might or a prince who was so rich that he wore pants of gold. The only glory to be found in marriage was in making one that was far above your station, and how was Reed supposed to manage that when her hero princess looked like the backside of a mouse?

"Kleia Gloria had best brace herself for a modest offering."

Silco snorted in agreement. Since they'd arrived in Cassor he'd made no secret of what he thought of their plan, kicking and stomping and walking so slowly that for a while she had to dismount and drag him along behind her.

"You know, you could be supportive now and then," she said when she was again mounted, and Silco jerked his head away. He was a warhorse and she a warrior. She was not suited to quiet or delicate heroes, and the goddess knew that. Which was why she had given this princess to Lyonene instead.

Reed wiggled her toes, uncomfortable in the slippers, which had gotten wet and stained as she walked in the Cassan mud. But she didn't dare trade the dress for her armor—this was one hero for whom the Aristene must remain a secret. No father was going to want an armed fighter preparing his daughter for the ways of marriage.

Overhead, a grumble of thunder rolled through a canopy of low gray clouds. There had been no rain, just puddles and water-filled ruts from the last deluge. Reed recalled her teachings from her years of map study in the Summer Camp: Cassor, the jewel that sparkled under angry skies. In Cassor it rained often and all year round. But perhaps to make up for that, the wilderness was full of bounty and relatively free of hazards: no venomous snakes, and if she got hungry she could leave the road and forage in the woods for any number of ripening berries and edible mushrooms.

Movement in the corner of her eye made her and Silco's heads rise. It was probably only a bird in the bushes, but even so, Reed twisted in the saddle. The red dress bound her, made her feel vulnerable, confined and slow. *If you see one of these creatures, kill it.* That's what Tiern had said. But if one attacked her in the red dress she would fall over and die in an annoying twinkling of silver bells.

As they crested the next hill, the walled city that surrounded the castle came into view, and the quiet landscape began to be dotted with habitation: a farm here, a hovel there, increasing in density as they neared the city. Reed nodded to people with mud-streaked cheeks, working fields of wet, tilled earth. Much of the country's labor force mined iron and mineral deposits—making Cassor rich in coin and in steel—but nearer the castle the land was pastoral. A man passed by, leading a cart pulled by oxen, and touched his forehead. "Lady," he murmured, and watched her warily. "Take care," he said, "and keep to the road."

Reed's magic prickled the back of her neck. Why would he say that? What did she have to fear so near the castle and under the light of the afternoon? *It must only be that I look so inept and helpless in this getup,* she thought, and tugged on the dress's collar. *Now stop thinking of war and start thinking of gowns and dancing.*

She was determined to do so, yet as they rode closer she couldn't help noticing the readiness of the castle against attack: the moat in the process of being dug, the turrets added above the battlements. And a newly built gatehouse, the work of a king constantly worried for war and with not enough sons to train for it.

One of the gatehouse guards stepped out to inquire about her business.

"I seek an audience with the king," she replied. "In the interest of his daughter Princess Yngarue." Her accent gave him pause, but after one look at her dress called for the gate to be opened. Reed looked up. The castle itself was a modest fortress of pale gray stone with four watchtowers. Inside the outer wall were ramparts of the same pale stone, but taken over by moss. Several sheep grazed the grass that topped them—small, hardy creatures with black legs and unruly gray wool. Great gray whorls of it, like they'd been bred less for meat and more for thread. Silco nickered to them in a friendly way and their little black muzzles sniffed at him before returning to the grass, uninterested.

"I would welcome a chance to sack this place," Reed whispered as Silco carried her deeper into the castle. "To test these new defenses, lead an army to their doorstep and lay a siege. . . . How long has it been since Erleven has attempted a proper attack?"

Silco snorted and twisted his neck to peer at her. *Listen to yourself,* that look said. *This scheme is never going to work. No one will believe you an expert in matters of matrimony. The moment you're off my back no one will even believe you have worn a dress before.*

Reed scowled. Her horse could convey quite a lot of meaning with just one eye.

Near the castle keep a boy set aside his broom and came to help her dismount.

"Where will I find the king?" she asked.

"The maids will take you to 'is hall. Your horse is lame, lady."

"And there's nothing to be done about it." She flinched when Silco lashed her with his tail. "But see that it gets a nice warm soak." She reached into the purse at her belt and removed a fat silver coin. "He is a very special horse," she whispered. "His keep and care are worth much."

"Aye, lady," the boy said with silver reflected in his eyes. He took Silco's reins. As the boy led him away, Silco tried to bite one of the bells off her stupid hat.

"You . . . nasty colt," Reed muttered as she walked inside. Though she wished he'd have gotten one. The bells were horrid.

Inside the keep, fires burned in every hearth and kept the air warm and dry. It also smelled sweet, and Reed spied fragrant bundles of herbs stashed in corners. Upon the walls, tapestries depicted scenes of wealth and war, though tapestries often struck her as less a recording of history than fabricated boasts.

The maid Reed followed into the hall was dressed in a gown of finely spun wool that had been dyed a pretty yellow. One of the queen's ladies, perhaps. As they walked, the king's laughter could be heard ringing along the corridor.

"Do not smile! No smiling! It will give away your strategy!"

They stepped into the great room, which was large, with two hearths burning. In the corner of her eye Reed registered guards stationed beside the entrance, and more at the exit. Each had a hand upon a long golden spear.

The lady's maid cleared her throat.

"King Urdien. The lady Machianthe requests an audience." The maid dipped, and Reed did the same, casting her eyes to the floor. King Urdien of the house of Ythyll was seated near the farthest hearth, across from a young boy in a blanket and a young man also in a blanket. The king and the young boy were playing a game with beautifully painted game pieces. At the maid's announcement, all three raised their heads. The boy resembled the king. He must be Prince Ullieth, the youngest child. The man beside him resembled neither one. He had dark brown hair, clipped short, and brown eyes in a handsome face. An adviser to the king, perhaps, though he seemed young to hold such a position.

The king rose from his chair and swept back the cape he wore, a heavy fabric edged in short gray fur. The boy remained seated, wrapped in blankets. What little of him Reed could see was thin and pale.

"Lady Machianthe," King Urdien said. "Of?"

"Of many places," she replied. She smiled, meaning to convey an air of playful mystery. The king glanced at her soggy shoes upon his floor.

"Lady Machianthe of many places," he said, his tone implying that "many places" really meant nowhere of note. "And why do you seek an audience with Urdien of Cassor?"

Reed hesitated. If Yngarue had truly been hers, the Aristene magic may have risen with an explanation. But Reed was a lie, wrapped in lies, and there was nothing to do but go on lying.

"I have heard that Princess Yngarue seeks a husband."

"And would you *be* that husband?" the king asked. The young man and boy remained silent, but the king's attendants laughed from the corners of the room. "I would be pleased were I to gain a son-in-law with such broad, strong shoulders." More laughter, and Reed sank her hands into the folds of her dress to touch the hilt of the poisoned knife. Surely the Outfitter had provided it for her to throw into the neck of this old, laughing ass.

No, no, she thought, and calmed her temper. For if the knife was to be used to cut a throat, then what was the point of the poison?

"King Urdien, of the house of Ythyll," she said, with just enough strength in her voice to pause the laughter, "I am a matchmaker. And I have been sent to you as a gift."

The king straightened. "A gift? From whom?" He studied her again, closer this time, noting the fine stitching of the stained red dress, and the gold and silver thread in the embroidery.

"From Cerille." Reed bowed low, to hide her nervousness. This was the plan she'd concocted on the road. Cerille was strong in military and heavy with coin; the king of a small nation like Cassor would never dare turn away their offering. And, should the king send a messenger to the Cerillian court to see if she was truthful, Lyonene and Alsander would be there to intercept it.

Urdien glanced at the brown-haired man before he stepped closer. "We have no diplomatic ties to King Alectos. Why would he send me such a gift?"

"I come not from King Alectos," Reed said, "but from the crown prince. Alsander."

The king's eyes began to dance. Alsander was one of the richest princes in the world. Reed could practically read Urdien's mind as he scrambled to discern what possible advantage a prince like that could see through a Cassan alliance. He wouldn't come up with one, of course. Because there was none. Alsander wasn't really interested in Yngarue. But that didn't matter. Reed only needed to use his name as a way into the royal circle.

"Surely the crown prince of Cerille has better prospects," Urdien murmured.

"He does. As well as the luxury of not needing them." She looked at the faces at the table. The young man's expression had tightened and he watched her with suspicion. Reed shrugged. "If you see no use in the friendship of my lord, then I am happy to return and tell him so. Perhaps he will send emissaries to the sons of Erleven instead."

At the mention of Erleven, Urdien snapped his fingers, and the lady's maid who had escorted Reed into the hall reappeared. "Bring my daughters to me," said the king. "I would introduce Wyrnnigrid and Yngarue to this gift." The maid dipped a curtsy and was gone in an instant, her sunny-yellow gown poofing from the corner of Reed's eye like colorful smoke. "While we wait," the king said, his demeanor shifting toward warmth, "I would like you to meet my son, Prince Ullieth." The small, pale boy slipped out from underneath his blankets and went to his father's side.

Reed bowed to the prince. He seemed sweet, the poor, sickly thing. He couldn't be more than seven seasons old, and it seemed to Reed that he would not survive long into adulthood. But that was less a concern in Cassor than it would have been in other nations, since King Urdien had already named his daughter Wyrnnigrid as his heir.

"And this is Parmenin." The king held out an arm, and the young man rose from his seat and removed his blanket to reveal the robes of a priest.

Reed stiffened. But priests were found in most places in the world, and this one's robes were not gray but brown, and well kept.

"He's a monk, but he gives good advice."

Parmenin smiled at this introduction, and inclined his head in greeting.

The king bent to his son's ear. "Run down to the kitchens and tell them to bring something warm for our guest, and some of the spiced wine."

"Yes, Father."

"Run fast!" Urdien watched as the boy ran joyfully to fulfill the errand, his face tinged with foolish hope. *The boy is well; let him remain well.* It was the prayer of every parent, and Reed found herself regretting her earlier urge to knife King Urdien in the throat. "Come," Urdien said. He beckoned her closer, to stand before his long table as he sat back down.

"You have traveled far, coming from Cerille," he said.

"Indeed," Reed replied. "Sometimes the journey has felt like traveling from another world."

"Tell me of your talents. What skills do you bring for my Yngarue? I cannot imagine you a matchmaker for long, young as you are."

Reed flexed her hands against the stinging memory of the Outfitter's needle and thread. "I excel at dressmaking. I am a fine dance master, a tutor, and am well versed in the fashions of the Cerillian court."

The king snorted. "A most useful gift. But the bulk of Yngarue's appeal will fall to me. I will make her charming indeed through her bride price."

"I am also an expert on prices." Reed gave a closed-lipped smile.

"At least, those discussed by the crown prince."

"Then you are a matchmaker, and a negotiator perhaps?" Urdien asked, but she didn't answer. There was no need to promise too much too soon. After all, Alsander was false bait—she would use him to get her in the door, and then make a better match from the suitors who were no doubt readying themselves to come to court. She would need a list of them. And maps to chart their countries.

Prince Ullieth returned with two servants who carried plates of warmed bread and small cuts of freshly seared meat, along with dried fruits and a delightful paste of mushrooms that Ullieth showed her was to be spread across the bread like butter. The little prince stood beside her and watched her eat. He fussed when one of the servants placed a blanket over his shoulders.

"I would gladly share that blanket," Reed whispered, kneeling down. "I'm unused to the rain, and look at my slippers, all ruined and wet."

"Have some wine. It's warm and full of spices." The boy ordered some poured, and then reached to the platter to get her the best of the dried apple. But he still refused the blanket.

"Father says there are great men coming for my sisters, and I won't be in a blanket when they arrive. There will be hunting and sport. And I will take part in it all."

Reed smiled wanly.

"Ah, here they are," the king announced. "My daughters."

Reed stood and braced herself for whatever plain faces she might see. Wyrnnigrid came first, older than her sister by several years. It was a shame Kleia Gloria hadn't sent Lyonene for her, as she was tall and lovely, with smooth, pale hair like wisps of early sunlight.

She wore a gold circlet upon her head, and her eyes were a chilly blue—almost gray, like the Cassor sky.

At the first glimpse of Yngarue behind her, Lyonene's words of warning sounded in Reed's mind.

Her eyes are brown, her hair is brown, both browns as unremarkable as the backside of a mouse.

Yngarue stepped forward to curtsy.

Reed blinked. Yngarue had bright brown eyes and shiny chestnut hair that peeked out from beneath a white veil.

Oh, Lyonene, Reed thought. *Only one as beautiful as you would ever think this girl a mouse.*

"And where is my wife?" Urdien asked, and looked at the maid. "Elizabeth, go and fetch her. I would have her meet my guest."

"Mother is abed today, Father," Yngarue said. She turned to Reed. "Last month my mother lost a child. A little boy, who came too soon."

"A great loss," Reed said, looking at the king.

"And poorly timed," Urdien muttered. "When we have so many guests to greet. But Elizabeth will see you installed with the princesses. So you may begin your . . . tutelage, straightaway."

"Tutelage?" Wyrnnigrid asked.

"Lady Machianthe is a matchmaker. From Cerille," Urdien added meaningfully.

"Cerille?" Wyrnnigrid's gray-blue eyes widened and she grasped her little sister's hand excitedly. "Alsander of Cerille is coming to court? When will he arrive?" Both princesses turned expectantly to Reed.

"As soon as I have had time to make my assessment," Reed said.

The princess and the king frowned. Perhaps she'd miscalculated. The way Wyrnnigrid had reacted to the mere mention of Alsander's name—Reed had thought the princess might faint from sheer joy. If they became too enamored with the idea of Alsander and his gold, she would never be able to persuade them to accept another suitor. Yngarue would wait forever for Alsander, who would never come.

But she would solve that problem later.

"Well," said King Urdien. "While we wait, you may help Yngarue practice her charms on the first suitor."

"Of course. Alsander of Cerille is not afraid of competition."

"Good. Then prepare her to receive Prince Hestion of Glaucia. He is to arrive with his entourage in a matter of weeks."

"What?" Reed blurted.

The king startled at her outburst, and the princesses looked at each other doubtfully until Wyrnnigrid said, "Of course, it may be uncomfortable for Prince Alsander to find himself competing with his ally for Yngarue's hand."

"Yes," Reed said blankly.

"I had planned to extend the invitation to Prince Belden," Urdien explained, "and though Glaucia is not so rich in coin, it is rich in warriors. . . ." The king droned on, as Reed's mind spun. Hestion was coming here. To court the hero princess she was assigned to guide.

Only I wasn't, she thought miserably. *It was Lyonene who was to be here, not me. The goddess had thought to spare me this, and I, like a fool, have blundered right into it.*

16.

THE YOUNG KING

Hestion grunted as morning sun cut through the open window and cast itself across his sleeping face. Day was breaking far too early in Glaucia for his taste. And the days were turning far too long. Good weather and sunlight left fewer excuses to shut himself away inside, in the dark, slumped over a barrel of ale.

"We must wake."

He half turned, startled to see the girl in his bed. She was sitting with her knees drawn up under their sleeping fur, her arms hugging them tightly. She was pretty, with bright blue eyes and gold hair that lay soft against her bare back. "I'm sorry," he said. "I thought I was alone."

"A lovely thing to hear," the girl said. "Almost as lovely as last night, when you could not stop calling me 'Reed.' *Reed, Reed, oh Reed . . .*" She crooked an eyebrow. "It is not pleasant to know your lover is imagining that your body belongs to someone else." She glanced at his chest. "No matter how skilled that lover is."

Hestion sat up, hoping the cool stone of the wall would ease the pounding in his head. The girl's tone was light. She didn't know how much it pained him to hear that name, or that she was not the first girl he had called by it. He was glad he'd had too much to drink, so he didn't remember the words passing through his lips. "I had too much ale," he said. "I was out of my wits." He reached out and ran the backs of his fingers down her spine. "You must forgive me—" He stopped. Balls and ass, he had forgotten the girl's real name. "Forgive me . . ." She turned to glare at him, but better to hazard no guess at all than to shout out another wrong one.

"You are a drunkard!" she spat as she pulled her dress over her head. She shoved her feet angrily into her boots and tossed her hair so hard that it struck him in the face like a golden whip.

"I am," he said. "I will remember if you give me but a moment—" He searched her face, or what he could glimpse of it as she finished dressing and cursing at him. He knew her. He had known her for a long time. But her name remained just past the edges of his memory. Frenella. May? Rose? Mayrose? He could see her in his mind, smiling and pretty, much less hateful toward him than she was now. He remembered her leaning against a pillar, with a smear of flour on her chin.

"The baker's daughter!" he exclaimed, and she balled up his shirt and threw it in his face.

"The baker's wife," she hissed, and stalked out, growling the whole way and nearly shoving Sar into the wall as he approached the open door.

Sar watched her go, and then turned back to Hestion. "Another lady well pleased, I see."

Hestion threw his shirt at him, and Sar caught it and grinned. The Ithernan was fresh and alert, the dark paint around his eyes free of smudges. But there was no blue upon his cheeks. There rarely was these days. For a while he'd kept it off in mourning for Belden. And now . . . the men of the Docritae simply didn't hunt, or hold the war games anymore. Instead, they drank. They chased women. They waited for Hestion to return to them from the depths of his grief.

"Why was Clara so upset?" Sar asked, gesturing toward the girl's angry wake.

"*Clara*," Hestion groaned, indirectly answering the question. "Of course. Clara." He took his shirt back from Sar and pulled it over his head.

"You forgot her name." Sar nodded. "But at least you didn't call out the Aristene's name again."

Hestion paused, and Sar growled.

"You must stop behaving this way. You have always loved the girls." Sar grasped his shoulder. "But you have always *loved* the girls, do you understand? I know you have pain—but you can't treat them like—"

"I know, Sar." Hestion pressed his palms to his eyes. How much ale had he drunk? Even his eyes throbbed. He needed water, a whole flagon of water. "How are you so fit? Didn't you have as much last night as I did?"

"Nowhere near it. An Ithernan knows how to celebrate life without waking the next day to wish for death. Now get up. Your aunt is asking for you."

His aunt Morna, his father's sister. She had been the one to rule the kingdom of Glaucia while its king and prince had lost themselves to sadness. She had overseen the summer hunts and fall harvests. She had facilitated the trading, commissioning and establishing new cargo ships, new schedules and routes for the imports from the conquer of Rhonassus. She'd done it without complaint and without declaration, because King Arik could not. The once robust king lived now in shadows and sickness of mind. His broad shoulders curled in like the legs of a dying beetle; his back sloped as the muscle beneath his cloak wasted miserably away.

King Arik had poured all his hopes into Belden, so much so that the darkness of his loss blotted Hestion from his sight completely.

But Hestion was glad. Because what would his father see if he looked at him now? Nothing but a drunkard like Clara had rightfully said.

"I can't go before my aunt like this. Will you stall her for me, my friend? Give me time to make myself well, and visit the altar of the prophet in prayer."

"I can," Sar said doubtfully. "But I do not know for how long." He left, and Hestion listened to his footfalls grow distant as he passed through the lodge. He heard him open the door and be greeted happily by someone outside. No one greeted Hestion that way anymore. Now no one laughed unless he laughed first and they could see his cheeks were ruddy with ale. Without the ale he'd become mean and sullen, his heart coiled in his chest like an angry snake, hissing against being trampled, its scales cut deep and hardened over with scars.

Hestion heaved himself up and shut his eyes as the walls spun. Then he strode out of the room he'd slept in, which was not his, and half stumbled down the stairs. When he pushed the door open and plunged into the daylight, he hunched as if it would burn. Someone murmured, "My lord," and he managed a friendly grunt. He still loved his people. He knew they deserved better.

They deserved his brother.

Hestion walked through the quiet shade of the wood path until he reached the river and plunged in to his waist. He dunked his head underwater and took a few swallows from his cupped hands. The pounding in his head lessened to a throb. He drank more, and combed through his wet, gold hair with his fingers. A little more of this and a quick change of clothes and he could face Morna.

Your stable is most comfortable. I may have slept there, too.

Her voice in his head was so clear that he looked to the riverbank, sure he would see her there. But it was only a ghost, and the memory of seeing her that day, so vivid he could almost hear the echo of the words against the water and see the splashing feet of her unlucky black horse.

"Stop haunting me," he whispered. "You were never real." She had said that she loved him, pretended that they might have a future. And then she murdered his brother to gain her own immortality. The girl he'd known, the girl he'd thought she was, had never even existed.

He looked downriver and imagined those black hooves, and her bare, tan legs walking behind them. He could stay there all day in the cool water, lost in memories. Or he could get up and change his clothes and go to meet his aunt.

Hestion walked out of the shallows, imagining that Reed was watching as he turned his back and left her behind.

Hestion found Morna in the oat fields, walking with three farmers among fresh green shoots that were already tall enough to reach their ankles. She was deep in discussion with the farmers, and one of the shepherds who tended their large herd of goats.

"The deer will have to be kept out," she was saying. "We'll need some of your dogs. The king's dogs are old—they can't do it alone."

"It's coming in thick," Hestion said. She glanced at him and he smiled the crooked half smile he had used to soften her edges since he was a boy. She was less susceptible to it now. Or perhaps he was no longer as good at it.

Morna dismissed the farmers. "Good weather," she said to Hestion. "There'll be enough in these fields to clear half for winter hay before it goes to seed. You look nearly awake." She beckoned him closer and gave him a sniff. "And you hardly smell like ale."

"You're a hard woman to find," he said, ignoring the insinuation. "You aren't like Father, who could be tracked by his booming bellow, and was more often than not in the great hall."

"I am a woman," she replied. "I'm unused to such idleness. Besides, a woman can't rule that way. She must rule through work and deed. If I sat in that fur-covered throne and issued orders, one of the lords would drag a knife across my throat."

Hestion's expression darkened. "None would dare."

"And who would stop them? You spend your nights drunk and your days asleep. I have had to turn from high lady of this house to steward of the Crown, and all without your help."

"I know, Aunt." Even drunk he hadn't been oblivious. He'd seen the messengers slowly stop seeking an audience with King Arik and ask for Lady Morna instead. He'd seen her pushing carts, haggling with merchants. He'd noticed when she began to carry a dagger in her belt, and watched the white streaks grow thicker through her dark gold hair.

"Why have you sent for me this morning?" he asked.

Morna squinted at the sun. "Morning turns to afternoon."

"I'm sorry, Aunt. But I am awake now—look! And standing without help. I know I've left you on your own. I know I've left my father."

Morna sighed, and after a moment, her expression finally softened. "Your father is not really here to leave. I know he drew away from you first. But there is something that could yet bring him back."

Hestion turned to her. To make his father well again, he would seek any medicine, perform any task. To see King Arik as he once was, he would quest across the sea.

"A grandchild," Morna said. "Another young prince to look into his eyes, and in whose eyes he might again see the joy of his line."

"In whose eyes he might again see Belden."

"In whose eyes we might *all* again see Belden," she whispered.

Hestion exhaled. The thought of a grandchild had never occurred to him, not even after all the girls he'd bedded. He supposed it fell to women to think about that, like it had fallen to Morna to pick up the pieces of their broken house, and to carry a dagger in her belt. He clenched his jaw, ashamed. He had been thoughtless, and careless, and his pain was no excuse.

"Is one of the village girls carrying my child?" he asked.

Morna snorted. "I wouldn't be surprised. But that is not what I meant, and in any case I imagine it will be weeks before we can say no to that for certain. Though at least Clara will pass it off as her husband's." She cocked an eyebrow. "I mean an heir. Some time ago, a messenger arrived from Cassor. He told us of a king seeking a husband for his second daughter, and with her will come gold, and land."

Hestion knew of Cassor. It was small and landlocked, perpetually at war with its neighbor. Some time ago, Morna had said. So she had already mulled this over. Already made up her mind. He looked out across the fields as if he would be able to spot the distant nation over the lip of their bay. "What is the girl like?"

"It doesn't matter what she is like," Morna snapped. "It is a good match. A chance to show again the might of Glaucia." She looked at him from the side of her eye. "A way for you to remember the young king you were raised to be."

But Hestion hadn't been raised to be a king. Belden had. It was Belden who should have courted this girl. Belden who should marry this princess, and whose son should inherit the crown.

Morna sighed and went on. "We would gain use of their river port and another route of trade. New waterways would please the men of the Salt Flats; they grow restless.

"And you," she said, "will finally be able to forget about that lying bitch who took your brother from us."

Hestion's jaw twitched. *Don't speak of her so*, he wanted to say. *She is mine alone to hate, and no one else may say one word.*

"I knew from the moment I set eyes on her that she wanted something from you," Morna said. "Always putting herself in your way. Sneaking out of the ladies' rooms that I had so graciously offered . . . I feared she would try to make herself your bride, but it was worse! Ambitious, greedy mercenary—"

"The fault was also mine," Hestion said. "I should have protected him."

"If you had, you'd have been killed, too. Looking after you is the only thing we have to thank that bitch for." His jaw tightened, but she stopped and put her hands on her hips. "You'll sail for Cassor as soon as your ship is prepared. You'll need servants, maids—*none to sleep with*—and men to charm the ladies of the court."

"No," Hestion said quietly.

"What?"

"I am sorry, Aunt. Perhaps someday. But not now." He turned away before he could see the fury ignite on her face, but he heard her curse him as he fled. Her words followed him all the way back to his father's lodge, where he drowned them out with ale, like a coward.

17.

THE OUTFITTER'S GIFT

After King Urdien announced that Hestion would be the first suitor to arrive, Reed had almost taken Silco and ridden back through the Veil, promise to Lyonene or no. But then she remembered what Lyonene had told her. Or rather, Silco had made her remember it, when he bit her in the arm.

The girl's first choice will be the wrong one. It will seem hard to believe, but if Yngarue aims high enough, she could unseat a queen.

She'd been so unsettled by the announcement that she'd forgotten. But Hestion had no queen to unseat, and if he was the first choice, then she wasn't there to push him into Yngarue's arms. She was there to steer him away.

She'd sighed into Silco's neck with relief, and the nasty colt had bitten her again. And he was right. Just because Hestion wasn't meant for Yngarue didn't mean he was meant for Reed. And she would still have to watch him court her—in fact, he would probably try to court her harder just to annoy her.

But it was still a relief. And though she was loath to admit it, part of her yearned to stay and see Hestion again, one more time. Perhaps in Cassor there would finally be space to say what was left to be said between them.

"Or perhaps he'll see me, expose my true identity, and swing his sword right at my head," she muttered.

"Lady Machianthe!"

Princess Yngarue and Princess Wyrnnigrid came toward her through the corridor. They stopped and curtsied; Reed tried to copy them, graceful as a swan on land. Beside Yngarue and the other Cassan ladies she stood out like a torch, dressed in red and as tall as the men. But Yngarue didn't seem to notice; her eyes were warm and lit like stars, the brown flecked with gold.

"Princesses. I'm surprised to see you away from your sewing." When Reed had arrived in Cassor, the household was already bustling with preparations for suitors. But the prospect of welcoming Alsander of Cerille spurred the preparations into a fevered pace. Even the princesses had been set to work embroidering the Cerillian crest onto a tablecloth.

"One of the merchants has brought new fabric," Yngarue said. "I thought you would want to oversee the selection of my new gowns."

"Of course I would want that," Reed said as Yngarue led the way. Fabric for gowns couldn't be too much trouble. She had seen gowns before. Even in the port city of her youth she'd seen beautiful gowns on the wealthiest women, when they would descend from the docks on sea-wobbly legs with handkerchiefs pressed to their noses against the mingled smells of the spice and fish markets.

"Princess Wyrnnigrid," Reed said. "May I ask why you are not yet married? Why does your younger sister have suitors before the heir?"

"That is precisely why," Wyrnnigrid replied. "I am to be the queen of Cassor. No king will leave his kingdom to sit beside my throne. I must find some second-born prince, or a well-connected noble. All the kings"—she touched Yngarue's elbow fondly—"are for our Ynga."

Reed noted that Yngarue's smile did not quite touch her eyes. She was less excited by the prospect of kings than Wyrnnigrid, and Reed couldn't blame her. Kings were a prideful, boastful lot; the idea of them parading around, strutting with their chests out like cockerels in the yard while they fought for her hand through hunts and contests that had nothing to do with her—

"Here we are, Lady Machianthe," Yngarue said as they arrived at the doorway to the throne room.

Reed threw her shoulders back and held her head high. But when she shuffled inside and saw the multitude of fabrics laid out across the king's table, she nearly fell out of her slippers.

"My matchmaker, as promised," Yngarue said to the merchant. He bowed, and the feather of his impressive hat flopped forward to tickle Reed's arm. She looked around. They weren't alone in the room; a few of the princess's ladies were seated in chairs, as was Parmenin, the priest in the brown robe. And all eyes were trained on Reed, as if selecting fabrics was something worthy of spectators.

Which it might be, she supposed, if she messed it up badly enough.

The princesses, no strangers to such tasks, were already leaned over the table, perusing the offerings; Yngarue caressed a soft-looking silk and raised it to press against her cheek. "Perhaps this one, edged in gold thread. Or this one, paired with a veil—" She paused as Reed looked at the two she held. They were both blue; was there supposed to be a difference? One was perhaps shinier? Or did the variable lie in the weight? She glanced at Parmenin, hoping the king's adviser had already grown bored, but his eyes followed her with interest.

"Wyrnnigrid doesn't like me to wear gold," Yngarue said. "She is the crown princess—gold is for her." She tossed a golden fabric teasingly at her sister, and Wyrnnigrid caught it and wrapped it around herself like a cape.

"I promise to look as plain as I can, little sister, to keep your suitor's eyes from floating."

"Her bride price will do that already," Reed said absently, trying to sort through similar damask, and their smiles disappeared.

"Lady Machianthe," said Wyrnnigrid. "What a cruel thing to say."

Reed straightened. She was about to apologize when Yngarue said, "No. It is a practical thing to say. And it is true." She nodded to Reed. "But that doesn't mean I shouldn't have the finest of dresses."

"Indeed, it means you should have more of them." Wyrnnigrid stepped back from the table and gestured to Reed. "Well, matchmaker. We await your selections."

That was close. She would have to be more careful.

Reed bent over the fabrics. It was piles of colors and softness, and nothing so useful as a good thick fur or a swath of leather. Was there truly glory to be found in this? Glory in catching a prince or a king? But perhaps there was. It was a kind of hunt, after all, and there was plenty of glory to claim in a hunt.

Just imagine the princes as stags, with great racks of antlers. And the gown we will forge from the fabric on this table is the spear that Yngarue will throw right through him.

Reed circled the table. So many shades of blue—fewer purples and oranges. That must mean blue was a fashionable color. Unless fewer indicated rarity? Were those fabrics more difficult to get? She frowned, and reached out to touch one and feel its softness.

But instead, her fingers spidered to the right and grasped a length of deep red brocade, adorned with all manner of livestock in silver thread.

"Oh yes," said Yngarue. "Father will like that one. He will say the animals make me appear bountiful and fertile." She raised an eyebrow, and Wyrnnigrid chuckled, but Reed barely noticed. She was too busy marveling at her hand.

It had moved on its own. As if guided by some invisible force. It was the gift of the Outfitter, she realized. The one she had sewn so painfully into Reed's fingers. Still not quite believing, Reed walked around the table and let her hands drag. As she went, her fingers walked this way and that, touching one fabric and throwing another aside, slipping down into the piles to select ones near the bottom. A heavy blue paired with an under-fabric of cream. A subtle brown made to shine with gold. Cloth of silver layered across purple silk. It must have seemed strange when paired with the dazed expression on her face, but when she was finished, the room broke out in applause.

"That was quite the show of skill," Wyrnnigrid said.

"I know my trade," Reed said, flexing her fingers. Or at least, the Outfitter knew hers.

The merchant gathered the selections into a pile, his eyes glittering with all the gold she'd just spent. He snapped his fingers and his boy began to pack up the rest of his wares.

Reed turned away to see what Yngarue thought of her performance, but the princess was deep in conversation with Parmenin the priest, their voices low and heads bent together.

"Oh, that is nothing," Wyrnnigrid said quietly when she caught Reed watching. "Parmenin and Yngarue have been friends for years."

"He's quite handsome for a priest. And young," Reed noted.

"True. But he *is* a priest. And he is the only man who our father allows to be alone with us, so truly, you have him to thank for anything Yngarue knows about the ways of love." Wyrnnigrid leaned closer, so close that her flaxen braid swung out and thumped Reed in the arm. "Or is that what you are here to teach us? A matchmaker must know much about pleasing a husband."

Reed's mouth went dry. If Lyonene were here, she would give some clever retort, and later would show them tricks that would leave the princes—and the princesses—panting. But what did Reed know about such things? Only what she'd learned from Hestion, rolling around in the stables of Rhonassus. And they had never . . .

"Wyrnnigrid! What are you saying to Machianthe? She appears positively scandalized."

Reed snapped out of her mortification, and Yngarue laughed. "Don't pay her any mind," Yngarue said as Wyrnnigrid giggled. "My sister has a wicked streak, and an eccentric sense of humor."

"It's quite all right," Reed mumbled as her cheeks flushed with heat. So much for her brief triumph as a fabric finder.

She glanced up as a servant entered and delivered a whispered message to Parmenin. Whatever it was wasn't pleasant; the priest's brow creased and his mouth turned into a frown.

"Excuse me, princesses," he said.

As he left the room, Reed's magic rose in his wake.

"Excuse me as well," she said, and went after him.

She kept her distance until he entered the king's chamber, then crept close to overhear. But she needn't have bothered. Urdien's bellows were loud enough to carry down the corridor.

"Erleven raiders!" the king cried, referring to the country that bordered them, the great enemy of Cassor.

"We do not know that," Parmenin said.

"Another wife comes to me to tell me her husband has been taken—another comes to tell me that her son is gone, and who else would be so cowardly as to attack us so? To take our men in the night?"

"But why would King Medes and Prince Denros do so," Parmenin reasoned, "in such small number, and to such little consequence? More likely that these men have left their homes in search of better work in the mines, or better wives."

Reed frowned. She had no love of raiders, but Parmenin's explanation did seem far more likely. Why take men in ones and twos? To what end?

"Very well," Urdien said, still seething. "Let them continue to raid our lands when we are reinforced by the soldiers of Cerille. Then they will see. What of the hunters?"

"I have posted notices," the priest replied. "They should be dispatched within the month."

"Good," said Urdien. "You may go."

Reed stepped back, but not fast enough. Parmenin nearly ran into her as he turned from the room.

"Matchmaker," he said in surprise. And then, "My apologies. Lady Machianthe. Was there something you needed?"

"I couldn't help overhearing. Is there something that troubles the king?"

"No," Parmenin replied. "Or nothing that you or the princess must concern yourselves with." He began to walk away, and Reed followed closely.

"He mentioned hunters?"

Parmenin flashed a placating smile. "We've had reports from the countryside. Bandits, raiding sheep herds and cattle. The shepherds are fearful for their flocks and have begun to spread rumors about great beasts prowling the woods."

"Beasts," Reed said, and in her mind she saw the curved claws on the hands of the fallen hero. "Do you think it's true?"

"Frightened farmers say many things. We will send our best hunters, and they will scare off the raiders, or they will kill the wolves. If you would excuse me." He bowed to her and hurried off.

Wolves and raiders, Reed thought. They were the most likely culprits. But if the Cassan hunters did not return from the woods, she would be the one to go in after them.

18.

OATHS AND CROWNS

Lyonene lay in Alsander's arms, listening to the soft, dozing sound of his breath.

It was midday—they should be doing something, not sneaking away to his chamber for a frantic, hurried embrace and a tumble into bed.

Alsander mumbled and moaned. He smiled when she prodded his ribs.

"We can't linger here," she said.

"Can we not?"

"If we are always in bed, the court will see me as your concubine instead of the adviser behind the throne."

"You are neither of those things," Alsander said, his hand sliding down the length of her arm. "You are my queen."

Lyonene's smile faded. The joy of their marriage had been so brief. Since Veridian had left Cerille, Lyonene had not been able to sleep.

Alsander rolled onto his elbow.

"Are you still worried about that?" he asked. "Veridian won't say anything. She is no Aristene; she said so herself." He trailed a hand down her arm. "They are a world away, my love. You and I have made our own destiny, created our own crowns."

"This was a mistake."

"Don't say that, Lyonene."

"We weren't thinking. This cannot last—I have duties, obligations. And you need an heir."

"I don't care about the heir."

"Alsander, you must care. Without a line of succession, Cerille will fall to civil war."

"I mean I don't care"—he pulled her close—"that you can't bear it. When the time comes we'll find some fine boy with black hair and beautiful green eyes." He brushed her temple with his thumb. "We have the coin. And we can keep the secret."

He sounded so sure. So confident. "I've taught you too well."

"The value of lies? My love, that at least I knew all along." He grinned and kissed her, but Lyonene flinched when she felt the tug of her magic. Alsander frowned. "Is it the hero?"

"Yes." Lyonene pressed her fingers to her forehead. "Somewhere far across the sea, a princess the color of a mouse must be in need of counsel." Since Lyonene had looked into the well, her magic had given her no peace: *Go to the port*, it whispered. *Take a ship. Make your way to the Cassan court.* "If Reed doesn't get the girl married soon, I'm going to develop a twitch."

"Well, we can't have that," Alsander said. "I must admit, I was pleased that your other hero was a princess and not a prince."

"She's only the first. I will have many. Men and women. Queens and princes."

"Well," he said. "We shall see." He kissed her again, slowly, until the kisses and touches turned serious. But Lyonene couldn't stay in bed. Not with her magic thrumming in her blood like the plucked string of a lyre.

"Come now," she said. "Time to mingle with the court." At first he gave a lazy, royal groan, but soon she felt his hands helping her with the fastenings of her pale blue gown.

They emerged from his chamber a short time later, her hair braided modestly and him in full royal regalia and an overdress edged in soft rabbit fur. With the golden circlet upon his head he already looked like a king.

"My love," he said as they walked the colonnade that wound past the fountain garden, where the air was always patterned with flitting orange and yellow butterflies, "is midwifery among the skills of an Aristene?"

Many of the Aristene had delivered babies—had delivered several, over the course of their long lives—but Lyonene had not.

"I only wonder if you would be there when Isadora's child is born," Alsander explained. "The women of Cerille bear witness to a birth. It is custom."

"You want me at the birth," she said. His eyes were furtive beneath his long, dark lashes. "You want me to kill the child. Alsander, I will not; it will be your little brother, or sister."

"I would never wish death on a sister," he said. "She would be treasured. I would let her marry for love and she would never want for any happiness. But you're right." He shook his head, ashamed. "It is not the child's fault. Even if it is born a boy he'll still be subject to my father's cruelty. I only wish . . ."

He turned those furtive eyes on her again. She knew what he meant; she'd already considered it. But Isadora and Alectos were no fools. They waited longer to inform the court than they'd said.

Now that Isadora's belly was on full display it was clearly a belly of five or six months—far too late for herbal remedies slipped into the girl's tea. "Were anything to happen to Isadora or the child, we risk losing the alliance of the nobles. They support you because you're a soldier; a hero. They support you because you are not like your father."

They swept into the king's throne room. It was almost empty, only the king speaking with one of his advisers and Isadora, seated beside him, padded with pillows and cradling her stomach. A scattering of a dozen nobles populated the rest of the space, gathered around tables, playing games or chatting over cups of wine. But though there were few, Lyonene relished the looks of admiration on their faces when she and Alsander entered.

We are Aristene and prince, she thought. *Young and strong and beautiful as gemstones. We are the ones you want on your throne.*

One of the nobles broke away to speak to them: Fournio, tall and thin, in robes of red. He was one of their allies and father to six daughters, all of whom he had offered to Alsander in marriage, separately, or all at once.

"Another blessed day," Fournio said.

"Indeed." Alsander glanced at the king. "My father has rarely seemed so jocular."

"You can hardly blame him." Fournio snapped his fingers for a servant, and handed both Alsander and Lyonene a goblet of wine. "For a man of his age, to welcome a new child after so many years?"

"I would expect a man of his age to be grateful for what he has," said Lyonene.

"Few men are grateful for that, Lady Lyonene. And even fewer kings. But he will not forget you—" Fournio lowered his voice as he spoke to Alsander.

"You think not?" Alsander asked quietly.

"Never," said Fournio. "It is only that a new prince offers new chances, and the promise of more time."

"Alectos will have the time he has," said Lyonene. "Like all men. That promise you speak of is an illusion." But illusions were often more seductive than truths.

Fournio tugged on the ends of his soft, groomed beard. He favored the rule of Alsander, but until the outcome of Isadora's pregnancy was known, not even he wanted to be seen taking sides.

"Let us speak of more pleasant things," Alsander said, his arm out to lead Fournio away before Lyonene and the noble could start to bicker. "Tell me, how are your daughters?" *"So many daughters,"* he mouthed to Lyonene over Fournio's shoulder.

Lyonene hid her smile behind her wine. With King Alectos present, few would speak with her unless she was at Alsander's side, but she didn't mind. She was perfectly happy to listen to their gossip. Eavesdropping on the court was always a bountiful source of information. Unfortunately, today it was also ugly, dusted with pointed jokes aimed at Isadora about what a man was to do with a mistress after she'd finished bearing for them.

"Mistresses come and mistresses go," said a rotund noble named Ascanio. "Even beloved ones. Surely the girl must know that."

Lyonene frowned. The slander was far from Isadora's ears, but Ascanio was right that she must know. In becoming the king's mistress, Isadora had reached higher than she'd ever dared hope. But that would only make the fall that much worse.

Isadora was still so young and so lovely, with hair like muted flames and rose-colored lips. She and Lyonene were alike, in a way; both awash in a sea of powerful men who only sought ever more power. But unlike Lyonene, Isadora had no safe haven to escape to. Of all the men in the throne room, only Lord Vengia, who had kept her as a ward, would look out for her interests. And only he because her interests were his as well.

Lyonene went before the king and swept into a deep bow.

"Lady Lyonene," Alectos said. "With us yet another day. I thought surely my son would have tired of you by now."

She kept her eyes lowered to the floor as her sword rumbled behind the barrier of the aether. She could call it up and drive it straight down Alectos's gullet. Or perhaps she wouldn't use a weapon at all, and twist him in two with her bare hands.

"Not yet, King Alectos," she said. Never "my king" nor "my lord." Those words would have stuck in her throat. "But any day now."

"Yes, any day now." Alectos's eyes glittered. "Look there—perhaps old Fournio has finally fathered one who will charm him."

Lyonene turned. One of Fournio's daughters stood with her father and Alsander. She was pretty, in a bland, overbred sort of way, with high cheekbones and beautiful tan skin. Her hair was a deep brown, but it had no opportunity to shine, braided tight to the back of her head and covered with a veil of blue fabric. Lyonene had noticed that whenever some noble or another paraded their daughters past Alsander's nose they always dressed them in blue, because Lyonene often wore blue. As if the color was the thing that Alsander liked and not her. She sighed. So stupid.

"That one there is the youngest," Alectos noted. "Fournio's

oldest two are already married, and I have heard they share three sons between them. Three fine, strong sons." Lyonene looked at the girl again. Fournio's daughter appeared different to her now. Suddenly all she could see were virtues, the qualities that would combine with Alsander's into one perfect child. *You are my queen*, Alsander said. But only in secret. They'd been married with no witnesses except for the priest who performed the ceremony, and the priest was loyal to the Crown. Alsander could throw her over with a snap of his fingers if something better came along.

Lyonene turned back to the king, who was smiling like a little boy who had just pulled the tail of a cat. "You should be more grateful to me," she said. "After the victorious campaign in Rhonassus and the riches we brought back to you."

"Oh, I am grateful," Alectos replied. His smile turned cruel, and in the seat beside him, Isadora shrank back to keep out of his sight. "Grateful that you've shown me what a *man* my son is, how he lets himself be ruled by a woman. How he's led around my court by the nose." He thrust his hand out to his mistress and Isadora took it quickly. "But one day soon, that will be no more concern of mine."

It will be no more concern of yours, Lyonene thought, looking at their joined hands, *because Alsander and I will sweep over you like a storm across a field, and tear you up by your roots.*

As it often had in the year since Belden's death, it fell to Sar to pull Hestion out of his darkest depression. After Hestion's meeting with Morna, when he'd refused the hand of the Cassan princess, Hestion had tried to drown himself in a barrel of ale, and might have succeeded had he not also been drinking it so quickly. He'd remained drunk and out of his mind for days, until finally in the depths of his stupor, he'd felt Sar's hands taking him by the arms. He heard Sar's voice, and awoke on the deck of his flagship.

"There you are," Sar said. "Now you can get off your ass and help us. We've been preparing your ship to sail for Cassor."

"I am not going to Cassor."

"And yet this ship is." Sar nudged him with his foot. "And if you don't sober up, how will you know anyway? We could sail you to Cassor and back again and one day you'd open your eyes and find a strange girl smiling at you and holding a baby."

Hestion snorted. "That would be quite a bit of drinking, indeed." The flagship on whose deck he sat wasn't even his, or not really—it was Belden's. As he watched, his men went to and fro with ropes, while others went down into the hold like ants into a tunnel, carrying supplies over their shoulders. He heard larger movements below as well, where the cargo door had been opened to load the gifts they would bring to impress the princess: gold plate and jewels, bolts of the best of their soft, dyed wool.

"She will be disappointed," Hestion said.

"If you arrive looking like you do now? I have no doubt," said Sar.

"She'll be disappointed anyway," Hestion said stubbornly. "When I am not Belden."

"The Cassan princess didn't even know Belden."

"It doesn't matter. They all want me to be him. As if Hestion was only a mask I wore until I could finally take it off." He stood. "It should have been me who died in that war."

"No one wishes that. No one wants you to be anything—" Sar cocked a brow. "Except not drunk." He stopped coiling the length of rope in his hands and came to clap Hestion on the back. "Come now. What is so wrong with this Cassan bride? New trade, an heir—and it would be an adventure. . . ."

"I don't want an adventure."

"You don't want to be alive," Sar said, his tone suddenly serious. "But you are. You don't want to be a king. But you are. You are what Glaucia has left and if your brother has looked upon you from the afterlife he has been ashamed."

"And are you ashamed?" Hestion asked.

"No," Sar said. "I understand. But it is enough, Hestion. It is now time for you to return to the land of the living."

Hestion rolled his shoulders back and they stretched and creaked. He ran his hand over his stomach and the layer of fat he'd gained. He didn't know what strength remained inside him or how much of what he'd lost he could recover. But suddenly he wanted to try.

"I don't like it when you use my name." Hestion turned sharply, and Sar's eyebrows rose above his kohl-dark lids. "And I don't like it when you're serious."

"Nor do I, brother." Sar grinned. "It drags on me. Like a bear-skin cape."

"This girl," said Hestion, "this princess of Cassor. Does anyone know what she's like?"

"She is bountiful. She has gold and lands."

"What about the rest of her? What if she has a cruel heart and a dull wit?"

"Then she will still have gold and lands," Sar replied. "And it doesn't really matter, does it?"

Hestion looked at his friend. Sar had liked Reed. Sometimes, when Hestion had gotten into the ale, he would ask Sar to tell the tale of the ambush on the legendary herd in Lacos, where they had first seen Reed don the silver armor and white cape, and she and her mean black horse had charged through a dozen men. She had snatched a crossbow bolt out of the air that day, before it could sink into Sar's eye.

"You're right," Hestion said. "I would rather not care about the princess at all." He patted his abdomen. "We ought to be more worried about what she'll think of me. I won't be the only prince competing for her hand."

"Fat or not, you can still beat them in open combat. But you are not fat," Sar added when Hestion frowned. "Or you won't be after I run you back and forth on the decks, every day of the journey."

Hestion laughed. His eyes ran over the ship from prow to stern, up the sails, across the oars. She was ready, as was the rest of the small fleet that would accompany them.

"So we go?" Sar asked.

Hestion nodded. "There is only one more thing I need to do first."

He left Sar to finish with the fleet and made his way to his father's hall. When he placed his hand against the wood he heard no voices, yet when he opened the doors the sight of his father's empty throne was still a disappointment. It was not so long ago that King Arik had been in it. Not so long ago that he had hunted the woods with his sons, sending his baying hounds into the ferns to flush a hiding stag. Hestion could still see him there in his cape of white wolf fur, leaning on one elbow and pounding his fist against the other arm of the throne, his eyes crinkling at the corners.

Hestion walked slowly through the lodge, past the feasting

tables that were in need of cleaning, crusted with spilled food and stained by dark rings of ale. So different from what it once had been. Even through his year in a stupor, Hestion had seen the spaces left between his soldiers and friends, empty places where others might have sat who hadn't returned from battle.

He left the hall, and passed through the rear doorway that connected to the royal house. On his way he met Clara, the baker's wife he had bedded. "Clara," he said, pointing to her as if he had just remembered. She narrowed one eye and fought a smile.

"Who told you?" she asked, and he laughed. He hoped she'd forgiven him. He also hoped she hadn't told her husband the baker, and it was still safe for him to eat the bread.

His footsteps were loud as he walked through the quiet house to his father's chambers on the second floor. When he opened the door, his nose wrinkled against the sourness of the air.

King Arik was seated by the window. The fire in the hearth had burned down to embers and dust motes floated in the slanting light.

"Have you brought a meal?" the king asked. "Set it there." He gestured to a table without looking.

"No, Father. It's me."

Arik turned. It was hard not to flinch from the sight of his sunken cheeks. His once bright brown hair hung limp and unkempt, and his beard had grown long and snarled—pure white, when six months ago it had only been shot through with gray.

"Father, I came to . . ." *Say goodbye* was what he meant to have said. But to say so when his father sat with his back hunched beneath a coat of stitched-together wolf pelts seemed like a bad omen. If he said goodbye, his father would fade away completely. Hestion would sail home with a bride only to find his father gone, long ago burned on a pyre and released with Belden to the afterlife.

"I come to ask your blessing to marry the princess of Cassor."

"The princess of Cassor," his father repeated. Hestion should have asked for her name. And he should have brought a meal, something hearty to enrich the blood, a stew heavy with meat and soft bread to warm his father's hands.

"Well," the king said. "Well. We must have a toast!" Hestion helped him as he stood. His balance was poor and his legs were weak and for a moment Hestion's sadness flashed to anger: his father's legs were still strong; they could still carry him upright if he would only use them. *This is how Sar felt about me*, he thought, *when he spoke to me on the ship*.

"Someone bring ale! Or wine!" Arik cried as Hestion half carried him to the table. A servant brought jugs of both, along with two cups. Hestion poured for his father as Arik sat back down. "To the princess of Cassor," the king said. He raised his cup and Hestion frowned as wine seeped from the corners of his father's mouth to run into his beard. "Ah, that is good. I wish you luck."

"Thank you, Father."

"Is Belden sailing with you?"

Hestion looked at him in surprise, but his father didn't notice. He'd begun to move the cups and jugs around idly on the table. "Mm?" he asked after a moment, when Hestion hadn't replied.

"No, Father, Belden is . . ."

"Well, he ought to. No young woman can resist Belden's charms. He would win your bride for you! He could throw a spear—" He drew back one bent arm. "So far that . . ."

"Perhaps you should sail with me instead," said Hestion.

"Me?" The king grunted. "I am too old."

"You are not old," Hestion said quietly. His father was not old. Yet he had aged. Loss had aged him. It had come for him once, when it took his queen, and what damage it failed to do then it succeeded in when it came for his son.

Hestion stared at him sadly, but this was why he had come. Not to try to bring his father back, which was impossible despite Morna's hopes. He'd come so he could look upon King Arik with clear eyes. To admit to himself what Morna and Sar had known for nearly a year.

That he was already king of Glaucia.

19.

TO PLAY THE PART

Reed watched from the doorway of the throne room as King Urdien presented Ullieth with a jeweled dagger. He handed it to the boy in a fine leather sheath, and in his excitement the lad drew it so carelessly that Reed feared for the tip of Urdien's nose.

Poor little lad, Reed thought. She wondered what it was that was stealing his life away at so young an age. A childhood illness, perhaps. A fever that had eaten away his heart beyond hope of repair. There had been a little girl in the Summer Camp who had suffered that. She'd died in a hut in the shadows while Reed and Gretchen and Lyonene raced and wrestled in the sunny fields beside the mountain.

Reed had come to the throne room to listen for news about the monster slaughtering livestock in the countryside. Hunters had been dispatched, but so far none had returned with the head of a great wolf, or tales of bandits. After another few moments watching Urdien and Ullieth, she sighed quietly and backed away. She shouldn't be in the shadows, tailing priests and listening for monsters. She should be with the princesses in the solar, using her Outfitter-enchanted fingers to sew circles around them.

Reed walked away down the corridor, silver bells tinkling softly. Since she'd been in Cassor she could sometimes reduce the number of bells by trading the red skirt and wrapped bodice of the matchmaker for warmer wool and darker colors. But she was always at the mercy of the stupid hat.

As she reached up and silenced the bells, she heard voices, carried through a shaft in the wall.

"I shouldn't—" someone whispered.

No doubt a pair of lovers, cavorting in the kitchens. Reed was about to leave them to it when the whispers turned harsh and she heard the unmistakable sounds of a struggle.

Without a thought, she darted down the hall, down carpeted hallways and two tightly twisting sets of servants' stairs. When she reached the corridor that led to the bread ovens she ripped the hat off her head to stop the jangling and shoved it into her bodice. Then reached into her skirt for a knife and found the handle of the poisoned blade.

No, not that one.

Her fingers walked ahead. She carried two, and a third in her boot, now that slippers were no longer an issue.

The man and the maid were hidden inside a small pantry. The girl had her eyes squeezed shut, her mouth a trembling frown. The man was, surprisingly, dressed as a priest. At first Reed thought that it was Parmenin, but this man was blond, and his skin was far paler. She knew because his robes were currently hiked up so far that Reed could see the backs of his pasty thighs.

Since those pasty legs were there for the kicking, Reed kicked the inside of his left ankle hard. The priest's feet spread and he fell forward. Then he yelled as she pressed his face against the stone wall to allow the maid to slip free.

"What do you think you are doing?" he demanded. One eye rolled toward Reed. "Matchmaker!" He tried to push off the wall and was surprised when it didn't work.

"I am indeed a matchmaker," Reed said. She turned to the maid. "Is this a good match?"

"No, my lady."

"I thought not. Go on now."

"Yes, Lady Machianthe."

Machianthe. Reed nearly looked around to see if someone else was in the pantry. She would never get used to that name. She watched the girl disappear up the stairs, and took a few moments to enjoy grinding the squirming priest's head against the stone.

"Let go of me," he said. Now that they were alone, his voice was far more reasonable. Reed stepped back and he smoothed his robe. He stared at her hand, the one that had held him to the wall so easily, and then glanced at the other that held a knife. She could read his thoughts as clearly as if he'd spoken them aloud: *The matchmaker kicked my feet. The matchmaker carries a blade.* She had to admit, watching his confusion was a little delicious.

"Where is your hat?" he asked.

Reed sighed. She dug it out of her bodice and placed it, wrinkled, atop her head. She was a ridiculous woman again, clad in bells.

"Next time," he said, "mind your business."

"Next time you will mind my knife." Reed flipped it in her hand and slid it back into its hiding place. "Get out of here. Shoo."

He narrowed his eyes in what she thought was meant to be a withering glare and straightened his robe one last time, very brusquely. Then he turned on his heel and walked away.

When he was out of sight, Princess Yngarue crept out from around the corner.

"You are very interesting, for a matchmaker."

"Princess Yngarue." Reed cleared her throat. "Matchmakers are supposed to be interesting. How else would we teach our charges to be interesting themselves?"

Yngarue's eyes moved over Reed's clothing, trying to spy where she concealed her blades. "Your knife. May I see it?"

"No." Reed moved the fabric of her skirt. "Had I known you were there, I wouldn't have put it on display."

"So you would have let him go on?"

Reed pursed her lips. "In some places in the world, a priest like that would be flogged and thrown in a dungeon."

"In some places, but not in Cassor. In Cassor, women must guard their virtue, yet are given no means by which to defend it."

With a frown, Reed reached back into her skirt and took out the knife. She handed it to the princess. Then she reached into her boot to pull out another.

"I have seen him in the castle with her," Yngarue said as she turned the knife back and forth. "Lurking in her shadow. Whispering in her ear. For weeks he has picked bits of ivy and wildflowers to tuck into her hair. So many smiles and so much kindness, all to get her alone. And once they were alone, where did all his kindness go?"

"Sometimes the powerful only wish to exert their power over something weaker," Reed said. She tensed as Yngarue thumbed the blade. "Have you really no experience with a knife?"

"Princesses are to be looked at," Yngarue replied. "To sing and dance, and sew if we want to be of use. There is no need to know how to use a blade. Not to butcher meat. Not even to whittle."

"I'm no good at whittling, but a knife has plenty of uses that a woman should learn." Reed flipped the small blade she'd taken from her boot handle out and gave it to the princess. "This one is a dagger so you must take care with both edges. This one"—she turned the knife in Yngarue's other hand—"has one sharp edge and one blunted. Better for cutting. You can lever down on it. Through a finger, or . . . a piece of fruit."

"Why would a matchmaker need to lever through a finger?" Yngarue asked.

"She wouldn't. It was only an example."

Yngarue studied Reed quietly. "You know my mother is ill. Childbed fever. When you first arrived I thought perhaps you were not here for me at all, but for my father. To find him a newer, younger bride." Yngarue's eyes had turned cold. "Do men always become so heartless when a woman is no longer of use to them?"

"No," Reed said.

"I have only as much experience with men as I have with knives," said Yngarue. "But I have watched. I have listened. This castle is an eavesdropper's paradise." She smiled. "I've heard the ways men speak when the women are not listening. It makes me cautious to trust one."

"Hestion of Glaucia is not like that," Reed said without thinking. "Nor is Alsander of Cerille. And your father hasn't spoken to me of any match besides your own."

"You speak of the princes of Glaucia and Cerille—you know them both?"

"I know of them," Reed fumbled. "I was with them. From afar—"

"You were there, during the War of Rhonassus." Yngarue stepped closer. "That is why you know so much about weapons. I would like to hear your stories."

"All the good stories are told by the bards."

Yngarue smiled again. "And I would like you to teach me how to use these." She held up the knives.

"No, princess. I'm here to teach you to dance, to sing, to flirt—"

"I already know those things." Yngarue tossed the dagger, a little clumsily, and Reed dipped to catch it. An easy catch from a short distance, but impressive to a girl who could barely cut meat.

"You're right, I suppose. Father says I am everything that could be wanted in a woman: a pleasing face and a fertile womb, all laden down with coin."

Reed pressed her lips together. Such an assessment made her blood run hot. She looked at the princess, noting the small gold flecks in her eyes, and the way those eyes simmered. Behind the trained silence, Yngarue was fierce. She didn't need a matchmaker to help the suitors fall in love with her.

"Very well," Reed heard herself say. "In addition to dancing, I will teach you knives."

"Will you really?" Yngarue grabbed Reed's hands and squeezed them. "Thank you, Machianthe. Truly." She kissed Reed's cheek, and spun quickly away before she could change her mind. "I will find you later so we can begin. Right now I must see Parmenin and inform him of Brother Clafin's behavior."

20.

THE GLAUCANS ARRIVE

Reed watched with interest as Yngarue mixed a paste of herbs and nuts ground with honey into the bottom of two hand-hewn wooden cups. They were at a table in the walled garden, where Reed had been helping the princess to practice her knife skills. As she watched, Yngarue lifted a hot pot and poured a pale orange liquid into both cups. Then she stirred it with a wooden whisk until the surface was a cap of foam. She sprinkled each with a brown powder and handed a cup to Reed.

"What is this?" Reed asked.

"It's made of goat's milk and fermented carrots," Yngarue replied. "We drink it at our winter festival, but I thought you might enjoy it now."

Reed took a sip. The taste was rich and sweet. The paste of nuts would settle to the bottom and become infused with it, and was to be scraped off the bottom of the cup and eaten. That, Yngarue said, was her favorite part.

"I've never tasted anything like it," Reed said. "I think if I drank much more I'd be curled up in a sunbeam like a cat."

A hint of color rose to Yngarue's cheeks, pleased by the compliment. Her lessons with the blades were progressing nicely. She had not much stamina, which was to be expected, having lived her whole life moving between the palace gardens and the solar, but she was eager and focused. And in the privacy of the walled garden she'd not hesitated to tie her skirts up on one side, so Reed could advise her steps. "You must have tasted a great many things," Yngarue said. "Seen a great many things. Been many places."

"How do you know I have not spent most of my life in Cerille?"

"I have met folk from Cerille. You are not like them." Yngarue tapped her cup with a fingertip. The princess saw things that others missed, a skill developed from a lifetime of being silent and watching. It was a shame that a girl so eager for knowledge had been sequestered in her father's court.

She would have done well in the Summer Camp, had things been different.

"It's true, I have been many places," Reed said.

"Where? Where is the farthest you have been?"

Atropa, Reed thought. But she said, "The port at Preta, on the northern side of the continent of Orillia."

"What is it like?"

"Like many ports. Busy and loud. Smelling of fish and spices. What is this spice you've placed on the top of our drinks?"

"Mace," Yngarue said. "And what did you do there?"

Reed shrugged. "Made matches. Traveled the country. The seasons are hot, and the air so heavy it feels like steam upon your skin. In quiet bends of the river, the water is as warm as a bath." She swallowed, remembering what it felt like to wade into the shallows with Mama to check the nets. Such a small sliver of her life that had been.

Yngarue leaned back with a sigh. "That is what I would wish. To go places, and see things. That is what I look forward to, traveling to some new place with the man who is my husband." She touched the edge of her cup. "All of the new tastes. The new customs."

"Glaucia and Cerille are both fine places," Reed said.

"You have been to Glaucia?"

Reed shook her head. Foolish to just let herself talk. It never went well. But before she could explain, Prince Ullieth raced into the garden.

"Sister!"

"What is it, Ulli?" Yngarue asked. She put out her hands to steady the prince. Reed could see that it was on the tip of her tongue to tell him that he shouldn't run. But to her credit, she didn't actually say so.

"I've been sent—I sent myself to find you," the boy said excitedly. "The Glaucans have arrived!"

The Glaucans. Reed's stomach lurched, and she regretted drinking so much of the rich beverage.

"Then let us go and greet them!" Yngarue pulled the little prince close and spoke into his neck, making him giggle.

"Wait," Reed sputtered. "You must be presented."

Yngarue and Ullieth looked at each other, disappointed.

"Must she really?" Ullieth asked.

"Now, Ulli, we must listen to the matchmaker," Yngarue said. Then she grinned. "But we can still watch their approach! Matchmaker! Come with us!"

"Wait!" Reed called. But the princess and prince were already far ahead, and she had no choice but to hike up the skirt of her dress and follow as they raced to the uppermost room of the keep.

Reed crowded around the window with them, careful to grip a hand onto Ullieth's shoulder so her bulk wouldn't knock him right out into the air. And also so she would have something to dig her fingers into, when she saw Hestion.

The Glaucans were less impressive traveling overland than arriving by sea—they didn't have the gilded coaches of Cerille, or the jeweled sabers of Roshanak. They came as what they were. A nation of warriors, riding a line of fast, muscular horses, swords and spears on full display. They were not great in number; Reed counted thirty armed men and a handful of attendants; a few pretty women with braids in their hair and silver bangles at their hips. Dancers, perhaps, though Reed hadn't seen much dancing during her time in the hall of King Arik.

"Which one is he?" Yngarue wondered, her neck stretched. "Which is the prince?"

All the armed men wore battle helmets save two, and even across the distance Reed knew one by the blue on his cheeks: Sar. The other, Reed could scarcely bear to look at.

"He's that one." She pointed.

"How do you know?"

"A matchmaker knows how to spot a prince."

Ullieth leaned out the window until Yngarue grasped him by the shoulders and tugged him back in. She placed a fur over him to stave off the drafts and the boy tried to shrug out of it. "I will not greet the prince in a blanket!"

"It's not a blanket, it is a cape," Yngarue tried. "And besides, we are not greeting anyone—it is like Lady Machianthe said: we must be presented. And Father will present you in your new armor."

"He will?" Ullieth looked at Reed.

"Of course," she said. "As befits a prince."

Ullieth leaned again out the window. "He's very strong and tall."

"How can you tell?" Yngarue asked, and laughed. "He's still outside the gates, and he's on horseback."

"You can tell," Reed whispered.

As the caravan drew closer the castle came alive, guards readying to their stations, the sounds of servants echoing through the corridors. Reed watched as Sar prodded Hestion in the back, and Hestion slowed his horse to land an elbow to the silver of Sar's chest plate. He seemed happy. Did she want him to be sad? Did she hope for some sign that he was incomplete?

I don't want any of that, she told herself. But she was lying.

"We will be sent for soon," said Yngarue. "We should return to my rooms and select a gown. One of the new ones."

"Every gown you own is new to him," said Ullieth, which was a good point.

The caravan stopped below them and Reed looked down. The banners of Glaucia drooped wetly in the light breeze. They must have been caught by one of Cassor's frequent rains. Hestion dismounted and stretched his back. She had never seen him in such finery before. She'd certainly never seen him with a silver circlet of royalty on his head.

"He is tall," Yngarue said. "And handsome. I wonder if he will like me."

"He will like you very well," Reed said numbly, and stepped back as on the ground, Hestion looked up toward the window.

* * *

Hestion straightened his armor and adjusted his sword—not an ornamental sword, but his real one, sharpened and blooded in many battles. Swords of ornament were clumsy and too long. They dangled with chains and were heavy with gemstones. He was glad that Glaucia had never really been rich enough for such indulgences, though perhaps that would change with his marriage.

He looked up at the castle, a formidable structure built for defense but also for opulence, the turrets and towers ornamented by faded tiles of blue and yellow. Carved stone gargoyles served as waterspouts, and shadows moved in a window of the upper keep. His future bride perhaps, catching a first glimpse of him.

"Make yourself look bigger," Sar said, looking upward as well. "She may be watching."

Hestion grinned. "I've never needed to look bigger to catch the eye of a woman."

"True, but you've never been presented when you're wet as a fish from the voyage." The Ithernan shook like a bird trying to ditch water from its feathers. "This place is too damp. Half the men will return home with a cough."

"You sound like an old woman," said Hestion fondly. But he squared his shoulders as the king emerged from the castle. Urdien threw his arms out wide, throwing back the cape he wore, which was edged in long white fur.

"Prince Hestion of Glaucia. Welcome to Cassor."

"King Urdien." Hestion went down on one knee. His men followed. Some dropped awkwardly, stiff from the ride and attempting to aim their knees away from puddles.

"I see your men are unused to bowing," said Urdien. "Come

inside. Warm yourself by my hearth and meet my son. The attendants will see to your horses and men."

As Hestion and Sar walked through the throne room, studying the wall hangings, the king called for warmed wine. It arrived with soft bread and bowls of dark red berries. Sar quickly sat at the long table and helped himself—first one cup of wine disappeared, and then a second, and then enough berries to permanently stain his chin.

"Your friend has a good appetite," the king observed. "Is it because he is a . . ." Urdien gestured to his own cheeks and eyes, and then to Sar's, painted blue, and ringed dark with kohl.

"He is Ithernan," Hestion replied. "But he is also Glaucan, or he may as well be. He is a fighting man, as I am. None of us are known to be light eaters."

"Of course. Glaucia is renowned for the might of their swords, the heft of their shields. And a fondness for war, which I am aching to wage as the bastard king of Erleven continues to press against our borders." As Urdien's expression darkened, the folds of his scowl aged his face. Then he took a breath. "But we will not speak now of statecraft. I would hear your tales! How was your passage?"

Before Hestion could speak, a boy raced into the chamber. He stopped on skidding feet and stared at Hestion with an open mouth, his small chest heaving under what appeared to be hastily donned and newly made silver armor, laid over dark leather.

"Ullieth!" King Urdien smiled proudly, and Hestion's chest tightened. Would the sight of every good father sting, now that his own had faded to nothing? "Prince Hestion," said the king, "I am pleased to present my only son, Prince Ullieth." The boy bowed, and Hestion bowed even lower. Prince Ullieth. Not Crown Prince

Ullieth, despite being the only son, and with a second glance the reason why was plain. The little lad's chest had not stopped heaving, and the flush in his cheeks had nothing to do with Hestion's good looks. The boy was dying.

"I thank the king and the prince for their warm reception," said Hestion. "That is fine armor, Prince Ullieth. I must have one of my scribes sketch it, to show to our smiths in Glaucia." Prince Ullieth beamed. He followed along for a few moments as the king walked Hestion through the chamber, pointing out this or that bit of history, this or that trinket taken in some long-ago battle. But it wasn't long before he caught sight of Sar and was lost to them. The little prince planted himself beside the Ithernan and in moments, both were laughing.

"And where are your daughters?" Hestion asked. "I long to see the princess."

"As any man would," replied the king. "As many men do. But I think to present her at dinner. She will want time to make herself ready."

They spoke with the king awhile longer, and then left the castle and went to the stables to see that their horses were settled.

It wasn't hard to find his stallion in the royal stables—Target stood out bright white against almost everything. Hestion entered the stall and ran his hands down the horse's legs. The mud, which had stained the horse to the knee, had been washed off, and all his hooves were sound.

"Look at him. Already asleep." Sar leaned over the door of the next stall as he looked upon his own horse, which had once been Belden's, the blood-bay stallion that Hestion had gifted to him after he and Reed had claimed the legendary herd of Lacos. "Weren't these stallions once the best of the best? The fastest and the strongest? We're making them soft. It's good that we brought them, for the exercise, even if they took up extra space on the ship. And even if I feel strange riding your brother's horse."

"Belden would want you to," Hestion said. "And I couldn't leave him behind. Even now, someone might have tried to sacrifice him above my brother's grave. And many times he told me that he didn't even want a goat to accompany him to the afterlife."

"Your brother will find much company there anyway. I never knew a man who did not become a friend to Belden. Or any girl who did not fall in love. Unless they fell in love with you first, eh?" He patted Hestion's shoulder. "Come. These lazy mules are fine. We need to rest and clean you up. Shine the gold plate you are to woo your rich princess with."

They stepped through the doorway of the stables, and Hestion turned to give Target one last pat. As he did, he caught a flash of black farther down the corridor. A horse head, emerging from one of the farthest stalls.

A horse head in a horse stable shouldn't have given him pause. But there was something about the way the horse moved. Sneakily, like it had been hiding and waiting for them to leave. Hestion peered closer, and the black head froze. Then it slowly drew back into its stall and disappeared.

"What is it?" Sar asked. His hand went to his sword.

"Nothing," Hestion muttered. "It is only . . ." He walked toward the stall, his steps slowing as he approached. A tightness had risen in his gut, and his heart had begun to pound. He stepped in front of the stall door as if about to face a dragon.

But inside the stall was only a horse, tall and black. Hestion exhaled. He reached out an arm to pat it, and the horse promptly and happily bit him.

Hestion yanked his hand away. "Silco! I knew it was you!" The horse stepped forward, found out, and Hestion patted both sides of his face. When he looked for the injured hoof the stallion lifted his foot to show him. It had healed, but badly, and would give him a prominent limp.

Sar joined him at the stall, kohl-ringed eyes wide. "That horse belongs to the Aristene. What is it doing here?"

Hestion stroked Silco's nose. He knew with one look into the animal's eyes that Silco was no longer a horse but an Areion, and it made him wonder if the changes in Reed were equally apparent.

Silco blinked slowly. He looked from Hestion to Sar and back again, as the happiness Hestion felt upon seeing him faded and turned into something colder.

"If he is here, then Reed is here. So the real question is, why has she come?"

21.
REVOLUTION

In the Cerillian court, it was preferred to conduct one's most bloody business in the dark. Lyonene knew that well. And yet when the play for the throne of Cerille was carried out at night, with hushed voices and blades shining silver in the moonlight, King Alectos's attack still managed to take her by surprise.

"What is the meaning of this?" Alsander shouted as torchlight illuminated the faces of the Cerillian guard. Armed soldiers had barged into his bedchamber. Beside him, Lyonene edged away from the point of a blade only to feel another dig into her back. There were twelve soldiers piled into the room and twelve sets of eyes fixed on her. They knew what she was.

"Prince Alsander," said a broad, thick man named Marvingan. He was the general of the Cerillian army, and in Rhonassus, Lyonene had seen the swing of his sword cut a man's arm clean from the shoulder. "You are placed under arrest for plots against the Crown."

"Marvingan," Lyonene said through clenched teeth. "We have fought beside you. Is this how you repay your allies?" She tried to look the general in the eye, but it was as if she hadn't spoken.

"My father is old and the crown is mine," Alsander hissed. "Why would I plot against myself? Marvingan, you have known me many years—" His tone softened. "Since I was a boy."

Lyonene's heartbeat flickered like the wings of an insect about to fly. The king had given the order. Alsander's appeals would change nothing. Yet there was regret in Marvingan's eyes when he said, "An oath is an oath, my prince. And mine is to the Crown."

"And when I wear the crown?"

"Then I will gladly take my oath to you; and you will remember this night as proof that my oaths are not lightly taken." He jerked his chin toward two soldiers, who moved toward Alsander with ropes.

Lyonene tensed. She could take her chance now, call her armor and sword, slice their way out of the bedchamber. But what then? Would they fight their way through the palace, and then the city? And then to where? If they left now, their coalition of nobles would break apart, and all their plans would have been for nothing.

"You don't need to restrain us," Lyonene said. "But we would know why you suspect us of this treason."

Marvingan nodded to one of the soldiers, who held up a sack of golden cloth, the bottom soaked through with dark liquid. "Your friend Fournio confessed all," he said, tossing the sack to their feet. Fournio's decapitated head rolled out across the floor.

Alsander gasped.

"The king is killing his own nobles," said Lyonene. She looked at the soldiers. "You think this evidence of a sound mind?"

"Silence, witch," Marvingan growled, and struck her across the face. It didn't hurt. But it was humiliating. And by the look on Marvingan's face, it was clear that though they had fought together, had laughed and drunk together, hitting her had been something he'd wanted to do for a long time.

"When this is over and I am king," Alsander seethed, "you will pay dearly for that."

"Get them up." Marvingan motioned to the soldiers, and Lyonene and Alsander were shoved from the room and marched along the colonnade.

As they went, Lyonene felt Alsander watching, waiting for guidance or a cue to start to fight. But she couldn't think. Madly, she found herself wishing for Reed. Where was her lucky Ox, to bash through these men?

As if in a dream, Lyonene looked out upon the sleeping city. She saw the torches of soldiers moving through the villas of Fournio, of Ascar, of Nephelos. All those nobles she had placed in Alsander's pocket. Every one of their necks would meet the sword, and their heads would fall into bloodstained sacks.

Lyonene turned to Alsander, but there were no threads of golden glory tying him to the palace. He stood tall, his back proud, but he no longer glittered with possibilities. The night around him was as black and dull as the void.

The only glow came from the direction of the stables, which were burning.

"General," a young man shouted as he came running from that direction. "Someone has set fire to the stable and loosed all of the horses!"

"Who?" Marvingan shouted back, confused.

The soldiers moved to surround the prisoners and Lyonene huddled close to Alsander as they waited tensely in the dark, listening to the sounds of the fire burning and the thunder of fleeing hoofbeats. And then Lyonene saw the face of her mare, lit orange by the patrol's torches.

"Strawberry," she said as Veridian and Everfall exploded from the shadows.

Veridian wielded her sword on the right, cutting low with the force of her red gelding driving the blade. She charged so fast and so fiercely that she seemed not to see them, and Lyonene leaped onto Alsander and shoved him to the ground to keep him from being culled like the rest.

"Impossible," Marvingan shouted as Veridian disappeared, horse and rider swallowed by the darkness. "Where has she come from?"

"She comes from nowhere." Lyonene got to her feet and called her armor. It burst forth, the thick leather a cold and comforting weight. "But she's been that way for years." Quick as a cat, Lyonene attacked. The point of her blade sank deep into one throat and swung left to slice another. She turned her magic loose as Veridian emerged again, riding down the men who ran for their lives. One poor lad turned and threw Fournio's head at her, a last-ditch effort before Everfall trampled him beneath sharp hooves.

In mere moments, all were dead save Marvingan. The general of the Cerillian army hadn't even drawn his weapon when Alsander stepped to him and buried a dagger in his gut.

"You shouldn't have taken my father's side, old friend."

"I had no choice," the man whispered, but Alsander twisted the blade cruelly before removing it and cutting his throat. Marvingan fell to the grass.

"That was unkind," Veridian said as she rode up to them.

"He was a traitor," said Alsander.

"*You* are the traitor. He was a soldier, doing his duty. It wasn't his fault that he didn't have an Aristene as a pet." She turned Everfall in a fast circle and whistled to Strawberry. The sturdy roan mare trotted to them with a leggy bay horse tied to her saddle. "Get on and let's go."

"You want us to run," Alsander said, incredulous.

"Only if you want to live."

"Here is where I live! Here is where I rule!" He pointed the blood-coated dagger toward the palace. "My father is yet inside and I would see him kneel!"

"To what end? You've massacred the general of your army and those nobles you bought are dead. Even if you win a crown this night, how long do you think you'll keep it?"

"I won't abandon my kingdom."

Veridian turned to Lyonene. "You don't know what waits inside that palace. We have a chance now to get out. A chance we might not have again."

Lyonene looked past Alsander toward the city. She wanted to stay, perhaps just as badly as he did. But Veridian was right. She'd been outmaneuvered. "Get on the horse," she said as she leaped into Strawberry's saddle. "Tonight is not a victory. But as long as you're alive you're still the crown prince. And the people will wait for your return." Alsander hesitated, and she held out her hand. "Don't you trust me?"

He cursed under his breath and slapped her hand away, but did as she asked and got on the horse. "I want my stallion," he said, and jerked on the bay's reins. "Where is Phaeton?"

"Too fast for me to catch, that's where Phaeton is," Veridian said. "Now move." She put her heels to Everfall and galloped away into the night. Lyonene waited until Alsander did the same before she and Strawberry followed.

At least they were alive. That was what she told herself as she watched her husband stare at the palace that should have been his. He didn't look at her, and her heart sank, because she knew that he was right. Once they left Cerille, there would be no taking it back.

22.
ONCE A MENTOR

Aster, have you felt anything wrong within the order?

In the weeks that followed Reed's departure from Atropa, that question pestered Aster like an unreachable itch. What had Reed meant by it? And why had she been so full of sudden questions about the World's Gate?

Aster sighed into a hot mug of tea. It was still too hot to drink; she'd left the pot over the fire for too long, lost in her thoughts. The pot hung nearby, swung away from the heat and still softly steaming. Barely a year ago she'd had an initiate to do these kinds of things, to sweep the ashes from her hearth, to prepare her tea just right. She missed those times and that place, the hut she shared with Reed in the Summer Camp. It was barely more than a thatched roof and four walls, but it felt like more of a home than her fine house in the white city. She remembered the mornings of being awoken by initiates' shrieks as they chased each other outside her bedroom window. She remembered the little garden, constantly infested with slugs. But mostly, she remembered Reed.

Aster, have you felt anything wrong within the order?

No, she hadn't. Yet if that were really true, the question would have stopped its echo.

Aster stood and slipped a shawl around her shoulders to stave off the chill of the morning. She took a fast slurp of her tea and burned her tongue—still too hot—and wiped her mouth before heading out of her house.

The streets were quiet, as they almost always were, especially near her home, where many of the buildings stood mostly vacant, only one or two Aristenes living inside them. Aster looked one way and then the other. Then she simply started walking, allowing her mind to go quiet and her legs to carry her by some invisible force. She'd been an Aristene for a long time and had done this often: letting her mind open like an eye inside her head and for her body to be pulled through the city as if by a string. She thought of that pull as her innate gift. It was her magic, it was her intuition, it was her pathfinder ability—it was Kleia Gloria herself. It brought her to the things she sought.

Today it brought her all the way out of Atropa, to where the streets changed from paved stone to dirt. It tugged her farther and farther away, until it was grass beneath her feet, and then grass to her knees, tangles of it strung through with clover and wildflowers, the air dotted with honeybees already at work in the growing warmth. She let the shawl slip from her shoulders. When the tugging stopped, she stood in the middle of an empty field. Or so she thought, until the Veil opened and Aethiel tumbled out of the darkness covered in blood.

"Aethiel!"

"Aster." The big Aristene raised an arm in greeting and then promptly lay back. Aster raced to her side. She tried to help her up but her grip slipped—Aethiel's wrist was a wet, red glove.

"We must get you to Mia and the healers."

"No," Aethiel corrected her. "To the elders. This scratch can wait."

What she called a scratch was actually several cuts, many of them deep. Aster used her shawl to bind them, wrapping it tightly around Aethiel's ribs. "What did this?"

"Take me to the elders. They will explain. Or they won't—you know how they are."

Aster helped her to rise, and they started back to the city at a slow and hobbled pace. "You ought to claim an Areion," Aster said.

"Nah. I'm not fit to look after one."

"It's the Areion who would do the looking after," Aster mumbled. She adjusted her grip on Aethiel and felt her fingers warm and sticky with blood. She reached down into herself and called to Rabbit. The mare would be dozing in the stable at this hour but she would hear the call and come, jumping gates or breaking through doors in order to reach them. Aster twisted to look at Aethiel. She wasn't badly hurt—the blood flow had slowed, and though Aethiel seemed tired, her eyes were bright. Still, wounds like these to an Aristene were infrequent, even to reckless, war-hungry ones.

"Tell me how you've come to this. What battle did you find yourself in where you'd take so many cuts?"

"I can't say."

"Because you've lost so much blood that you can't remember?" Aster dragged Aethiel to a halt and let her stand there, dripping. "I know that something is wrong. And you'd best tell me what it is."

Aethiel's black eyes shifted between Aster and the Citadel. For a long moment she said nothing. Then she reached into her belt. She pulled something out of it and tossed it through the air.

Aster caught it, but just barely. The moment it touched her skin she wanted to drop it into the dirt. It was a dark fragment of bone, wet with blood, no larger than a coin.

"It's a piece of the prophet's skull," Aethiel said.

"The skull that Reed fought against during her Hero's Trial."

Aethiel nodded.

"Where did you get it?"

"I dug it out of a monster. Who used to be a man. A month ago, the elders dug another out of a different monster, who used to be my hero."

Someone was turning their heroes into monsters. So that's why Reed hadn't wanted her to take a new hero of her own. Reed had known.

Aster looked down at the bone in her palm. She rubbed the blood from it with her thumb, felt the smooth sides and the sharp edges where it was broken from the rest of the head. It felt foul. It felt alive, like an insect that would bite and burrow under her skin. But it was just a bone. Even if it had such a will, it had no legs to see it to purpose. "Who is doing this? Why?"

"The whos and the whys are for the elders," Aethiel replied. "I am only for removing the limbs and slaying the beasts."

Aster curled her fist around the bit of bone. "That isn't true. It is said that the war queens of Fennbirn Island are great strategists."

"Those days are long behind me," Aethiel said, nostrils flaring. "And if you have not noticed, I am still bleeding. So might we . . . ?" She gestured toward the Citadel as Rabbit cantered down the dirt road toward them. When the horse saw that Aethiel was injured, she pulled up short and sidled close to kneel so both women could mount.

"Good girl," Aethiel said once she was astride. She patted Rabbit's gray neck and left behind a red handprint. "Perhaps I should take on an Areion. A nice, mean black one, like that one of Machianthe's. All hooves and teeth."

"You would have to promise not to fist-fight with it," Aster muttered. She nudged Rabbit with her heels and the mare eased into a gentle trot. "And first, let us get you to the elders."

Aster and Aethiel waited for the elders in the great half-circle room with the balcony that overlooked the city. The healer, Mia, was summoned to treat Aethiel's wounds. She unwrapped the shawl from Aethiel's ribs and leaned down to sponge the cuts.

Aethiel had refused to lie upon any of the furniture—not worth ruining a pillow over, she'd said—and instead lay upon the floor. As the healer's fingers slid over the silver of Aethiel's armor, she glanced at Aster. Aethiel had been cut in sets of four, as if by claws. The marks continued from her skin onto the armor.

"Send your armor away," Mia said. "I need to get underneath it."

Aethiel did as she was bid, her armor flickering back into the aether like a blinked eye. In its place she wore a plain tunic and leggings, both dyed an expensively deep black. The queens of Fennbirn Island wore black, Aster knew. Aethiel was dressing like one of them again.

"It tried to cut through my crown," Aethiel whispered as Mia dabbed at a wound on her forehead. A thin red line bisected the band of black that ran across her brow.

"It won't scar," Mia said. "And that is not a crown anymore." The healer drew back and rose to her feet. She walked out without another word.

"I should not have said that," Aethiel whispered. "The Aristene wear no crowns."

"It's not as if you can cut it off of your face," Aster said. "It doesn't make you less of an Aristene. Or less of a sister to me." She held out her hand. "You know, you're like Veridian in many ways. You make demands; you are uncouth—but you are no apostate, and you shouldn't greet the elders lying on the floor." The big Aristene grinned and Aster helped her to her feet.

No sooner was she upright than Ferreh and Tiern entered.

"Aster," Tiern said, waving a hand in her direction as Ferreh swept past her to assess Aethiel's injuries. "You may go."

"I would like to stay."

"Aethiel will be fine." The elder waved again. "Go. We have much to discuss."

"Like this piece of the prophet?" Aster opened her palm to reveal the piece of bone, dry now, all the blood rubbed red into her hand. She closed her fingers over it quickly when Tiern moved to snatch it. The elder's eyes had taken on a ghastly gleam, as if she would have grabbed it and gobbled it up. "Ferreh," Aster said. "What is happening?"

Ferreh approached Aster and gently pried her fingers apart. She stroked the flat coin of bone with a forefinger and slid it from Aster's palm. "Was it another of your heroes, Aethiel?" Ferreh asked.

"After what happened to the last, I thought it best not to take another," Aethiel replied. "This was an attack, by a beast that seemed half man and half dog."

Aster looked again at the wounds, the long lines of claws and a deep set of punctures through Aethiel's forearm. A bite. From a monster.

"But you killed it," Tiern said.

"Not this time. It bore an open wound upon its chest. I dug inside and pulled out the shard of bone. And the beast became a man again."

"It returned to its prior form?" Ferreh asked. "Then there is a way to undo it."

"The priests in shabby robes took him away after that," Aethiel said. "They called him by name; I think he was one of them."

"How many of these creatures must we face?" Aster asked. "How much of the prophet's skull is unaccounted for?"

Ferreh shook her head. "We don't know. We sent riders to the boy king in Roshanak, but he has refused to relinquish the bones to us, nor even to allow us to view them."

"Roshanak," Tiern said. "That must be where these priests saw us. Twice now, Aethiel has been attacked. As if they know her."

Aster stiffened. "Then they'll have also seen Reed, and Lyonene. Ferreh, we must bring them back. Now."

"We don't know if they're being hunted, and Machianthe at least knows of the danger," Tiern said, and Aster's eyelid twitched. The elder shrugged. "But you are right. Go and get them. Make sure that they are safe."

After Aster and Aethiel departed, the elders remained.

"Is this wise?" Ferreh asked, amber eyes watching as Tiern dragged a toe through the vaguely woman-shaped smear of blood Aethiel had left on the marble floor. "To go to the initiates? We may be leading our enemies right to them."

"You'd rather take the chance?" Tiern rapped her knuckles against the bare table. No cups of tea or wine, no bowls of dried fruit sat upon it. No flowers. The only scent in the room was that of Aethiel's drying blood, and underneath that, the faint, cloying rot of the creature who had drawn it. "Two attacks in less than a moon cycle." Tiern exhaled hard through her nose in disgust. She reached into the pouch at her belt and withdrew her shard of bone to worry at it with her thumb. Ferreh rubbed hers as well, taken from Aster and still slightly stained.

It had been an age since any had dared to attack the order. They dared now only because the Aristene were weak. But glorious death would fix all that. Reed would fix it, fortifying them through the deeds of her heroes and their sacrifices as precious as the purest gold. Through Reed their link with the goddess would be reforged. A vision rose before Ferreh's eyes, the same nightmare vision that had come from the depths of the well: Machianthe, shrouded in darkness and blood. The eyes of her black Areion shot through with red.

"This creature," Tiern said. "Aethiel said he was like a dog. Why not 'like a wolf'?"

"She said it was one of the priests. Priests are like dogs. Loyal and devoted."

"So the skull made them into dogs. And it made of Oreas a great and monstrous king. . . ." Tiern set her fragment on the table. It winked there in the light, its edges sharp and wicked. "To Aethiel's sailor it gave fins with which to swim." Her brow knit thoughtfully. "The skull of the Scylloi Prophet seems to make a person *more* like themselves."

Ferreh eyed the other elder. Tiern's voice had turned cunning.

"You would put that into our Reed," Ferreh said, disbelieving.

"You would corrupt an Aristene with this . . . filth!"

"No, don't you see? It would not corrupt her. It would make her what we have seen in our dreams."

Ferreh blinked. Tiern was an elder. She was Ferreh's equal. It was they who had stood in the shadow of the goddess, they who had built Atropa from the dust and ash of their fallen worlds. She and Tiern had watched the ages turn together, seen the rise and fall of thousands of years. So how could Tiern be led so astray? She'd received the same vision, shown to them by Kleia Gloria as a warning. A tragedy to avert, not a prophecy to fulfill.

"I won't let you do that, Tiern."

Tiern paused. She drew her lips back. Showed her teeth. "You do not *let* me do anything."

Never in the elders' long history had they crossed swords, not even in jest. Both knew that they each contained too much power for even a jest to be safe.

So Ferreh remained still. And Tiern's weapons remained sheathed.

"Machianthe will be the greatest of us all," Tiern said. "The most terrible—"

"The most terrible monster. And how, sister, would you think to control such a creature?"

For a moment Ferreh thought that Tiern would see reason. But Tiern had been an elder for too long. The thought that there would be a beast she couldn't conquer—the thought of her own death—was inconceivable. She picked up the shard of bone and returned it to her belt, then went to Ferreh and drew her close. So close that her chin rested on the taller elder's shoulder. "It will not be long now," she whispered, "until Machianthe will wield a power so great that she will obliterate all who come after. And then we will be safe."

She kissed Ferreh's cheek and walked out.

"This is not the way," Ferreh called after her.

"It is the way," Tiern called back. "You have seen it."

In Ferreh's hand, the wickedness of the bone shard vibrated like a fast pulse. She didn't want to stand against Tiern. She didn't want to fight the woman who had been her only partner. But if they could not agree, then who else but Ferreh had the strength to do it? The task of saving Reed, of saving the order, and of saving Tiern as well, would fall on her shoulders alone.

As Aster readied her Areion for travel, her mind swirled with thoughts of the skull of the Scylloi Prophet and the priests who seemed to serve it. And as always, she thought of Reed. Her thoughts were consumed by what they meant to do to Reed.

She threw a blanket over Rabbit's gray back and thumped the saddle down on top. She tightened the cinch too sharply and the mare grunted.

"I'm sorry, girl," she whispered, rubbing the horse's belly. But Rabbit was as eager to be off as her rider, and only bobbed her head toward their saddlebags. "I'm lucky you're you and not Silco. Silco would have taken my arm off."

The mare nickered when someone entered the stable, and Aster turned to see Aethiel. The big Aristene was leading a horse she'd caught from the meadow, a black mare with two white socks and a wide white blaze down her face. Aster knew that horse. She was an Areion who had belonged to an Aristene named Beatrixe, who had fallen in battle ten years ago.

"What are you doing with Nightfly?" Aster asked.

Aethiel shrugged. "I just went to the pasture and asked which of the lone Areion would like to carry me into battle. I am going with you." Aethiel tied the mare to a post and picked up a brush. Then she started grooming her, if indeed one could call it that. Aster and the horse traded a look. She didn't need to have been there to know that Nightfly was the only Areion who had volunteered.

"Aethiel, you're wounded. You should rest."

"I need no rest." Aethiel flexed her chest and shoulders. The movement squeezed blood from her wounds like juice from a handful of berries. It was a gruesome sight, but Aethiel smiled. It was said that the war queens of Fennbirn Island reveled in blood. Aster had thought that an overblown rumor, until she met one.

"And besides," Aethiel said. "There is something I must tell you about Reed and Lyonene. They are not where you think they are."

Aster and Rabbit looked at her sharply. "What do you mean?"

"The day Lyonene claimed a new hero, I overheard them in the Citadel. They've switched places. Lyonene has returned to her princeling and Reed—"

"Has taken a hero who is not hers." Aster threw her saddlebags into the dirt. "What were they thinking? Aethiel—"

"I don't know," Aethiel replied, shrugging away when Aster grabbed her shoulder. "And don't ask me questions. I'm injured."

"Why did you say nothing? Why did you not tell me?"

"I do not inform on my sisters. Not even the littlest ones, when they make stupid decisions." Aethiel went back to brushing Nightfly. "So I am going. I will retrieve Lyonene from the princeling, and you will get Reed from her false hero. No one will be the wiser."

Aster looked at Rabbit, and Rabbit pawed the ground. *Our children are in danger*, the movement said. *So let her come. We will need her help.*

"Fine," Aster said.

Together they walked their horses out of the city, into the hills where they would open the Veil and pass through to the world of men. But when they reached the sun-soaked grass, they found another Aristene already there waiting. Mol sat astride her large white stallion. She was wearing Ellora's silver headband, as she often did when the other Aristene was away with a hero, and it glinted in the light.

"There you are, sisters," she said. "Tiern says I am to go with you, to retrieve the initiates."

Aster and Aethiel looked at each other. Rabbit snorted under her breath, a curse word if Aster had ever heard one.

"That isn't necessary, Mol," Aster said. "I'm going to collect my initiate Reed, and Aethiel has volunteered to go to Lyonene. Two initiates, two Aristene." She smiled warmly, and Mol smiled back with narrowed eyes.

"Then three will be even better," Mol said. "And we will stay together. For safety. The elders have told me of the threat we face."

"But that will take longer," Aster protested.

"These are the instructions of Tiern. Do you wish to go against them?" Mol raised her brows. Then she turned her Areion and rode to the top of the hill, where she began to speak to the Veil, conjuring it with a whisper and the twirl of a finger.

"If she comes, she will know that they traded—" Aethiel grumbled, and Aster silenced her with an elbow to the gut.

"I'm sorry," Aster whispered, when Aethiel winced and clutched at her bandages.

"It's all right," Aethiel replied. "I kind of liked it. But what are we going to do?"

"I don't know." She and Aethiel mounted their horses, and trotted up the hill where Mol waited with the Veil yawning open before her.

"Reed," Aster muttered through her teeth as she watched Mol disappear into the void. "You foolish initiate. What were you thinking?"

23.

A BANQUET OF FORCED SMILES

Reed stood to one side as ladies moved past with arms laden with colorful gowns. Each of the new ones delivered by the dressmaker, in blue brocade and orange taffeta, in wine red with an under-fabric the color of fresh milk. They were in Yngarue and Wyrnnigrid's shared chamber, preparing for the banquet at which Yngarue would be presented to her first suitor, Hestion of Glaucia.

"The purple silk with cloth of silver is so beautiful," said one of their ladies, a young matron called Evie who was married to a lord twice her age.

"It is," Wyrnnigrid agreed. "But this one—" She ran her hand over the brown dress layered in cloth of gold. "This is the one in which *you* will be the most beautiful. The gold cloth will cause the gold in your eyes to sparkle. You must save it for something special. Save it for the night when you know which suitor you will choose."

Yngarue smiled gently at her sister. "Don't you mean when Father knows which suitor he will choose? All of this is just for show; that I really have a choice is an illusion." She looked past the gold cloth and purple silk to reach for the red brocade embroidered with silver livestock. "This one," she said. She turned to Reed. "Yes?"

Reed nodded. It was a very pretty gown, well cut, and the dancing goats were charming in silver thread. Also, Reed was too preoccupied with thoughts of the Glaucans to hear half of what they were saying. She smoothed the skirt of her dress. The matchmaker's costume had never felt more red or more full of bells. Even standing still she thought she could hear them lightly tinkling as she breathed.

It doesn't matter, she thought to herself as the ladies hurried to help Yngarue into her gown. *No one will be looking at you.* Both princesses were beautiful, Yngarue with burnished brown hair stuck through with seed pearls and Wyrnnigrid, her pale blond twisted into an ornate crown atop her head. The thought of standing beside them made Reed feel slightly sick. Hestion would indeed not be looking at her.

"You know, there still may be a choice to be made," said Wyrnnigrid to her younger sister as she took a box of jewelry from Evie and picked through its contents. "If Lady Machianthe will help us."

Reed snapped to attention. But Yngarue only glanced at her apologetically. She pushed aside the pin her sister offered, encrusted with gemstones and lapis lazuli, and instead chose a small ring of hammered silver. "Machianthe has been a friend to us," Yngarue said, "but she is here on behalf of Alsander of Cerille. Of course she will advise Father in his favor."

"No, Wyrnnigrid is right," said Reed. "I am a matchmaker by trade, and I will make the best match. If I deem you and my prince to be poorly suited, I will make you the finest match from the other suitors. It is on the prince's orders that I do this," she added, because what was one more lie piled atop the stack?

Yngarue's eyes slitted slightly. "Is that true?"

"My prince is fair," Reed replied. "And when he gives a gift, he intends it to be just that: a gift." She bent her knees into one of her awkward curtsies, and Yngarue smiled the first real smile Reed had seen on her face all night.

"I am lucky you are here. And so happy. You do not know how happy." Yngarue reached back into the box of jewelry and withdrew a strand of carved amber beads. "Here," she said. "You must wear these tonight. And let us loosen your hair, which is so lovely."

"Perhaps a veil of red silk," Evie suggested, coming at Reed to pull out her braid and rake fast fingers through the back of her head. Reed leaned away like a snake about to strike as Evie secured the amber necklace. She held her arms tight to her sides as they fitted her head with red silk. Once her hat was back on it did nothing to improve her appearance, but perhaps she could use it to hide behind, if Hestion's gaze passed too closely.

"There," Wyrnnigrid announced as Yngarue turned in a circle. "Is this not a young lady with whom Hestion of Glaucia will fall in love with at first sight?"

"Is he the sort of man who can fall in love with one look?" Yngarue asked, and laughed. She turned to Reed. "Does such a man exist?"

Reed thought back to her first battle at Hestion's side. To the awe in his eyes when he first saw her in her armor of silver and white. "All men are mysteries," Reed said. Quickly, she turned away, amid a twinkling of bells. *All men are mysteries?* She squeezed her eyes shut. What kind of nonsense was she spouting? What in balls and ass did that even mean?

Another lady's maid came into the chamber to announce the arrival of Parmenin; he was dressed in his usual brown robes but had adorned his fingers in gold rings and wore a bright gold medallion around his neck.

"Princesses," he said. "You look splendid. Your father will be so pleased."

"Thank you, Parmenin," Yngarue said. She stepped forward to kiss the priest on the cheek and Reed saw something flicker across his face as she stepped back. The expression was there and gone in an instant but was recognizably a look of shared intimacy.

They are friends, she thought. *Wyrnnigrid says they have been friends for years*. Perhaps it was only that. The knowing look of one friend to another as they embarked on a new phase of life.

"I have come to escort Princess Yngarue to the banquet."

"I think I would prefer to enter alone, just behind Wyrnnigrid," Yngarue said. "But I have a better idea: you must escort our matchmaker. Come, Machianthe, and take Parmenin's hands!"

Reed and Parmenin met each other's eyes with surprise. But the priest quickly recovered and held out his arm.

Reed didn't care one way or the other who escorted her into the feast. Were she to have her way she would not go at all, or would arrive rolled up in a rug, or hidden in a trunk. She took his arm, and thankfully found that they were placed at the back of the processional, where with any luck she would simply be overlooked.

Hestion and Sar awaited the princesses at the head of the same chamber the king had welcomed them into. Their soldiers were somewhere behind them, standing with hands folded like good, tame nobles. He'd only heard a few grumbles since the horn had announced the princesses' imminent arrival—it was lucky they'd not kept them waiting longer, after more of the ale had flowed. Beside him, Sar looked down at his chest. They'd cleaned the dried gore from the points of their spears and banged out the recent dents in their armor, but they still looked less like a royal entourage than a raiding party.

"Perhaps we should have removed our armor," Sar whispered. "We could be frightening to a princess."

"Then let her be frightened," Hestion muttered back. "To win this dowry is only to pretend to win the princess while in truth I win her father. And what her father wants are men who can rout Erleven and paint the streets in blood."

"I don't think your aunt meant for us to pledge a war."

"My aunt meant for me to secure this princess at any cost. And the only surety in these lands is that the peace between Cassor and Erleven does not last."

Sar's jaw tightened. Hestion glanced around the room, at his men shifting their feet, and the nobility of Cassor standing beside them, well fed in tunics and capes of blue and yellow. King Urdien sat upon his throne. Prince Ullieth was stationed beside the entrance to the rear hall, presumably to take the princess's arm and guide her to her suitor. He caught Hestion's eye and smiled.

Hestion smiled back. His gaze swept the room again. He'd already searched the attendees for Reed, and she wasn't here. But she must be somewhere. He'd waited in the stable with Silco for as long as he could, hoping to catch her unaware. Sar finally had to drag him away to dress for the feast.

He caught movement in the crowd and turned. Only a woman adjusting her veil. Not Reed.

Sar elbowed him in the ribs. "Stop looking for the Aristene," he said through the side of his mouth.

"I wasn't," Hestion whispered. And then he promptly turned to look for her again.

Footsteps sounded in the corridor and King Urdien stood.

"Last chance to pray," Sar whispered. "That she is not too plain. That she is not too beautiful."

"Not too beautiful?"

"Too beautiful and I will wed her instead." Sar grinned.

"My daughter," King Urdien announced. "Princess Yngarue."

Hestion straightened. The first girl to enter was a tall blond with gray-blue eyes and wearing a gown of deep green, embroidered with gold leaves. She was beautiful—so beautiful he heard Sar's sharp intake of breath—but the look on her face was too playful, as if she couldn't wait for him to see what walked behind her.

"Er," King Urdien said, "allow me to present my elder daughter, and heir, Princess Wyrnnigrid."

"Thank the gods of my people and yours," Sar said happily. "Had she been the one I would have had to fight you for her."

Hestion laughed. He looked past Wyrnnigrid to the arched doorway, and the shadows that approached. His pulse quickened. Was that a flash of white cape he saw? Was it her laugh he heard? He blinked hard. None of that was real. Nothing about her had been real. He was haunted by phantoms.

"Ah," King Urdien said at last. "Here we are. My daughter, the princess Yngarue." He stood and came down from his throne to embrace her and kiss her cheek. She was beautiful like her sister, though in a softer, warmer way. Her hair was loose and brown. Her eyes when they met his were bright, and she smiled pleasantly. The gown she wore was red and embroidered with—he squinted—goats.

"Prince Hestion."

"Princess Yngarue."

She held up her hand and he took it as the guests and his soldiers cheered, and the king announced the commencement of the feast. But as he escorted Yngarue to the high table, he turned his head back to the doorway.

Where was Reed?

Reed felt her heart jumping in her chest like a cornered cricket as the sounds of those gathered in the hall grew louder. Her hand upon Parmenin's arm was damp with sweat.

"Are you unwell, Lady Machianthe?"

"No." She looked at Parmenin. Then at the arched doorway. They were almost there. Yngarue was stepping inside.

"Yes," Reed said. She dragged Parmenin back, not caring that her strength must have surprised him. "Forgive me, I—don't like being placed on display. Could we perhaps enter after the feast has begun, and sit at one of the farthest tables?" She knew he had to say no. He was Urdien's primary adviser. She was the royal matchmaker.

"Of course," he said. He patted her hand kindly, and for the first time she noticed that he had gentle eyes, a soft brown flecked with green. "We may sit wherever you like. It will be better, perhaps, for you to observe Yngarue and Hestion from afar?"

"It will be most useful, Parmenin. Thank you."

"We will enter beside the servants once the feasting has begun." He turned them around. "Though we may be seen anyway." He nodded to her dress, and flicked a fingertip against the nearest bell on her hat. Reed looked at him in surprise. Then she laughed.

"Indeed, I am sorry you must be seen with me," she said, and he laughed, too.

They waited at the servants' entrance for a raucous moment, and when the heads of the room had turned toward the king, they stole inside beside the cover of a platter of roasted fowl. Parmenin led her to a far corner, and Reed maneuvered herself so her back was to the head table, before remembering she was supposed to be watching Yngarue and repositioning herself to one side. They greeted the others seated with them, lesser nobility in fine clothes but few jewels, and adornments in plain metal. They seemed confused by the presence of the royal adviser, but weren't about to question it. It was no doubt the closest they'd come to the king all year, and they wasted no time before bending Parmenin's ear to the concerns of their households. He'd barely gotten a swallow of wine before one of the ladies was beseeching him to ask the king for an easement onto land whose property line was contested by a neighbor.

Poor Parmenin. Such was life in the royal circle. She caught his eye over the rim of her wine cup and waggled her eyebrows.

As soon as she dared, Reed snuck a glance at the high table. Sar was there, seated beside Wyrnnigrid and regaling her with some wild tale; he was all arms as he reenacted a great battle, and Wyrnnigrid's eyes were wide. The king was laughing with little Ulli as he showed his new dagger to a few of Hestion's soldiers, Dacron and Stavros, who Reed remembered from the war.

Reed turned farther, tugging the red veil across her cheek. Hestion sat beside Yngarue with his elbow resting comfortably upon the table. His dark gold hair was slightly longer than when she'd last seen him, but he still kept one side back with a small braid. His shoulders still looked strong, and he looked well for having just made a sea and overland voyage. He actually looked, she thought, and smiled, a little heavier around the middle.

I still love him, she thought with a sinking heart. But of course she would. He'd done nothing to make her stop. He smiled at something Yngarue said, and his head tilted back as he laughed.

"Is something wrong, Machianthe?" Parmenin asked.

"No," Reed said quickly. She took a swallow of wine, and then, on second thought, took a lesson from Veridian and drained it. "More wine?" she asked the priest as she refilled her cup. He held his out so she could replenish the small amount he'd consumed.

"I forgot to thank you," he said, raising his cup gingerly to hers as she drained it a second time. "For your help with Brother Clafin." Brother Clafin, the man who had tried to rape the servant girl in the pantry. "Yngarue told me you were the one who spoke against his actions."

"Spoke," Reed said. "Yes."

"I've sent him back to the abbey to receive his judgment from our Holy Father. It is a shame he proved so abhorrent; he was the only other man of my order here in the Cassan court."

"You must be lonely, with so few of your faith near," said Reed.

"At times," Parmenin admitted. "Are the men of Glaucia pious? I enjoy speaking with men of other faiths, in the absence of my own."

"In Glaucia they revered the Scylloi Prophet," Reed said. She watched the priest carefully.

"It was a grave fate which befell the prophet. We did not worship him in my sect, but we knew of him."

"I thought the Scylloi Prophet was the prophet of all."

"Perhaps he had not made it to us yet," said Parmenin. "Perhaps he would have come to our Abbey of the Calumnian Brotherhood, had he had more time."

Reed sent her magic out into the air to coil around Parmenin, searching for any trace of the malevolent magic that infused the prophet's bones. She felt nothing. She sensed nothing about him that was monstrous or cruel, and was relieved.

"I will enjoy speaking with the Glaucans of him," the priest went on. He looked at the high table and smiled. "They seem to be fond of one another already."

Reed looked back at Hestion and Yngarue. They did indeed seem fond of one another. Their heads were bent closely together, their fingers upon the table almost touching. They might have been the only two people in the room for all the attention they paid to anyone else, and Reed felt foolish for hiding herself away. It hadn't been necessary. She could have stood right in front of him, and Hestion would not have noticed her.

The princess was lovely enough. She was lively and clever; easy to speak with. Though perhaps not as easy as her sister—behind him, he heard Wyrnnigrid compliment the blue upon Sar's cheeks. Beautiful, she called it, and suggested their own nobles adopt the custom and do the same, painting their cheeks in blue and yellow.

"I would like to see blue upon your cheeks," Sar said back. "Yet you do not need the adornment with those eyes, like the sea, and the stars."

Hestion stifled a snort by eating a piece of roasted suckling pig.

"My sister seems to be taking a liking to your general," Yngarue noted.

"Now you know why I brought him. When Sar is near there's no need for me to speak." He smiled at her, and glanced again toward the arched doorway. The Aristene must be there somewhere. He hadn't imagined her horse inside the stable.

"You have some very fine horses in your stalls," he said, and Yngarue's brows rose at the sudden shift in conversation.

"Ah, yes," she said. "I have been told you are fond of horses. In fact, I've heard that yours—" She looked down and touched her chin as if remembering. "That yours is so bright a white that he attracts enemy arrows like moths to a candle, and it is a wonder you are still alive."

Hestion and Sar set down their bread. "Where did you hear that?" they asked together.

Yngarue laughed. She turned to the crowd to motion to a figure in red. "From my matchmaker."

The matchmaker. She hadn't been there when the feast began, waiting among the nobles—there would have been no missing that ridiculous hat.

Hestion's eyes bored into her back so hard she must have felt it like an itch. It had to be her. But the dark waves of her hair were hidden beneath a veil, and she stubbornly kept her face turned away.

"Matchmakers are an old custom in Cassor," Yngarue explained. "Young women have them as others have tutors. I had not had one until recently; I thought my father had decided against the expense. And then she arrived. As a gift."

"A gift," Hestion murmured.

"A gift from our father," Wynnigrid added. She looked at her sister meaningfully, but Hestion wasn't paying attention. He stood, and Sar grasped his elbow.

"Don't," Sar said.

Hestion tugged loose and walked around the long table while Sar made excuses in his wake: "Forgive him, he has always been an impulsive brute. . . ."

Hestion didn't hear the rest. His eyes were on Reed and the hat dripping with silver bells. On the priest beside her who was vying for her attention. *Turn and face me*, he thought, growing angrier with every moment she did not. As he neared the table, she was so willfully ignoring him that he doubted himself. But it was Reed. The same serious line of her mouth. The same long, dark lashes. When would she stop pretending she didn't know he was there, that she hadn't been his companion in a voyage across the sea and his ally through the siege of Roshanak—that she hadn't been his Aristene!

His fingers jerked for the hilt of his sword, but before he could draw it and watch the red dress dissolve to reveal the silver-armored truth, the priest rose to greet him.

"Prince Hestion," he said. He bowed, and as he did, Reed slipped away, excusing herself from the table. "I am Parmenin," the priest went on, and Hestion noticed that he was young and handsome. "Of the Calumnian Brotherhood. And also adviser to the king. And . . . you have just missed Lady Machianthe, our royal matchmaker."

"I am . . . pleased to meet you," Hestion mumbled. His eyes tracked Reed as she fled between tables. "Excuse me." He went after her, leaving the priest standing openmouthed, and knocking guests forward into their food. He cut around the end of a long table and reached Reed before she could leave. He relished the way she tensed as he fell in step beside her.

"How did you know I was here?" she asked.

"I saw Silco in the stable," he replied, and heard her curse. "Did you really think to hide from me the entire time I was here?"

"I did," Reed said, her voice infuriatingly even. "I hoped."

Hestion's jaw clenched. People had begun to watch them as they took their turn about the room. "So you got what you wanted after all. Does she know what you are?" He bared his teeth. "Glorious Death?"

Her eyes darted to his and he nearly froze; it was only a look, but after so long it felt like she'd reached out and grabbed him.

"No," she whispered furiously. "And you will not tell her!"

"I will tell her. I won't stand aside and allow that young woman to be walked to her doom—"

"She is not one of mine," Reed hissed, smiling at a table as they passed.

"What do you mean, 'not one of yours'?"

"I mean she is Lyonene's. I am only here as a favor."

"And where is Lyonene?"

"In Cerille. With Alsander."

Hestion stilled. "So not all of the Aristene are as faithless as you." For a moment she looked as if she'd been slapped, and a dark part of him felt joy. "And now you're here," he said. "To guide this princess. Right into my arms? One more mission, to put your last hero to bed and rid yourself of him forever?"

"This has nothing to do with you!"

"And why should I believe you, Reed? Only that is not even

your name anymore. What did that pretty priest call you?" He paused. "Machianthe."

"You may call me whichever you like. Both are me."

"I shouldn't like to call you anything. I should like for you to never again be in my sight."

"Then take Sar and the others and return to Glaucia," she said, and that dark part of him delighted in the sight of tears welling in her eyes. "And I will try to honor your wishes."

Reed left the feast with her back straight. She had enough pride to manage that much. It was only when she was alone in the shadowed hallway and the sounds of the guests had faded that she allowed her head to fall into her hands. Veridian had said when she next saw Hestion he might greet her with a knife to her throat. She supposed that this was better. But it didn't feel that way.

"Aristene!"

She turned, wiping at her eyes, and saw Sar, charging straight for her. Before she could wonder whether he meant her harm, they collided, and he bent down to wrap his arms around her backside and lift her in a spinning embrace.

"Sar," she cried, and suddenly she was truly crying, crying and laughing as tears leaked from the corners of her eyes.

"Aristene," he said more softly. He set her down.

"Don't call me that." She wiped her eyes again. "They don't know I am that here."

"I didn't mean to make you sad."

"You didn't. You made me happy. At least one of the Glaucans is pleased to see me."

Sar grinned. The blue on his cheeks was bright, as were his kohl-ringed eyes. There was a good deal of wine on his breath, and he'd tottered a little as he spun her around. But then, she was quite a lot to spin.

"This Glaucan Ithernan will always be pleased to see you. And he will always owe you his life." He looked her up and down. "You look . . . nice."

Reed snorted.

"But what are you doing here?" he asked.

"I am guiding Princess Yngarue into a glorious marriage."

Sar's brows rose. "This was an unkind mission for your goddess to send you on. Are you being punished?"

Reed laughed. "Yes. And I've done it to myself. But what of you? I've never seen you in so many clothes." When she had seen Sar in a tunic it had been open to the navel. He was a warrior and a wild man. He often preferred to go without shoes.

"Neither you nor I belong in a court like this," Sar replied. "We are meant to bear shields, not . . ." He reached out and flicked one of the silver bells dangling from her hat. Then he grew serious. "Hestion must make this marriage. A bride and a child to one day rule, these are the things he must have."

"And the things he will have. But not with Yngarue of Cassor."

"Why not? She is very beautiful, though perhaps not so beautiful as her sister."

Reed smiled. Of course Sar would be swept away by Wyrnnigrid and her striking gray-blue eyes. And it wasn't such an outlandish hope. Sar was a royal son of Itherna. A second-born prince, just like Wyrnnigrid would require. Perhaps if Reed put in a good word . . .

Kleia Gloria, she thought, *I have truly become a matchmaker.*

"I should not tell you this," Sar said, snapping her out of her marriage-broker daydreams. "I should not even speak to you, so hated are you by my countrymen. All of Glaucia blames you for the loss of Belden, and for what Hestion has become since the war. But I cannot blame you. I know you. And I was there." He smiled at her sadly. "If you want to have Hestion again, you need only to reach out your hand."

Reed inhaled sharply. That couldn't be true. What she and Hestion had had died the moment that Belden did. It died again in the sacred cave, when she drove a sword through her heart and it stopped beating. "I can't have him back," she said quietly. "I don't want him back."

"Then I do not understand. Why do you oppose the marriage of Glaucia and Cassor?" Sar lowered his voice. "Do the Aristene have plans for us?"

"I can't tell you that."

He waited a few moments, as if she might change her mind, and then he reached out and touched her face with surprising tenderness. "I know you still care for him. And I am glad to see you. But if you were ever my friend or his, you must let him go."

24.

THE HUNTING PARTY

Mol, Aster, and Aethiel stepped from the Veil and into Cerille in the hours just before dawn, when the light was blue gray. They'd been deposited in a quiet clearing in the foothills to the south of the city. The Veil always opened in a place where they would be alone. When she was a young Aristene, Aster had wondered how it knew. Later, she was only grateful that it did. It would be jarring to step into the world amid the screams of someone who'd just witnessed a black void open up right next to their chickens.

Mol and her horse, a great white Areion called Verger with feathered feet, rode to the edge of the trees and looked out upon the capital. "I haven't been here in many years," she said. "I am surprised your initiate is here, Aster. Was this not where Lyonene's hero from her trial hailed from? And was this not where you last found her?" Mol turned back and cast Aster a look from a slanted eye. "What could they possibly have in Cerille to make our little sisters return so faithfully?"

"Just tell her," Aethiel murmured when Mol looked away. "She is about to find out anyway."

Aster pressed her lips together. She'd been so distracted on their journey through the Veil, trying to think of an explanation for why Reed and Lyonene might be in the wrong places, that she'd twice dropped the chant and felt the darkness pull at Rabbit's hooves, eager to take them into the black and keep them there. But there was no plausible explanation. The only thing she could do was tell Mol the truth, and try to convince her not to tell the elders.

That would be no easy task. Already Mol carried resentment toward Reed for being allowed to join them after failing her trial. And she had advocated for killing Reed, after she'd brought Hestion into the white city. Aster grimaced. If only Sabil had come with them instead. If only Tiern had sent anyone other than Mol.

Rabbit turned her head to look at her. She cocked an ear toward Mol and Verger and kicked her foreleg out, miming shoving the pair of them off the side of the hill.

"That isn't funny," Aster whispered. "Mol and Verger are our family."

"It was a little funny," Aethiel said. The big Aristene looked slightly uncomfortable in Nightfly's saddle. "But I suppose they'd only roll down and come right back up."

Aster nudged Rabbit toward Mol with her heels. "Mol," she began.

"Wait." Mol held up a hand. "Something has happened. Soldiers are gathering near the palace."

Aster and Aethiel rode closer, but though their Aristene eyes were good, they could barely make out the lines of soldiers at that distance. It was only Mol who could see any detail, as her Aristene gift came with hawksight.

"What else do you see, sister?" Aster asked.

"I see bodies without heads," Mol replied. "And an old king standing before his army and raging. Is this the work of your initiate?"

Aster scanned the palace grounds with worried eyes. It was not the work of her initiate. Nor was it the work that Lyonene intended, if the old king still lived.

"Someone has burned the stables. To keep them from mounting a fast pursuit?"

Small herds of loose horses dotted the clearings and meadows around the palace. A few horses had made their way into the forests. Aster sent her magic out and knew that Mol and Aethiel were doing the same, seeking the glimmers of glory in the hopes it would lead them to answers. If Veridian were there, the apostate could read the beats of battle and tell them what had occurred.

"We need Sabil," Aethiel whispered.

Mol turned to her sharply. "Why? Her initiate was not to have been here; what use would Sabil be?" She looked between Aster and Aethiel. "What is it you are not telling me?"

"Never mind that now," Aster said. "Right now all that matters is that we find Reed and Lyonene."

25.
REFUGE IN EXILE

Lyonene, Veridian, and Alsander rode hard and fast throughout the night, fleeing the carnage of Cerille. When dawn rose, they cut into the forests, and took refuge deep within the trees.

"Can we afford to stop?" Lyonene asked as Veridian dismounted.

"If we don't, that bay gelding is going to fall dead right underneath your prince." She nodded to it, the poor creature's sides flecked with foam and dark with sweat, head hanging as it blew air miserably in and out. "Cool him slowly and dry him off. I'll get us something to eat." She pulled her small crossbow from her saddlebag and went off into the woods, leaving Lyonene and Alsander to tend to the horses and start a fire. Or rather, leaving Lyonene to do it, since Alsander seemed able to do nothing but oscillate between rage and despair.

"We're safe for now," Lyonene said as he wandered between the tree trunks. "Even had Veridian not scattered their horses, no one could have kept up with our pace."

Alsander stared back in the direction of the capital. "We could have ridden farther had she thought to saddle Phaeton before she torched the stable."

"There may have been no time. She—"

"How did she even know?" he asked. "What was she still doing in Cerille?"

"I don't think she was in Cerille. I think she was camped nearby. Watching over us." Lyonene looked into the trees. Despite what Lyonene had done, and how angry and disappointed she'd made her, Veridian had stayed. The apostate was behaving like a mentor.

"Alsander. Help me with the horses."

Alsander shook his head. "How could you let this happen?" He looked at her then, finally, and what she saw in his eyes almost made her flinch. She'd failed him. She hadn't seen Alectos's attack coming.

"I'm sorry," she said quietly.

"I have nothing now, Lyonene. No crown. No country." He stared at the exhausted bay gelding. "Not even my own horse."

She took a step toward him but he backed away.

"I'm going to find some wood for the fire," he said, and walked off.

Everything inside her wanted to follow. To comfort him, to list all the things that they still had. But she knew better. Alsander could be cold when he was angry. So Lyonene took care of the horses instead. First the gelding and then Everfall and Strawberry. Strawberry pulled out of her bridle the moment the leather was off her ears and dashed off into the forest, apparently not fatigued in the slightest.

Lyonene stared after her, holding the empty bridle in her hands. She heard the crunch of Veridian's footsteps as the apostate returned holding two rabbits by the ears.

"Where's the princeling?"

"Gathering wood. I should go and help him."

"Don't coddle him." Veridian picked a spot and knelt to start a fire, sweeping dried leaves and twigs into a pile on the ground. "He's not a child. He's a warrior. He's led an army across the sea. Break those dry branches off." She pointed to a dead sapling. "Where is your Areion? Skin those rabbits."

So many questions. So many orders. But Lyonene didn't object. She and Alsander owed Veridian their lives. And if Veridian was irritated with them, they had earned it.

"She ran off," Lyonene said, taking up a rabbit and her knife. "I don't know to where. I haven't forged a bond with her like Reed has with Silco."

"No one forges bonds like Reed." Veridian struck her flint and rained down a shower of sparks.

"I suppose that's true. Aster, Silco. Ferreh. Even Gretchen loved Reed best."

"Does it make you jealous?"

"No. Because I love her best as well."

Veridian cocked an eyebrow. "Even better than that princeling?" she asked, but when Lyonene would have protested, the fire caught and Veridian piled it higher with thick twigs. "I know you love Reed. But your mind has been tangled up in that boy. He's making you do foolish things."

Lyonene pulled the skin from the second rabbit and placed it on a spit. Veridian wasn't wrong. She'd stayed in Cerille for Alsander. She'd allowed Reed to risk punishment for Alsander. And she'd broken the Aristene's laws. All for Alsander. And look what she had to show for it.

"Perhaps the bonds Reed forms only seem extraordinary in comparison to me," she said quietly. "Perhaps there is some flaw in me that holds those I love at a distance."

Veridian reached for the spitted rabbits. "There's nothing wrong with you, Lyonene. Reed loves you. That princeling pouting in the woods loves you."

"What about my Areion? Everfall is always at your side; Strawberry can't wait to be free of me."

Veridian looked at the red gelding where he dozed nearby. "It will be the same for you and Strawberry someday. The bond between Areion and rider is different for each pair."

Alsander returned with wood, armfuls of long, thick branches that would need to be cut. He broke a few with his foot and added them to the fire, and soon enough the flames were licking the spitted rabbits. Lyonene's mouth watered as they cooked. She could have devoured an entire rabbit on her own. And already she missed the sweetened wine of the Cerillian court.

"Where do we go?" Alsander asked. "What is our plan?" He looked to Veridian, as did Lyonene, but the apostate acted as though she hadn't heard. This was not her fight, not her mission, not her business. This was Lyonene's mess, and Alsander was Lyonene's responsibility.

"We go to Reed in Cassor," Lyonene said.

"Cassor? Why not sail to Roshanak—there are still soldiers there, soldiers who served under me."

"Not enough to retake the city."

"Not alone, no, but perhaps with Rhonassan reinforcements. Young King Oren and I are close allies—"

"Then don't put him in the position of choosing an exiled prince over a rich trading partner," Veridian interjected. "Not until you're ready to wage a war."

"Veridian is right," Lyonene said. "We must gather strength first. Cassor offers us a place of respite. We will say you are there to court the princess; news of your disinheritance won't reach them for weeks—perhaps months, and King Urdien would never turn away the crown prince of Cerille. While we hide there, we'll send word to Oren, and Prince Hestion in Glaucia."

"And you can finally do your duty to your hero princess," Veridian said as she lazily turned the spits.

Lyonene frowned and ignored her. "Oren and Hestion will support your bid for the throne."

"For a hefty price," Alsander said. "I will claim my birthright only to find myself in a pauper's crown."

"Did you whine this much when you were at war?" Veridian asked. She threw one of the rabbits across the fire to him.

"That's not fair," Lyonene said quietly. "This isn't war. It's exile." But instead of growing angry, Alsander simply began to turn the rabbit.

"Do not defend me when she's right. What good does it do to dwell on the loss? I am a prince in exile, but I'm still a prince. One day I will go home, and I will rule as I was meant to."

26.

TO CASSOR AFTER ALL

They made their way toward Cassor as quickly and quietly as they could. The opportunity for sleep didn't come often, and when it did Lyonene's was uneasy and light, one ear always listening for the approaching hoofbeats of pursuers. Alsander's was also troubled; even with his arms wrapped around her there was still a crease between his brows. Only Veridian rested well. And only because her horse would lie down for her to use as a pillow.

Lyonene couldn't even ask Strawberry to do the same. Because Strawberry was gone. The roan mare had abandoned them the very first night.

An Aristene abandoned by her own horse, Lyonene thought as she clung to the back of Alsander's saddle. Perhaps she hadn't spent as much time with Strawberry as she should have, but they were immortals. She'd thought they would have years of adventures.

Ahead of them, Veridian and Everfall slowed.

"What is it?" Alsander asked.

"We approach the coastal road. Where we'll lose the cover of the trees."

"Is that the best way to go?" Lyonene looked around at the trees, ghostly in the low light of evening.

"The likeliest port to find passage to Cassor is that way," Veridian replied.

"Isn't the Styrian port closer?"

"Yes, but the southern port is larger. Easier to hide in and quicker to get out of. We'll be all right." Veridian looked up at the darkening sky. "Traveling at night."

They continued on as the sun sank below the cliffs. When they left the cover of the forest, the wind whipped across Lyonene's face and she turned her cheek toward the warmth of Alsander's back. Out in the open, Veridian increased the pace, but when the bay gelding tried to keep up, he stumbled.

"Slow down," Lyonene called. "Our horse is still tired."

Veridian circled Everfall back to them. "Of course he is when he carries two. Come up behind my saddle. Ever is more than strong enough." Lyonene slipped down from the gelding and stretched her legs. Everfall was strong enough to carry two, or three, or however many as could fit before they slid off his tail. But Alsander and the bay horse needed real rest. She was about to recommend they stop for a time when they heard the rumble of hoofbeats.

"What is that?" Lyonene spun in the dark. Alsander's horse knocked into her and she grabbed its reins.

"Horses," said Veridian. "Several of them." She drew her sword.

"More than we can take?" Lyonene asked as she drew her own.

"Let's find out. Yah!"

"No! Veridian!"

The apostate and her Areion thundered away into the darkness. "Wait here," Lyonene ordered Alsander. "And if it's not us you see returning, run this gelding back into the forest."

Lyonene charged away from the road on foot, following Veridian toward the approaching hoofbeats. The moon that night was slender, and in the scarce light her eyes could barely make out the shapes of horses and riders. She counted five. They rode in a group, and Veridian and Everfall were barreling straight for the center to scatter them, making it easier to pick them off one by one. But just when they would have collided, Everfall pulled up short and tossed his head.

Fear slammed through Lyonene. Had he been struck by an arrow? She hadn't seen one shot, but her eyes were no good in the dark.

As Everfall whinnied, Veridian launched herself through the air and dragged one of the riders from their saddle, bearing them to the ground as the rest of the party stopped and broke into a wide circle.

"Veridian!" Lyonene pulled a knife from her belt and took careful aim. She threw the blade straight at the nearest rider's throat without breaking stride.

And the rider caught it.

When the rider turned her face to the light, Lyonene almost fell into the grass. The rider was an Aristene. Mol, the one who had glared at Reed when they'd ridden into Atropa.

"Gloria Thea Matris," Mol said as Lyonene slowly approached. *"Initiate."* She tossed the knife back and blood splattered across Lyonene's forearm. Mol had caught it by the blade.

"I'm sorry, Mol—I thought you were attackers." Lyonene looked at the other riders. One was Aethiel, the great Aristene with the band of black inked across her forehead. And sitting upon the ground in Veridian's arms was none other than Aster.

"That was my fault," said Veridian. "When I saw Aster my blood was up and it was too late to change course." She grinned, and Aster shoved her playfully before kissing her hard.

Lyonene smiled tentatively. Aethiel already had a grin upon

her face, but Mol sat motionless astride her white horse. The only sounds in the darkness were the chirps of nighttime insects and the slow drip of Mol's blood striking the hard surface of her saddle.

"Sisters," Lyonene said, willing her voice to return to normal. "What brings you to the Cerillian countryside?"

"We came expecting to find Machianthe," Mol replied, "and instead found a palace reeling from recent bloodshed."

"We were attacked by the king," Lyonene explained. "Alectos seeks to disinherit his son."

"And what business is that of yours? Why are you not in Cassor, with the hero you were given by the well?"

Lyonene glanced at Aster. The mentor's expression braced for the worst. She already knew. As did Aethiel, judging by the similar grimace on her face.

"I'm not in Cassor because Reed is there instead."

"Instead?" A brief flicker of confusion knit Mol's brow, but it was quickly replaced by anger. And not only at Lyonene. "This is your fault," she said to Aster. "Allowing these initiates to bend the rules until they do not hesitate to break them. And you—" She pointed to Veridian.

"What did I do?" Veridian asked, palms up.

"An apostate has no place beside sisters of the order."

"If not for this apostate, that initiate would be dead."

Mol shrugged. "Then that would have been the price for her folly. It was not for you to intervene!"

Veridian got up off the grass. Aster kept a calming hand on her wrist. "And what will you do about it, Mol?" Mol bared her teeth.

The moonlight glinted off the silver headband holding back her short blond hair.

"Stop this, sisters," Aethiel boomed, and all obeyed.

"The elders will hear of this," Mol said.

"Mol—" Aster stepped forward, but Mol wheeled her horse away.

"Don't worry, Aster," she said, her voice full of disdain. "Despite the fact that she had no respect for our ways, I am sure that none will dare punish your precious Reed."

"She has a point," Veridian said, and Aster shoved her. Veridian tugged her close and planted a smacking kiss on her neck. "Ouch. You have always been a brute."

Aster snorted. "But there will be consequences for this," she said to Lyonene. "None of us are above our laws. Even the elders themselves would be subject to justice, were they to break or bend them."

Lyonene lowered her head. That was how it should be. Yet she had to admit, she'd truly believed that she and Reed would get away with it. She'd thought that Reed could get away with anything.

"Is that why you've come to find us? To take us back to the elders?"

"Yes," Aster replied. "But not because you broke the rules. The threat that rose upon the throne of Rhonassus has returned. Pieces taken from the skull of the Scylloi Prophet are being used to create monsters to move against us."

Lyonene felt a sudden chill. She remembered well the monster that the skull had made of King Oreas. How it had increased his size and strength. How it stretched his limbs and popped his joints. "I thought the skull was destroyed."

"It seems not," said Aethiel. "I have seen men corrupted by it, made monsters by fragments of it driven into their skin."

"Two of those fragments we have," Aster said. "But we don't know how many remain. We think it is the work of a sect of priests. And any Aristene who were seen at Roshanak may be in danger."

"That means Reed. I was riding to her now. With Prince Alsander in exile, we intended to present him as a suitor to the princess, and hide from Alectos in Cassor."

"A good enough plan," said Mol, who had not ridden far and was still listening. "We will go with you."

Lyonene stifled a frown. She could think of few things worse than traveling to Cassor under the watchful eye of the order. Crawling on her belly to the hero she'd been meant to serve in the first place. And presenting her own husband as a suitor for her hand.

As she stewed upon her thoughts, she heard a familiar nicker and looked up to see Strawberry. In the commotion she hadn't noticed that the two extra horses who accompanied the Aristene were none other than her own Areion and Alsander's golden stallion, Phaeton.

"We found her running with the gold one," Aster said as Lyonene wrapped her arms around the roan mare's neck. "It was she who led us to you."

"I suppose you can't be blamed for that," she whispered to the horse quietly. "Thank you for going back for him."

Veridian came to the mare's side and patted her shoulder. "So that's where she ran off to. It seems her rider isn't the only one with a soft spot for Cerillian princes."

"Are you coming with us, Veridian?" Lyonene asked.

"I think I will. If for no other reason than Mol doesn't want me to." Veridian chuckled. "And I would see Reed and throttle her for coming up with this foolish scheme."

"What are they going to do to us?" Lyonene asked quietly.

Veridian looked back in the direction of Alsander. "Not nearly as much as they would do if they discovered your other sin," the apostate said gravely. "So do not let them discover it."

It didn't take long for them to find passage on a ship. Aethiel spoke the secret language of sea captains, and within hours they were sailing for the port at Preta, on the northern coast of Orillia. From there it was a short sail to Erleven, and overland travel to Cassor. They could have sailed to Erleven directly, but they'd have had to wait for three days, and Lyonene had advocated for speed. Alsander's father could still be in pursuit. Better that they disappear from the port like ghosts, and leave Alectos to wonder which of his supposed allies' shores his firstborn son would wash up on.

The ship rolled, and Lyonene pressed a hand to her stomach. She disliked ships. Aster saw her discomfort and brought her a cup of cool water. As Lyonene drank, she felt Aster's eyes wandering over her, perhaps looking for bruises or cuts, wounds taken in the attack in Cerille.

"We were ambushed," Lyonene admitted. "I never saw it coming."

"You're not used to that, are you?" Aster asked. "Failure. Defeat."

"An Aristene doesn't accept defeat," Lyonene said sullenly, and Aster laughed.

"Of course they do. It's in defeat that an Aristene discovers what kind of woman they are. Winning is easy. Failure, defeat, despair . . . those are the things that make you."

Lyonene smiled grudgingly. "You know, I used to tease Reed

about you. That you were nothing special."

"Oh?"

"But really I was jealous. Because you are special. No one in the order spoke of Sabil the way they speak of you. And there are no tales of her like there are of Veridian's archery."

"There are if you know who to ask. Sabil is a fine mentor. And a fine Aristene."

"I know that," Lyonene said. "But at the time . . . I think she sensed that I was unhappy with her. I shouldn't have—"

Aster shook her head. "Sabil knows you as you know yourself. She was always proud. She would have been here, had she not been caught away from Atropa." Aster looked across the deck of the ship. "How is Prince Alsander?"

Lyonene shrugged. Having Phaeton returned to him had lifted his spirits, but only briefly. When they'd boarded the ship he'd gone straight to their cabin and hadn't reemerged.

"Well," said Aster. "Why don't you go below and see Aethiel? I think she's worried you're cross with her for telling your and Reed's secret. Which I would be very cross with you about, was I not certain that it was Reed's idea."

Lyonene pursed her lips. It had been Reed's idea, but she'd been all too eager to go along with it. She left Aster on the deck and went down into the hold, where the horses were, and where Aethiel's hulking shape was curled over a barrel.

"Aethiel? Are you seasick?"

"Mm?" The Aristene came up from the barrel munching on something as a horse munched on hay. "No. Only helping myself to the pickled cabbage." She held out a handful.

"No, thank you."

Aethiel hung her head and shrugged. At times the way she moved reminded Lyonene of a great black bear, fuzzy and hapless, until its claws rent your arms from your body. "I only told Aster what you and Reed had done. And I would not have told even her, had it not been important. These creatures . . ."

"I know," Lyonene said. "I remember." She might never get the image of King Oreas out of her mind, bellowing and covered in blood. She'd charged him, fought him. But it had taken all the courage she had to do so.

Aethiel nodded gravely, but then she grinned. "It will not be so bad. This is a strange sect of priests. Zealots. They are shabby and few in number. We will best them easily."

Aethiel sounded confident, but the elders were worried. They must have been, to send Aster out to secure their glorious death.

"Do the priests worship the Scylloi Prophet?" Lyonene asked. "And if they do, why then are they not our allies, when we were among those who avenged him? Why have the bones of the prophet turned against us at all?"

Aethiel's jaw slowed on the mouthful of cabbage. She seemed to be thinking long and hard about this, in a way that suggested to Lyonene that she'd never before even considered the questions.

"I do not think it is the prophet who has turned against us. I think the magic in his bones is being used by men for their own ends. In life the Prophet of All was a man of peace. He cannot be blamed for what others do with his body, after he's left it."

"But why? Why would these zealot priests wish for the destruction of the Aristene?"

"I come from a place men sought to destroy simply because it was reigned over by a woman." She shrugged. "There are many strange reasons for desiring conquest. I once waged a war to celebrate the spring."

"When you were the War Queen of Fennbirn Island," Lyonene said. She had long been fascinated by that small and isolated place ruled by a line of queens who wielded great magic. It was said that some queens could command the fiercest of beasts. That others could control the wind and the waves.

"*A* war queen," Aethiel corrected her. "Not *the*. Queens of Fennbirn are born from all of the gifts. Elemental and naturalist. Oracle, and even poisoner."

"I've heard that the war queens of Fennbirn can control the direction of an arrow with their minds." Lyonene smiled. "Is that true?"

"Arrows. Daggers. The swing of a sword."

"Can you show me?"

"I am not a war queen anymore." She touched the black mark upon her forehead. "Though the image of my crown remains, it is not real. You know that."

"No oaths," Lyonene whispered. "No vows save those made to the goddess."

Aethiel closed the barrel of cabbage and walked to Everfall to pat his neck. A little hard, judging from the way he pinned his ears. "I was born a daughter of the goddess of the island. But when my reign was ended my vows to her were also at an end."

"Why?" Lyonene asked. "What did you do wrong?"

"I did nothing wrong." Aethiel straightened. "I ruled, and then I gave the goddess her next set of triplets."

Aethiel had daughters. Lyonene knew that—she'd come across the lore of the triplet queens of Fennbirn in her readings in the Summer Camp. The concept had caught in her mind because of its strangeness—into every generation a set of triplet girls was born to the queen. One of those triplets would inherit the crown: the one who survived bloody battle with her sisters.

"Which of your daughters survived?" Lyonene asked.

"I do not know. And they were not my daughters. Queens of Fennbirn Island give birth to the goddess's children. They do not raise them."

"Did you kill your sisters or did they kill each other?"

"I killed both," the big Aristene replied, a little surprised. "I am me."

"Is that why you're so devoted to us now? Out of guilt, for the first sisters you had and murdered?"

"There is no guilt. It was our way. Tolerating other queens is not within a Fennbirnian Queen's nature. But I am enjoying having new sisters. I am enjoying not killing you."

"Will you take me someday, to visit?"

"A queen does not return once her reign is over."

"We could go in secret," Lyonene whispered.

Aethiel shook her head. "Kleia Gloria and the goddess of the island keep to their own. But I would like to see it again. See who reigns there now. We've not heard of war there, so it cannot be one like me. And the time of my own triplets has long passed."

"It's strange to think that you had children."

"Of course I did," Aethiel said, insulted. "An oracle queen and a tiny little poisoner. One fire elemental. She burned." She made a face of wincing pain that still seemed to convey that she'd enjoyed it. "I had a husband, as well! Does that also shock you?"

Lyonene grinned. It did, actually. She wondered what he was like. And whether Aethiel had murdered him, too.

"He is long dead," Aethiel said, her voice sad. "And my island is lost to me. Let these priests come, I say. Them who threaten my new sisters. I will enjoy putting them to my blades. I will enjoy digging for bits of bone beneath their skin. I will not let them take the home that I have found."

"Neither will I," Lyonene said quietly.

Veridian and Aster tucked themselves into a quiet place against the ship's starboard rail. The vessel was fast and the crew was used to the route; they would make good time to the port. Veridian reached out to tuck a wisp of Aster's brown hair behind her ear. Aster smiled, and a flush rose to Veridian's cheeks. Still, after all this time.

How precious this woman is to me, she thought. *How lucky I've been, to have had this time with her.* But even as she thought so she held Aster tighter, as if she was only a dream and Veridian would wake to find her hands empty. *I love you*, she thought. *I have always. I will always.* They never spoke such words aloud. It wasn't their way. For as long as they'd been together the feeling had run so strongly between them that both knew, without being told.

"I'm glad that you are with us," Aster said. "It feels like old times. And perhaps—" She ran a finger along Veridian's lip. "Like times yet to come."

Veridian looked down.

"You can't be happy this way," Aster pressed. "Without us. Without me."

"I'm not," Veridian admitted. "I am not happy." Sometimes she felt so adrift that she could scarcely breathe. Sometimes the color bled out of the sky and turned to black. Even beside Aster now, she felt the tug of that darkness like a sucking current just beyond her sight.

"Then come home. Maybe, if the order changes . . ."

"There is no order within either of our imaginations that I can accept," Veridian said, her pale green eyes gone hard as stones. "Because there is nothing wrong with it. The Aristene are what they are. And I am not that, that's all."

"Then what do we do? How do we fix this?"

"There is no fixing this, Aster," Veridian said, her voice harsher than she'd intended. "There is no fixing what is wrong at the center of me."

Aster's eyes grew soft. She kissed Veridian's face, her lips, trying to provide some comfort. "I will never stop waiting for the day you return to us," she said.

"I know," Veridian whispered, and knew with sad certainty that Aster would wait forever.

27.

THE GLAUCAN SUITOR

It was supposed to have been easy. Go to Cassor, make a marriage. Help her friends. Instead Reed found herself standing by, watching as a hero princess and the hero of her trial wooed each other in disgusting fashion. They were out on the grass, in a field strewn with small white and purple wildflowers. Hestion had put down a thick blanket to protect them from the dewy ground. He'd plucked so many wildflower blossoms for Yngarue that the skirt of her gown was speckled. And he whispered. So close to her ear and her neck that Reed knew his lips must be brushing against her skin. Reed remembered well how that felt. She relived those moments every day in her memory.

"Did you know?" Reed grumbled quietly to Kleia Gloria. "Did you know from the start that I would come to this hero instead of Lyonene?" She curled her lip. That morning, Reed had stood listlessly behind Yngarue as her Outfitter-enchanted hands had woven Yngarue's hair into a comely and complicated braid. How much did the goddess foresee? How much did she control, moving them around like pieces on a game board, apparently for her own amusement?

"No, truly, she will tell you," she heard Yngarue say. "Machianthe! Prince Hestion would like to know the extent of my lessons with a blade."

Reed smiled tolerantly as Yngarue waved her over. But to the goddess she hissed, "You place me here as a matchmaker and now I am my former lover's chaperone! Yes, princess," she said when she had reached them and curtsied. "What may I tell him?"

Yngarue laughed. "Please, give an honest assessment." She bent her head toward Hestion's. "Machianthe's teachings have been extraordinary. She is a matchmaker of rare skill."

"I am sure," Hestion replied.

Reed lifted her chin. "Princess Yngarue's ease with a weapon grows daily. Her footwork is a little heavy, but that's to be expected in a long gown."

"And we can't be tying up my skirts anymore," Yngarue noted with a wry smile, "with Prince Hestion and his soldiers frequenting the castle."

"More's the pity," Hestion noted, and Reed wanted to retch. He reached for his cup of wine and drained it, then stood. "Show me."

He pulled the princess to her feet.

"I would see what you have learned. I'm sure Machianthe has a blade we could use." He smiled, and Reed glared at him as she reached into her skirt to get one.

"We have been using a man of straw," Yngarue said as she took it. "What do I demonstrate on?"

"On me," Hestion said, and held his arms wide.

"Killing blows only," Reed said, and Yngarue laughed. The princess took a breath, then flipped the dagger for a better grip and stabbed straight for Hestion's eye. He dodged the blow, but just barely. And had Reed imagined it, or did the air around Yngarue brighten for just a moment as she struck?

"That is good," Hestion said as he caught her by the wrist.

"I didn't mean it," Yngarue admitted. "I don't know if I could ever truly stab a blade into living flesh."

"You could if you had to," said Reed. "If a soldier was attacking Wyrnnigrid. Or Ullieth."

"Yes," Yngarue said. "Then I could."

"Your Machianthe speaks like a soldier," Hestion said as he held Yngarue, one hand around her wrist and the other about her waist. "But what can a matchmaker know of real combat?"

"Every woman knows something of combat," Yngarue said. "Would it displease you to have a queen who could carry a sword?"

"No. Though I would hope she would never have cause to use it. And this is no sword." He twisted his hand and gently disarmed her, making Yngarue gasp.

"I haven't taught her that yet," Reed muttered.

"How to keep her weapon? That would have been the first thing I taught her. And what of breaking holds?" He slipped both arms around the princess's middle. "Unless this isn't a hold that she wishes to break." He pressed his lips to Yngarue's neck. "Perhaps you could send your matchmaker away. I'm happy to teach you all."

"Perhaps the matchmaker will report to King Urdien that Prince Hestion is pawing his daughter." Reed reached down for Yngarue's wine cup and took a swallow. But instead of letting Yngarue go, Hestion pulled her closer.

"A strange way for a matchmaker to behave," he said. "You should encourage the princess to explore. We're innocent enough in this field, but our aim is the bedchamber—better to practice now, so that there are no surprises on the wedding night."

"Prince Hestion," Yngarue said. She rolled her eyes, but she made no move to get out of his embrace.

"You see?" Reed raised her chin. "I told you he was coarse."

"I have been trying to tell Machianthe of your virtues." Yngarue removed his hand from her waist. "I've told her of your stories, and your country—"

"Sunlight and trees," Reed said. "What wonders." She crossed her arms.

"But what about the eels?" Hestion said.

Yngarue's brows rose.

"The eels that run upriver in the spring and summer. Countless numbers of them, brown and wriggling and delicious."

As Hestion recounted the various methods of eel cooking known to his people, Reed's heart sank. The eels, and Hestion's disgusting love of them, had been a jest that they had shared. It had been special. Or she thought it had been.

"I really don't think this is behavior becoming of royalty," she said, but no one seemed to hear.

"You won't really make me eat an eel," Yngarue said.

"Only once." Hestion touched her lips with his fingertip. "And then never again, if you do not like it."

Hearing him speak so to Yngarue, and seeing him look at Yngarue the way he had once looked at her—Reed turned and left the meadow without another word, her arm reaching behind her for a sword that wasn't there. She needed something to fight, something to stab. She needed to be away from there. Perhaps away from Cassor completely.

Alas, Reed still had a task to fulfill, and she would see it done— even if she did so with her back slumped and her feet dragging.

She'd looked so miserable and moved so slowly that afternoon that Parmenin had asked her if she'd hurt her leg. And she felt no better by the time of the evening meal, when she had to sit beside Yngarue as Hestion fed her sweet, soft grapes.

Reed stabbed her dining knife into the side of a roast goose and wished she could trade places with it.

"You left me alone," Yngarue whispered in her ear.

Reed startled. The princess had gotten up from her seat.

"Come," Yngarue said. "Walk with me."

Reed got up and followed the princess through the banquet.

"You left me alone with him," Yngarue said once they were off on their own, away from the prying ears of the court.

"Not entirely alone. You had my dagger."

Yngarue's lips quirked. "That is not funny. I am not to be left alone with him, Machianthe! My chastity must never be allowed to be questioned!"

"Of course. I'm sorry, princess," she said, and was surprised to find that she meant it. It was Yngarue's life with which they toyed. Coming to Cassor for Lyonene had seemed a small thing, a simple trade for a sliver of glory. But if Reed failed, it would be Yngarue who paid the price.

"It's all right," Yngarue said. "After my betrothal is made, I will be sorry to see you go. Growing up in this castle—" Yngarue looked toward the sturdy walls built to repel the forces of Erleven and also to trap Cassan princesses inside. "I have had few friends. Our maids and ladies are nothing but a constant rotation of Father's bedmates." She looked at Reed and stifled a smile. "He hasn't tried to lure you into his chambers, has he?"

"Ha! No." Reed laughed. "Perhaps he's seen my knives." She studied Hestion as he sat at the head table, talking with King Urdien and pretending not to pay attention to what she and Yngarue were doing. "What did you and Prince Hestion discuss, after I had gone?"

"He spoke of Glaucia. Of a mother he lost, who had many talents." She sighed. "He spoke of an aunt he seemed vaguely afraid of."

Reed snorted. "Yes, she is—" She stopped when Yngarue looked at her in surprise. "Everyone has a mean aunt."

"And he asked about you."

"Me?"

"I think he fears you will poison me against him in favor of Alsander of Cerille. Truly, he did not remain with me for long after you left. Hestion is not half so attentive to me as his Ithernan friend is to my sister. They have scarcely left each other's sides."

Sar's and Wyrnnigrid's heads were bent close.

"Sar is a second-born prince, you know."

"Is it so?" Yngarue's face lit like stars. "Then perhaps Wyrnnigrid at least could be happy."

"You may still be happy, Yngarue."

Yngarue shook her head. "It is impossible for me to have the one I want."

But before Reed could ask what she meant, King Urdien beckoned the princess back to the high table. Reed remained on the outskirts of the great room, beside the window, where a cool breeze cut through the close air and she wouldn't have to watch any more of Hestion's courtship.

It troubled her to think that Yngarue was unhappy. She was fierce and beautiful and rich. There were fine matches to make in her future, matches that could yet see her fall in love, and once Reed had stopped Hestion's ill-fated pursuit she would find her one. She would find Yngarue the best of men. She would see her wed in a veil of golden glory.

Reed took a deep breath. Suddenly she felt better than she had in weeks. But it didn't last long.

"You left so abruptly from the field today," Hestion said. "Yngarue was so worried you were upset that she could barely concentrate on our embraces."

Reed clenched her teeth.

"Are you trying to blame me for the dullness of your kisses? I had to leave. The meadow had taken on a sudden stench." She narrowed her eyes. "Yet the smell seems to be here now, too."

Hestion smiled. He leaned against the window. "You are such a child. I see how you turn whenever I touch her. I don't know what I enjoy more: Yngarue's surprisingly passionate kisses . . . or your scowl." He raised his brows. "No, it is definitely the kisses. Yngarue is skilled with her tongue when it comes to speaking, and also—"

Reed drew her blade and shoved the handle into his chest. "I don't care what you do with your tongues. No doubt every girl in Glaucia has had to experience that particular unpleasantness—"

"Strange, then, that you raced from the field like your skirt had caught fire."

Reed returned the knife to her belt before she truly stabbed him. "It wasn't your pawing of Yngarue that drove me from the garden. It was—" She stopped. She couldn't tell him about the eels. It sounded so foolish now. So childish, like he said.

"What was it, then?" Hestion asked.

"King Urdien!"

Heads turned throughout the hall. The servant who had called out to the king stepped aside as two men hobbled into the banquet.

Gasps erupted. They were covered in blood, both fresh and dried. One walked with a pronounced limp, his leg wrapped in dirty bandaging from the knee to the ankle.

"A healer," Urdien bellowed, and the servants raced to find one as the men made their way slowly to the floor before the high table. Even tired and wounded, they each attempted a bow. Urdien waved his hand. "Enough of that. Tell me what has happened!"

"It attacked us," the man holding up his friend replied. "It came at night. Despite our number. Despite the cooking fire. It came for us and—" He lowered his head and collapsed onto one knee. His friend slid from his grasp to lie panting at his side.

Reed craned her neck. These were the hunters that Parmenin had dispatched. The ones sent to hunt the beast that had been slaughtering the sheep and the cattle.

"Are you all who remain?" Parmenin asked now. The priest came forward to kneel before the men and place his hands upon their wounds.

"Yes. I don't know." The hunter lowered his head. "We ran."

"Where?" Parmenin pressed gently. "From where did you run?"

"We'd tracked the beast into the forest near Ixion Village."

Cries broke out through the hall. "Ixion Village!" they exclaimed. "That is not far from here!"

"It is not far but it is not within the walls," Urdien said. He held his hands out for calm. Reed began to go toward the wounded men, and Hestion caught her by the elbow.

"And what would you do for them, matchmaker?" he asked quietly. But for the moment, her disguise was forgotten. She needed to see the wounds. She needed to know if it was a monster who'd made them.

She gently slipped out from Hestion's grip and knelt beside the men. "Let me see." They nodded, and she slowly unwound the bandage upon the prone hunter's leg.

Four deep wounds shredded the flesh of his calf, so deep it was a wonder that the muscle had held together at all. At the tables, nobles groaned and turned their eyes away. Women pressed cloths to their mouths. At the high table, where all were on their feet to look, Sar drew Wyrnnigrid into the crook of his shoulder.

"A bear?" Hestion asked, crouching beside Reed.

"It didn't move like a bear," the fallen hunter said.

The man's wounds were grave. Reed didn't know if they were survivable.

Tentatively, she pushed her magic out. Would it sense glory lingering from the fight? Or would it recoil from the stain of the prophet's bones?

She let it swirl about the two men, let it fall over their cuts. But it neither glittered nor retreated. Whether the wounds were inflicted by a creature such as the one Tiern had thrown into the World's Gate, she couldn't say.

She looked up at the high table, at Yngarue's stricken face. The princess's betrothal would have to wait for just a while longer. Reed had to go into the woods.

28.

THE BEAST OF CASSOR

When Reed reached the stable, she found Silco had sensed her coming and broken out of his stall.

"I know, I know," she said as he nosed his saddle blanket hanging upon a hook. The black colt stomped and pawed as she tacked him up. For as much as he enjoyed lazily dozing in a warm pile of straw, even he could only nap for so long before he needed something to do.

"This is just the thing to stretch our legs," Reed whispered as she tossed the reins over his head. An adventure, and a dangerous one, if indeed the beast in the woods was a creature of the prophet's bones.

Reed stroked Silco's neck, suddenly hesitant. Then she heard the voice of the elder in her head.

If you see one of these creatures, Tiern had said, *kill it*.

Reed swung into the saddle and rode away from the castle, following the map of the Cassan countryside retained in her memory. The village of Ixion lay across the river, before a wide swath of forest. Silco had stamina to spare, and even with his slower gait, she would reach the forest in a few hours' ride.

They hadn't gone far when Silco tossed his head and snorted. Reed looked back and saw a large, moving patch of white. It was

Hestion, coming after them on his enormous white stallion. Silco whickered questioningly.

"Yes, of course I see him," she said. "If he wanted to hide he'd have taken a different horse." She looked around. They were passing through the sheep fields. There was no cover to take. And with his bad hoof, Silco's days of outrunning Target were over.

Hestion rode at them hard, charging Target as though he meant to plow right through them. But Reed wasn't fooled. No matter how angry Hestion was with her, he would never hurt her horse.

He pulled his white stallion up in a few jolting strides.

"What are you doing here?" she asked him.

"I'm hunting a beast."

"Then where are your long spears? Where is Sar?" She peered around his horse like the Ithernan might be hidden in his saddle-bags. "You're following me."

"I suppose I am. But what can you be thinking, Reed? What will you tell Yngarue when she finds you gone?"

She paused. She hadn't thought of what to say. She hadn't thought to be missed. "I'll make something up."

"You do not think. You only act."

"Well, then, since you are the thinking one, why don't you return to the castle and make my excuses?" She turned Silco back onto their path, and Hestion steered Target right beside them.

"And miss the chance to slay a beast and win a princess's heart?"

"You'll slow me down."

"Target is faster than Silco. And the woods are not far."

Reed spun Silco into Hestion's stallion, and the horses stomped and squealed as they were pressed together. "Go back, Hestion!"

Hestion put his heels to Target and knocked him harder into Silco. He raised his hand to grasp the back of Reed's neck.

Reed's breath caught. Looking into his eyes, she wanted to tear him out of his armor. She wanted to throw him to the ground. It hadn't been like this before, and she wasn't sure if she was moments away from kissing him or biting him.

"You're angry," he said, fighting to control his horse as she also fought to control Silco, who stomped and lashed his tail. "Do you hate me?"

"Yes," she said.

"Good." He shoved her away. "Because I hate you, too." He turned Target in a tight circle and rode away toward the forest.

Reed and Hestion waited just before the tree line, listening for movement, or howls in the dark. Their stallions tested the air and Target pawed and tossed his head at the scent of blood. But both horses were brave. Neither would run.

"We should have brought hounds," Hestion murmured.

"So we could be responsible for the deaths of sweet dogs?" Reed watched Hestion as his eyes searched the trees in the moonlight. He didn't know what awaited them in the woods, but he'd seen the wounds on the hunter's calf. And he'd been a hunter long enough himself to have a sense for danger.

"Do not suggest that we go in separately," he said, and Reed nodded. "The man said they'd camped a quarter day's walk into the trees, beside the river. We should start there. Perhaps there are yet men who survive."

Reed nudged Silco with her heels and they plunged out of the moonlight and into the dark, following Silco's nose.

They didn't have to wonder when they'd reached it. The air was thick with blood and foul with split entrails, and the smell of death jolted them back in their saddles. The horses danced nervously. In the darkness they couldn't see enough to make out which shadowy shape was a shrub and which a fallen man.

"Stop," Hestion said. "I will start a fire." Reed heard him dismount and move through the underbrush in search of dry wood. The sound of snapped twigs set her on edge—though the carnage that had occurred here had taken place long before, she thought she could still feel eyes, following them from between the trees.

Hestion returned with the gathered wood, and searched through his saddlebags for a flint and the prepared tinder he kept in a pouch, tufts of fiber that had been soaked in oil and would catch quickly. The familiar, acrid smell as it caught was as much a comfort as the sudden light cast by the flames.

"You know," Hestion said as the fire grew. "We're far from the castle now. Perhaps you should—" He waved his hand at her. "Change." Reed looked down at the matchmaker's dress. It was stained and torn, the hem of the skirt frayed and dirty. Nowhere near as fine as it had been when the Outfitter had presented her with it. "Unless you think our quarry will not be alerted by those bells."

Reed reached into the aether and drew on her armor. It was a relief, to be garbed in her own attire, and to have the flames reflected off the plate of silver upon her chest and the bright white of her cape.

Hestion stared at her, his eyes cold.

"It's not the same."

"No," Reed said. "This is my true armor. Not borrowed, through Aster's magic." Ridiculously, she wanted to ask him if he liked it.

Hestion looked back to the fire. "Is that Silco stamped into the arm guards?"

"It is."

He grunted. "A good likeness." She heard a small whoosh and the ground beside the river brightened considerably. When he handed her one of the torches he seemed amused by the look on her face. "Some of us think ahead when we are going to stalk a beast through the woods at night."

"Shut up, Hestion." She swung down from the saddle, and they walked into the middle of the camp.

"Kleia Gloria," Reed breathed. The camp was a killing field. Bodies lay strewn in all directions, faces turned toward the sky in wordless screams above the cracked-open caverns of their rib cages. Reed knelt to study a hunter, barely more than a boy. His body appeared unharmed, but his throat and the whole of his right cheek were missing, bloodstained teeth laid bare in a macabre smile.

"More claw marks," said Hestion, beside another hunter.

"A mountain cat?"

Hestion cast his torch to another dead man. "I don't think so." There was an ax buried in the man's back.

"Perhaps a friend killed him by mistake," Hestion said. "Amid the chaos." Except as they looked they saw more of the same. Throats that had been cut. Ax wounds to the belly. Strange, bloody handprints beneath the flesh sliced by claws.

"A man could not do these things," Hestion said as he crouched.

"What if it's not exactly a man?" She knelt beside him and looked into his wary eyes. "I know what it is we hunt. It is another like Oreas. A monster, made from the bones of the prophet."

She waited. She knew it hadn't been easy for him during the war, to see the bones of his revered friend twisted and used for such a dark purpose. "But the skull was destroyed," he said. "And Oren guards the bones."

"Not all were found. He told me, before I left Roshanak. There were fragments missing. And the bone of the jaw. We thought they'd just been lost in the fighting."

They stilled as something moved in the trees. Reed let her magic rise, so its retreat might give her a moment of warning. But it sensed no danger.

"You knew this," Hestion said. "And yet you thought to face it by yourself." He rose to his feet. "Unfortunate that becoming an Aristene has made you no wiser. You're the same as you always were, never thinking of the consequences."

Reed stood, understanding his meaning. "I knew what I was doing when I threw that sword to your brother. And I knew the consequences. Have I not accepted them?"

"Accepted them?" Hestion asked. "There have been none! You sent my brother to his death like you wanted. Forced me to be a king in his stead like you wanted. Became an immortal Aristene like you wanted. You have lost nothing."

"I have lost you," she cried. She stepped back. She hadn't meant to say that, but Hestion only looked away.

"You never really loved me, Reed. Or at least not as much as you loved the idea of living forever." He squinted with disgust at the bloodshed at their feet. "Let us slay this beast. So I might return to the princess who will become my queen." He glanced at Reed coldly. "When I came to Cassor I didn't think I could find it in myself to want her. But it has been surprisingly easy."

Reed cast her torch into the dark as she followed him through the trees. "Yes, surprisingly easy. Your charm always seems to come so easily. With Yngarue. With me. How many girls have you gotten into your bed with disarming jests about eels?"

"You were never in my bed, Reed," he said meanly. "At least, not in the way others have been."

"And thank the goddess for that," Reed spat. "Now I might choose a man who is not so faithless, who—" She thought of him laughing with Yngarue and closed her eyes. It shouldn't matter that nothing that had passed between them had been special. But it did.

"Reed."

She opened her eyes.

"I only thought of the eels because you were standing right there."

"What do I care?" she said. "Use the same charms and tell the same stories. In fact, I may use the same stories myself."

"On who?" Hestion asked mockingly.

"Parmenin." He was simply the first name that came to mind, but he was a good one. Handsome and of a high station.

"The priest?" Hestion laughed.

"Why not? He has very good shoulders, underneath those robes. And he is quite fond of me."

Hestion seemed displeased when she spoke of the priest's shoulders. But then he smiled. "Reed, my sweet. Getting him to look past that hat would take far more allure than you have."

Reed drew her sword. "Why don't you?"

"Reed," Hestion shouted in the instant before the creature dropped onto her back. She screamed in surprise and went down beneath its weight, her torch knocked from her hand and the flame smothered. Fangs gnashed beside her ear and she punched back—the beast bit down hard; she felt teeth pass all the way through her hand. But the teeth were not what she feared most. An arm wrapped around her torso and claws raked across her armor.

Hestion swung his weapon down and the beast roared. Reed pushed against it, frightened by how much effort it took. Her magic was lessened, sapped by the nearness of the prophet's bone. But her armor was still with her. It didn't want to be, and she could feel it trying to pull back into the aether, but it remained.

She heard Hestion grunt, and the light from his torch dimmed. She scrambled to her feet and he was again beside her, casting about in all directions with his sputtering flame.

"Did you get it?" she asked.

"Not enough. What was that thing, Reed? It looked like a man, and yet . . ."

Reed didn't reply. She'd been unable to see it when it had her pinned. The fragment of bone placed inside Aethiel's hero had turned him into a sea monster. She had no idea what this man may have become.

"Stay together." She glanced up into the trees. Distracted as she was by their argument, her magic had given her no warning of its presence. How long had it been waiting there for them to pass underneath?

"It may have run off," Hestion said. "I wounded it, and we're no longer caught unaware." But unless the wound was grave, Reed didn't think the creature would care. It had attacked and slaughtered seven capable, armed hunters, seemingly for sport.

"Silco," Reed called, her voice low. "Get Target out of here." Hooves splashed through the river. She heard his whinny of reassurance when they'd reached a safer distance.

"Was that wise?" Hestion whispered. "He is very mean. He could've helped."

Reed smiled grimly. But she'd sent Silco away more for his own safety than for Target's. The Areion magic was linked to the Aristene. The beast would be sniffing him out as well, and she didn't know how the horse might be affected by the prophet's bones.

The beast crashed through the underbrush and jumped at Hestion, knocking him to the ground. It pinned his sword tight to his body so he fought with the torch instead, scorching the monstrous face, jamming the flames between its teeth as it tried to bite.

In the torchlight, Reed was able to get a clean view of it, and the sight made no sense to her eyes. It was unclothed and it was a man, yet it also was not; it had haunches like a rodent, and its forearms were elongated and ropy with muscle. The hands were tipped with long, curved claws. The face that bit at Hestion's torch was strikingly, disturbingly human as it groaned and snapped—the eyes had taken on a watery pinkness, the nose reduced to the small slits of nostrils.

"Get away from him!" Reed shouted.

Immediately she wished she hadn't. The creature sprang off Hestion and scrabbled toward her, its watery eyes fixed upon the silver of her armor, the white of her cape. It leaped and she braced against the impact; her feet skidded until she struck the broad trunk of a tree. She brought her sword up and the beast bit into her arm guard. It was then that she saw it: a puckered, poorly healing wound in the meat between its shoulder and neck, the edges of which were blackened as if by rot.

Reed wrenched her off hand free and tried to dig inside the wound, to remove the fragment of bone, but she needed a knife, something to cut into it with.

"Hestion, help me." He was there already, hacking into the creature's back, which was protected by strange deformities of bone, as if a new, longer cage of ribs had sprouted above its spine. "The wound—cut into it! Dig out the fragment of bone!"

He drew his dagger and sliced deep, then reached inside. The creature bawled miserably and raked Reed's side with claws that cut all the way through the leather of her armor.

Hestion seized the bone and the beast jerked its head back viciously, sending him sprawling. As it did, it loosed Reed's sword hand and she angled the blade upward. She thrust as hard as she could.

The creature looked into her eyes. Hestion had held on to the bone fragment, and with it removed, the monstrous parts of the creature began to fade. The face that looked back into Reed's became again that of a man, whom she caught as they sank together toward the ground.

"They took us," the man said as blood leaked from his mouth.

"Who took you?" Reed asked. "The priests? Who are they?"

"The-e . . . the-e," the man sputtered. He spat more blood. And then he died.

"Reed!" Hestion slid to his knees beside her as she pressed her hand to the claw wounds on her side. "Let me see." He pushed her hand away. But the armor had done its job, and the cuts, while ugly, were not deep. They would heal quickly, and without a scar, thanks to her Aristene magic.

Hestion pulled her close. He kissed her face, her eyes, her hands. "You could have been killed."

"I wasn't," she said quietly. But he didn't let go. They stayed like that for a long time, holding each other in the darkness of their extinguished torches.

When dawn came and the light was strong enough, she and Hestion searched for the fragment of bone, which had been dropped in the struggle. They went over and over the dirt, crouched low or on their knees, but it was nowhere to be found. Reed even sent her magic out to search, but though she could feel the sickness of it there somewhere, she couldn't find it. It had been such a small piece. A thin, sharp shard no longer than her fingernail.

"I may have flung it when I was knocked back," Hestion said. "If it is too small for your magic to seek out, there is no hope. It is lost."

Reed exhaled. He was right. But if such a small shard could create such a creature, she shuddered to think of the pieces that remained.

They loaded the bodies of the fallen hunters onto their horses' backs and prepared to return to the castle. They'd spoken little since the sun rose, and in the daylight the terrors of the night felt far away. But Reed hadn't forgotten what she'd seen in Hestion's eyes when he held her. What she heard in his voice. It had come as a shock, but it couldn't be denied. Despite what he said, Hestion still loved her.

She gave Silco's grim cargo one last tug to make sure it was secure. Her armor was gone, and she was dressed once again as a royal matchmaker, albeit one with a slight limp and a hand wrapped in blood-soaked bandages. Silco whuffed gently at the healing cuts in her side and rested his chin on her shoulder. He was always at his most affectionate on the days right after she'd almost been killed.

"What do we do with this?" Hestion asked. He stood over the creature's body. Some of its monstrosity had faded, but though the face looked much like the man it once was, the fingers were still tipped in claws, and the rear legs still bent in an odd, rodentlike fashion. "I doubt that either of the horses will agree to carry it."

"It's certainly no basket of eels," Reed said, but he didn't smile. "I'm going to get rid of it."

He looked at her.

"The last thing King Urdien needs is fresh rumors," she said. "And this attack was not about Cassor. It was about us. The Aristene. A sect of priests is moving against the order. Somehow they are tracking our movements. Targeting our heroes."

"How is that possible? Who would know the Aristene secrets?"

"I don't know. These priests serve a dark god; who can say what tools he has given them to use against us." She knelt beside the twisted corpse and looked into the man's face. He'd suffered. He hadn't known what he'd done; he hadn't been one of the priests. "I just don't know why."

"Can you think of no reason? Not every man enjoys being a

puppet in the name of glory."

Reed cocked her eyebrow. "That may be, but I can still think of none who would dare." Hestion scoffed, and she gathered the body in her arms and carried it into the river, where she sank it and weighed it down with stones.

"What, then, will we say did all this?" Hestion asked.

Reed wrung out the skirt of the matchmaker's dress as well as she could. She was cold and wet to the neck. "Bandits who travel with trained wolves. Urdien may send men out to seek them, but when they find nothing they'll assume they've just moved on."

Hestion shook his head and began to walk back to the castle, leaving her to lead both the horses.

"Are you angry with me?" she asked. And when he didn't reply, added smugly, "You didn't seem so last night."

"Last night was an old impulse," he said. "Today I don't even know if I am relieved that you are not dead."

Reed's mouth hung open as Hestion sighed wistfully.

"Now I am only eager to get back to my Yngarue."

Reed pulled the horses forward. Target didn't like the scent of death strapped to his back and sidestepped into the water, nearly making her lose her balance and fall back into the stream. The silver bells on her hat jangled wildly and Hestion looked back and smirked.

"She is not *your* Yngarue," Reed hissed, tugging on Target to catch up. "She will never be your Yngarue, so long as I am her matchmaker."

"The way she kisses me, Reed, I doubt that you will have much say in the matter."

"She kisses everyone that way," Reed snapped, and didn't care if the words made sense. "She is not for you, Hestion. If you continue to pursue her, you may ruin her. Is that what you want?"

"What are you speaking of?" His eyes narrowed; he looked her over as if it was her magic that stained the matchmaker's dress instead of water. "Do not speak to me of destinies, or of the wishes of your goddess. I have given enough to that cause."

"Do you fight the gods of your homeland with such fervor? How have you fared there when you've posted yourself against their will?" The moment she spoke the words she wished she could have bitten them back. She couldn't imagine how he'd fared in Glaucia, after the loss of Belden.

Hestion's jaw flexed, and she braced herself for whatever he would say. But she was unprepared for his hand, grasping the back of her neck, or for his mouth, pressed against hers.

Reed dropped the reins of the horses as he pushed her back against the hard bark of a tree. She opened her lips to speak and instead found his tongue.

This kiss was unlike the others they had shared. In Rhonassus their stolen moments had been sweet and seeking; this was bruising, given in self-loathing, given as punishment. His hands on her were not soft, and nor were hers on him—for so long she had ached to see him again, to touch him; now he slammed her against the tree trunk, and though she winced from her injuries, she would not tell him to stop.

Hestion drew back with a growl. Their breath was fast, his lips so close to hers. But when she moved to kiss him again, he turned aside.

"You are not worth desiring," he said. "Not worth the life I'd have given you, nor the life that you took."

He shoved her away. But not in time. A gasp sounded from upriver and they turned to see Princess Yngarue and Parmenin the priest, mounted on a pair of palfreys and staring at them, aghast.

29.

YNGARUE'S SECRET

No Aristene magic Reed had ever heard of could erase past moments of time, so there was nothing for her and Hestion to do but walk up the riverbank to Yngarue and Parmenin and face them.

"Machianthe?" Yngarue asked. Her eyes flickered from Reed to Hestion, to Reed's wet clothes, and to their horses laden down with the bodies of Cassan hunters. As the stallions carrying the bodies approached, Yngarue's palfrey shied and snorted; Parmenin dismounted quickly and took hold of its reins.

"Princess Yngarue," Reed said. "What are you doing here?"

"Looking for you," Yngarue replied. She looked at Hestion dazedly. "Your man Sar said you'd gone after the matchmaker, in search of the beast who had injured the hunters. Though what business a matchmaker could have on such an errand we didn't know."

"Sar," Hestion grumbled. He looked at Reed. "Princess Wyrnnigrid must have batted her eyes."

"We were worried," Yngarue went on. "But it seems we needn't have been."

"What is the meaning of this?" Parmenin demanded. He looked to Reed. "Lady Machianthe?"

"I—" Reed began. "That is . . . Parmenin—" She searched her mind for an explanation and found none.

"Tell her," Hestion said.

"You see, I—"

"Tell her."

"Don't tell me how to handle my heroes," Reed hissed. But he was right. There was no way out. She reached into the aether and called her armor. It settled upon her in a glimmer of gold and white light, and she let her magic rise, let Yngarue and Parmenin glimpse the Aristene she was, dazzling them the way Aster had done to her, all those years ago.

"Trickery," Yngarue murmured.

"No, not trickery," Parmenin answered in an awed voice. "She's an Aristene! I have heard tales of them. It is said they are the servants of glory, that they come to heroes to help them forge great destinies." He looked at Yngarue. The princess was silent, staring at Reed. But the priest's words seemed to please her.

"And you were sent to Hestion," Yngarue said tentatively.

"No," said Reed as Hestion muttered yes. "This time I was sent to you."

The journey back to the castle was uncomfortable, to say the least. Reed didn't know what to say to Yngarue, and Yngarue seemed uninterested in speaking to anyone, riding quietly on her white palfrey. Reed didn't know what to say to Hestion either; she could hardly look at him without blushing. Luckily Parmenin was there to break the silence by asking near constant questions about the order.

And about her armor, which she banished back to the aether after he'd poked and prodded at it.

And about her Areion, until Silco bit him for inquiring about his bad hoof. In the end, she'd smiled and said, "You know, Parmenin, the Aristene do keep some of their secrets," and he'd looked abashed and bowed his head.

"I'm surprised you dared take Yngarue on an errand like this," Hestion said to the priest.

"When you have known the princess as long as I have, you will understand that there is little one can do to stop her once an action comes into her mind. It was unwise, but we feared for you—even you, Prince Hestion. This part of the country is dangerous." Parmenin gestured to the river, and the valley beyond the trees.

"Do you see that strip of land there? A road lies in the heart of that valley and follows the river. This route carries the main flow of goods in and out of Cassor, and the house of Ythyll has fought with Erleven over it for centuries. Caravans and barges traveling here often find themselves ripe targets for plunder."

"But Erleven has its own ports," Reed noted.

"They do."

"So they fight only to keep Cassor from having the valley, even though they have no real need of it themselves." She cast Hestion a look, and he shrugged. It was an argument of state, yet it sounded like a disagreement between children.

"One man feels slighted, and the ground runs red with blood," said Parmenin. "We are all at the mercy of the kings we serve."

"Or the goddesses," Hestion muttered.

When they reached the palace, Yngarue dismounted and spoke for the first time.

"Parmenin, tell my father what has befallen the hunters. Tell him that Prince Hestion and one of his soldiers have taken care of the threat and returned the bodies for burial. Machianthe, come with me." She lifted her skirts and turned to hurry inside, assuming that Reed would follow.

Reed looked at Hestion.

"I will take care of Silco," he said, and took the black horse's reins.

"But—"

"Go. There is no more I wish to say to you." He led the horses toward the stable, and with no other recourse, Reed went after Yngarue. The princess awaited her inside her chamber.

"Yngarue?" There was no one else there; the ladies must have been in the solar or the gardens, and perhaps Wyrnnigrid had snuck off somewhere with Sar. Reed took a deep breath. "Please let me explain. What you saw by the river—"

"I do not care about that."

Reed blinked. Yngarue didn't care? But Reed had apologies and explanations at the ready, having thought of them on the long ride from Ixion Village.

Yngarue smiled. "Though he is quite a good kisser, isn't he?"

"I wouldn't know. I mean, I know, clearly. But I've no other to compare him to."

"Really? But you are so traveled. And you are so beautiful in your armor."

"In my armor," Reed said.

"You are beautiful in or out of it," Yngarue said kindly. She looked at Reed's matchmaker's dress. "Though that hat does not do you any favors."

"I'm relieved that you know," Reed said. "I haven't enjoyed playing a part to you. It was my duty, and I am not ashamed, but I have not enjoyed it."

"So many things about you make more sense now," said the princess. "Your skills with knives. The stiff way you dance, like your upper body is unattached to your feet. Yet I still feel you are much the same. Still my matchmaker."

"I am still your matchmaker. That is what I wanted to tell you. What I said was true: I have been sent to you, to make you a glorious marriage. Just because Prince Hestion and Prince Alsander are not the correct matches doesn't mean—"

"Prince Alsander was a lie as well?"

Reed winced guiltily. "He is a friend. I used his name to get your father to allow me into his court."

Yngarue laughed. "I knew it. I knew this was the reason that you were sent."

Reed's brow knit. The princess was acting strange, and Reed got the sense that their roles had changed, and she was the one being kept in the dark. "We will still find you a glorious match from the other suitors. . . ."

"There are no other suitors."

"What?" Reed asked. The list of suitors for Yngarue's hand was long and distinguished; she'd heard the names of two royal houses of Valostra, and the prince from warlike Salkades.

"My father decided that I would wed Alsander of Cerille the moment you arrived," Yngarue said. "He sent messengers in secret, to rescind the other offers of suit and inform the princes that another has already won my hand. After all, why go to the expense of hosting them if it is all just for show?" She cocked her head. "Parmenin told me."

"And you didn't think to mention this to your matchmaker?"

Yngarue shrugged.

"But—" Reed's head buzzed like a swarm of bees. "Then why keep Hestion here?"

"Father thinks the competition may improve the deal he forges with Cerille. Alsander has no need of my bride price. But he may pledge more protection, more soldiers, if I am seen to be desirable, and pursued by another man."

"But Yngarue—Alsander is not really coming. There is no choice, then, besides Hestion!"

"No." Yngarue smiled. "There is. Come. There is something I want you to see." She bent over a heavy trunk at the foot of her bed, beckoning Reed closer as she opened it and began to riffle through its contents, removing boxes and fine fabrics to pile onto the floor until she had almost reached the bottom. "Can I trust you? Will you tell no one?"

"Tell no one of what? Yngarue, what do you have in that trunk?" Whatever it was, it was wrapped in a large swath of stitched-together ermine. Yngarue picked it up and cradled it to her chest, unwrapping it slowly. "A book," Reed said, when it was laid bare. But not only a book. Stuck between the pages were letters. Dozens of letters, written in fine black ink. Yngarue took one out and handed it to Reed.

Reed unfolded it and read. Within moments she was blushing. *My darling, Yngarue*, he wrote. *How I long to be in the warmth of your embrace, to kiss and caress you as your lordly husband. . . .* Reed flipped ahead. *Not far is the day when our loneliness will be at an end, when this cruel separation gives way to a most ardent uniting. . . .* She flipped again. Peppered in between passages describing Yngarue's unsurpassed beauty were long sentences decrying the cruelty of their situation, and vows to raise an army to one day claim her. Some of the things he wrote—she couldn't imagine what Yngarue had written in return.

"Yngarue, these letters are unsigned. Who are they from?"

She looked through them again. The penmanship was too fine for a servant. One of the Cassan nobility, perhaps? Was the princess carrying on a secret affair with the son of a noble lord?

"They are from Prince Denros of Erleven," Yngarue said. "The son of my father's greatest enemy."

Reed gaped at her. "You are in love with Prince Denros of Erleven?"

"And he is in love with me." Yngarue lifted her chin proudly, eyes blazing as if she was daring Reed to oppose the match. How wrong Lyonene had been to call her a mouse.

"How have you achieved this?" Reed asked.

"With the help of Parmenin. He came from Erleven, long ago. It is what made him my father's favorite—the idea that he'd fled Erleven for Cassor. It has long been our desire to see the strife between our two countries at an end. And this is how we do it."

Reed could have tossed the girl up onto her shoulders and danced her around the room on her Outfitter-enchanted legs. Erleven and Cassor had been bitter enemies for generations. A royal marriage between them would cause the rumblings of war. It would call for a clash of kings. And from that, if the prince and princess survived, both nations would rise. A new allegiance in the region. A new stronghold of power.

And glory, for the hero queen and the Aristene order.

"This is why we were sent," Reed whispered. "This was no

simple errand, no task for a marriage broker. It was—" She stopped, remembering Lyonene's words, given to her by the sacred well. *The girl's first choice will be the wrong one.* She looked down at the paper in her hands. The letters went back years. This was Yngarue's first choice. The first prince she'd reached out to, the first she'd loved. Prince Denros of Erleven.

Reed's hopes crashed to the floor as quickly as they'd risen. The first choice would be the wrong one. This match with Erleven was not to be. And if Denros was the wrong choice, and Alsander was a false choice, then only one option remained.

Yngarue must marry Hestion of Glaucia.

30.
THE WRONG SUITOR

That evening, Reed dressed for dinner in a simple shift of dull red linen. Since her arrival red had been deemed "the matchmaker's color," and the other women at court had slowly ceased to wear it. It gave Reed an unintended mark of status. The men of the court bowed to her when she passed them, and the ladies often pulled her aside to ask for her advice.

They would not if they knew of the blunders she'd made.

On her way to join the evening meal, Reed stopped beside a window. Outside, Cassor was softening in the fading light. It was lovely there, she had to admit. The country was like its princess, a small, hidden jewel, rich in charm, and surrounded by forces who sought to keep it pocketed away.

If Yngarue were truly my hero, we would carry out her plans, Reed thought. The princess would ride into battle beside her. They would use those long years of love letters with the Prince of Erleven to secure a secret entrance into the kingdom, and together, she and Reed would burn it to the ground. Yngarue could even take the vanquished prince as a husband, if she wanted. He could be half a consort, half a political hostage. It would be glorious.

Except if Yngarue were hers, she wouldn't survive the battle. The heroes of a glorious death did not live to wed their beloveds.

They found their glory impaled upon the end of a blade or thrown from the top of a tower.

Laughter sounded from the great hall, and Yngarue's and Parmenin's rose above the rest. They thought themselves close to a victory they'd planned years for. Reed didn't know how to tell them it wasn't to be.

She left the castle, fleeing, as she often did, to the comfort and security of her horse. But when she reached the stable she was surprised to find that Silco wasn't alone. Sar was there, miming a battle in sweeping strikes of a sword and dramatic falls.

"Sar?"

Sar startled, caught. The red that rose to his cheeks made the blue streaks upon them all the more becoming.

"They say the Areion speak to those who are worthy," Sar said. "I was telling him of my deeds during the war in Rhonassus."

Reed smiled. "And?"

"So far he has no comment." Sar recounted a bit more of his story, punctuating the tale with grunts and thrown elbows as Silco listened with pricked ears. Sar shook his head and laughed. "This is what becomes of a warrior when there is no fighting."

"I'll fight you." Reed reached out to stroke Silco's nose. "I could use something to punch."

"Because of Hestion?"

"Yes," Reed said. "And no. I have made a wreck of things, Sar. And I don't know what to do."

"Hestion has told me of the threat to the Aristene," Sar said. "That it has found you here."

"Yes." It was the only thing that made her not regret her choice to come—that she had been here to face that beast instead of Lyonene.

But there was too much at stake now for her to continue on. She had to return through the Veil and tell the elders what she'd found, let what she and Lyonene had done come to light. But first she had to make sure that Yngarue got the marriage that she deserved. She had to get out of Hestion's way.

"Sar," she said. "I need to ask a favor of you."

"Anything, for the warrior who saved my life."

"Can you get me into Hestion's chambers?"

Sar smuggled her into the Glaucan's lodgings wrapped in a cloak. He drew the hood down over her face so far that she was half-blind, and kept his arm thrown around her so if anyone saw them they would think he was only bringing a girl back to his own chamber.

Reed looked down at the dark red linen of her skirt, which showed plainly. "They will know you are with me."

"I don't mind that rumor," Sar replied. "Though if it reaches the ears of Princess Wyrnnigrid, I will expect you to tell her the truth!"

"That you snuck me into the bedchamber of her sister's suitor?"

"No. That I am an excellent lover."

"Sar!" Reed cried, and smacked him, but the Ithernan only laughed.

Reed returned her eyes to the floor, trying not to become dizzy with the turns. The apartments where the Glaucans had been housed were in a part of the castle she had never been to, and she hoped she would be able to find her way back out.

They reached Hestion's door, and Sar opened it and shoved her inside.

"Should I tell him you are waiting?" he asked.

"No. Yes." Reed shook her head. "It doesn't matter."

Sar grinned. "Good luck, Aristene." And then he left her alone.

Reed looked around. It was a fine room, finer than hers and even than the large chamber the princesses shared. The floors were padded with thick furs and the bed protected from drafts by a heavy drape. It was kept warm by a fireplace, and every candlestick was made of gold. This was the room of a king, wealthy and refined, and she saw nothing of Hestion in it. But Hestion would be a king someday. Because she'd made him one.

The door clicked open behind her. Sar must have wasted no time in telling Hestion where she was.

Reed took a deep breath. She remained facing the window, afraid that if she faced him she would forget what she had come to say.

"I've come to say goodbye," she said. "I never should have come to Cassor, or tried to stand in your way. I have to return to Atropa tonight, and Hestion, you *must* stay here and convince Yngarue to marry you. It is important, and you are her finest match; you will make her happy—"

Hestion crossed the room. He took her arm and turned her around. Reed looked into his eyes, and he stepped closer and swept her up in a kiss.

"I don't understand," she said when they broke apart.

"Do you wish us to remain angry with each other forever?" he asked, his voice gruff. He kissed her again, gently at first, as if in apology for his harshness in the woods, but soon the fire in him grew. He tore her shift and pulled it down her shoulders.

"I never wished to be angry at you at all," she whispered as Hestion laid her upon the bed.

31.

A ROYAL GUARD OF ARISTENE

Reed didn't know how long they slept, or how many times they woke each other for more. But by the time the gray light of dawn began to creep across the castle grounds, the fire in the hearth had burned itself out, and Hestion lay dozing upon the pillows, his lashes dark against his cheeks. Reed laid her hand upon his chest. She never wanted to leave the bed. She never wanted to leave his side.

"Reed?"

She looked up. He'd opened his eyes.

"What's wrong? Did I hurt you?" He touched her lip. "Should I have been more gentle?"

"Did it seem like I wanted you to be more gentle?"

Hestion smiled. He tugged her closer, farther onto his chest. "Then why do you look so?"

"I'm sorry about Belden," she said, and his mouth turned down grimly. "I should have said that, long before."

"You did say it," he said. "But I was not ready to hear." He moved to kiss her, but Reed saw the light growing brighter through the window.

"We shouldn't have done this," she cried softly. "It will only make it harder, what we have to do."

Hestion shushed her gently. He brushed her hair back from her forehead. "We do not need to do anything. I will take my men and ride from here. I will take no queen but you."

"You know I can't become your queen," Reed said. "And Glaucia needs an heir."

But Hestion's jaw flexed stubbornly. "I love you, Reed. Only you."

In the night, there had been no questions. No tomorrows. But one night didn't change who they were, or the paths they had been set upon. A tear slid from the corner of Reed's eye and Hestion pressed his forehead to hers.

Sometime before dawn had fully risen, she slipped from his chamber and hurried through the castle on silent feet, the red of her torn dress covered in Sar's dark cloak.

She leaned against her closed door and absently touched her lips in the quiet. Her recollections of the night brought a flush to her cheeks and a rush of joy so wild she might have laughed aloud. She clapped her hand across her mouth. It had been bliss. And it had been foolish. Hestion was only on the other side of the castle, but he may as well have been across the sea. She felt different, but nothing in the world had changed, and when night fell, she had to go back to Atropa.

But she would allow herself one day of dreams. Unfortunately, that day required that she change back into the traditional match-maker's gown.

She pushed her arms into the sleeves and the bells jangled. "How can I let him see me in this now?" she muttered. "He will have nothing but regrets."

After the sun had fully risen, she joined Yngarue and Wyrn-nigrid in the solar. The sisters were meant to be working at their embroidery, but their heads were bent together, smiling and chuckling, gossiping as sisters did. Reed distinctly heard the word *Ithernan*.

"Machianthe, what are your opinions of a man such as Sar?" Wyrnnigrid asked with bright eyes, and more color in her pale cheeks than Reed had seen since arriving.

"I think if you wish for your husband to live long, then you do not marry a man like Sar." Her response gave them pause, and she laughed. "I know Sar well. You cannot find better."

Wyrnnigrid sat back with a pleased expression.

"Are you well, Machianthe?" Yngarue asked. "You were not at the feast last night."

She smiled at Reed discreetly, and Reed noticed that she'd dressed in the gown made from the brown fabric and threaded with gold. The one that had been saved, to wear when Yngarue's match had been decided. She wore it now to signify that she had chosen Denros of Erleven.

Reed frowned.

"Your Highnesses!"

Their lady's maid Evie burst through the door of the solar.

"Evie, what is it?" Wynnigrid asked.

"It is Crown Prince Alsander! He arrives at last! As promised," she added, and dropped a curtsy to Reed.

The princesses rose. They filed out of the solar, and Yngarue cast Reed a furtive glance.

"I thought Prince Alsander was a falsehood," she whispered as they trailed Evie through the castle. But Reed had no explanation. *He is. He was.* She stopped the princesses outside the entrance to the throne room.

"Does the king not want the princess to be formally introduced?"

"No, no, in his excitement he commanded she come immediately!"

Immediately. There was no time to gather her wits. Reed stepped to the front. At least she could precede the princesses inside. With luck she could greet Alsander and whisper a moment into his ear. But what she saw when she entered the great hall stopped her dead.

Alsander was not alone. Five Aristene stood behind him. Or rather, four Aristene and an apostate. Reed had to clench her teeth to keep from crying out as she passed Aster, Veridian, Aethiel, and Mol, the surly blond warrior who kept her hair back with a silver headband. Lyonene stood just behind them, and gave Reed a warning lift of her eyebrow.

Urdien turned. "Ah, at last, your matchmaker appears!"

Reed fumbled into a bow. "Prince Alsander, I am so happy you have finally arrived."

"Indeed," Alsander said, eyes twinkling.

"Where are my daughters?" Urdien called. "And my wife, she too will be with us soon."

At the mention of their mother, the princesses hurried inside.

"Father, is it true?" Wyrnnigrid asked. "Is Mother well?"

"Yes, yes," Urdien said, tugging her to one side to give Alsander a better view of Yngarue. "I spoke to the physician this morning and they say she is much improved. But do not speak of that now." Introductions were made between Yngarue and Alsander, but Reed barely noticed. Her eyes remained fixed upon the Aristene.

Only black-crowned Aethiel appeared at ease, her thumbs tucked behind the silver buckle of her belt. And perhaps Veridian. But Aster's eyes were serious, and Mol appeared ready to beat Reed black and blue.

What were they doing here? What had happened? She looked at Lyonene, but Lyonene gave no clues, seemingly paying rapt attention as the king regaled Alsander with a long list of Yngarue's virtues. Behind the king, Parmenin looked vexed; he kept stealing glances at Reed as if to ask whether her prince was going to upset their plans. Reed shrugged at him, overwhelmed. There were too many sudden complications for her to pay Parmenin any mind. When Hestion arrived with Sar, she could have screamed.

"Here's some healthy competition for you, Prince Hestion," King Urdien said as Hestion approached.

Hestion's eyes flickered to Reed before the two princes greeted each other with an embrace. "I'm glad to see you, brother," Hestion said. "Even if you are here to win the hand of my intended." He turned and extended his arm to Yngarue, who didn't seem to know what to do. *That makes two of us*, thought Reed.

"First you compete with me for a city," Alsander said, "and now a bride."

"The city we share."

"But I doubt that the princess can be shared similarly."

An impertinent remark, and Reed saw Lyonene frown. Luckily, Urdien laughed. "True enough," he said. "Though any father would be blessed to have two such royal sons-in-law. Now, you have journeyed far. Let us take some ease in sport. We will have some wine on this fine day and we will all come to know one another."

To welcome Alsander and his party, King Urdien had archery targets set in the long field behind the castle. Servants brought fine chairs for him and the other royals to sit in, and the cloth the princesses had embroidered with the crest of Cerille was set upon a table. Lesser chairs and blankets were set out upon the grass for the Aristene, who had been introduced as Alsander's personal guard. But they preferred to stand. Reed stood stiffly to one side in her red dress as trays crowded with cups of pale gold wine passed among the guests, and platters of preserved fruit and berries were set upon the table. There were cheeses and soft breads to be dragged through butter or dolloped with jams and jellies. It was, quite frankly, torture.

Of Alsander's "guard," only Aethiel took part in the archery. The big Aristene couldn't resist a contest of weapons. It didn't take long for her to best the princes, and when she was finished, she held a bow out to Veridian.

"Come," she said. "Show us what it truly means to fire an arrow." Veridian shook her head, and Aethiel frowned deeply. "Was a time," Aethiel said, "when my gift with an arrow was rival to yours. But it's been many years since I have seen that kind of mastery."

She sounded so sad, and Aster inclined her head, entreating Veridian to do as she asked. Veridian sighed. She walked to Aethiel and took up the bow, taking an arrow from the ground quiver.

"The members of my guard are elite marksmen," Alsander hastened to explain to the king. "Veridian is one of the best."

"One of the best," Veridian muttered under her breath as Parmenin put an arm across Yngarue and Wyrnnigrid, as if "the best" instead meant the most reckless. Veridian nocked the arrow and took aim at the target. After a moment of consideration, she lowered the bow and took up two more arrows. She nodded to Aethiel's goblet of wine. "How far can you throw that?"

The Aristene drew her arm back and heaved the goblet into the sky. It spun end over end across the field, and just before it reached the height of its arc, Veridian drew and fired. The first arrow hit the goblet with a ping and sent it sailing farther. She drew and fired again, and again, so fast, each shot pinging into the goblet and flinging it off on a new trajectory. When it finally landed, Prince Ullieth ran to recover it, and the poor little lad would be running for a very long time.

All in attendance clapped in astonishment. The other Aristenes clapped in pride, even Mol. It had been a show, and somewhat foolish—Parmenin stared at them now as if frightened—but at least it put an end to the archery, as no one wished to follow such a grand display.

"There," Veridian said, and set down the bow. "Now, if we may be excused. Alsander's guard needs to settle their horses. Matchmaker. Come and help us."

The moment they breached the quiet of the stable, Reed hurried to Aster and her mentor folded her in an embrace. "What are you doing here?" Reed asked.

"It's I who would be asking that of you." Aster lowered her voice. "Reed. What could you have been thinking?"

"She was not thinking," Mol said loudly. She returned to them after a quick search of the building to oust the grooms and servants. "At least it seems there has been minimal damage. And you two will return to Atropa tonight, to face the elders' judgment." She forked her fingers at Reed and Lyonene.

"I can't just leave," Reed objected. "What will the king think when the matchmaker is simply . . . gone?"

"And what about my hero? Her marriage?" Lyonene added.

"You didn't care about your hero before."

"She was in good hands before," Lyonene said. For a moment, Mol and the recent initiates stood silently, gritting their collective teeth. And then the apostate spoke.

"Oh, come now, Mol, be reasonable. Delay your snitching until this marriage business is concluded. It will be barely a blink in the span of an immortal order."

"Veridian," Mol growled, "this is not a joke."

"Mol," said Aethiel, and Reed looked at her in surprise. "You have a love for your order, but do you not also have love for your sisters? Allow them the grace to fix what mistakes they have made. Their punishment will still be waiting when they are ready to return."

Mol frowned, staring first at Reed and then at Lyonene. "Tiern expects Machianthe. It was a direct order that she be returned."

"So Reed can go," Aster suggested. "Tonight."

"Lyonene can't remain here alone," Reed said. "The abominations have come to Cassor. I slew one not two nights ago, in the forests not far from the castle. I was going to return tonight, to inform the elders." She looked at Mol, who only pursed her lips.

"Fine," Veridian said. "I will protect Lyonene as she finishes her duty. Are you happy?"

"No, I am not," Mol grumbled. "The rogue initiate stays without consequence and only an apostate to guard her flank? This is not what the elders intended."

"It is not without consequence," said Aster. "They will face their punishment. When the time comes."

Mol scowled. But there was nothing she could do. She was outnumbered.

"Very well," she said. "But I will remain, too. To make sure Lyonene and the apostate are"—she cast them a withering look—"safe." She looked at Aster. "I will trust you to return Machianthe to Tiern directly. And Machianthe—you have my word: none will hear of what you have done until this business is concluded."

Reed bowed her head, but before she could thank her, Mol's hand shot out to grasp her hard. She glanced down as Mol tapped her pinkie finger against Reed's arm. It was curiously shortened, as if it had been cut off at the knuckle.

"I am not so unreasonable," Mol said. "I, too, once had to learn to follow the rules."

32.

LITTLE SHARDS OF BONE

Reed and Lyonene stayed behind after Veridian and the Aristene returned to the castle. For a moment neither knew what to say, and they stood in silence, listening to the Aristene bicker as they walked through the yard.

"Aethiel," they heard Veridian tease, "you sounded almost like a queen back there." Giggling followed, as did Veridian's "oof!" when Reed assumed Aethiel socked her in the ribs.

"So," Lyonene began. "This has gone well." They stared at each other. Then both burst out laughing.

"It is not funny," Reed choked out after several long moments.

"I know." Lyonene held her ribs. "I don't know if I'm laughing . . . or crying!"

"Lyonene," Reed said as the laughter subsided. "I'm sorry. I have made a mess of this."

"Don't apologize. You did it for me, and I agreed to it." She turned toward the stalls and reached out to stroke Strawberry's and Silco's noses, who watched their hysterics with judgment on their faces. It was a stable full of Areion, except for bright white Target and Alsander's golden Phaeton, and most of the horses wore similar expressions. Only the black mare with the white blaze down her face whom Aethiel had ridden in on seemed not to care one way or the other.

"Did you see Mol's finger?" Reed asked.

"Yes. And now I am thinking of every scar I have ever seen on another of our sisters. Wondering whether battle put them there or the elders did. How deep could a lash cut us, do you think, before we would bear the marks?"

"I'd rather take the lashing than lose a finger," Reed said.

"No, you wouldn't. I would, perhaps, but not you. A lost finger is pain and payment; but to be struck by the elders? That is pain *and* indignity."

An image of herself bent beneath the elders flashed behind Reed's eyes. She knew how to bow, but never in disgrace. "So you're vain and I'm proud," she said.

Lyonene chuckled. "Yes. What a pair we make."

"Lyonene, what happened in Cerille? How has Alsander come to be here, with an Aristene escort?"

"There was a coup," Lyonene replied. "King Alectos killed all our noble allies. We would have been executed were it not for Veridian's swift intervention."

"But you were so confident in your position."

"Yes, well." Lyonene lips twisted ruefully. "Now Alsander finds himself a wandering prince of nothing. And he blames me for it."

"He doesn't really. He's only hurt and—" Reed searched for a word. "Unmoored. Besides, you are an Aristene. You have all the years of Alsander's life to work your plans. If you want to return him to the throne of Cerille, then you shall."

"Such faith you have in me, Ox."

"It isn't unearned. I know you, Lyonene. No old king, and no young prince, no army is going to get the better of you." She thought a moment and frowned. "I suppose this means that Alsander is no option for Yngarue. If he has no crown and no army, no riches to offer Cassor."

"And just how is my little brown mouse?" Lyonene asked.

"She is no mouse. She's aligned herself with Prince Denros, the son of Urdien's great enemy, King Medes of Erleven. She means to marry him and join the kingdoms."

"No," Lyonene said, and such a light grew in her eyes that Reed knew her magic was at work. Had Lyonene been in Cassor like she should have been she would have seen the malevolent strands winding around Yngarue from the start. Had Lyonene been there, she would have known what to do. But at least she was here now.

"*The girl's first choice will be the wrong one.* I know," Reed said. "You'll have to talk her out of Denros's arms and into someone else's. Perhaps if you're very skilled you can even come up with an alternative to keep her from marrying my Hestion."

"*Your* Hestion." Lyonene's eyes widened. "You've finally done it. You've bedded your hero."

"He's not my hero anymore," Reed muttered.

"So," Lyonene pressed, "how was it?"

Reed flushed. "You said it would hurt, but it didn't."

"I said it *might* hurt," Lyonene corrected her. "Though of course it wouldn't for you, the vaunted foundling, for whom everything comes easy: Ferreh's shield, a painless first— Ow!" She rubbed her arm where Reed had punched her. She laughed.

"I'm happy for you, Reed. Though I thought this would have

happened already. During the trial you were always at each other's sides. How did you wait?"

"My sights were set on other things," Reed said. "My sights still are. The gifts of the Aristene are many. But there are some things we do not get to have."

Lyonene looked down.

"I have to tell you something, Reed."

"What?"

Lyonene looked again at the stalls, where the long faces of the Areion gazed at them, dark eyes full of innocence.

"It's not as though they can repeat it," Reed said. "For that they'd have to lower themselves to talking."

Lyonene tugged Reed outside. Her voice was barely a whisper when she spoke.

"I've done something foolish."

Reed waited. "What?" But Lyonene didn't reply. Her green eyes were imploring, as if she wanted Reed to guess. "Lyonene, you're making me nervous. What's wrong?"

"It's Alsander," she said finally. "Reed, I married him."

The words rang through Reed's ears. She married him. Married him! But that wasn't possible. Lyonene couldn't be that stupid. As the words died in the air, Lyonene looked up at the sky. Out into the forests. Anywhere but into Reed's eyes. She was ashamed. And she was afraid.

She should be.

"Undo it," Reed said.

"I can't."

"Of course you can; it isn't real. You can take no oaths save those made to the goddess. You can wear no crown. It isn't real, Lyonene. It doesn't count. Does no one else know?"

Lyonene shook her head.

"Then it never happened." She took her friend by the shoulders and shook her, hard. "Do you hear me? It never happened."

"It never happened," Lyonene whispered. And then she curled into Reed's chest and wept.

Reed's knuckles had scarcely touched the wood of the door before Hestion swung it open.

"Where have you been?" he asked. "I feared you were unable to get away."

"I had to be sure everyone was abed before coming." She stepped into his embrace, and for a moment they stood still. But she had no time. She kissed him as one of his hands moved hungrily to her chest. The other tore her cloak and she hurried with the fastenings of her dress before he could tear that, too. Reed shoved him toward the bed.

"Quickly," she said. "And then slowly, after."

Hestion grinned. "I'm glad you came. And I'm glad you didn't wear the hat."

Later she lay with her head beside his on the pillow, her body relaxed but unwilling to sleep. She couldn't sleep. She had to return with Aster that night, through the Veil.

"I have come up with a plan," Hestion said, staring at the ceiling.

"Oh?" She smiled.

"I will not marry Yngarue. I will not marry anyone."

"Hestion—"

"No, wait, listen. You will come to me in Glaucia, whenever you can. In the weeks or months when you have no hero to guide. And in the meantime, I will broker a marriage between Sar and Princess Wyrnnigrid. They are already much attached, and though I will miss him, he will be happy here, ruling by her side in Cassor."

"But what about an heir for Glaucia?"

"I will ask Sar to send me one of his children, to raise as my ward. To raise for the throne. The people love Sar; they will accept his child. And both of the nations will be happy." He touched her face. "I will be happy."

Reed frowned. "You would be giving up a child of your line, a marriage—"

"Yes, I know. I am the one who thought of it." He looked into her eyes. "I love you, Reed. I will never love another like I love you."

"It is a good offer," Reed whispered. And it was. It was a sweet dream, and she wanted it, so badly. "But it won't be enough for you. Eventually you would want more. More than I could give."

"I know myself," Hestion said. "I know what I want. Do not make us spend our lives apart."

Reed slid out from beneath Hestion and started getting dressed, fussing with the cloak like she hoped to magically fuse it back together where he'd torn it. If she had a needle and thread, her Outfitter-enchanted fingers could be of real use for once.

"I don't know what to do."

"You said you were not even supposed to be here," Hestion said. Gently, he drew her back against his chest. "Yet here we are. Our gods have put us together. I think they don't wish us to be parted."

"The gods place us in each other's paths. But gods are just as often cruel as they are kind." He kissed her shoulder and she sighed. "Hestion. I can't stay."

"Yet you can't go. It is a problem." His expression turned serious in the low light from the fire. "When can you return? When can you come to me in Glaucia?"

"I don't know. These priests wage a war against us. We must all return to Atropa until that threat is vanquished."

"You know that the Glaucan army will defend the Aristene; you aren't without allies."

"The Glaucan army has its own lands to protect. And we can handle these priests. We can slay these monsters."

"I know that you can," Hestion said as he rolled on top of her.

"Hestion. Aster and Aethiel are waiting."

"Once more," he whispered against her lips.

"Once," she replied.

THREE

SEEKER OF THE BONES

33.
INITIATES IN THEIR PROPER PLACES

The Veil opened, and Reed, Aster, and Aethiel stepped through on their horses into the sunlit hills of Atropa. Reed had never been sorrier to be back. Mol was not there to tattle on her, having remained in Cassor with Lyonene and Veridian, but it still felt like she was returning in shame, that Tiern would take one look at her and know what she had done.

"Don't ask me to put it off," Aster said when Reed glanced at her plaintively. "I promised Mol that I would bring you to Tiern, and that is precisely what I intend to do." Then she turned to her with softer eyes. "But don't be afraid. I am here with you."

Ahead of them on Nightfly, Aethiel put her hand up to shield her eyes from the sun and said, "I do not think it will be necessary to bring her to Tiern." She jutted her chin to the road that led into the white city. "She comes."

Tiern rode toward them on a chestnut-brown horse, her many-colored hair and silver-touched armor unmistakable. Reed didn't know the horse, and thought it odd. Normally when Tiern required a mount she chose Ferreh's Areion, Amondal.

"Gloria Thea Matris," Aster said when she charged up to them.

"Gloria Thea Matris indeed," Tiern replied, her eyes on Reed. "You have found her."

"We found Lyonene as well; Mol remains with her as she settles matters with her hero, and then they will return."

"Good, good," said Tiern, "Machianthe, are you ready?"

"For what?" Reed asked.

"Another journey through the Veil. You and I are for the city of Roshanak, and your friend the boy king. We are going to bring home the bones."

Lyonene met Hestion just before dawn, not long after Reed had left Cassor through the Veil. Hestion stared out of a small window cut into the stone. The light was so soft in the corridor that Lyonene could hardly see his face, and to him, she must have been all shadow.

"You're going already?" Lyonene asked.

"She is gone, and so I go," he said quietly.

"I think she wanted you to stay," Lyonene said. "I think she wanted you to marry Princess Yngarue."

But instead of seeming hurt, Hestion snorted. "Well. We cannot let her get her way all the time." He smiled, and despite the predicament his departure would leave her in, Lyonene found herself smiling back.

"Are you sure? Cassor and Glaucia would make a good match," Lyonene said. "And you could have Reed, too—she's not jealous."

Hestion smiled wider. He looked good as a crown prince. All that wild gold hair and one braid woven into it, tied with a strip of leather. Still no circlet upon his head. Only the silver stag, pinned to his shoulder. "But she is the only one I want." He pushed away from the window. "Farewell, Lyonene."

"Farewell," she sighed after he was gone. Another suitor, lost.

The only suitor besides Alsander, thanks to her and Reed's foolish scheme. Lyonene would have to find more men. Send for more princes. Surely there were many who would jump at the chance to win the hand of the rich princess of Cassor.

"At least she isn't plain," Lyonene said as she walked back to Reed's old chamber—the matchmaker's chamber, and her chamber now. "Or at least not as plain as she seemed to me in the well."

Hestion had roused the Glaucans with the sun, and by the time he left Lyonene they were ready to depart. Belongings had been packed. Last words of friendship had been exchanged with those companions they had met in Cassor. Hestion bid a hasty and apologetic goodbye to the still-half-asleep King Urdien. As his men pulled their horses from the stable, Hestion placed his hand on the door of Silco's empty stall.

"We do not have to leave," said Sar. "Alsander is no match for you in the hearts of women, coin or no coin."

"I know," Hestion replied.

"Then why are we departing with no bride? And much poorer after the gifts of fine plate and jewels?"

"Perhaps those gifts will keep you in the mind of Princess Wyrnnigrid."

For a moment, Sar was uncharacteristically speechless. "We are not here for that," he sputtered. "You must get the Aristene out of your head!"

Hestion squeezed the door of the empty stall. "I can't."

"What will you tell your aunt? She will not be pleased! And I am not going to tell her for you," he called as Hestion walked outside.

"Prince Hestion!"

He looked up and saw little Prince Ullieth running to the stable yard, his small chest heaving.

"Must you really go?"

"We must." Hestion clapped his hand on the lad's shoulder. Sar came out to say goodbye as well, and reached into his saddlebag for a small clay jar. He dipped his fingers into it and leaned down to streak blue pigment across Ulli's cheeks.

"May the eye of the gods be always upon you."

Ullieth stepped back as the Glaucans mounted their horses. Many seemed eager to be going home, but none looked forward to the journey. It was a long ride through Cassor to the port.

"Don't make it easy on Alsander," Hestion said to the little prince. "Make him earn your respect, and the hand of your sister." He tousled the boy's hair and got on his horse.

"And tell him how much tougher we were," called Sar as he rode away. "Tell him he is soft and pampered, compared to us!"

Hestion laughed as he turned Target back toward the waiting ships. And home, to Glaucia.

Lyonene waited outside the queen's chambers to tell Yngarue that Reed had gone. Since Lyonene had arrived she hadn't seen much of her, as both princesses had spent most of their time with their mother, who had been ailing but was apparently now quite recovered. Good news, which would perhaps put the princess in a better state to hear that her gift of a matchmaker had abruptly been taken away.

Lyonene paced back and forth, listening to the sounds of comfort issuing from the other side of the door: soft laughter and gentle conversation. She stepped out of the way of a servant who was carrying a tray so piled with cups and fruit that it nearly blinded them, and they glared at her as they passed. Already the Glaucans' sudden departure was causing tensions within the Cassan court. Hestion and his men had been genial and popular, and now he was to be replaced by another who arrived only with a band of armed women, and no fine gifts, no minstrels or jugglers, and not even any clothing of his own.

"Could he not have stayed for a week, or even a day?" Lyonene groaned, imagining Hestion riding gaily through the countryside on his luminous white horse. While she was trapped in the castle with a surly lover and a hopeless princess, under the watchful eye of Mol.

The door of the queen's chamber opened. Yngarue stepped out, holding a pretty glass vase.

"Aristene—"

"Lyonene," Lyonene supplied, and offered the girl her most charming smile. Reed was right; Yngarue was much prettier than a mouse. She had lovely, soft lips and a small waist, and her eyes had flecks of gold in them.

"Lyonene," Yngarue repeated. "I was just going to the garden, to arrange some flowers for my mother from the early blossoms. Did you have need of me?"

"I trust you've heard that Prince Hestion and the Glaucans are gone."

"Oh yes," Yngarue said, not sounding terribly concerned. "Has it displeased my father? Wyrnnigrid has been weeping—she fears that if the Glaucans anger him he will not allow Sar to seek her hand."

Lyonene didn't know anything about that, and nor did she care. "Reed—your matchmaker, Machianthe—has gone as well."

"She left with Prince Hestion?" As Lyonene considered how best to reply, Yngarue pushed past her and walked down the corridor. "But she can't have just left us! Without saying goodbye?"

"Wait, Yngarue—"

Lyonene followed the princess through the castle, all the way back to Reed's empty room, which she stormed into as if certain that Lyonene had been lying. But all that remained of Machianthe the matchmaker was what Reed had left behind. Everything the Outfitter had given her, from the red dress to the mud-stained slippers, to the ridiculous hat edged in bells. How she must have delighted in leaving Lyonene that. It all lay folded and set into a pile, the knife with the poisoned edge resting on the top. Yngarue picked it up.

"How could she go?" Yngarue asked. "She was my friend."

"She didn't want to." Lyonene held her hand out for the knife, but Yngarue spun the blade expertly and tucked it into a sheath.

"I will keep it. As a remembrance. She had been giving me lessons. Before I knew what she really was, it had seemed strange to take instructions on weaponry from a matchmaker. But I suppose I've received some of the finest training in the world."

"You and I could continue it, if you like."

Yngarue studied her for a moment. Surely what she saw must look a far sight more capable than Reed had, in the red dress. "I do not know you," the princess said. "I will think on it." And then she left the room.

Lyonene's head fell back. "Ox," she said to the ceiling, "we never should have done this. You never should have come here—"

"Lyonene?"

She turned. Alsander watched her through the doorway. He slipped inside and closed the door behind him.

"I thought I would never get away from Urdien." He took Lyonene in his arms. "Now that Hestion has slunk away he seems determined to feed and entertain me at every moment. What did you say to the princess? She seemed upset."

"She'd grown attached to Reed."

"Ah," said Alsander. "Well, she cannot be blamed. I too wish Reed had stayed. I wish they all had. Did they not think for a moment how odd it would look to have half of my royal guard disappear overnight?" It was more than half, actually—the moment Aster left, Veridian had taken her horse and disappeared into the forest.

Reluctantly, Lyonene removed his hands from around her waist. "For the sake of appearances, you may not touch me."

"You are my wife," Alsander said, beginning to brood. "I do not expect to do without you." He touched her face, and she allowed him a few brief kisses until they grew more insistent and his hands began to wander.

"Discretion, then." Lyonene gently pushed him back. "We can't be seen. To every eye and ear in Cassor, you must appear aimed for the princess."

"Is that all I am to do? Play my part for the Aristene's charade? Remain in hiding while my father formalizes my disinheritance and removes me from the line of succession?" His eyes narrowed, and Lyonene searched for a way to curb his temper.

"My love, pleasing the order is not without its benefits."

At once, his expression brightened. "You think the Aristene would help me press my cause?"

"You are one of their heroes. You are mine," Lyonene lied. *But it isn't truly a lie*, she told herself. She would see Alsander in the crown of Cerille. She just needed to buy a little more time.

34.

THE BOY KING

Reed and Silco burst from the Veil, gasping, and Tiern looked back and laughed. "You look ill as a pair of fish tossed up on the beach. I'll never tire of watching initiates traverse through the darkness." Reed eyed the elder as she swallowed, trying not to vomit. There was a lot wrong with that statement—fish tossed up on the beach weren't ill, they were dying, and she was an Aristene now, not an initiate—but Tiern was an elder. It wasn't for the likes of Reed to correct her.

Reed squinted against the bright sunlight. They were in Rhonassus—she could tell by golden sandy dirt beneath Silco's hooves. By the dryness of the air. And by the trees, the bark a grayish color, their trunks wizened and twisted with branches that sprouted scant silver-green leaves. Rhonassus felt just as it had when she'd first arrived there for the war, and she realized that it must have been the same season, one year ago.

Reed nudged Silco ahead, out from beneath the sparse cover of trees. The Veil had opened high in the northern hills, along the coast. The city was visible below, built into the valley that sloped toward the beach, protected by a vast stone wall and tall city gates. It hadn't been breached in a thousand years before Glaucia, and Cerille, and the Aristene came. She and Lyonene had helped their heroes to break through the gates and take the wall. Tiern and Aethiel had battered down the drawbridge to let them sack the palace.

"So much has been repaired," Tiern said, riding close. "In so little time. I would like to stand here for a few months and watch the ants reconstruct their anthill."

"So you could kick it apart it again?"

"No." Tiern shrugged. "Perhaps. Someday." She began to ride down the winding path. Reed and Silco followed slowly, his bad hoof making him cautious as he navigated the steep incline. Every few steps he would snort, and she wondered if he was objecting to the terrain, or to returning to Roshanak. It couldn't have been a place of good memories for him.

She looked down at the harbor, where ships flying the flags of Cerille and Glaucia were docked in the port as the nations engaged in trade and received tribute from the defeated Rhonassans. Farther inland the city gates stood open in times of peace. Reed's gaze crept to the villas on the hill, and the one that had been Belden's. It looked much the same, but quieter now that it was returned to its proper owner and no longer swarming with soldiers.

"How well do you know this boy king?" Tiern asked, referring to Oren, the boy king of Rhonassus. When he'd been their captive Reed had saved him from execution, and as a thank-you he had unwittingly betrayed her into a golden cage.

"I know him well enough to often want to beat him," said Reed. "But that's part of his charm. Before I take you to him, you must promise he won't be harmed."

"Promises are for children." Tiern reached into the pouch she kept tied to her belt and took out the flat piece of bone, which was beginning to turn smooth and shiny where she worried at it with her thumb. It was hard to imagine that it had once been embedded in the skin of a hero. That a zealot priest had forced the bone into the flesh.

She didn't know how Tiern could bear to hold it in her hand. "Doesn't it make you weak?"

"Not anymore. It knows me now." Tiern looked down at the piece of skull and closed her fist over it. "The skull of the prophet is not evil in itself. The evil is done by those who wield it. We will claim all of these fragments and once we have them, they will do us no harm."

"You said the order would fall if I didn't become a Glorious Death. But I have become one, and still we're threatened."

"You thought that's all it would take? One decision, one choice, and all would be as it should be?"

Tiern turned in the saddle. Even in the bright light of day she seemed an otherworldly beast, as if the woman's skin she wore was only a costume, a stretched-thin covering for the being barely contained inside. From the time she was a child Reed had heard tales of her. Hushed and whispered tales of terrible feats. That every streak in her hair was a hero whose flesh she devoured.

Tiern held the piece of bone up between her fingers. "Small, isn't it? Hard to imagine what it can do when it is placed inside a hero. Aethiel says that even I would have difficulty slaying a monster with one of these beneath its skin. I think that sounds like a challenge. What do you think?"

Reed thought that not many challenges remained for an elder to face. Perhaps that was why Tiern sounded so strangely eager.

"These shards infuse a person with power. They take what is

already inside them and increase it a hundredfold. It makes them more of what they are." The elder turned the bone back and forth, studying its edges, the light against its darkened sides. "What do you think it would do to me?" She held the fragment out to Reed. "What would it do to you?"

Reed swallowed. She was a Glorious Death. What it would make of her would be an Aristene like the world had never seen. Fiercer and stronger, greater than all. She could protect all of those she loved. Through her, the order would be kept safe.

If it didn't also turn her into a monster.

Reed looked away. "I don't think I want to know, elder."

Past the shard of skull, Tiern's lips pulled into a smile. "I don't believe you."

She slipped the bone back into her belt.

They passed easily through the city until a pair of guards stopped them at the palace gate. Guards who recognized them, judging by the resentful fear that came into their eyes. Both wore the marks of the war: scars upon their arms, and one had suffered a burn. Smooth pink flesh snaked up the side of his neck as if he'd been licked by a dragon.

"We come for an audience with the boy king," Tiern said, pausing for the barest of moments before knocking aside their spears and continuing on like the guards hadn't been there at all. Reed smiled at them apologetically as they glowered and shouted their arrival to a messenger who raced ahead. Tiern dismounted in the southern courtyard and looked appreciatively over the palace grounds.

"What a lovely hedge maze," she said as they turned to walk up the palace steps.

"Yes, it's very pretty," Reed said, and curled her lip.

It was strange to be led inside the palace of Roshanak rather than prodded by a spear at her back. The very air reeked to Reed of the blood of betrayal, and the memory of being locked inside Oreas's golden cage made her break out in sweat. Had Aster been there, she would have sensed Reed's unease, but Tiern was oblivious. Yet Reed was safer with Tiern than with anyone; if anything went wrong, the teeth of the order could tear through men like they were wet bread.

They walked through the archway of the brightly lit throne room, and Oren greeted them immediately.

"Aristene," he said, and Reed was surprised to hear that his voice had grown deeper. She bent her head in a short bow and Tiern tsked her. The Aristene didn't bow. Except they did, when it was to their advantage.

Oren stepped forward. He wore a finely spun tunic of pale orange linen, overlaid with a green robe embroidered in gold. His long black hair was braided to his nape and secured with wide gold clips, and he was flanked by no fewer than a dozen servants and handmaidens.

"Reed." He grasped her wrists and she felt the large rings around each of his fingers.

"King Oren," she said. "Our captive prince."

He laughed. "And you, the woman who thinks herself the equal of a man." Reed laughed as well, and surprisingly, so did Tiern. Her laughter was loud and barking. She growled a little at the end of it, and Oren uncomfortably shifted his weight. "What brings you again to my shores, my friends?"

"An unpleasant errand," Reed replied. "Though you are a surprisingly pleasant sight."

Oren flicked his wrist and servants entered with trays of refreshment. He guided Reed and Tiern to the long feasting table near the open wall of marble columns and gestured for them to sit. Once there, the elder seemed content to eat and ignore them, leaving Reed to do the work of diplomacy.

"I must admit, I worried about you," Reed said. "Ruling here in a land freshly torn by war, without your brother to guide you."

"Prince Alsander remained for a time." Oren reached for an olive. "He was a great help. But how odd that you would worry for me, when I also worried for you. You were not well when last we met."

"I wasn't injured."

"Not outwardly. But anyone could see what the war had cost you. I, too, wished that Belden had not died. Of all the princes who have kept me captive, he was the kindest. The most noble."

"Of all the princes who have held you captive so far," Reed said, and the boy smiled. "But don't worry about me. I'm well. I've made my peace with the choice I made. And I think I've been forgiven."

"So you will pass my greetings along to Prince Hestion, then." Oren smiled wryly. Reed would have punched him in the arm if the act would not have brought a slew of armed guards.

Reed wrapped her fingers around a gold goblet of wine and stared down at the deep red liquid. It smelled of sunshine, and ripe red fruits. It had been sweetened with honey. Oren had banished all traces of his father from the palace. He had scrubbed the blood clean. When Reed looked into the corner of the room, she could hardly conjure the image of the body of the prophet that had once lain there, shrouded and decaying.

"Oren," she said quietly. "We must ask a favor of you."

"Ask and I will give it."

"We wish to see what remains of the skull of the prophet."

"Done."

Reed blinked. "So easily? I was told you refused a request."

The boy king nodded. "You must forgive me for that. I did not know them. And they would not provide me the reason for their request." He peered at Reed. "What is the reason for your request, Aristene?"

Reed glanced at the pouch hanging from Tiern's belt. "Do you remember what you told me, about the pieces of the skull that were unable to be found?"

"Yes, of course."

Reed looked at him gravely. "We have begun to find them."

Oren took them to the bones of the prophet himself, on foot, with an escort of armed guards and servants drifting in their wake. As they walked, the signs of battle were evident all around them: piles of rubble remained from burned-down structures, the hastily dug moat had been drained and the populace had begun to use it as a refuse dump. Yet despite their defeat, the mood of the people seemed full of hope.

A woman leading a donkey laden with clay pots made a gesture of respect to Reed as she passed. The war for Roshanak had been brutal, but in the end, their attackers had become their liberators. It would have been easy to think that the war had been righteous for all, were it not for the frequent sight of scarred flesh and missing limbs, of mothers dressed in mourning veils. And for the undercurrent of fear that Reed sensed in every pair of eyes that dared to meet hers.

Oren led them down a quiet street that twisted into the foot of the mountain. He signaled for his entourage to remain behind, and he, Reed, and Tiern traveled alone up a trail not unlike the one that Reed and Tiern had just come down. It led to a cave, and when they approached, a guard stepped from inside carrying a spear. He dropped to one knee at the sight of the king.

"We keep it always under guard," Oren said as he went inside and took a torch from the wall. Reed took one as well, and passed the flame across the golden breastplates of four more soldiers. "None but the guards, myself, and the holy priests of our temple know what lies inside. I would give no one temptation to steal it. I would have kept it in one of the palace vaults, except . . ."

"I wouldn't want it near me either," said Reed.

The path within the cave was straight, but the light from the opening faded quickly. Reed didn't like to think of the skull lying somewhere ahead, alongside its own skeleton. She remembered too well the way it had seemed to move on its own, turning and twitching in King Oreas's grip.

To her great relief, the light of their torches was soon met with the light of others.

"The guards keep this illuminated at all times," Oren said, as if he, too, didn't wish for the bones to be lurking in the shadows.

Reed stepped aside as Tiern swooped upon the raised stone platform. The smashed skull lay in the curve of one withered arm, as if the Scylloi Prophet was carrying his own head. But had he really been carrying it, he would have needed a bag, as it had been shattered into pieces. The elder's eyes moved greedily over the fragments, and she inspected the body as well, squeezing the bones hidden beneath the prophet's robes with both hands, from collar to knee. When her attention returned to the prophet's head, Reed took that to mean that none of the other bones were missing.

"The jaw is gone, that is apparent."

"Yes," Oren said. "Its absence was the most glaring, when the priests were sent to recover it. I mentioned it to Reed before she departed the city."

"Yet *she* mentioned it to no one," Tiern mumbled. Oren cast Reed an apologetic glance, but there had been no reason to inform the elders of the missing pieces. No one had known yet what the bones could be used for.

You should be dead and gone, she thought as she looked at the bones. In her memory she saw Alsander as he raised the skull high over his head. He'd dashed it against the ground, over and over, sending cracks racing through it like rivers on a map. They thought by destroying it, they'd won. But Oreas had risen again, and killed Belden. Would the skull rise again as well, to finish the rest of them?

"Has anyone tried to reconstruct it?" Tiern asked. She picked up two pieces. The shattered skull had been laid in an approximation of its former whole shape: the largest intact piece consisted of most of an eye socket and the prophet's right cheekbone. The cracked bits of the left eye socket were placed beside it, and below that a piece of the upper jaw, with teeth still affixed. The right side of the upper jaw had been split into three, and a few of the teeth had been knocked out. They lay in a careful row just below it. The other pieces, from the dome and the rear of the skull, were spread out between the prophet's bent arm and his rib cage like a smattering of stars.

"The priests have done what they could," Oren replied. "I wished to honor the prophet, but after what happened to my father . . . truly, I just wanted these bones locked away."

Reed agreed, but Tiern looked displeased, as if she thought him living up to his moniker of "the boy king."

"Is that—?" Oren craned his neck as Tiern drew her bone fragment from the pouch at her belt.

"Yes," Reed said. "It's another piece."

"Will you tell me now what is happening?" Oren asked.

Tiern looked at her sharply, a caution to speak carefully. "Someone," Reed said, "is making monsters with the fragments of bone."

"But why?" Oren asked, aghast. "Are my people at risk?"

"We have no reason to believe so."

"I hoped that once broken, the skull would become only bones," said Oren. "Do you have need of me? To combat this threat?"

"You volunteer your army?" asked Tiern.

"I must. It was my father who created this abomination."

A kingly response, Reed thought, but Tiern only sighed.

"We've no use of your army, King Oren," she said. "But I will take these bones."

Oren's eyes widened. "All of them?"

"They're too dangerous to be kept in the worlds of men."

He looked at Reed.

"In Atropa they'll be kept safe," she said. "In Atropa the prophet can rest, and no longer be the warped weapon that Oreas made of him."

For a moment she feared that Oren would argue. He'd been more than welcoming so far, but he was a king, and kings didn't like watching their treasures be carted away. Not even sinister relics like this one. He looked down, considering, and Tiern's grip moved to her dagger.

Oren looked up, and Reed relaxed. "Very well," he said. "Take the bones, and with my thanks. Roshanak was never meant to be the prophet's keeper."

35.

A PRINCESS'S GLORY

Yngarue didn't like her. No matter what Lyonene tried, how many compliments she paid, or how dutifully she stood in the girl's shadow. She'd even briefly donned the ridiculous red matchmaker's dress, for who could be cruel to a person when their clothing was cruel enough already. But nothing worked. It wasn't all Yngarue's fault; in fact, it wasn't even mostly hers—it was Lyonene and Reed who had made a mess of what should have been a simple mission. Get a pretty, rich girl married. What could be easier?

It wasn't so long ago that Lyonene thought she would be one of the greatest Aristene to wear the silver and white. At her Joining, she'd gone into the cave with the little roan mare and thrust her sword into her chest the moment she reached the chamber. No initiate in history had ever emerged any faster. Now she wondered if she'd turned that sword on herself so quickly so there would be no time to consider her doubts.

As Yngarue and Alsander strolled the small orchard that lay to the east of the castle grounds, Lyonene waited in the shade. She'd dressed modestly, in a plain, woven gown the color of wine. She was trying to be patient, to be quiet and pleasing, to earn the princess's esteem. There was probably no point. Yngarue barely acknowledged her. She was even cold to Alsander, and Lyonene could see him growing frustrated. He wasn't used to a woman who spurned his advances.

But Lyonene didn't mind that part. The courtship was supposed to be fake, so let it remain fake. Alsander was still hers. Her hero, and her husband, even though it couldn't remain so.

She watched Yngarue and Alsander as they walked. She was too far away to hear what they spoke of but close enough to tell they were bored. She could hardly blame them. She was bored as well and let her gaze wander away, until she felt her magic give a curious tug.

Yngarue had dropped her book and Alsander bent to pick it up. As he handed it back to her their hands touched, and the air around Yngarue began to glimmer, expanding around her and Alsander in filaments of golden chains.

There would be glory for those two, were they to join together. Glory for them, and glory for the goddess.

Lyonene's breath caught as she looked at them. There were other princes. Other paths. It didn't have to be this way. It didn't have to be him.

And even if it did, he wouldn't go, Lyonene thought. *He loves me. And only me. He gave up an heir to make me his queen.*

"Prince Alsander." He looked away from Yngarue as Lyonene approached. "The day grows late."

The prince and princess glanced into the sky. The sun remained high overhead. But Yngarue folded her hands before her and nodded.

"Indeed it does," Yngarue said. "And I should return to the castle and see how my mother fares." She gave Alsander a short bow and turned to walk away up the path.

"I was just beginning to charm her," Alsander said after Yngarue was gone. "Why did you stop me? Did you not like it?"

"The only thing I didn't like was how long it took her to be charmed. She must be cold indeed to resist you for so long."

"Not like you," he said, and smiled. "Who can never resist me."

Lyonene scowled, and he laughed and pulled her close.

"You think I would satisfy you now," Lyonene asked, "when your thoughts would wander to the princess?"

"I think only of you, Lyonene. You in this Cassan gown. We must encourage the women of Cerille to adopt this fashion. . . ." Of course in Cerille that fashion would be too warm. Women would pass out during the midday heat. But Alsander only gave thought to how tightly the garment adhered to her shape. He kissed her and pulled her farther into the orchard.

"Prince Alsander."

He and Lyonene froze.

"I waited some distance away and heard sounds," Yngarue said.

"Yngarue," Lyonene said. She untangled herself from Alsander's arms.

"Many have said it odd that your personal guard consisted of all women. And since that guard departed, others have whispered about why the loveliest ones have remained behind."

"Mol is not so lovely," Alsander muttered.

"I do not understand the Aristene," Yngarue said. "Machianthe told me she was sent to make me a glorious marriage. Of course she only said that after I'd caught her kissing one of my suitors"—Alsander coughed to cover a chuckle—"and now you?" She turned to Lyonene. "Did you not say that you were meant for me now?

That you were the next Aristene in service to me?"

"I am."

"Well, it is a very strange service that you provide." Yngarue gathered her skirts and left. For real this time—Lyonene could trace her path all the way back to the castle in a thin golden thread that tethered the princess to Alsander. Lyonene fought the urge to draw her sword and slice right through it.

"Well, that made it worse," Alsander said.

"Do you think King Urdien will send us away?"

"Because his daughter accuses me of tumbling a few maids?"

Lyonene shoved him in the chest. "I am not 'a few maids.' And I will take care of this."

She strode out of the orchard. When Lyonene had looked into the sacred well, the girl had seemed little more than a mouse. But the real Yngarue was surprisingly feisty. Dealing with her would require more tact. More skill. She didn't know how Reed had managed it so well.

She searched the castle for the girl, but could find her nowhere: not in the solar, nor in the fountain garden with her sister and their still-fragile mother, not with Ulli in the great hall playing a game with a blanket around his shoulders. She would certainly not be with the king, who had taken a shine to Mol and had engaged her in a contest of knife throwing. Finally out of other options, Lyonene checked the stable but found only the knowing expression on her Areion's long face.

"We've made a mess of this, haven't we, Strawberry?" she said, but the mare didn't reply. If she had, she would probably say that she regretted ever following Lyonene into that cave, regretted being struck dead as by a bolt of lightning and rebuilt—or whatever happened to a horse to make it an Areion. Lyonene hadn't been conscious for that part. As she stroked the mare's mottled nose, she found herself gazing into Everfall's empty stall, and wishing that Veridian was there to give her advice. The apostate often gave sage advice. Not that Lyonene had ever taken any.

Two figures stormed into the far side of the stable and Lyonene instinctively ducked down behind her horse. It was Yngarue, her gown covered in a charcoal-colored cloak, her chestnut hair hidden beneath a hood. She was accompanied by the handsome young priest, Parmenin, adviser to the king. The priest pulled two long-legged geldings from their stalls and began to saddle them.

Lyonene stepped out from behind her Areion. "Where are the pair of you going in such haste?"

"You!" Yngarue gasped, her voice pitched low. "You will not stop us!"

"Stop you from what? What are you doing, princess?" The girl's cheeks were flushed. She wore boots for riding and at her waist Lyonene glimpsed a belt with a knife in a sheath.

"Aristene." The priest, brown-robed and of the Calumnian Brotherhood, if Lyonene recalled correctly, bowed to her.

"Do all in the court of Cassor know what we are?" Lyonene asked.

"It is none of your concern." Yngarue tried to vault into the saddle, and Lyonene was obliged to grab her by the cloak and plop her back down. "How dare you touch me!" She drew the blade and slashed it through the air, dangerously close to Lyonene's face.

"Stop that," Lyonene said. "And tell me where you are going. I am your Aristene, as the priest said. I will not impede you, if where you go is in service to your glory."

Yngarue's eyes flicked between Lyonene and the horse, measuring her chances of knocking Lyonene aside and getting away. "The princes brought before me are unsatisfactory," she said finally. "So I go to make my own match. With the prince I have wanted to match with from the beginning."

Denros of Erleven. *The girl's first choice will be the wrong one.* Those words flooded into Lyonene's mind just as they had when she gazed into the ripples of the well, but she pushed them aside. She glimpsed a packet of opened letters, tied with a string and tucked into the priest's robes. "Are those his letters? Let me see."

"Parmenin, don't!" Yngarue cried, but the priest quickly handed them over.

"The letters stop just before Reed's arrival," Lyonene said when she'd finished leafing through them.

"I wrote to him of my father's plan to send for suitors," said Yngarue. "He never responded. He was hurt."

Or angry, at seeing his carefully woven web come apart thread by thread. That was what Lyonene's magic said. Her magic tugged away from the letters so hard that she nearly dropped them before handing them back to the priest. What Denros promised was nothing but a scribbled fantasy. A pretty daydream put forth by a spoiled boy whom the bards had told too many romantic tales. *Alsander*, Lyonene's magic said. *Alsander and Cerille is where this woman's glory lies.*

Lyonene clenched her teeth. Was this Kleia Gloria's punishment for Lyonene's betrayal of her oaths? If it was, then the goddess was cruel, and Lyonene had no wish to serve her any longer.

"You mean to ride to Erleven."

"Through the valley passage," Yngarue said. "And on to the capital of Erlengard." She raised her chin, daring Lyonene to stop them. It was easy to see why Reed would want to teach her how to use a blade. She didn't belong in any marriage, glorious or otherwise. She should have been with them, training in the Summer Camp. She should have become one of their sisters.

"I will go with you," Lyonene said. "And in uniting Cassor and Erleven, we will find your glory."

36.

A DARK ROAD

As Reed and Tiern left the city of Roshanak behind, Reed leaned over the side of her saddle to peer down the sheer edge of the cliff path. Silco was more sure-footed on the ascending climb than he'd been on the way down, but the drop was still dizzying to look upon.

"Don't worry, Machianthe. I won't let you fall."

"Forgive me, elder." Reed nudged Silco farther into the center of the trail. "But your words fail to comfort me."

Tiern chuckled. "Yes. I've heard that before."

They'd not remained long with Oren. Just long enough for him to feed them a meal, an invitation that was only accepted so as not to appear rude. Tiern spent the whole of it with the prophet's bones on her lap, one arm coiled around them like a mother snake around a clutch of eggs. In the cave, she'd tied the prophet's musty and rotting rags into an improvised sack, but in the palace Oren had sent for something more secure: a bag of black silk. Tiern had lowered the rag-wrapped bones into it, and the servant tied it tightly closed. Now it lay slung over the pommel of her saddle. So much power in those blackened and broken pieces.

One sliver of bone, Reed thought, *pricked beneath my skin*. That was all it would take. One small, sharp pain, and she would be the instrument by which all battles were ended.

She watched the movement of the bones from the corner of her eye. They shifted with the horse's strides, but sometimes it seemed that the bag also moved by itself. *Why shouldn't we try it? Why shouldn't we use it, when we have it in our grasp?*

"We will open the Veil and return to Atropa as soon as night falls," Tiern said, and Reed tore her gaze away. "Until then we ride. I want distance between us in case the boy king regrets his choice to give up the bones." She turned and saw the look on Reed's face. "What? Is something wrong?"

"No," Reed said. "I was just thinking." Which was true, but she didn't want to tell the elder what she'd been thinking of. She scanned the hills, and her gaze settled on Silco. "Will you never take another Areion?"

The elder looked at her quizzically. "Perhaps. If a beast comes along who is fierce enough. One who is fast, and smart, and stronger than Ferreh's Desert Fire." She nodded to Silco. "I would also take one like him," she said, and both Reed's and the colt's ears pricked. None of the Aristene looked at Silco. Few anywhere did, once they noticed his limp. "You know what I thought of the idea of a permanently lame Areion. But he has since changed my mind. The sight of him charging with a foot like that is glorious. Monstrous. He is a mount for an Aristene who would strike fear into all who look upon her."

"That sounds like you," Reed said. "And I'm not about to trade him."

"Ha! That does sound like me. And it will sound like you as well. Someday." The elder turned her eye to Reed, and Reed felt her magic glimmer, swelling with pride. "I see what you could be,

Machianthe. As elders we have only one gift to give in our blood. One. I thought Ferreh was mad to give hers to an initiate."

"Why did you try to give yours to Veridian?" Reed asked.

The elder's face soured. "Veridian. She is the worst apostate I have ever seen. When will she admit that she never really left us? When will she admit that all of her running, all of her moaning . . . has been nothing but the passing of a tantrum."

"A tantrum?"

"Yes. Directed at me because I dared to give her the gift of the glorious death. I thought her worthy of that elevation. She was to be our great protector. Our guardian. And now you, Machianthe, must do it in her stead." Tiern bared her teeth. "She should have been killed. We should have killed her, when she turned from us."

"But you wouldn't have really killed her," said Reed. "Didn't you love her?"

Tiern's nostrils flared. The teeth of the order was built small like Veridian was, and wild like she was, her hair of many colors whipping in the wind. Perhaps that was why Tiern had chosen her to be a Glorious Death in the first place. When she'd looked at Veridian, she'd seen herself. "Do you know what my gift is, Machianthe?" Tiern asked. "It is to take in the essence of the heroes I serve. I carry each within myself, every new hero giving more strength, more speed, more intelligence—a new streak of color in my braids."

"I have heard that, yes."

"And have you heard that it happens when I eat their flesh?"

Reed cleared her throat uncomfortably. "The order loves a good rumor."

Tiern slipped her fingers into the pouch at her belt. She took out the shard of bone.

"You didn't put that one with the rest?" Reed asked.

"No." Tiern rubbed the shard with her thumb. "This one no longer belongs with the others." They rode, farther and farther from Roshanak toward the sunset.

"You said that I tried to give my blood to Veridian." Tiern flipped the bit of bone between her fingers. "But I did not only try. I gave it."

"What do you mean?"

"I mean that you are not the only Glorious Death of the order," Tiern said. "Veridian is one also. She drank the blood. It was only afterward that she realized she did not have the stomach for it."

Lyonene rode hard and fast through the valley passage with Yngarue clinging to the back of her saddle. In the interest of speed they had both ridden on Strawberry; even with two riders the Areion could gallop all day and into the night without tiring. Parmenin the priest she put upon Mol's horse, Verger, and for the first leg of the journey she was constantly looking back, to make sure Mol's white beast hadn't turned back to report them to his rider. She'd have much preferred to borrow Everfall, but Veridian hadn't returned him to the stable.

However, Veridian and Everfall were there now. Twice Lyonene had glimpsed them behind them in the trees: a flash of the red horse and his apostate rider. It could be no one else. No other horse could have kept a similar pace.

At first she'd been annoyed, but the closer they drew to Erleven the more the apostate's presence became a comfort.

"May we slow?"

Lyonene drew back on Strawberry's reins. Yngarue had said nothing for the entire journey, Lyonene thought out of nerves or resentment, but now she realized it was probably due to the jarring pace. As Strawberry came to a hopping stop, Yngarue gasped into Lyonene's ear, and Lyonene had to grab her arm to keep her from toppling to the road.

"Forgive me," said Yngarue shakily. She slid from Strawberry's haunches and massaged her jolted limbs. "I held on for as long as I could."

"Don't apologize. I should have considered how taxing the journey would be for one not of the order." She watched Verger come to a halt beside them with the priest slumped in the saddle. When Parmenin slid to the ground, he cried out like both his legs had been broken.

"We've been too long on gentle palfreys," Parmenin said, rubbing his backside through his robes. "When I was a boy, I used to ride all day through rough terrain."

"And with me on the castle grounds," Yngarue said, bending to support him. "Teaching me to jump my pony."

Parmenin smiled. "You were a brave girl, even then." He patted Yngarue's hand and stood taller, stretching his back. He must have been almost the same age as Yngarue was now when they met. A young priest, in a new country. Lyonene saw the way he looked at her, almost the way a parent looks at a well-grown child. He had been planning for this betrothal since before he'd arrived.

"May we slow?" Yngarue asked. "I've no wish to meet Prince

Denros stooped over like a crone."

The light in the valley had begun to darken, and Lyonene looked back the way they'd come, searching for signs of Veridian. She sensed that the apostate was not too far away.

"We may slow, for a while," Lyonene conceded.

She reached into Strawberry's saddlebag and leaned down to hand Yngarue a chunk of bread and a long drink from her waterskin.

Yngarue was pale as she and Parmenin passed the water back and forth, taking large, panting gulps. There was a bit of dirt on her cheek, perhaps from being struck by a branch, and her braid of chestnut hair had started to come undone. She looked up at Lyonene with a fair bit of envy.

"How do you yet look so well?"

"I always look well," Lyonene said. She scanned the landscape. Even in the cover of dark the valley made for treacherous travel. The hills on both sides were too steep to provide routes of escape, but offered a clear shot to anyone posted above. Their only cover was a sparse border of trees on either side of the road.

"If we are to walk, we keep to the trees," Lyonene said. She turned Strawberry from the road. Parmenin took Verger by the reins, though the horse made a point of walking a few strides ahead.

"When I meet Denros I'll be in such a state," Yngarue said, and gave a laugh. She turned to Parmenin. "Do you think I will disappoint him?"

"Impossible," Parmenin replied. "The prince has been thoroughly bewitched."

"Perhaps he will think me truly a witch and will call for my head the moment he sees me."

"Is that what you do to witches here?" Lyonene asked, her eyes on the hills.

Yngarue looked up. "Is it not the same in your country?"

"There are no witches in Atropa, unless you count the Outfitter. But those who like to scream about witchcraft would say that every member of my order was one."

Walking at her horse's side, Parmenin huffed. "It has long seemed to me that 'witch' is merely a word men use for a woman whose power they fear." Lyonene and Yngarue traded amused looks.

"But you do not fear a woman's power, do you, priest?" Lyonene asked.

"I do not," he declared. Then he glanced at her. "Or I fear it in just the right amount."

Lyonene smiled. "When I was a girl," she said quietly, "long before I was sent to my convent and long before I knew anything of the Aristene, I saw a woman taken away in a cart. I asked my nurse why, and she said that the woman was a witch, and was being taken to be buried alive."

"Were you frightened?" Yngarue asked.

"I don't remember. But if I was, it wasn't the witch I was afraid of."

Yngarue paused thoughtfully. "But now you are afraid of nothing. You are an Aristene who can fight for her own safety, and controls her own destiny. Who commands great men as easily as she commands this horse." Strawberry stretched her head down for a bite of grass, and perhaps to cover her snort.

"That is a nice thought, Princess Yngarue," Lyonene said. "But I think you know little of my order. And little of my horse. Are you ready to ride again? We may go a little slower."

"Perhaps a lot slower?" Parmenin suggested. He tried to get back into Verger's saddle, hopping and wincing until Verger cast Lyonene an irritated glance and bowed down to make it easier for him.

"A little slower," Lyonene replied with a smile. She went back over the maps of Cassor and Erleven inside her mind. It was not much farther to the capital city of Erlengard.

They left the trees and entered a broad, grassy meadow, and Lyonene halted the horses. In the distance, the nighttime silhouette of Erlengard was lit by torches. On its other side, the sprawling capital of Erleven was a seaport, but coming from Cassor they approached what had the appearance of a hill fort, a city of stone protected by a high stone wall. Lyonene glimpsed the shapes of archers stationed atop it, bathed in torchlight. She felt Yngarue's fingers tighten about her waist. All that remained of their journey was to cross the wide river bridge and approach the gate.

"I will ride ahead," Parmenin said, putting heels to Verger. The horse jumped ahead and gave a buck of warning. "Sorry, friend, sorry," Parmenin said, and patted him. He looked back at Yngarue. "I will tell them you have come. A princess must be announced and presented, as your father always says."

"You must be happy to be returning home," said Yngarue.

Parmenin smiled. "Cassor is my home. But Erlengard is where I was born, and I have long wished to see those two places at peace. I will not be long! I will send you an escort!" He waved to them as he and Verger cantered away, and Lyonene could not help laughing as she listened to him cry "ouch, ouch" every time his rear bounced in the saddle.

Lyonene turned to Yngarue in the silence. As her Aristene, she should offer some advice. Provide some words of comfort or courage. But she didn't know what to say. She reached for her magic but it was no help; it didn't even want to be there. She shifted in the saddle, and Strawberry gave a low, motherly nicker.

"Are you afraid?" Lyonene asked.

"Afraid?"

"Well, letters are one thing, but being face-to-face with a man is another. Perhaps you're afraid that his letters were all in jest. Or that you'll arrive and find that he's not at all how he described himself, and is a toad."

"A what?" Yngarue gasped.

"A warty toad. I know you've been presented with Alsander and Hestion, but I assure you, not all princes look like they do."

Yngarue laughed, surprised by Lyonene's levity. "When I first saw you I thought you seemed cruel. A beauty who never smiled."

"I could have said the same to you." She studied Yngarue in the moonlight. "Though perhaps not now."

The princess's hands flew to her cheeks.

"Here." Lyonene lowered the girl's hood and, with hands that required no enhancements from the Outfitter, rewove Yngarue's hair into a crown of braids, with sections left long and loose and wavy down her back. She wiped the smudge of dirt from her face, and plucked twigs from the fabric of her cloak.

"You and Machianthe," Yngarue asked. "Are you friends?"

"Best friends," Lyonene said as she continued to dust the princess off. "We grew up together. Became Aristene together."

"You seem so different. She is strong and awkward, like an—"

"Like an ox?" Lyonene suggested.

"Yes, rather." Yngarue peered at the edge of Lyonene's white cape, showing beneath the dark cloak. "Even your armor is different."

Lyonene pushed her cape back to show hers—silver fitted over brown leather. "Every Aristene has their own variations, our own flourishes. It is hard to see in the dark, but my arm guards are inlaid with gold etching—" She tried to catch them in the light. "Our elder Tiern has armor made to house a second sword of ancient bronze."

"Ancient bronze?" Yngarue's eyes widened. Tiern's bronze sword was sheathed beside her new one of superior steel, and for the entire battle of Rhonassus, Lyonene hadn't seen her use it. The sword had carried over from a different time, and perhaps one day would disappear forever. The elder would call for her armor, and the sword would simply be gone.

"What of the ragged one? The archer." Yngarue asked.

"Veridian is no longer one of us. I don't even know if she can call her armor anymore." But Lyonene would have loved to see it. The archer's intricate silver bracers must have been beautiful.

Yngarue looked past her to the city, lit with torches. "I am nervous," she admitted. "And I do wish Machianthe was here to witness this. Even if she did turn out to be something of a terrible matchmaker."

Lyonene chuckled. "She was, wasn't she? But it wasn't her fault. She was never supposed to be here. It was I who was summoned to your side. And then I, too, failed you, by bringing you another prince you never could have had."

"I might have," Yngarue said. "If my heart had not already been pledged to Denros."

"No," Lyonene said. "You could never have married Alsander. Because he is already wed to me." She looked away from the princess's eyes. "It wasn't supposed to happen. I am sorry, Yngarue."

For a moment, Yngarue was silent. Then she touched Lyonene's hand. "You do not need to be sorry. We cannot control who we love."

"I thought I could. How many times did I tell Reed not to lose herself over one hero? How many times did I say to Gretchen, 'Don't lose your head; he's just a boy!'" She sighed. "In my order we are forbidden from marrying."

"So you wed in secret," Yngarue said quietly. "How romantic."

"It cannot last."

Beneath them, Strawberry snorted, and pricked her ears. Five riders approached on horseback. Two carried torches, and Lyonene noted that, though their garb was less fine than that of the guards of Cassor, they were better armed.

Lyonene tensed. As they rode closer, her magic sensed arrows being put to bows.

"Yngarue," she said calmly. "Hold tight to me."

"We've come with the priest Parmenin," Lyonene said as the guards neared them. "Has he not announced us?"

"You are Princess Yngarue of Cassor?" the head guard asked.

"I am Yngarue, of the house of Ythyll," Yngarue said. She removed her glove and showed them her signet ring. Most of the guards relaxed. But the one in the lead kept his eyes on Lyonene, studying the sword strapped to her saddle and the hilt sticking up from her back.

"So much trouble for two ladies," Lyonene said.

"Unexpected for ladies to arrive so late," the guard replied. "Take them inside," he ordered. "Take them to the prince."

37.

BETROTHAL

The sounds of Strawberry's hooves against the stones were sharp as four of the gate guards escorted them along the road inside the city. The road was walled on either side by barriers twice the height of a man. Every ten steps, an archer peered down at them, and the arrows they kept trained on Lyonene felt like biting insects alighting on her skin.

"I wish I were riding in front of you," Yngarue said, and Lyonene felt the princess's hands trembling on her waist. "So the prince wouldn't see your beautiful face first!"

Lyonene patted her hand as they approached a low stone archway. She nodded to Parmenin when she saw him standing just inside.

"There is Parmenin," Yngarue whispered excitedly. "But where is Denros?"

The guards took hold of Strawberry's bridle and Lyonene and the princess dismounted. As they walked to the archway, Lyonene thought she saw a shape in the shadows, and caught a flash of what could have been a golden circlet upon his head. Until now she'd been too afraid to call her magic, afraid it would admonish her for going against its guidance. But she must know if there was any glory to be found in this match, whether she could wrench free the golden threads that bound Yngarue to Alsander and wind them instead around Prince Denros.

Lyonene took a deep breath and sent it forth. The golden glimmer rose in a gentle current, stretching toward Denros and Parmenin, before it snapped back like a scream in Lyonene's blood.

"Yngarue," she said, too late.

They stepped inside the archway and Yngarue cried out as she was dragged away by armed soldiers. Men grabbed on to Lyonene and though she was calm and didn't fight, there were enough men on her to create a pile. She was driven to her knees and heard Strawberry whinny as they stretched Lyonene's arms out to either side and pointed a spear at her throat.

"Wait, Prince Denros!" Parmenin held up his arms. He stepped between Lyonene and the prince. "This woman is part of the princess's escort!"

Denros stepped out of the shadows. He was no toad but slender and well-muscled, with brown hair that fell softly around his face and dark, hawklike eyes that fixed upon Yngarue.

"Yngarue?" he asked. "Is it you?"

"It is me, Denros." The color had returned to Yngarue's cheeks from the shock of the ambush and Denros was clearly pleased by the sight of her. He touched her hair, nearly the same shade as his. "Tell your soldiers to release my companion. She is my escort, only armed because we were on the road."

"Of course," he said. "Release this woman into the custody of the brotherhood."

"The brotherhood?" Parmenin asked, confused.

More men entered the small space, and these were tall and hulking, larger than the prince. Their robes were dull and gray.

Shabby. And there was something wrong with the way they moved.

Lyonene's skin went cold. These were the priests the elders had warned of. The shabby-cloaked brothers who created monsters. She hadn't expected that they would be monstrous themselves.

"This is not necessary," Yngarue objected. She looked at Parmenin. "Parmenin?"

"It will be all right, princess," he said. But he was staring at the priests with unease. "Lady Lyonene," he said, "this is not my brotherhood."

"I know," Lyonene said. She summoned her magic and felt how it recoiled, how it wriggled against her hold like a caught snake. "I know who they are."

The soldiers attacked. The unfortunate gate guards died first, as Lyonene drew her sword and swung, taking care of both in one arc.

"Parmenin," Lyonene shouted. "Protect Yngarue!"

He tried, grappling with Denros as the prince held Yngarue by the arm. Fueled by Yngarue's cries, Lyonene cut and dodged, stepping deftly over bodies. She fought coolly and kept her movements small in the confined space. She needed only to get to Yngarue and Parmenin. Strawberry would take a few arrows from the archers as they fled, but a few arrows wouldn't even slow her.

One of the gray-robed priests moved into her path and up close she saw that his face was long and warped. Her magic wavered, and for a moment she was struck through with fear, that it would be as it had been against Oreas and her armor would disappear. But though they were similar, they were not the same. Her magic didn't like them. But it didn't leave her. They could be beaten.

The priest swung his fist, faster than she'd anticipated, and she felt the full, rattling impact as it struck her jaw. She tasted blood. She looked at Prince Denros and saw that he was smiling.

Lyonene never fought in anger, or in panic. But looking into Denros's smug face, Lyonene felt rage.

With a roar she kicked the priest in the chest, and the painful reverberation in her leg only made her angrier. How dare they make her feel weak? She was no initiate; she was an Aristene. Sword in two hands, she carved a path through arms and knees and the thick trunks of bodies. Her blade got stuck, and she had to shove the dying off the end of her sword with her foot before she could face the next. But though their deaths were satisfying, Prince Denros had called for reinforcements. More soldiers. More gray cloaks. One of them hit her square and Lyonene's vision swam.

Large hands grasped her arms. Their touch disgusted her, but she couldn't jerk loose. She heard Strawberry's whinnies, and the stomps of her hooves. Lyonene's head lolled toward Yngarue, and her hero princess's eyes were wide with disbelief.

"What have you done to these men?" Parmenin demanded of Denros. "Are they even men anymore?"

"They are more than men. More than you. Take the bitch," Denros said to his men. "Silence the priest."

Parmenin flailed as he tried to fight. They dragged Lyonene past the prince, and she tried to curl her lip in defiance. But she couldn't be sure that Denros had seen it. Her lion's mane of hair, dripping blood, had fallen across her face.

Yngarue stood frozen amid the fallen bodies. Lyonene was gone. Parmenin had been taken. She watched as a puddle of blood expanded toward her feet and drew up her skirts so it wouldn't stain them.

"Yngarue."

She began to tremble. Denros, her prince, the young man she'd loved through letters, still held fast to her arm. *Run*, her mind screamed. But run to where? She was far from Cassor and she was alone in an unfamiliar city, surrounded by bodies scattered on the ground.

"Yngarue," Denros said. "Look at me."

But she didn't want to. "You didn't need to attack us," she whispered. And Denros laughed. He actually laughed, low and soft and wicked, so close she could feel the movement of his breath on her skin.

"Yngarue, my love," he said, his voice dripping with condescension. "It wasn't you we attacked. It was the one you brought with you."

"But why? Lyonene has done no wrong—"

Denros ignored her and touched her cheek, his movements slow as one trying to stroke a cat with an arched back. "You are frightened. Do not be frightened."

"What will you do to her?"

"Do not worry about that."

She saw Lyonene's roan mare being led out of the tunnel. She didn't want to go, and tugged backward until the man leading her lashed her on the neck with her reins.

"Don't! Stop that!" Yngarue tried to twist out of Denros's embrace. He jerked her back to face him. Hard enough that her breath caught in her throat.

Denros's eyes were brown and handsome but not warm. He

didn't seem nervous or shy, or yearning after all their years spent exchanging letters. He didn't even seem happy to see her. His gaze traveled lower, to her lips and then lower than that, to her breasts beneath the cloak. It filled her with revulsion that he could think such thoughts when they stood surrounded by death.

"Who are you?" she asked. "Where is the man who wrote me those letters?"

"I am he." Denros smoothed her hair with a rough hand. "You and I will wed, and we will rule over Cassor and Erleven together."

"My sister, Wyrnnigrid, will rule over Cassor. And I wish to return there now, to my father the king."

"Yngarue." Denros pulled her closer. "You cannot leave. I've waited a long time for my betrothed."

"Stop!" She tried to push him away and he only held her tighter.

"What did you think would happen when you rode to me?" he asked, and lowered his head to kiss her.

Yngarue moaned. It wasn't like she'd imagined, nor like what he'd written in his letters. There was no softness, no nervous smiles, only the cold hard stone against her back and his lips, forcing hers to open.

"Wait!" She twisted away.

"Do not struggle, my love." He lowered his head to kiss her neck, and bit into her shoulder not too gently.

"Denros! Stop," Yngarue shouted. But he paid no attention.

Yngarue didn't think. She simply did what Machianthe had taught her. She drew the knife from her belt and sliced the back of his hand.

Denros shoved her away. He stared in disbelief at the cut, and then at Yngarue as she pointed the tip of the blade at him.

"You've been corrupted," he spat. "You are a woman, Yngarue. Who made you think you could wield a weapon?"

"One like Lady Lyonene," Yngarue said. "So stay away." She stepped sideways and adjusted her grip. She didn't know what she meant to do. She didn't want to kill him. She'd only wanted him to listen. He bared his teeth and darted forward, fast as a snake.

"You disappoint me, Yngarue," he growled, catching hold of her wrist and twisting it. "Give me the knife!"

But she held on. If he got the dagger, he would hurt her with it. She could almost feel the blade dragging across her throat.

"Such a disappointment," he said as he ground the bones of her wrist together, and through the pain she began to grow angry.

"You are not the only one who is disappointed," she gasped. She drew her arm back and struck him across the face.

Denros let go of her and doubled over. Yngarue blinked. That slap couldn't have hurt him much!

She stepped back as Denros clutched his arm and then his chest. The flesh of his face had turned red. Her lips parted as a blood vessel burst in the white of his eye.

"You—" he groaned, and tried to grab her, clawing the air with hooked fingers. Then he fell to the ground and began to convulse.

Yngarue didn't know what was happening to him but she wasn't about to waste her good fortune. She looked out of the tunnel's arch and saw Lyonene's mare, still fighting the soldiers who were trying to lead her away. Yngarue glanced back at Denros upon the stones.

"Help!" she shouted. "Someone help the prince!"

The soldiers came running, and as they attended to Denros she snuck past, sprinting along the darkened road until she came to Lyonene's horse and the lone man still holding her.

"What's happened?" he asked.

Her response was her knife thrust into his throat.

There was so much blood. She hadn't been ready for that, and let go of the dagger, leaving it in the man's neck as she grabbed on to Strawberry and struggled into the saddle. "Please go," she cried, and the mare took off down the road, without needing so much as a touch of Yngarue's heels.

38.

GRAY ROBES

Veridian knew there was something wrong the moment the gate guards led them into the covered archway. She'd been watching since Lyonene rode out of Cassor with the priest and the princess, she and Everfall galloping steadily behind them, keeping to the trees and mostly out of sight as it was obvious the group didn't want to be followed. She gave Lyonene and her Areion a glance of them, now and again, so they'd know they weren't alone. And as a warning against doing something stupid.

Veridian should have known better. She should have asked Everfall to outrun Strawberry and Verger and corralled them all back to Cassor the moment she saw them leave.

"Don't follow them in there," she'd said as she watched Lyonene and Yngarue approach the tunnel. But of course, Lyonene did.

There was no cover between the edge of the forest and the walled roads of Erlengard. Veridian had to track north, following the trees until she could slip into the shadow of the hill. By the time she made it back, slinking along the base of the wall, the fight was already over.

"Help! Someone help the prince!"

That was the Cassan princess's voice. Veridian heard running feet, and heard Yngarue speak to someone. Then came the distinct sound of a man being stabbed in the throat.

"Balls and ass," Veridian muttered as hoofbeats rang out against the stones. She jumped onto Everfall's saddle and used his back to boost off, landing silently atop the wall. Below, on the road, the princess was fleeing back to the gate, and every archer between here and there had arrows trained on her. Strawberry was fast, but already the little mare was riddled with shots, arrow shafts sticking up out of her haunches.

Veridian grabbed the nearest archer and turned him, using his already nocked arrow to kill the man posted on the opposite side of the road. Then she drew her sword and skewered him through the back. The poor fellow had barely known what happened. She took up his bow and fired shots—counting in her head, one, two, three; four, five, six—and as many archers dropped dead along the top of the wall, slumped over their bows, or toppled forward to fall over the side.

One fell into Yngarue's path, and she looked over her shoulder, wild-eyed. She wasn't riding well, clinging to the saddle, her hair streaming behind her in the moonlight. But she was going to make it. Her path was clear now all the way to the gate.

Veridian dropped off the wall onto Everfall's back. He grunted.

"I am *not* too heavy," she said. She touched her heels to his sides. Ahead, Yngarue and Strawberry burst through the gate and galloped through the meadow, the mare taking such long strides that she stretched out nearly to the ground. Veridian and Everfall followed, Veridian turned in her saddle to look back at Erlengard with bow at the ready until they were out of range.

"Yngarue!" She called twice more, but it was Strawberry who

actually heard her, and slowed to a canter even as Yngarue tried to get her to run on.

"You," Yngarue gasped as the mare trotted in a circle to let Everfall catch up. "Aristene Veridian!"

"Not quite," Veridian replied. "But close enough." They'd reached the cover of the forest, and the branches cut through the moonlight. Veridian looked over the roan mare's injuries. Two arrows stuck out of her rump and another had broken off in her right shoulder. The mottled reddish white of her coat was stained and dripping with sweat and blood. Veridian reached a hand out to stroke her steaming neck, and the sweet little horse nickered.

Yngarue made a sad sound at the sight of the arrows. "I only thought to run. Will she live?"

"She'll live. More than that: she'll recover. An Areion is tough." Veridian looked at the princess. "What about you? Are you hurt?"

"No. Only frightened. And angry." Yngarue's voice trembled, and the breath came fast from her lungs. But even in the moonlight her eyes were bright and fierce. Veridian's dormant Aristene magic began to prickle her skin like an itch, like hot sweat dripped down the back of leather armor. Rarely did it rise anymore to sniff for glory. But tonight she'd woken it with the excitement of the pursuit, and the arrows loosed effortlessly in the dark. She didn't like to fight. She didn't like to fire arrows into a man's back, and feel how easy it was, that even now the arrows seemed connected to her eye, and to her thoughts, as if she couldn't take a wrong shot.

She didn't like to remind her magic, or herself, of what she was.

She turned Everfall back toward Erlengard.

"Wait!" Yngarue cried. "Where are you going?"

"To get Lyonene. How many were there, that she was overpowered?"

Yngarue paused in the dark. "Five to start . . . perhaps ten to follow."

That was strange. Veridian would have thought she could handle that many.

"Wait here for us," she told the princess. "You'll be safe until we return."

"No!" Yngarue rode Strawberry into Veridian's path. "You can't."

"Don't be afraid. I've broken initiates out of worse."

"I mean you can't. There was something wrong with those men. Denros called them priests, but . . . Parmenin asked Denros what he'd done to them. He said they were not of his brotherhood."

Veridian stared at the shape of Erlengard in the dark, the fortress upon the hill, the gray stone lit by torches. For the first time in many years, she asked her magic to rise, and to travel across the fields to slide into the city like snakes. It broke apart long before it got there.

The priests the Aristene feared were in Erlengard. And now they had Lyonene.

"Balls," Veridian growled quietly. "And ass."

She dismounted, and dragged Yngarue out of the saddle.

"What are you doing?" Yngarue cried, slapping at her.

"Trading horses. Strawberry is too hurt to travel quickly, and besides, she should come with me, to the healers."

"The healers?" Yngarue asked. Veridian boosted her onto Everfall's back.

"Can you make it to Cassor?"

Yngarue took up the reins and nodded.

"Ride fast." Veridian pulled the big red gelding's head to her and gave him a squeeze. "He won't tire. He can carry you straight through. Just don't fall off." Yngarue leaned forward, grabbing a handful of mane as the horse bolted. Veridian and Strawberry watched them go until they could no longer hear the sound of hoofbeats.

Veridian turned to face the darkest part of the forest. She wrapped her fist around Strawberry's reins and raised one finger, swirling it, shyly at first.

"Now let's see if this bitch will still let me in." She whispered the words, just once, and the Veil yawned open. Too fast, in her opinion, as if it had been waiting all this time. She and the horse traded a look. Veridian took a deep breath, and they stepped inside.

The warped priests set Lyonene in a large rectangular hall. It was shadowy and the firelight was low, but she saw tapestries on the walls, and the heads of animals. Before the hearth were rugs of fur and woven cloth, though her knees rested on bare stone. An ornately carved throne sat to one side, empty, as the king, Medes of Erleven—or who she judged to be him by his crown and pin of gold—stood before the fire with a priest.

This priest was not malformed like the ones who had brought her. He was simply a man, in robes of a similar cut as Parmenin's, except gray and ragged. Lyonene thought they looked purposely ragged, the kind of attire worn by someone for whom poverty and simplicity were performative. She was further convinced of it when she saw his silver signet ring, and the chain of gold that held a jewel-encrusted medallion hung around his neck.

"Where do you get all these lovely gray cloaks?" Lyonene asked. There were far more men inside than the ones who had brought her, hulking shapes lined against the walls, each wearing a swath of torn gray fabric.

She shifted to make room for Parmenin as he was dropped onto the floor beside her. "Lady Lyonene, are you all right?"

"As all right as you are. You said these were not of your brotherhood. Do you know whose brotherhood they are of, then?"

Parmenin studied them. Some of the warped ones wore the robes of priests while others the armor of soldiers. He stared hard at the elder priest as he spoke with the king. "I do not. It has been many years since I have returned here. Things have changed."

Indeed, Lyonene thought. The man guarding her on her right had bulbous, bulging eyes. The one to her left, elongated hands. She sensed that their strength was linked to the bones of the prophet, but these soldiers weren't monsters. They were simply warped. Increased in size.

"I know him," Parmenin said.

"Who?"

He gestured to the man with bulging eyes shot through with blood. "That is Clafin. He was not long ago in Cassor. I sent him away as punishment, but I did not realize I was sending him to this."

The elder priest stepped away from King Medes and came to stand before them. There were streaks of white in his hair and lines at the corners of his eyes, which betrayed no emotion as he studied Lyonene upon the floor.

"This is a fine pack of monsters you have here," she said. "Did you make them yourself?"

"These warriors are my brothers," the old priest replied.

"And are there pieces of the prophet in all of these brothers?" Lyonene asked. She didn't really expect him to answer, but he shook his head.

"The sacred beasts who carry the bones are far more fearsome than these."

More fearsome than these, Lyonene thought as she looked around at them. The idea of that was . . . unpleasant. "But how did you create them then? If not with the bones?"

"In time," the priest replied, "you will find out."

Parmenin narrowed his eyes. "I do not know you. That medallion, it is not of the god Caloxiornis."

The priest lifted the flat gold pendant. "This honors the Adonumrian. And I am his priest, Nestor." He inclined his head, civilized, as if they exchanged pleasantries over a cup of wine.

"Adonumrian," Lyonene repeated. "Never heard of him."

"He who walks in shadow has no wish to be heard of by the likes of you."

"Then he's failed. For the likes of me know very well what his priests are up to."

Parmenin glanced at her and lowered his head.

"I wish you would be silent," he whispered.

"Why?" Lyonene whispered back. "They're going to kill us anyway."

King Medes walked to them and gestured to Lyonene.

"Take off her cloak."

She looked up. The king gave the order, but it wasn't carried out until Nestor nodded his consent. It didn't take a scholar to see that the authority of the king of Erleven hung by a thread. It was the Adonumrian priests who ruled here now.

The guards tore the drab cloak from her shoulders, and Lyonene knelt in her white cape and armor, streaked with blood both her own and not.

"This is it," asked the king. "This is the one you fear?"

"She is but one of many," Nestor replied.

"She's barely more than a child."

"Don't be fooled, great king. That is what she was made for. Tricks and deception. Thinking herself so high that she may mold the destinies of men."

"The women of my order are servants," Lyonene said quietly. "I traveled here tonight to bring Prince Denros his bride when these soldiers attacked me without provocation."

"A bride?"

"Yngarue, of the house of Ythyll. The second-born princess of Cassor."

For a moment the king simply stared.

"You bring me a daughter of Cassor," he said, "and expect me not to cut her throat?" He turned to Nestor. "This is what you require my army for? This girl is your great enemy?"

The priest stared at Lyonene. "They are an order of vipers," he muttered, almost to himself. "In thrall to a vile, false goddess. These . . . *women* . . . wind themselves into the hearts of men. They corrupt the mind." He grabbed her jaw with trembling fingers and Lyonene grimaced with revulsion. Nestor's lip curled as though he was similarly repulsed. "You think yourselves so high that you may decide the paths of your betters."

"Through our service our heroes ascend to glory. It is their choice."

He squeezed. "And you have never used the wiles between your legs to twist a man to your will?"

"Only once," Lyonene said. "It worked so well I haven't needed to do it again." The priest shoved her backward. "This Adonumrian," she pressed. "Pray to him. Ask him for the wisdom to turn away from this madness. You can't pick a fight with the goddess of glory. Many before you have tried."

"But none but we have tried and succeeded. Long ago, when the outsider goddess came to lay waste to men, the forefathers of my order stormed the pale city. They assailed it with rock and arrow and drove it into hiding, where they hoped it would wither and perish. But instead you return, rising from the earth like swarms of cicada."

Lyonene leaned forward.

"You were the ones who attacked Atropa in the ancient days." She'd seen the scars of arrows in the stone of the Citadel, and knew the Citadel had been built to be a fortress. But when she'd imagined the threat that forced Kleia Gloria to sweep it away behind the safety of the Veil— "I thought you'd be taller."

The elder priest gripped her by the throat.

"Stop!" Parmenin cried. "Do not touch her!"

Nestor cast him a withering glance, but he released his grip. "She has bewitched your mind, brother. Her kind is an invasion."

Lyonene couldn't help but scoff. They were mad, these priests. Her kind was an invasion? She would have liked to tell them that she'd been born in the northern forests of Bevellet, in a city not so different from the hill fort of Erlengard. But it would have been wasted breath.

"Show us how to reach the pale city, witch."

"Gladly." Lyonene glanced at the soldiers who held her. "You'll have to release my arms." The elder priest nodded to them and they let go. Lyonene rubbed her wrists. She took a deep breath and extended her fingers to spin them in a lazy circle, whispering the sacred words, too quietly to be heard and deciphered. The soldiers shrank back as the mouth of the Veil swirled open, large enough to swallow them whole. "Step through," Lyonene said, nodding invitingly.

Of course as soon as they did she would let the gateway snap shut, and they would tumble through the darkness, to be driven mad and die with the sounds of their own screams in their ears and their own clammy skin smothering them like a soaked blanket.

Nestor edged forward. "To see it, open before us . . ." He stretched out his hand, then drew it back as if burned. "Pure darkness. Can it be held open?"

Not without me, Lyonene thought. But as Nestor opened his palms to the Veil she felt her magic lurch, and apprehension spiked through her. These priests possessed great magic. They had tracked the movements of the Aristene across the world. They had known where to find their heroes. She stopped her chant and lowered her hand. The Veil vanished like fog breaking apart in a valley.

Nestor spun, his face furious, but he had no time to yell at her as Erleven soldiers raced into the throne room.

"King Medes! Your son! Prince Denros has been injured!"

Lyonene and Parmenin twisted their heads as the prince was carried past upon the soldiers' shoulders. They set him before the fire upon the soft rug of white fur.

Lyonene cocked her head curiously as Prince Denros writhed, his handsome features contorted by pain. Through the slits of his eyelids his eyes were red as blood, and every vein in his face and neck seemed poised to burst from his skin. She saw no mortal wounds, and the fur beneath him remained white as he convulsed. The only mark on him was a cut on his hand.

Her mind traveled back to the chamber of the Outfitter, when the mystic had enchanted Reed with the abilities she would need in Cassor. She had sewn talents into her fingers and adorned her in the ridiculous red dress. And before they had gone, the Outfitter had opened one more box. Inside was a knife with a poisoned edge.

King Medes moaned as he bent over his son.

"Who did this to him?"

"It was the princess, sire," one of the soldiers replied. "Yngarue of Cassor. She cut him and left him to die. When we came to see what had happened, she killed one of the guards and escaped on the abomination's horse."

Lyonene leaned back and closed her eyes, imagining Yngarue and Strawberry galloping out of Erlengard. She turned to Parmenin and they smiled at each other.

"What have you done to him!" The king struck Lyonene across the face.

"Ow," she said, though it hadn't hurt. "Not me! Didn't you hear? Yngarue!"

Medes's lips twisted in fury. He turned instead to Parmenin and kicked him in the gut until he vomited.

"All right, stop!" Lyonene yelled. "There's no need to hurt

Parmenin. It's poison. There's nothing we can do about it."

Medes turned wild eyes on Nestor.

"Can you save him?"

"It will take much," Nestor said. His voice was grave but his eyes were not. They glittered.

"I'll give you anything Erleven has to give." Medes removed the gold pin from his shoulder and pressed it into the priest's hand. "Save my son and it is yours."

"Even your army? Even your soldiers?"

"I wouldn't," Lyonene cautioned, and received another strike to the face.

"Do it," Medes commanded. "Please."

Nestor knelt beside Denros as he gasped for air. He spoke words in a language Lyonene didn't know and moved his hands over the young man's body. Whatever he meant to do, he'd best be quick. Lyonene knew the gasps of the dying when she saw them.

"Rise, Prince Denros. Rise with the light of Adonumrian, the gray-robed god, he who walks in shadow. Rise by his grace and by the bones of the uniter—" He reached into his own gray robes and pulled out a dagger.

Lyonene felt her magic shudder. The dagger was made from the jaw of the Scylloi Prophet, the teeth polished bright white and the bone darkened and sharpened to a razor's edge. This was how they'd made the warped men around her. By cutting into their flesh with the prophet's jaw.

Nestor used the bone-blade to slice deep into Denros's hand. He carved away the flesh around the shallow wound that Yngarue had made. But the prince continued to gasp, the time between each breath longer than the last.

"It's not enough," Nestor said after a moment. "The poison has gone too far."

"You said you could save him," Medes said, anguished.

Nestor looked at the king. "I can. But to save him now . . . he must become a servant of the bones."

"No," Medes whispered. "You can't."

"Without the light of the god inside him he will die."

"So let him die!" Lyonene struggled to her feet. She jerked against the soldiers who held her, soldiers with elongated faces, with stretched fingers, who had the gall to say that she was the abomination. She knew what the priests meant to do to Prince Denros even before she saw the fragment of the prophet's skull between Nestor's fingers. "Don't let them do it!" She twisted toward King Medes, not caring that the soldiers' spear tips sliced into her skin, or that the bones of the prophet tugged at her magic, sapping it from her blood. "You're his father! Don't let them turn him into a monster!"

"Do it," Medes said. "Save him."

Nestor used the sharpened jaw to carve a pocket of flesh over the prince's heart. Then he worked his fingers into the wound, shoving the piece of the prophet's skull deep inside. Lyonene's mouth flooded with nauseous spit. She could feel it as the skull took root, burrowing through the prince's flesh. She felt it as if they'd embedded it into her own skin.

When it was over, Denros lay still. His father crept closer, and curious soldiers moved forward. They obscured Lyonene's view as the prince began to change, but she saw plenty in the shadows thrown against the walls. Denros's spine bent and his arms lengthened; the sounds of his ribs cracking and being pushed outward were as the snap of green wood.

"No," Medes moaned. "What is he?"

Soldiers scurried backward as Denros rose to his newly formed feet. The corrupted soldier priests loosened their grip on Lyonene's arms.

"Where is my betrothed?" Denros asked, his voice thick and slow.

"She's gone," Parmenin growled. "Far away and safe from you."

Foolish priest, Lyonene thought, *to attract that monster's attention*.

Prince Denros of Erleven turned. He towered over all in the room and looked at them with eyes red as blood. His arms and legs were bulging veins, sinewy muscle.

Lyonene edged closer to Parmenin. They had to get out of there.

"Kleia Gloria," she whispered, "be with me now."

Fast as a blink, she twisted out of the loosened grip of her captors. She wrenched one of the spears from their hands and threw it straight into the chest of King Medes of Erleven.

Denros turned and bellowed as his father fell, and as the other guards shouted in shock, Lyonene reopened the Veil. Only Nestor saw her do it, and shouted, "She's getting away!"

But there was nothing he could do about it. Lyonene winked at him.

As she fell backward into the darkness, she grabbed for Parmenin, but just when she would have pulled him to safety, the soldier who held him jerked him back, and her fingers closed on nothing.

39.

AN APOSTATE'S RETURN

Reed stood at the window of Aster's home, the place she inhabited when she was in Atropa. It was grander than the hut they'd shared in the Summer Camp—a higher ceiling and white walls—but it wasn't all that different inside. The rooms were braced by dark wooden beams, just like in the Summer Camp, and the furnishing was spare, only one table and two chairs, and a bed in the corner upon the floor. There was also a hearth, and Reed watched Aster tend the cooking pot. It felt like something she ought to do. She'd been the one to do most of the cooking back when she was an initiate. But she wasn't an initiate anymore. She was a guest.

"It's only one meal," Aster said as she stirred the pot. "Can't you keep your mind off him long enough to eat one meal with your mentor?"

Reed and Tiern had returned with the bones that morning and presented them to Ferreh. She'd thought the elder would be pleased—the threat of the bones had been contained; all that remained was to reckon with those fragments that the priests still possessed—but Ferreh had simply taken the bones and turned away.

"I wasn't thinking of him," Reed said. Though she had been not long ago. Hestion. She missed him. She imagined him lingering in Cassor, waiting for her, and wondered if he had grown angry that she'd left.

"Still," Aster mused, and Reed noted the quiver at the corner of her mouth as she fought to keep from smiling, "you and Hestion were in Cassor a long time. Something must have happened." She raised her eyebrow.

"I can't talk to you about these things," Reed grumbled. "And besides, I really wasn't thinking about him this time."

"Then what?" Aster came to the window and handed Reed a cup of watered wine.

"I was thinking that you've had this home for longer than you've had me. For longer than I've been alive."

"Much longer."

"When I think of you all I see is our hut in the Summer Camp."

"It must be strange for all children," Aster said, "to know that their mothers had long lives before they were born. To know they will have long lives after. If you were to look around this place you would find memories of many things. Veridian. Selene. Old heroes tucked away in boxes or on shelves."

Reed looked around. She would very much like to search through it for those memories and the relics of heroes, and hear all the stories that went with them.

Aster wrapped the pot handle in a cloth and brought it to the table, and Reed cut bread from a dark brown loaf. They ate, dipping their bread into the pot and using it to grab chunks of stewed meat.

"Aster?"

"Yes?"

"If you had a chance to end this conflict with the priests, even if it cost you something grave, would you take it?"

"What is the cost?"

"I don't know." Reed shrugged. "Damage, to yourself."

"What kind of damage? Why are you asking this, Reed?"

"For no reason." She tore at her bread as her mentor stared at her, chewing thoughtfully.

"You've known of these abominations for longer than I have," Aster said. "That day at the library grounds, when you told me you didn't want me to take a new hero—it was because you feared I'd become a target."

"I'd just seen Tiern throw a creature through the World's Gate. I didn't want you to be harmed—"

"It is not for an initiate to look after their mentor," Aster said, angry. "Nor to keep secrets."

"I'm not an initiate anymore," Reed said softly. She was a Glorious Death. Safer in the world than Aster was in many ways.

"You should have told me, Reed."

As she opened her mouth to give the expected apology, Reed felt a soft click in her mind.

"Someone has opened the Veil." She dipped her bread again. Aristene coming and going through the Veil wasn't uncommon. But when she glanced at Aster, she saw that her mentor had turned as still as stone.

"It's Veridian."

Veridian lurched through the Veil and into Atropa, sweating and blinking in the sunlight. The Veil was a dark gauntlet of terrors;

she didn't know how Reed and Aster could bear to pass through it every time they needed to travel. She would rather a four-month sail at sea than take that particular shortcut.

"Did that seem worse than it normally is?" Veridian asked Strawberry. "Stomp your hoof if it was."

She looked back at the little roan mare. Strawberry seemed slightly refreshed—her sweat had been cleansed, the blessing of the goddess upon a servant's return—but her wounds were still bleeding.

Veridian patted her and gave the reins a tug to get her moving down the hills and onto the road that led into the city, but after a few steps the horse refused to move.

"What is it?" Veridian asked. "Can't you make it?" She peered around at Strawberry's haunches, dripping blood. The shafts of arrows stuck up like a porcupine's quills. They had to hurt with every step, but Veridian hadn't wanted to pull them out before they made the crossing. "Come on, girl, it's not much farther." But the horse simply stood there, fierce in her silver face plate. "Look, you're small, but not small enough to carry. And we are in a bit of a hurry—"

Strawberry's ears flicked backward as the Veil yawned open behind them.

Veridian's hand flew to the hilt of her sword. She released it when Lyonene fell through the darkness onto the grass.

Woman and horse hurried to her as she tried to struggle to her feet. The mare shoved her face into Lyonene's chest and Lyonene grasped the cheekpieces of the bridle.

"Strawberry," she said as the horse pulled her up. "Good girl."

"You got away," Veridian said. "Yngarue thought they'd gotten the best of you."

"Yngarue. Is she . . . ?"

"She's fine. Everfall is carrying her back to Cassor as we speak."

"It was foolish to go," Lyonene whispered. "Thank you for following me."

"An apostate's work is never done." Veridian grimaced as Lyonene tried to take a step and buckled. "We have to get you to the healers."

"No." Lyonene pushed away. "Strawberry needs the healers. I need the elders. They have to know what I saw. . . ."

"And what was that, exactly?" Veridian asked, but before she got an answer, she spotted movement at the edge of the field. It was Aster and Reed. Reed strode quickly to wrap Lyonene in an embrace. But Aster approached with caution, as if she feared Veridian was a trick of the eye. She didn't smile until she'd touched Veridian's arm and found it solid.

"You used your own magic to open the Veil," Aster said.

"I did," Veridian replied. "I wasn't sure I could. And then I thought I might be swallowed whole, but apparently she took mercy on the horse." She jerked her head toward Strawberry. "I brought the horse. Lyonene came separately."

"What happened?" asked Reed.

"I only have the strength to tell it once," Lyonene said. "Get me to the elders, Ox, and you'll know everything then."

They made their way down from the hills. A merchant saw them inside the city and called for acolytes, who came with buckets and gently pressed cloths soaked with cool water to Strawberry's hindquarters.

"Veridian," Lyonene said. "When I came through the Veil you put your hand to your sword. What were you looking to fight? What did you think would come out?"

Veridian thought back to the feel of it snapping open behind her. "Nothing." The apostate shrugged. "I thought it was coming back for me. I thought I was going to fight the Veil itself."

Reed and Aster brought Veridian and Lyonene to the elders inside the great half-circle room that overlooked the city. Mia came with herbs and hot water, and a sharp needle to sew Lyonene's wounds closed. After she was finished, Lyonene told Ferreh and Tiern what had transpired in Erlengard.

Lyonene, Reed thought as she listened. *You should never have gone alone.* She knew, *she knew*, that the Erleven prince was the wrong choice. But lately Lyonene seemed to think that she could carve glory out of stone.

"The priests we seek are in Erlengard," Ferreh said.

"Along with the jawbone of the prophet," Tiern murmured. "The last significant piece."

Tiern paced back and forth, her white cape swishing with her steps, her hands gripping the handles of the daggers at her belt.

Reed looked at Ferreh. The mind of the order stood pensive, toying with the gold rings upon her fingers.

"We will destroy the priests now," she said. "In their nest."

Reed's eyes widened. That was not what she had expected Ferreh to say.

"Ferreh," Veridian interjected. "Haven't you been listening to what the girl said? They've corrupted soldiers, given them strength to stand against even the Aristene. They've made themselves a monster."

"What are you doing here, Veridian?" Tiern snapped. "Why do you not just go, back through the Veil to wander as you have desired?"

"Because I only do as I desire. And now I desire to stay until this is done." Veridian shrugged. "Besides, you need me. I stood against this magic in Rhonassus. I wasn't to its taste."

Tiern's mouth tightened. "So what? We have Aethiel, who does not taste good either. And we have Machianthe. Who does her duty better than you anyway." Her eyes narrowed slyly, and Reed glanced around the room. Did anyone else know about Veridian? That she'd drunk the blood? That she was another Glorious Death, just like Reed. But the only eyes that met hers were Veridian's own.

"I will go," Ferreh said. "Myself."

The room stopped. Ferreh hadn't fought in battle for longer than most Aristene memories stretched. "Aethiel will also come. Jana and her spears. And I will take you, Aster. Where is Mol?"

"Protecting my hero in Cassor," Lyonene quickly supplied.

"No matter. We can show these priests what cowards they are without any further help."

"No," Lyonene said. "Forgive me, Ferreh. But even if you attacked with every Aristene in the city, I don't know that it would be enough."

She might have said more, but Aethiel burst into the room, her long black braid swinging. She wrapped her arms around Veridian and lifted her in the kind of embrace that looked like it hurt. "You've opened the Veil," she said. "You've returned."

"Aethiel," Veridian grunted, eyes bugging as she was squeezed. "I've returned in times of trouble. Nothing more."

"You say that, but since Reed's trial you have been as much an Aristene as any. You have returned, and I am not the only one who rejoices—" She nodded toward the open air beyond the columns, where voices could be heard rising from the square.

Reed, Aster, and Veridian stepped to the railing and looked down. Acolytes and merchants, donkeys and goats, and no small number of white capes had gathered below. Every Aristene in Atropa must have felt it when the Veil opened, and word that the apostate had been sighted traveled through the streets like wildfire. Reed frowned. Everyone loved Veridian so well. If the apostate returned, and took up her mantle as Glorious Death, where would that leave her?

"Shit," Veridian said, and leaned back before anyone caught a glimpse of her face.

"Ferreh, please listen." Lyonene slid off the table where she'd been stitched up, landing with a small wince. "Our magic—"

"These are not like Oreas, child. We are not powerless. You yourself were able to fight."

"But Prince Denros—and they have the jaw blade. Who knows how many corrupted soldiers will await you?"

"Then we shouldn't give them the time to make more," Tiern said. "And this is not a debate. Aster and Aethiel will ready themselves for battle. And you, Veridian, if you insist. The initiates may go."

"But—" Lyonene began, but Veridian took her by the arm and

motioned for Reed to take her other side.

"I can sense when I'm not wanted," the apostate said, "So we'll leave you to act like fools." She jerked her head, and Reed pulled Lyonene's arm farther over her shoulders as they slunk past the elder's glare. Aster watched them with worry but made no move to follow.

"Are we really just staying behind?" Reed asked as they went with Veridian through the hall of statues.

"Of course I'm not. I'm an apostate. I'm getting out of here." She reached out and stroked the marble nose of a horse, its head low as it charged beneath a rider preparing to throw a spear. "And you two are welcome to join me. Unless you think the elders are right, and they can do this all by themselves."

"We need an army of our own," Reed said.

Lyonene nodded. "We need heroes."

"And which heroes would the two of you be thinking of? I wonder." Veridian's eyebrow arched. "But you are right. We'll return to Cassor to raise an army. And to get my horse back."

They hurried out of the Citadel shadows and into the sun. Looking down upon the square, Reed saw many upturned faces, and when Veridian came into view the crowd gave a rousing cheer.

"Why didn't you tell me?" Reed asked her quietly. "That you are—"

"Because I am not," the apostate said. "Because it doesn't matter.

"Why is there no back way out of this place?" she growled. She affixed a smile to her face and waved to the people below. When they reached the bottom they were crushed by acolytes and Aristene. It felt nearly as overwhelming as it had when Reed and Lyonene had descended for the initiates' banquet. Ellora embraced Veridian and gave her smacking kisses on the cheek. A warmer welcome than Reed had ever received.

"Veridian, come to the tavern and celebrate," said Ellora. "We have missed you so. And I owe you an ale, for holding that crossbow on you when you returned after Aster was wounded in Rhonassus."

"It was nothing," Veridian said.

"Of course it was nothing," someone shouted from the crowd. "When she knew you could have drawn your own crossbow and split her bolt in two."

Reed remembered that day. It was when Veridian, Aster, and Aethiel had freed her and Hestion from the clutches of King Oreas. When they'd broken the sacred laws, bringing an apostate and a hero through the Veil. Veridian hadn't actually had a crossbow. Only her sword.

"Another time," Veridian said, and the crowd groaned in disappointment. "Oh, now. What does an immortal order have but time?" More groans, but they were allowed to pass through the square and into the stables.

"Do any of them even know about the threat we face?" Lyonene asked.

"Many probably," Veridian said. "Mia, certainly, as she's seen the wounds. But I'm betting they don't know how far the danger might spread. The elders like to keep their secrets."

"Well, they will all know soon, if we don't get back to Cassor," Reed said as she saddled Silco. Lyonene would need another horse, as Strawberry was still healing from the arrows.

As soon as Silco's reins were over his head, Veridian grabbed onto his saddle. "I will ride with you, foundling."

Reed pursed her lips, but before she could object, Lyonene shook her head.

"No, you can't. Reed has to go find Hestion."

"He's not in Cassor?" Reed asked.

"He left the day after you did," Lyonene said. "Refused to court Yngarue anymore. Took his men to sail for Glaucia."

But he wouldn't have been able to leave quickly. He would still be on the continent. "He would probably make for the port of Lhyrgia, on the border of Erleven and Sirta," Reed heard herself say.

"Go there, then," said Veridian. "Find him, and bring him back with haste."

Lyonene chose a sleek bay mare and threw a saddle onto her back. Veridian helped her to mount and then sprang up behind her.

"Let's get to the hills, initiates. It will take time for Jana to return from the Summer Camp, but we don't have much time if our army is to march to the elders' rescue."

"Perhaps they won't need it," said Reed. "Perhaps the priests will take one look at Ferreh in her armor and lay down their swords."

"I fear they're not that smart," Lyonene quipped.

"I never asked you," Lyonene said to Veridian as they rode out of the square, "but who was your mentor? Was it she, the statue whose horse you kissed in the Citadel?"

"No," Veridian replied from behind her. "That horse just saved my life once. My mentor is still alive."

"Who is she, then? Have we met her?"

"You've met her. You may have heard that Aethiel was mentored by Tiern," Veridian said, and Reed stilled. "Well. So was I."

"A Glorious Death and mentored by an elder. Our apostate is greater than anyone knew," said Reed, and Veridian laughed, failing to detect the chill in her voice.

40.

HEROES

Alsander prodded the logs in the fire, stabbing ashen bark with the tip of the poker. He was in the great hall with the rest of the royal family, but he was the only one awake. The queen sat with her back propped against a pile of pillows, asleep with two of her children. Princess Wyrnnigrid had laid her head on her mother's lap, and Prince Ullieth was curled up between them beneath a thick pile of furs. The king slept in a chair with his head tilted back, softly snoring.

When it was discovered that Lyonene and the princess were missing, Urdien had sent soldiers and servants into the forests to search, and the family had gathered in the great hall. Alsander looked at the queen. She'd just emerged from her sickbed, but she didn't look that ill. A little quiet, perhaps, and cowed by her husband. But she was fine enough to look at, with coloring similar to her eldest daughter: pale hair that hid any gray, and bright blue eyes. He wondered why King Urdien had really locked her away. Perhaps she was a little mad. Or perhaps he just didn't like her.

Alsander took a long swallow of wine and thought about his own wife. His queen. Lyonene of Cerille. She would have been magnificent. A queen of war that other men would fear to touch. She'd been concerned that she couldn't give him an heir, but he could have gotten one on another woman, a woman with Lyonene's green eyes and tawny hair, and none would have been the wiser.

He took another drink. That was a good dream, while it lasted. But his father had locked his bony fingers around the throne. He'd pushed Alsander into exile. Much as he loved her, Alsander could never take Lyonene as his queen now. Now he needed alliances. He needed coin. He needed an army. He needed Yngarue.

And Lyonene had run off with her.

On purpose? Had she gleaned what he intended? Not even the remaining Aristene could say. When he'd asked her why Lyonene had gone, Mol had just glowered and plunged off into the night, grumbling about borrowing horses without asking.

Alsander prodded the fire again, harder.

"Lyonene, my love," he whispered. "Where have you taken my bride?" He leaned against the stone of the hearth. The Cassan wine was sour and made him feel slightly sick. He hadn't slept, and the sun was about to rise.

He heard a hound start to bay outside, and rested the poker beside the fire. He walked out of the castle. The hound had ceased baying and the only sounds were the crunches of his footsteps on the path. But something approached. Alsander squinted into the darkness where the torches failed to reach and made out a creature with several heads and more legs than a spider. He reached for his sword, and then saw that it was no monster at all.

"Yngarue!"

The princess was being half helped, half carried by two soldiers. Another held the reins of a tall red horse he recognized as Veridian's gelding.

Alsander rushed to them and the soldiers relinquished the princess into his arms.

"Are you unhurt?" he asked. She mumbled a reply, and he raised his head to the soldiers. "Rouse the king!"

"I'm all right," Yngarue said, more clearly.

"What happened?" He blew on her hands to warm them, touching her fingers to his lips, and tasted copper. He looked at her hands—they were rusted with dried blood. "Where is Lyonene?" he asked. But Yngarue's eyes were dull with exhaustion. "Where is Lyonene?" he asked again. When she continued to simply stare, fear kindled in his stomach and he shook her and shouted, "Where is Lyonene!"

"The Aristene has been taken," Yngarue said.

Alsander knelt upon the ground, in shock as the princess was pulled from his arms and brought inside. He looked up at the red gelding. An Aristene could not be taken easily. So what had happened?

Alsander got up from the path and returned to the castle.

Yngarue was set in a chair beside the fire as her father barked orders for warmed wine and more logs. Her sister and little brother placed furs upon her lap and around her shoulders. Her mother couldn't seem to stop touching the girl's face. Alsander floated a small distance away and tried to be patient.

"Ynga, my sweet," the queen murmured.

"What happened?" asked Wyrnnigrid. "Where did you go?"

Yngarue accepted a cup of warmed wine, cradling it in both hands. "To Erlengard," she said simply.

All eyes moved to the king. Urdien was harried and unkempt, just roused from a night of poor sleep.

"What could you mean, going there?" he asked.

"Parmenin and Prince Alsander's servant Lyonene escorted me. I was to be betrothed to Prince Denros." She looked at Alsander as her father's face reddened with rage.

"And what has he done?" Alsander asked quietly, before the king could erupt. "What has the bastard of Erleven done to the princess?"

Yngarue gave him a discreet nod, in thanks for redirecting her father's anger. She was free now to tell them the rest, and as she did the fear in Alsander's chest was replaced by wrath.

The prince of Erleven had dared to take Lyonene. Dared to hurt her. Thoughts of what she suffered threatened to drive him mad as he listened to Urdien pace and bitch about his petty grievances of disrespect and land disputes. Eventually, he could take no more.

"Give me your army," Alsander said. "Let me lead the might of Cassor against this city of curs in the name of King Urdien."

Urdien looked at Alsander. Alsander knew what he saw: crown prince and a commander of many battles. A seethingly angry future son-in-law. And coin. In Alsander, Urdien saw all the riches and power of Cerille.

Urdien grunted and turned to the man nearest him. "Ready the soldiers to march."

When Hestion reached the port of Lhyrgia, he quickly set about securing goods and gifts, to please his sure-to-be-angry aunt Morna. He acquired linens and bast, delicately spun wool, and even silks in exchange for coin and salt from Glaucia's plentiful stores.

"It's good we're leaving," said Sar as Hestion watched the last of the goods be loaded onto his flagship.

"I thought you wanted me to stay, and return to the Cassan princess."

"I do. But since you won't do that, it's good that we go. I've heard whispers. The port is about to become unsafe. The truce between Essor merchants and the guild of Toruk has failed. We should sail before we are caught in between."

Hestion looked out across the port. It was crowded and chaotic, filled with people of differing backgrounds from different places, as port cities often were, and in such places, conflicts were bound to arise. But Lhyrgia especially was prone to bloody rivalries, as one side of the port belonged to Sirta and the other to neighboring Erleven.

"Don't start thinking we ought to linger," Sar cautioned, the blue paint flaking from his cheeks beneath the sun of midday. "The Aristene could be away for months—years!—you said so yourself."

Hestion smiled. What Sar said was true. He didn't even know where Reed gone. He wondered if she thought he was angry with her for going. She liked to pretend he was as a toddler with a toy, holding on to her with clenched fists, but he understood what being an Aristene meant.

"We sail today," he said, and Sar visibly relaxed.

But despite his declaration, Hestion was last aboard. He stood on the deck with his white stallion, patting the horse's nose as the ship shifted gently beneath his feet. The stallion snorted. Target wasn't fond of travel by sea. No doubt he remembered a time when a ship sank in a cove and he was forced to swim for it.

Sar came to them and held out his hand. "I'll take him below."

"I hope they left room," said Hestion.

"If they didn't, he can sleep on a pile of your silly silks," Sar grumbled, grabbing the stallion's rope.

"They're for Aunt Morna."

"Morna doesn't care about silks. She cares about brides. Heirs. And you should care about them, too."

Hestion chuckled. "What happened to the wild Ithernan? I remember when you used to scream for battle." But Sar wasn't only surly because Hestion had failed to win a bride. He was missing Princess Wyrnnigrid. His mood would improve once Hestion shared with him his plan, that the Ithernan marry Wyrnnigrid and they forge a line of succession between the two nations. He actually couldn't wait to tell him.

"What are you smiling about?" Sar snapped.

But Hestion only grinned wider, looking out at the bustling activity of the port. Reed had spent part of her childhood in a port city like this. He could almost see her there now, racing past the merchants' stalls on slim tan legs, the waves of her hair flying like a flag. He blinked, and when he looked again, he saw her there for real.

She was standing beside her black horse, and when she saw him through the crowds her eyes brightened. Silco whinnied, and Target bugled back; Sar had his hands full as the white stallion raised his tail and stomped.

"Hestion," Sar said, trying to control the horse as Hestion broke into a jog. "No!"

"You like Reed," Hestion said without slowing.

"I do like Reed. It's you who are making me dread seeing her face!"

Hestion leaped back onto the dock and pushed through people. When he reached her, there was plenty of space, even as an Areion Silco was unfriendly and pinned his ears at passersby, his head weaving in the air like a great black snake.

Reed jumped into Hestion's arms and kissed him so ardently that he forgot for a moment that they stood upon a crowded street. He only remembered himself when they bumped up against Silco and the horse snorted.

"I worried I wouldn't find you in time," she said against his lips, her arms still holding him tightly. "Are you angry?"

"Why would I be angry?"

"Because I had to leave."

"Well—" He gestured to the port. "I left, too." He pushed her hair back from her face. "What's the matter?"

"Do you remember when you said that the Glaucans would defend us?"

"Yes."

"Then I need your help."

Hestion could feel the eyes of his soldiers watching from the deck of his flagship, eager to sail for home. Glaucia was where they belonged. It was where he belonged, on the throne of his father.

He brushed his lips across Reed's fingers. "I'll be but a moment."

He leaped upon the deck. "We return to fight in Cassor!"

His men gathered around, barking questions.

"The Aristene, who fought with us at Roshanak, are in need of our aid," Hestion said. "I know you men have longed for home.

But any who have also longed for battle are welcome to come with me."

He reached for Target and took the stallion's reins from Sar. He didn't know how many of his soldiers would choose to stay. They were small in number, a courting party, barely a guard—but they were also brave and eager for glory.

"Hestion, brother—"

"We go, Sar."

The decks were a flurry of activity as men hurried to secure weaponry and bring their horses up from the hold. Hestion went to fetch a saddle for Target and Sar went with him, walking backward and trying for the prince's attention.

"But why do we go? What do they need us for? They are Aristene; you've seen how they fight!"

Hestion cocked an eyebrow at him patiently. "I know you want to go home, Sar. But your words begin to sound like cowardice."

"What they sound like is sense." Sar grabbed his arm. "You cannot do this. You are not a second-born prince anymore. Glaucia needs you. If you fall . . ."

Hestion paused. The words Sar spoke were true. His people depended on him. But Reed was depending on him, too.

"I hear what you are saying," he said. "That's why you must stay back."

"What? No—"

"If something goes wrong, you must return with the whole of the Glaucan army. You must lead them."

"No—forget what I said—I will go with you!"

Hestion took the pin from his shoulder, the silver stag of the

Docritae, and placed it in Sar's hand. "I won't fall," he said. "But I have to go."

"You don't have to go," Sar shouted as Hestion turned and climbed out of the cargo hold.

"I love her," Hestion called back.

"The things we do for love," Sar cried from the shadows, "make fools of us all!"

41.

THE ALLEGIANCE OF HEROES

When Lyonene and Veridian stepped out of the Veil on the back of the bay mare, they walked into a Cassor preparing for war.

"Looks like they started without us," Veridian noted.

"Something must have happened," Lyonene said. Something with Yngarue? But the princess was alive—her fate was linked to Lyonene through the vision of the sacred well and she would have felt it if she'd perished. She searched the faces of the men for answers, looking for Alsander, or for the king. Everywhere she looked, soldiers were on the move. Some tended to weapons. Others carried sacks of grain or rolled barrels of water. The gate was crowded with fresh recruits, called up from their farms and villages to have helmets placed upon their heads and swords into their hands. The castle was so busy that even their arrival through the Veil was met with only a few surprised blinks.

"Oi," Veridian called as a trio of freshly shod horses was led past. "Get your hands off that one." She slid off the bay mare's rump as Everfall tugged free of the groom holding his reins. Veridian smiled and scratched him on the forehead. "Thought you'd take advantage of my absence to get a pair of new shoes, eh?" she asked, and the gelding bumped her with his nose.

Lyonene swung gently down from the saddle, bracing for

pain. But Mia's healing touch was doing its work, and her injuries were already far less troublesome. However, the moment her feet touched the ground, someone grabbed her by the shoulder and a fist connected with her face.

"Where is my horse?" Mol shouted.

"Ow." Lyonene rubbed her jaw. "How many times am I to be struck in the face?"

"As many as I like until you return my horse," Mol said.

"Mol, stop!" Veridian hurried to them. "She's hurt."

Mol spun on Veridian. "And you—how do you come to be traveling through the Veil? Does no one tell me anything? I have remained here, in Cassor, to help you and—"

"You're right, Mol," Veridian said. It was such an unexpected response from the apostate that Mol calmed. "We owe you many explanations."

"Where is Verger?"

"He was taken inside the walls of Erlengard," Lyonene answered. "I'm sorry; in the midst of what was happening—I didn't even think to look for him. But"—she added when Mol looked pained—"he was ridden inside by Yngarue's priest—no one will know he's an Areion."

"Unless he shows them," said Veridian.

"Verger is smart," Mol said. "He knows how to hide."

"We'll find him during the attack," Veridian promised. "We'll bring him back."

"Attack?" Mol looked back and forth between them.

"I will tell you all," Veridian promised. "Lyonene, go inside and find your princess."

Lyonene nodded, and Veridian led Mol away to explain their plan.

Inside, the castle was just as hectic as the outside. As Lyonene made her way to the great hall, servants carrying all manner of things threaded by her as smoothly as fish navigating past rocks in a stream. The hall itself was cluttered with piles of shields and shoes, and servants set to cleaning and repairing them. But the royalty was nowhere to be seen. Lyonene reached out and snagged a passing soldier by the crook of his arm.

"Tell me what's happening."

"We muster to march on Erlengard," he answered, after trying and failing to pull free. "In recompense for attempting to harm the princess."

"Where is the princess?" she asked, and the soldier shrugged. She finally found Yngarue in the solar, with her sister and a tall older woman. Her mother, the queen, judging by the gold circlet upon her head.

"That pile there may go," Yngarue said, pointing to a stack of tunics. Little Prince Ullieth hurried to scoop them up and nearly tripped. He grinned when he saw Lyonene, and as soon as he passed her in the doorway he raced away, laughing. The women inside were sewing, making capes in the Cassan colors, and repairing torn shirts. Yngarue stood at a table, making piles and giving orders. When she saw Lyonene she sagged with relief.

"Aristene!"

"We have names," Lyonene said as she went to the girl and took her hands. "Yet as soon as one learns what we are, that's all we become."

"I'm sorry. Lyonene." Yngarue squeezed her fingers. "I am so happy you escaped! Where is Parmenin?"

Lyonene's face fell, and Yngarue moaned softly. The queen's hands flew to her mouth and Wyrnnigrid squeezed her mother's shoulder.

"I tried," Lyonene said. "I tried to take him with me, but I failed."

"It doesn't matter," said Yngarue angrily. "We will free him soon enough."

Lyonene inhaled. The air around the princess sparkled and glimmered with gold. She was standing in the middle of piles of sewing, but she could have been holding a spear for how much glory swirled through her. "Yngarue, you don't intend to ride to battle?"

Yngarue's eyes widened. Then her brow knit as she considered whether she could. "I am no soldier."

"I'm not so sure of that. You used Reed's poisoned knife."

"I didn't know it was poisoned. But I don't regret that it was."

Lyonene pressed her lips together grimly. She might, if she knew what the priests had turned Prince Denros into.

"Lyonene!"

She turned. Alsander stood in the doorway of the solar. He wore fine armor, borrowed from the king, and the sight of him flooded Lyonene's senses. He jerked toward her but could come no closer. To all watching but Yngarue, they were simply prince and servant.

"You look like a prince of Cassor," she said softly. She should bow her head, tear her eyes away from him. It must be obvious to everyone, the way that they looked at each other.

"Prince Alsander," said Yngarue. "Perhaps you would take your servant and see her properly outfitted."

"Of course." He inclined his head to the women and stepped aside so Lyonene could pass. As she went, Lyonene cast Yngarue a grateful glance, and the princess smiled slyly as they departed for Alsander's chamber.

Parmenin swallowed bile as he watched the dagger of bone slice through the soldier's hand like ripe fruit. The sound it made, and the ease with which it cut, made his stomach turn. Every time Nestor lowered the dagger to a soldier's hand, Parmenin was sure he'd sever it, slicing tendons and leaving fingers dangling. But even if it did, it wouldn't have mattered. Soldiers like the ones they made were lethal, with one hand or two.

Kneeling upon the stone floor, the soldier squeezed his fist around the blood. After the cut was made the change to the men was fascinatingly fast—almost instantaneous. And every transformation was different, a lengthening of legs here, a stretching of jaw there, but in all there came a general distension, muscles stretched and bulked beneath the skin. Every man added several inches of height, so that when they rose from their kneeling position Nestor had to look up into their eyes.

"You ought to bandage them," Parmenin said as the soldier walked away bleeding. The Erleven guards had chained him to the wall and kicked him like a dog; he was pained and exhausted, past knowing whether he still wished to survive. "Instead of letting them lick at the wounds and smear their own blood across their faces."

Nestor snorted. "We tried. They would often tear the dressing apart to get at the wound anyway. Kneel."

The boy next in line was young, his hair still thin and flaxen as moonlight. He was trembling; two of the other unspoiled Adonumrian priests had to shove him to the ground. Nestor grabbed his hand and dragged the dagger across his palm, and Parmenin looked away. When they had turned the soldiers of Erleven, many of them had been less than willing. But now they began to turn farmers and laborers from the fields, all to increase their ranks as they prepared for an assault from their great enemies, the Aristene.

"You must be very afraid of them," Parmenin said. "Will you recruit the ladies' maids next?"

Nestor's lip twitched. He dismissed the new soldier and the boy stood. Parmenin's breath caught in his throat. The boy's face had remained the same, but one of his eyes had deadened and turned gray. He walked away with knees stained by the pool of blood left by countless others who went before him.

Nestor cleaned the edge of the dagger on a cloth. "When the servants of the false goddess come they will not guess at what awaits them."

"Is that what you saw in your vision?" Parmenin asked, and Nestor curled his lip. Parmenin had overheard Nestor and the other priests discussing the cloudiness of the vision before it went dark. They were operating out of fear.

Heavy footfalls sounded against the floor, and Parmenin looked to the entrance. Prince Denros, or the beast that had once been Prince Denros, walked through the hall on legs that bulged with muscle.

He hunched before Parmenin and took him by the jaw.

"My old friend," Denros said. "My matchmaker."

"Are you still my old friend?" Parmenin asked. "Are you still you?"

He had known Denros as a boy, in the years before he'd departed for the court of Cassor. Denros hadn't been much older than Prince Ullieth then, and like Ullieth he'd been all legs and elbows, a quick-witted child who slept with his hunting dogs every night.

"Do I look different?" Denros asked, and grinned, showing his newly sharpened teeth.

"I am sorry," said Parmenin quietly. "It was never my intention that it come to this."

Denros sighed. He turned to Nestor. "How many of them will come?"

"Even I cannot say for sure, my prince," Nestor replied.

"The soldiers. They are strong?"

"Very strong, Lord Denros."

"Then you do not need me."

Denros turned back to Parmenin, piggish eyes peering out of a contorted face, the whites gone bright red with burst blood vessels—the lingering mark of Yngarue's poison.

"Come here, priest." Denros extended an arm. Nestor came near, and Denros took the jawbone blade from his hands. With two fingers, like he would use to pluck a grape, he grabbed on to one of the prophet's teeth and pulled it free.

"What are you doing?" Nestor cried. "You must not defile the prophet!" He tried to snatch the bone away, jumping at Denros like a hunting hound around a hung stag. Denros reached out and crushed Nestor's head in his fist. The priest dropped to the ground.

"Brother Nestor!" Two other priests of the brotherhood ran toward them but stopped short.

You fools, Parmenin thought wildly. *Now you are at the mercy of a monster of your own creation.*

"Parmenin," Denros said, his voice low and garbled from his elongated jaw. "You are a friend to my betrothed. To Yngarue." He seized Parmenin's head in his hand and the priest screamed. He clawed at Denros's fingers, trying to pry them loose. "A friend to her escort."

"Stay away from me! Don't touch me!" Parmenin cried.

"Her escort will be glad to see you," Denros said as he pushed the prophet's blackened tooth deep into Parmenin's eye.

In Atropa, the elders stood together inside the Citadel in the quiet moments before a great battle. It had been many, many years since Ferreh had experienced such a moment, that particular hum of anticipation in her blood, and even that faraway twinge of fear. She remembered this feeling. She was grateful that she could still feel it.

"This isn't like you," Tiern said. "Rushing in to face these priests."

"And taking Reed to Roshanak to collect the bones behind my back," Ferreh said. "Is that like you? Is that what we are now, Tiern? Separate?" She turned to look at her friend. "What else have you done without my knowing?"

Tiern looked away. "We have always been separate, Ferreh. United but separate. Nothing has changed."

"Everything has changed." Ferreh strode from the room.

"Where are you going?"

"To claim my sword."

The sword of Ferreh resided not in the aether with the elder's armor but within the Citadel, atop a wide pedestal of white marble. It lay upon cloth of gold, beside the broad silver shield that Ferreh had lent to Reed during the War of Rhonassus.

Ferreh stood before the marble and gazed down upon it. The sword was a thing of beauty, the grip wrapped in soft, dark leather and the pommel housing a large red stone.

This blade is a wordless song. That's what they'd said when they placed it into her hands.

How long had it been since she had held it?

She didn't remember.

She reached out and took it up. Light reflected off the metal and flashed into her eyes. Her hand around the grip felt like home. With this blade, Ferreh could carve through bone and cleave through bronze. She could banish the threat of the gray-robed priests.

"This sword has seen many things," Ferreh whispered. "And done many things. Yet I do not think we have seen all of what it may do."

42.

THE CASSAN ARMY

There was no time for warm welcomes when Reed and the Glaucans returned to the castle of King Urdien. There were simply too many preparations to make. Reed looked upon the mass of activity, soldiers and servants set to purpose, and was impressed. For an army that hadn't fought a proper war in a generation they were well underway.

Hestion touched Reed's arm. "I'll see my men settled and find you inside." Reed nodded as Prince Ullieth stopped before them. He'd been carrying too many bridles over his shoulder and when he lowered his arms he dropped them all into the dirt.

"Prince Hestion! You've returned!"

Hestion grinned and placed a hand on the younger prince's shoulder. "I couldn't let you and Alsander have all the fun. Where is there room for my men?"

Prince Ullieth looked around. "Nowhere," he decided finally, and tugged on Hestion's elbow. "But come, and we'll find some! Welcome back, matchmaker!"

"Ulli," Reed said, amused. Even in her armor, her presence was an afterthought compared to Hestion. She reached down to pick up the bridles the little prince had left behind.

Inside, the great hall was being set for a feast. Long tables had been brought and servants went to and fro, carrying armloads of cups and baskets of vegetables. The smell of roasted meat made her mouth water—they were using the hearth as an additional cooking fire.

Reed stopped the first servant she saw pass by with nothing in her arms. "Where is the king? Prince Alsander? The princess Yngarue?"

"The king is with Prince Alsander in the war room. The princess . . ."

"Never mind. Where is the war room?" She'd lived in the castle for months, and never heard of a space called so. "Never mind," she said again, when the girl looked flummoxed. The servant was a strange face in a sea of strange faces, called up from nearby towns to serve the Crown in a time of need. Reed pressed the pile of bridles into her arms. "These go to the stable," she guessed, and the girl hurried away. Reed spotted a boy carrying two cups of wine and followed him; he led her to the king's chamber, where Urdien and Alsander stood over a table, studying a map.

Alsander looked up. Fond surprise brightened his handsome face. "Reed." He extended his hand as she crossed the room and pulled her into an embrace. "She worried you wouldn't return in time."

"But I have, and with reinforcements."

"Prince Hestion?" Urdien asked. "And how many soldiers does he bring? More than what he came with?"

"Less," Reed replied. "But the ones who come are of the Docritae, the finest in all of Glaucia. Each one of them is worth ten."

"Or twenty," Alsander said when Urdien seemed disappointed. "We fought beside them in the war with Rhonassus. I have seen their skill."

Urdien pursed his lips. His eyes traveled over Reed's armor and flinched away from the bare skin visible above her greaves. He didn't know how to address her when he had known her so long in a red hat that jingled.

"Machianthe. That's still your name, isn't it? I shouldn't shake your hand as a friend after your deception—" He stuck his hand out. "But if you fight beside Cassor against Erleven, then all may be forgiven."

Reed glanced at the maps upon the table. An attack on Erlengard by land was a straightforward affair: the army would travel through the valley and form ranks after fording the shallow river. Urdien would ride with them; markers of carved stone representing Urdien's faction of soldiers and Alsander's had been placed outside the capital. The king would assail the castle from over the low wall, while Alsander was set to attack the gate.

"Do you have any suggestions, Aristene?" Alsander asked.

"None that Lyonene won't already have posed. And not a suggestion so much as a wish, for ships." She moved her hand to the port.

"Yes. Had we the luxury of time." He looked at Reed quietly. Both knew that time or no time, no ships from Cerille would come to Alsander's aid.

"We'll have no need of a navy," said Urdien. "My line of scorpions will form here and fire upon the wall. There is no shortage of artillery." He moved his pieces into place, his eyes glittering. War had brought Urdien to life. For so long he'd prepared for it, commissioning weapons and building fortifications. But he'd never engaged in it. All he knew of war were these toys, placed upon paper. Yet as Reed looked at the map, her Aristene eyes saw battle lines glowing with gold. She saw the borders of Cassor pushed outward and Erleven absorbed; she saw heroes and glory there for the making, and so much glorious death.

"Reed?" Alsander asked quietly.

"I should go and find Lyonene," Reed said. "Hestion will join you shortly."

When Reed walked into the solar, she surprised them all, so much that Wyrnnigrid dropped her sewing into her lap. Lyonene and Yngarue hurried to take her hands.

"Did you find him?" Lyonene asked.

"I did."

"And who has come with him?" Princess Wyrnnigrid rose from her chair; the sewing she'd been working on fluttered down the folds of her gown to land upon the floor.

"Not all," Reed replied. "And not Sar." Wyrnnigrid's face fell.

"Machianthe," Yngarue said. "It was only by your teaching that I knew how to use the knife. Thank you."

"I am so sorry, Yngarue. I wouldn't have left you, had I known."

"It was a mistake," Lyonene muttered. "I never should have taken her there."

"But had you not gone, we never would have known that the priests were in Erlengard. The goddess places us where we need to be."

"Or merely where she wants us," Lyonene said.

"Do you think we'll be in time to help the elders?" Reed asked.

"Maybe. Urdien feasts with his nobles tonight and we march the army tomorrow. If they march well, we may reach Erlengard on the third day. But even if they march very well, it's still slower than the Veil."

Reed glanced out the window, at the fading light. She knew they must move quickly. Yet somehow she also wished that they could stop. Men would die in this battle. Aristene may die. And these soldiers they rallied, even the Docritae, had no real understanding of what it was they would face.

That night, Reed found she had no appetite, and remained with the soldiers while the nobles feasted in the great hall. Outside, the battle preparations had paused, and soldiers gathered in groups to eat and sing. Their eyes and cheeks glowed, lit by the fires, and by Kleia Gloria, who wound through their ranks like a great golden snake. Her scales brushed a man's shield arm here, and wound around a sword arm there. Her tongue flicked out to test their courage. On nights like these, an Aristene had no need for wine or ale. The coming glory made Reed feel drunk.

"You are the one they call the Warrior in the Red Dress."

Reed turned. It was a young soldier. Younger than she'd been when she'd undertaken her Hero's Trial. And he was scowling at her.

"What is your name?" she asked.

"Macon," he replied, still scowling.

"How old are you?"

"Fourteen."

"Do you fight with sword or bow?"

"I've never fought with either." He glanced at the sword upon her back. "They say it's your fault that we march. Yours and the princess's. That we go to avenge some debt of honor, to give our lives because a princess feels slighted. Is that true?"

"No," Reed replied. "We march because that princess discovered a city full of monsters. Monsters who will come to your door. Who will come to your homes, and for your families. There is only one reason to fight a war, and it isn't coin, and it isn't glory. It isn't for revenge." The pretty lies dropped easily from her lips, to give him courage, and his scowl softened. Reed drew her magic over herself, laying her final trick, dropping her mortal guise to show the shining warrior beneath.

Macon's eyes shone like stars.

"And you'll fight beside us?" he asked quietly.

"I will. Beside you and for you, and so will my sisters."

The boy nodded. As he walked away, Reed sensed Hestion coming up beside her.

"He seems half in love with you," he said.

"No. Only dazzled. Down deep he doesn't like me at all." She frowned. "And perhaps he shouldn't. The Aristene are not supposed to take sides. We're not supposed to wage wars in service of ourselves." In the back of her mind, she'd thought that the goddess would be absent from this fight. That she would shun it. Yet she was there, moving among the soldiers, willing to drink of their glory no matter how it was obtained. "We lead these men to fight against corrupted soldiers and in doing so corrupt ourselves."

"To save yourselves," Hestion said, and Reed sighed. She supposed that was true. The order must persevere, no matter what the cost.

"Initiate and hero," Veridian said, and they turned as she and Mol approached.

"Veridian has told me that the elders will attack the city," Mol said. "She thinks that a mistake. I disagree."

"So what will you do?" Reed asked.

"I will remain here, with the hero princess. I will make sure that the order does its duty by her"—she cast a slanting look at the apostate—"while the rest of you lead an army away to rescue those who do not need rescuing."

"And your horse," Veridian said, and clapped Mol on the shoulder. "Do not forget about that." Veridian looked at Reed, and Reed was struck by the lightness in her eyes. It had been a long time since she had seen her so alive. "I will go tonight, ahead through the valley, to put arrows into any Erleven scouts. And you two"—she gestured to Hestion and Reed—"take your comfort while you can. For in mere days we may all be dead."

In the morning, Reed woke in Hestion's arms, her head upon his chest in the predawn watching the light outside the window turn from dark to blue. He was awake, too, just quiet, as he often was. She felt the brush of his fingertips back and forth upon her shoulder.

"All across the castle people are waking just like this," she said. "After passing one more night in the beds of their lovers."

"Yes," Hestion agreed. "Though none will have done that night quite so well as we have."

Reed snorted. "I'm sure Lyonene and Alsander would have something to say about that." She slid up from his chest and pushed away with a sigh, reluctant to leave him for the cool air and the cold stone beneath her feet. There was no point in building up the fire; they would be gone before it had time to warm them. As she leaned for her boots, Hestion grabbed her around the waist and pulled her back into bed.

"Do you wish to be last to the formation?" she asked, laughing, and pulled herself free.

"Wait." He rolled onto his elbow and looked her up and down. "Show me."

She knew what he wanted, and reached into the aether to draw her armor onto her body. For just a moment she saw the way it shimmered and the brightness of the white cape, all reflected in his eyes.

"Do not leave my side," he said. "For the duration of this battle, we fight together."

"As long as you don't fall back asleep," she teased, and slipped out the door.

On her way to the stable she stopped short as King Urdien strode from his castle to the ranks of his men.

He looked both older and younger as he prepared to march, his back straight beneath armor of leather accented with gold. Silver touched his shoulders and covered the greaves upon his legs. He wore a short cape in the Cassan colors and on his head a finely wrought crown that sparkled in his graying hair. Prince Ullieth strode behind him.

"Is Urdien mad?" Lyonene asked from beside her, and Reed jumped. Lyonene had softer footsteps than a cat. "The boy isn't well enough to fight."

"I'm sure he just means to ride out with us. A young man wouldn't want to miss it." Reed and Lyonene looked past the king and the prince at the women they were leaving behind. Yngarue and Wyrnnigrid stood on either side of their mother, their eyes fierce. The queen's eyes were fierce, too, and filled with tears. Her cheek was reddened by the handprint of her husband, which told Reed that she, too, would rather Ullieth remained in Cassor.

Reed and Lyonene approached the women.

"We'll keep him to the back," Reed said. "We'll look after him."

"Do you promise?" Wyrnnigrid asked.

"Promises are for children," Reed said, and Lyonene glanced at her in surprise. "But we will try."

"I wish I was riding to battle with you," Yngarue said.

"I, too, wish that," Lyonene said. "You should have been called to us, princess. And to think, I used to call you a mouse."

Reed looked at Mol, who stood beside the ladies. For all Mol's disapproval of her and of Lyonene, for all her disapproval of what they did now, Reed knew that the Aristene would look after the hero. Just as she knew that the moment it was over, she would inform the elders of what she and Lyonene had done. She nodded to Mol once, and Mol nodded back.

"Fight well," Mol said, and finally, she smiled. "Tell me what you see, when Ferreh takes the field."

"I will, sister," Reed promised.

Behind them, the army was ready to march. It was a small force compared with that which they'd commanded in Rhonassus, and Erlengard was not the impenetrable fortress of Roshanak. The battle they faced shouldn't chill her blood, but it did.

Silco whinnied as he cantered toward her, his silver chest piece flashing with every jolting stride. He was eager for battle, yet watching him, Reed felt doubt cut through her pride, and wished that he was back in Atropa, in a paddock, safe with Strawberry.

Reed swung into the saddle, and waited as Lyonene mounted her bay mare. As the army thundered away from the castle, Reed heard Mol's shout.

"Gloria Thea Matris."

43.

THE BATTLE OF ERLENGARD

The Veil opened in the trees just north of the city, upon high ground with good cover. Ferreh and Tiern, Jana, Aster, and Aethiel stepped out of the darkness and into the cool shadows on their horses. The air smelled like salt, and slightly of rotting seaweed. The ocean wasn't far from there—to the northwest, Erlengard was bordered by broad sand beaches and salt marshes full of birds. Below, the city seemed quiet, drawn in and suspicious. Aster couldn't be the only one to sense the loose snare of a trap.

"If it's as bad as the initiate feared . . . ," Jana said, and tightened her grip around her spear.

"Then we will know," Ferreh replied. "And we will retreat."

Aster glanced at her doubtfully. Ferreh hadn't picked up her sword for the first time in a thousand years just to retreat. They would fight, no matter what it was that they found.

"Leave the Areion behind," Tiern said, teeth bared and glistening. "They will have their chance to stomp any who escape our blades and tear them to pieces with sharp hooves."

Aster reached out to send away Rabbit, and the mare flapped her lips against Aster's fingers. "Keep your magic low, sisters," Tiern said. "Aster. Find us a path."

* * *

The Adonumrian priest stood in the main chamber that looked into the many tunnels of the hypogeum, the system of underground caves carved into the limestone sediment beneath the fortress of Erlengard. Before the brotherhood came, the caves had been used for burials, or the storage of pottery and goods. Now it was a stronghold of weapons, and the sleeping quarters of soldiers.

He stared down the nearest tunnel, past where the oval of natural light ended and farther beyond, where the orange glow from the torches died. He sensed movement there. And sounds. Breathing. Faint clicking as from the shell-covered wings of beetles. The army of Erlengard, given new purpose as the blades of the pale gray god, who would drive the serpent goddess back to the darkness.

The gold medallion hung heavy around the priest's neck as he prayed for visions, denying himself food and water, purifying his body through pain. Not long ago the medallion had hung around Brother Nestor's neck. But Brother Nestor was gone.

The Aristene would come soon. They would come and find a city that appeared dormant. Unprotected, full of no one but mothers and children, shopkeepers and stooped men with white beards. They wouldn't know that the army had gone underground.

The priest ran his tongue over dry lips and listened for the noises of his soldiers. Now that they had been changed, they no longer gathered around fires. They didn't wander the streets in search of trouble or play their games of colored stones. Instead they sought out the shadows belowground and waited there, their long fingers hanging and stretched skulls bent toward the dirt.

"Brother." He turned at the sound of another priest's voice, and a rivulet of blood ran from his nose. His tongue flicked out to taste it, the first drop of anything he'd had in days.

"Yes, brother?" he asked.

"They are here."

The line of Aristene followed Aster up and over the city wall, placing their feet after hers in the footholds, sliding their fingers into the same gaps between the stones that she did. Slowly and quietly they rose, twisting themselves up into Erlengard until one by one they reached the top. After a look to ensure no guards were about, they hopped over and crouched to gaze upon the fortress and the city beyond.

Aster squinted into the distance. Goats were bleating somewhere, and she saw small flocks of birds, kept birds fed by keepers who wore long tunics dyed the color of the red riverbeds of her youth. Farther off people moved through a marketplace, but not nearly so many as there should have been.

"Where is everyone?" Jana asked. The butt of her spear dragged against the stones.

"They are waiting for us," Ferreh said, and she led them onward, Tiern's eager breathing driving them from behind.

Ferreh moved as fast as a hound with a scent in her nose, and they passed through the interior of the castle like ghosts, until they found themselves again crouched behind a low wall, looking down on a cloistered square of green grass and pale sand pathways. In the center was a winding set of stairs that led down to a large underground chamber.

Aster craned her neck. The chamber was larger than it seemed—past the edges of the hole she glimpsed a swept-clean floor cast in shadow and piles of clay pots.

"Tunnels," Jana noted.

"Tunnels are a good place to fight," said Aethiel with a soft grunt. "They remove the advantage of numbers. And I like to smash men against one side and then the other."

"We all like to do that," said Jana, and Aethiel grinned.

Ferreh motioned for quiet as a team of four servants walked into view, carrying a whole roasted boar on a spit, suspended between four poles. The savory smell rose through the air, and Aster's stomach gurgled loudly. Her sisters gave her a sharp look, and she wrinkled her nose in apology. She was becoming as bad as Reed and Veridian.

Below, the servants descended with the boar, and the Aristene watched as they set it upon the ground. A moment later, the servants returned aboveground, and men began to drift into view within the chamber.

Only not men. Not quite. They moved strangely, with heavy, ungainly steps like children learning to use their legs. Some had malformed hands, or shoulders that jutted up at odd angles. One by one they fell upon the boar, kneeling around it and tearing at it with hooked fingers and teeth. They ate voraciously, their chins slicked with grease, shoving each other out of the way when too many swarmed the carcass.

"I've seen wolves with finer table manners," Jana noted, and Tiern curled her lip.

"What do you feel?" Aster asked. "Are they like Oreas?" Reed said that when she'd fought King Oreas, her magic had been dampened into nonexistence. But when Aster called her own in the face of these strange soldiers, she found it there, though her grip on it felt slippery, like it was a skittish cat who might at any moment wriggle out of her arms. She looked to Aethiel as the big Aristene tested her own magic, the silver upon her chest and shoulders shining brightly and then fading with her breath.

"They are like him," Aethiel whispered. "But not. Nor are they like the monsters I have faced."

"Lyonene said they created one," Aster said. "Prince Denros."

Aethiel stilled. She shook her head. "I do not sense one. Could she have been mistaken?"

Jana and Aster exchanged a glance. They knew Lyonene. They'd been there as she grew, watched over her during her training. "If Lyonene said such a one exists, then one exists," said Jana. "And we must be ready for it."

Thirty corrupted soldiers hunched in the pit below, tearing at the remains of the boar, and more darted in and out of view. "Elders," Aster said. "What is your order?"

Ferreh didn't look at her. She reached for her sword and drew it from its scabbard in one smooth motion. The blade whispered a melody against the leather and she raised it before her eyes, turning it back and forth in the light. "We will follow," she said, and before Aster could ask what she meant, Tiern leaped up onto the low wall and jumped down into the pit.

Aster, Jana, and Aethiel leaned forward, hands clutching the edge of the stones. Aster expected the air to be filled with the elder's rage, to hear Tiern's roar, but the only sounds were made by the soldiers as she kicked aside the bones of their meal.

Tiern fought with no shield, using the brute strength of her arms and elbows to create distance. In one hand she held a long dagger with the blade turned downward and with the other she wielded her short sword of bronze. Within moments of landing she'd killed five and spilled their guts into a pile—she stood on the twitching backs of the dying to kill still more. They tried to swarm her two at a time, three at a time, but she was too strong and shook them off like a bear shaking brambles from its fur.

Ferreh stepped up onto the wall and leaped gracefully down into the cavern. By the time Aster and the others followed, the fight was over, and Tiern stood, blood-streaked and delighted, her breath only a little fast.

Jana walked toward the pile of corpses, indistinguishable now from the carcass of the boar they'd been feasting on. She prodded a piece of one with the tip of her spear.

"What did you bring us for?" she asked.

"For them," Tiern replied. She pointed her dagger into the darkness as the cave tunnels came alive with movement and the groans of reinforcements. Corrupted soldiers flooded the chamber in a torrent, and knocked Aster backward to be caught under the wave.

The army of Cassor stopped in the heat of late afternoon to rest and take water. It was the third day of their fast march. Reed and Hestion rode together at the rear, while Alsander was forced to entertain King Urdien and little Prince Ullieth at the fore. Lyonene rode far ahead, and when she looped back, she still hadn't seen Veridian, nor had she found any bodies of Erleven scouts with arrows protruding from their chests.

She dismounted to stretch and find her bay mare something to drink. "It's not much farther. We'll be at the gates of Erlengard before dark."

"I'd hoped Veridian would have rejoined us by now," said Reed. "I worry what she'll do if she gets there before us."

"Yes," Lyonene said, walking away. "It is always a worry, what Veridian will do."

Reed and Silco wandered through the army as they sat in rows and groups, seeking out the shade of the trees, hunched over a dipper of water or a torn chunk of bread. She sensed eyes upon her and looked up to see the young soldier, Macon, watching from where he sat with his elbows upon his knees.

"There he is again," Hestion said, riding so close on Target that his knee nudged against hers. "When this battle is over he'll challenge me to fight for you."

"He looks fierce," Reed said. "I think you'll lose." She looked again at the boy. "If this was some other battle, I would keep him in my shadow, cut arrows out of the air before they could pierce him."

"Like you did for Sar."

Reed smiled at the memory.

"Thank you for riding with us," she said.

"I will always be here, Reed."

A horn sounded, and the soldiers snapped to attention to resume the march. They were grim and pale. Only the young ones seemed eager to fight and a few of them glimmered slightly. Many more than that would fall.

It was just as they reached the river that Reed felt a cold ball twist in the pit of her stomach.

"Lyonene!"

"What?" Lyonene asked, riding close.

"It's Aster. They're in trouble." Reed dug her heels into Silco's sides and he sprang, his stride jarring as he scrabbled with his bad hoof. "Find her," she said to him, and he stretched out to gallop, making for the gate.

The gate burst open. What came through it brought them skidding to a halt.

All that remained of Parmenin's brown robes were tattered pieces. They hung around his neck and dangled in strips where they had split to make way for his new form.

Hestion and Lyonene rode up beside Reed. "What is that?" Hestion asked.

"It's one of them," Lyonene said, and spat on the grass. "One with a fragment of bone inside. I can feel it; my armor doesn't want to stay."

Nor did Reed's. But she couldn't let it go. "It's not one of them," she said. "It's Parmenin."

"The priest?" Hestion asked, aghast.

The priest. Parmenin lurched toward them, bent forward, his shoulders bulging with muscle and his legs snaked through with veins as thick as ropes. Tiern said that the bones of the prophet made one more like themselves, and Parmenin was still a man. Just a warped one, stronger and larger and clearly suffering. There were no claws on his fingers nor fangs in his mouth. But one of his eyes had turned a sickening yellow, and the pupil stretched like a cat's in the dark. She couldn't see the other eye. It had swollen shut, the lid bright red as a boil.

"Aristene!" he cried. "Matchmaker!"

Reed and Lyonene looked at each other. At least he still knew who they were.

"Make this stop!" He fell to one knee, breathing heavily. Lyonene drew her sword.

"No!" Reed stuck her arm out.

"There's nothing else we can do, Reed."

"If we can get the prophet's bone out of him, he'll be well again."

"And how do we do that?" Lyonene looked at the priest with pity, and jerked her reins tight as her mare tried to bolt. "The bone could be anywhere."

Reed peered at the swollen eye. "Let me try."

Behind them, soldiers cried out in shock as the army joined them on the field and saw Parmenin.

"Tell them to hold, Lyonene. Give me a chance."

"They seem to be in no hurry to charge," Lyonene said, but she circled her horse and rode back to the lines.

"Reed," Hestion cautioned. "Be careful."

She walked slowly toward Parmenin. It was difficult to look at him. She could barely see a trace of the handsome, dark-haired priest he had once been.

But though his appearance was monstrous, in his heart Parmenin was gentle. If the bone truly made him more of what he was, then perhaps she had nothing to fear.

"Parmenin, I know what to do. Let me help you."

His yellow eye followed her hopefully. "Help me?"

"Yes." His breathing was ragged. His massive shoulders trembled and flexed. She drew one of her smaller knives, slowly, with her other palm open and raised.

Reed's armor shuddered. It hated the nearness of this thing, and shrank from the corruption of the bone flowing throughout it. And, as if the bone didn't like the armor either, Parmenin squeezed his eye shut and screamed.

"Reed, look out!" Hestion cried.

The impact caught her in the shoulder and knocked her to the ground. She scrambled back, and felt the soreness in her arm.

"Parmenin, stop!" she shouted as he swung again, stumbling blindly ahead. He squeezed his head between his hands so hard she thought he might crack his own skull.

"I don't want to hurt you! I don't want to fight you!" she cried, but didn't know if he heard her through his ceaseless screams.

Another blow rolled her across the grass. She tried to stab up with the knife and he knocked it from her hand. Reed gritted her teeth. She had to put an end to this. Aster and the elders were inside the city and needed their help.

She heard Lyonene shout just as the ground began to rumble beneath her feet.

Reed looked to the open gates, but the rumbling was coming from everywhere. It was loud as a herd of horses.

The army of Erleven erupted from every passageway. They flooded through the gate behind Parmenin; they clambered over the walls of the hill fort. Corrupted soldiers rushed over the army of Cassor in a sea of elongated faces and open mouths. Her eyes widened with horror as long fingers pulled the arms from soldiers' bodies like the wings from flies.

"Aristene!"

Reed flew forward onto her belly as Parmenin collided with

her. She'd barely rolled over when he leaped upon her, and it took all the strength in her arms to hold his teeth at bay. She looked for Hestion, but he had been drawn back to the army, fighting corrupted Erleven soldiers alongside his Docritae.

"Parmenin, stop this!"

"You." He leaned over her, his face close. "Were a liar from the start."

"You're not wrong," Reed replied, and thrust her fingers into his swollen eye.

It was feverish and disgusting, at once soft and yet hardened like leather at the edges. Parmenin bellowed and threw himself back to paw at his face like an animal. Reed looked at her dripping fingers. They were empty, but it was in there. She'd felt the smooth edge of a bone fragment.

From behind she heard a strange clicking and turned to see a corrupted coming toward her—before he could attack he flew past, knocked aside by Silco's hooves. Reed smiled.

"Good boy." Then she screamed as Parmenin lunged and grabbed Silco by the leg. He wrenched the horse off his feet and threw him across the grass.

Reed stared wordlessly as she watched her black colt land, legs askew, his black eyes fearful as he rolled. Her vision went red.

"Don't. Hurt. My HORSE!"

She drew her sword and charged, carving a red line into Parmenin's shoulder, ducking his blows, her anger quick and hot. She swung her arm and in the arc of her blade saw the tips of monstrous fingers fly—when he screamed she leaped on him and bore him to the ground. She dug into his swollen eye until she was red to the second knuckle, and then to her palm. She found the shard of bone and grasped it even though touching it made her arm go loose. She dropped her sword and used her sword hand to help her first hand pull free.

The shard came out, and Reed sat back, gazing at it in horror. It was one of the prophet's teeth. And most of Parmenin's brains had come along with it, attached to the root.

On the grass, the priest's face began to return to the one she remembered. The yellow faded from his remaining eye, and when Silco limped close to him to sniff, Parmenin reached out his hand to brush the horse's muzzle.

"Did I hurt him?" Parmenin asked quietly. He looked at Reed and smiled as his last breath left his shrinking lungs.

Reed squeezed the tooth in her fist. In a fury she thew it upon the ground and slammed down upon it with the butt of her sword, again and again until it was dust. The zealot priests had done this. From them, no one was safe, not even another man in holy robes.

She turned back to the battle with bared teeth. On Lyonene and Alsander's side of the battlefield closer to the gate, they had formed ranks, and the Cassan soldiers were fighting well, modeling their movements after those of Hestion's Docritae who fought beside them. But King Urdien's soldiers had scattered. Some had run for the cover of the trees, and the ones who did fight only did so because they were overrun and had no choice.

Reed searched for the king. She saw him near the cover of the bridge, turning and turning his tall gray horse. The air around him glittered with gold and Reed's magic rose.

"Urdien!" She shouted and waved her sword. Her Aristene

voice carried to him through the fray. "You are the king! Give them courage!"

Urdien looked back at her. As her magic touched him, his dazed eyes cleared. He put heels to his horse and charged along the lines with a great cry, using his shield and his blade to clear a path for his weaponry.

"Set the scorpions," she heard him shout. "Take aim!"

"More," Reed whispered, and pushed her magic further. She nodded to Urdien. "More!"

The king's eyes took on a wild light. He gave her a rakish smile and spurred his horse.

Before the awed eyes of his soldiers, Urdien ran down the enemy, his sword arm swinging, felling corrupted soldiers beneath his horse's hooves. Reed looked ahead of him, where one of the soldiers in his path wielded a long pike. She felt the goddess's jaws yawn wide.

The pike took down the king's horse, and Urdien tumbled to the ground. As his Cassan soldiers began to fire the scorpions from the space that he'd cleared, Reed's blood sang in her ears. Urdien of Cassor was set upon by the enemy and torn apart, screaming amid one final burst of gold. Kleia Gloria's jaws snapped shut.

Glorious death.

Reed jumped onto Silco's back and rode to Urdien's soldiers.

"Fire," she ordered them. "Fight! Fight for the king!" All around her, men and boys glimmered with gold as untested soldiers used their weapons to hack into their enemies, as farmers and shopkeepers became warriors beneath helmets and behind shields.

With glory fresh in her veins, Reed turned and sliced an Erleven guard clean through the middle to fall into two halves. She called to Lyonene and Hestion. "To the gate!"

She and Silco lurched across the battlefield, with Hestion and Target not far behind her. When they plunged through the gate, Hestion leaped from Target's back and sank his sword into the exposed throat of an Erleven guard. Reed jumped to the ground, and he covered her flank as she cut through the corrupted, and their war stallions kicked and fought with their hooves.

Lyonene raced in in their wake.

"What took you so long?" Hestion teased.

"I had to come on foot," she said as she stabbed a soldier through the gut. "My horse was shot out from under me."

"These corrupted soldiers have no bows," said Reed.

"I know. The shot came from our own men. They've never been to war." Lyonene shoved Reed lightly. "Why do you think I didn't see it coming?"

"Where is Veridian? We have to get to the elders."

"If we sensed danger for the Aristene, she might have sensed it as well," Lyonene replied. "She may already be ahead of us."

Hestion wiped blood from the blade of his sword as more warped soldiers lurched into the street that led to the gate.

"I don't like this road," Lyonene said grimly, and turned to shout for Alsander.

On the battlefield before the city, Alsander held the men together in King Urdien's stead, barking orders in a voice that left no space for fear. He and Phaeton were streaked in red, galloping through the lines. Giving mortal men the will to fight.

"He should stay," Hestion said. "They'll need him."

"Shouldn't you stay, too?" Lyonene asked.

"No," said Reed. "Where I go, he goes." She looked back at her black colt. "Silco," she shouted, "look after Target!"

The stallion whinnied, and Reed, Lyonene, and Hestion fought their way farther into the fortress, until they reached the interior of the castle. Fewer soldiers challenged them here, and they were able to take a breath.

"Where are we going?" Lyonene asked.

In the distance, they heard a great, deep bellow.

"Well," said Reed. "That'll be Aethiel."

Veridian stood upon the lip of the massive cavern, where the Aris-tene fought amid a sea of corrupted soldiers. Every now and again a priest in a ratty gray robe dotted the mass, issuing orders that the soldiers only seemed to be half following. It was hard to know where to jump into such a writhing mess. But the priests, at least, were a problem she could deal with.

Veridian took her bow from her back and placed an arrow on the string. She fired; her arrow went clean through her target's eye. His other eye fixed on her briefly before he slumped to the ground in a pile of robes and his soldiers trampled over the top of him.

"That's one," she muttered, and took aim again. "Two. Three." But by the third she had no longer gone unnoticed.

"Brothers!" one of the priests shouted. "Get into the tunnels!"

"Aster," she called from above, and saw her beloved's face rise like the sun, already bruised and streaked with blood.

Aster hacked through the soldier she held and Veridian leaped down upon him, her heels driving him farther into the dirt. She pulled Aster close and kissed her, hard.

"How can you fight here?" she asked. "We are ankle deep in blood and monsters."

"Before we're done they'll bury us to the waist," Aster panted, smiling. "But Aethiel and the elders will make us more room."

Across the chamber, Aethiel bellowed and ran through soldiers, her arms outstretched, head lowered like a bull. She was cut, and bleeding, but seemed not to care. On the other side of the main cavern, Jana formed rings of fallen foes, running them through with her spear before using it to vault to better ground.

"Where are the elders?" Veridian asked. She crossed blades with a corrupted soldier and was surprised by the strength in his arms. He knocked her weapon wide and struck her in the face, then head-butted her so her nose spurted blood. Aster brought the tip of her sword down between his shoulder blades and he sank to the sand.

"They're clearing tunnels."

Veridian scanned the space. She saw two tunnels leading east, both littered with corpses. From inside of one she heard the distinct sound of Tiern roaring.

"These things are like locusts," Aster said, pulling her blade free of the soldier's body. "Though the flow seemed to lighten a moment ago."

"That was Reed and Lyonene. They've brought an army of heroes to your rescue, and some of Erleven's fighters were drawn to the gate. You're welcome."

Ferreh strode out from one of the tunnels. The sight of the elder with her sword drawn and streaked in gore, her gold-flecked eyes hard and bright as stars, made the apostate take a breath.

"Once these tunnels are clear, we must go and help Reed and Lyonene at the gates," Veridian called.

"First we must kill all of the priests," Ferreh said.

"But you will never reach the last of us," one of the priests said, his voice rising from the shadows, echoing down one tunnel before issuing from another.

"Where is he? Find him!" Ferreh barked.

"You will never snuff us out, Abomination," the priest cried. "Not us, nor the god who walks in shadow. We will hunt your outsider goddess to the ends of the world. And beyond it."

"What does that mean?" Jana asked as the caves began to collapse.

"They've knocked out the supports," said Aster. "They're trying to seal us in."

"We have to go!" Aethiel shouted.

"No!" Ferreh turned around wildly. "Get the jawbone blade! Stay, and kill them to the last!"

"We'll kill them to the last later," Veridian said. She nodded to Aethiel, and the big Aristene grasped the elder around the waist, and leaped up and out of the cavern chamber.

44.

BETRAYAL OF DUTY

Reed, Lyonene, and Hestion found the Aristene gathered around the mouth of an underground chamber, covered in blood and dust. Ferreh stared down into the space, which appeared to have caved in.

"Aster," the elder ordered. "Find a path."

Aster extended a tired, shaking hand. Then she let it fall. "I can't. There isn't one."

Ferreh cursed.

"You're all alive," Lyonene said. "Where is Prince Denros?"

"No one has seen this monster you speak of," Tiern said. "All we faced below were twisted soldiers."

Lyonene touched Reed's arm. "He wouldn't run away," she whispered. "We need to leave this place."

"Agreed," said Tiern. But Ferreh lingered, pacing back and forth before the edge of the chamber. "Ferreh. Come. There is nothing more to be done here."

Ferreh slashed her sword through the air angrily, and Reed felt the air move across her cheek.

"Ferreh," Tiern said again, and finally, Ferreh turned her head.

Reed and Lyonene led the way to the gates. As they passed through the city, Veridian whistled, calling for Mol's horse, Verger.

There was no response.

"Perhaps he made his escape through the gate with the army," Aster suggested.

They reached the battlefield beside the river. Everywhere they looked lay the bodies of the dead and the dying. Aethiel moved from soldier to soldier, offering a kind hand and a cut throat to the suffering. To the corrupted she offered only the heel of her boot, stomped down.

"They don't revert when they die, like the monsters did," Tiern noted, staring down at the twisted spine of an Erleven guard.

"Perhaps because the corruption is in their blood," Lyonene said. "These are the soldiers made by the jawbone dagger."

"Lyonene!"

Alsander stepped out from behind his golden stallion and Lyonene raced into his arms.

"Where is Ulli?" Hestion asked, beside Reed. "Ulli!"

"He's here," said Alsander. The boy been weeping over the body of his father, but when he saw Hestion he ran to him and collapsed against the older prince's chest. Not far away, Reed saw Silco standing beside Target, and her shoulders slumped with relief.

"What will they do now?" Lyonene asked, looking at Urdien's body draped in his bloodstained cape.

"That is not our problem," said Tiern, but Ferreh was quiet, surveying the army.

"Help them collect their dead," the elder said. "We will return with them to Cassor."

The return journey to Cassor took much longer with the addition of wounded men, and the heaviness of the army's footsteps. But after camping three nights in the valley, at dusk on the fourth day they reached the small town that bordered the castle.

At first, their spirits were so dampened that none noticed the quiet. It wasn't until a young woman burst from her home screaming for the king and ranting about a great monster that they realized what had happened.

Prince Denros had come to Cassor for his betrothed.

"That's why he wasn't there," Lyonene said. "He came around behind us."

Reed put her heels to Silco, and she and Lyonene raced ahead with Hestion and Alsander close behind.

As the castle came into view, Reed drew her sword, for all the good it would do. She knew what the quiet village meant. She knew what they would find inside.

They dismounted and ran.

Yngarue stood in the great hall. Her pale blue gown was sprayed by so much blood that at first Reed thought it was a pattern upon the fabric.

"Yngarue?" Reed asked.

The princess turned to them with blank eyes. Reed and Lyonene walked to her slowly, past a pile of furs and fabrics. The fire in the hearth had burned out and the air was chilled.

"She's so cold her lips have turned to match the dress," Lyonene said softly. "Alsander, bring one of those blankets. Yngarue—" She took her hand. "Are you hurt?"

"Where is everyone?" Reed asked. The quiet was unnerving. Their voices echoed. Hestion's footsteps nearly made her jump.

"There should be guards," he said. "Servants. The castle wasn't left empty."

"Reed," Lyonene said. "Where is Mol?"

"No, don't!" Yngarue lurched toward Alsander as he reached down to take a blanket from the pile of furs.

He jumped back with a cry. It wasn't a pile of furs. It was a pile of broken bodies, and on the top lay those of Princess Wyrnnigrid and the queen.

"He killed them," Alsander said, staring with horror at their twisted shapes. He looked at Yngarue. "But he left you alive."

"Of course he did," Yngarue whispered. Her features twisted bitterly. "I am his betrothed."

Reed closed her eyes.

"Did you find him on the road?" Yngarue asked. "Did you kill him?"

Reed shook her head. "We didn't see him. We didn't know."

"Where is my father? Where is Ullieth?"

"Yngarue," Lyonene said gently, "where is Mol?"

Yngarue turned her head to the hearth. At first what lay inside looked like the ashen remains of logs. The white cape had burned completely away, and the silver armor had charred to black.

Footsteps sounded in the hall and the elders entered alongside the other Aristene. Soon all of Reed's thoughts were drowned out by the sound of Aethiel's screams.

The loss of Mol was a shock. The Aristene did not often lose their own, and they were no good at it. Hestion and Alsander stepped aside as Aethiel dragged the burnt corpse out of the hearth and onto her lap, and Jana collapsed beside her. Tiern struck the wall so hard that Reed saw blood bloom instantly on her fingers.

"Reed." Aster wrapped her in an embrace and tried to turn her face away. But she had to look. She had to see. Because otherwise she wouldn't be able to believe.

Mol was dead.

"Tell me how she fought," Aethiel said, between her sobs. "Tell me how she stood."

"She tried," Yngarue said listlessly. "She failed."

Prince Ullieth appeared in the doorway and raced to his sister. He seemed not to notice the bloodstains and buried his face in her dress.

"Father is dead," he said, and Yngarue rocked back slightly. One final blow.

Only not final, Reed thought as she looked at Ulli sadly. For soon the little boy would die as well. And then Yngarue truly would be alone.

"Ferreh," Veridian said. "What will you do?" She waited, and when the elder didn't reply, she turned to shout. "Ferreh! What do you do now?"

But Ferreh stood silent. She looked at Reed, just for a moment, and then her gaze wandered away.

"Denros and the priests will pay," Tiern said. "They will all pay." And then she, too, looked at Reed.

Reed stepped farther into Aster's arms. She heard shouts and saw Cassan soldiers and captains rush into the castle, calling out names of ladies and servants.

She thought of the young soldier, the boy called Macon. Had he survived? She'd searched for him in the aftermath of the battle but hadn't been able to find him.

"Collect her," Tiern said, referring to Mol. Veridian had gone to crouch beside Aethiel, gently sweeping the black-haired Aristene's tears away with her knuckles. "And get them up."

Veridian whispered to Aethiel and Jana, and Aethiel nodded.

"Take it. Cut it," Aethiel murmured. Jana drew a knife and cut the white cape from Aethiel's shoulders. She and Veridian spread it over Mol's remains, wrapping each part tenderly. Every Aristene in the room exhaled when it was out of sight.

Veridian turned as she crouched, facing the elders in profile. "They took her hand," she said.

Tiern went to the hearth and searched through the ashes. But Mol's right hand, the one with the missing fingertip, was not there.

"You are all cursed," Yngarue said.

Reed drew away from Aster. She moved toward Yngarue to comfort her and Yngarue shrank back.

"This is your fault," she cried. She pushed Ullieth behind her. "It was all put in motion by your coming here!"

Lyonene stepped forward, palms out, and Yngarue darted ahead, fast as a cat. She grabbed the dagger from Lyonene's belt and lunged at Reed.

Reed was so surprised that all she could do was stagger back. Hestion caught the princess gently by the wrist and the blade clattered to the floor.

"Yngarue," Hestion said softly. "They did not know." He tried to gather her to him, but she beat at him with her fists.

"Get out!" Yngarue shouted at Reed. "Take all of your cursed Aristene and go! And you." She looked at Alsander, who backed up a step, but Yngarue's attention shifted again to Reed and Lyonene.

"You call yourselves servants! Here to make me a glorious

marriage! Yet how did they intend to find me a husband when they had already taken those husbands for themselves?"

"Yngarue, no," Reed said, but it was too late.

"You bring me princes who are already married!" Yngarue pointed her finger between them. "Alsander to Lyonene, and Hestion to Machianthe!"

In the wake of the accusation the air grew still. Aster caught Reed's eye and Reed shook her head vehemently. But Tiern was watching Lyonene. The expressions on Lyonene's and Alsander's faces weren't of confusion but of fear.

"Take them," Tiern said.

"No!" Reed cried as Jana rose to point her spear to Alsander's chest.

"Take them, too," Tiern said, nodding to Reed and Hestion.

"Tiern," Aster protested. "She's done nothing wrong!"

"Then she has no reason to protest and should come willingly." Tiern picked up a length of rope. "Tie your heroes and get on your horses."

45.

FUNERAL PYRES BURN BRIGHT

"Did you even know Atropa had cells?" Lyonene asked.

"This isn't a cell; it's a cleared-out storeroom." Reed knocked the side of her fist against the door for emphasis and Lyonene rolled her eyes.

"It has a locked door and we're inside. It's a cell." She sat beside the small solitary window, reclined against a stack of barrels with one knee drawn up to her chest.

"A cell that we could break out of." Reed knocked against the wood, harder this time.

"Is that what they want us to do?" Lyonene asked. "To escape so they won't have to cut off our heads? Are we not taking their hint?"

"They're not going to cut off our heads." Reed tried to peer through the crack between the door and the wall. Somewhere else in the Citadel, Hestion and Alsander were pacing away in a similar room. Somewhere far enough away to keep the two pairs from shouting to each other.

"They're not going to cut off *your* head," Lyonene amended. "I don't even know why you're here. You didn't do anything wrong."

"But why did you?" Reed asked. She crossed the small room and pushed Lyonene's foot off the other barrel so she could sit down. Lyonene looked away. She was so beautiful, and for so long her beauty had seemed like another set of armor, one more layer of protection that made Lyonene impenetrable, invulnerable. But there would be no escape from the elders' justice. Reed just didn't know what form that justice would take.

"I loved him," Lyonene said. "And at the time . . . in that moment—it seemed like such a small thing. Just a little thing that I could keep for myself, in secret." Her lips twisted into a frown. "I never would have tried to be his queen. I would have found a way out of it. I just wanted it, for a little while."

Reed looked around their depressing cell, bare but for the barrels and a few sacks of grain. "I understand the impulse, if not the decision. I won't chastise you for it."

"You'd better not," said Lyonene. "You, who bends rules until they are circles."

"Rules, Lyonene. Not laws."

"Forgive me," Lyonene said sarcastically, and stuffed her foot back onto the barrel so it jabbed into Reed's thigh. "I forgot that you are the perfect Aristene. You must be annoyed that I will become a legend before you do."

Reed sniffed. "And how will you do that?"

"Because I will always be remembered when my head is stuck on a pike!"

"That won't happen to you."

"How do you know?"

"Because I won't let it happen." Reed leaned over and looked out the window. The sun had set, and bonfires had been started below, large enough to cast light all the way up to them in the Citadel.

Every warrior in the city gathered in remembrance of Mol, to sing and scream their grief into the flames.

"Glorious Death," Lyonene whispered, and for the first time Reed could hear how frightened she was. "Who thinks she has the power to do anything."

Reed reached out and slipped her fingers into her friend's, and Lyonene squeezed them, hard. "I won't let it happen," Reed said again. "I swear it."

Lyonene nodded, but she tugged her fingers away. "She's burning," she said, and Reed looked down. Mol's body lay upon the pyre, still wrapped in Aethiel's white cape. The acolytes had draped it with wildflowers before setting it alight.

"I wonder if they'll do the same for me," said Lyonene. "Or if they'll just throw my headless corpse into the sea."

"Lyonene. Enough." Reed watched the Aristene below dancing and tearing at their clothes. "We should have been there. She was our sister, too."

"Maybe that's why they held it in the square," said Lyonene. "So we could be."

Reed leaned away from the window as the wildflowers withered in the heat and the flames ate through Aethiel's cape. "Did we do this?" she asked.

"Did some small part of us know that Denros would return for Yngarue? Did we leave Mol there just so she would never be able to tell the elders what we'd done?"

Lyonene stared at her, horrified. "No, Reed. Of course we didn't. Mol was the one who said she would stay in Cassor. And we never could have predicted . . ."

"You're right," Reed said quickly. And in any case, the sin of trading a hero felt insignificant compared with the sin that had been exposed now.

"Veridian is again in the white city," Lyonene noted. "Perhaps that will be the good that comes of this—if she returns."

"Veridian will never return," Reed said, and Lyonene seemed startled by her tone.

"You sound so sure."

"I am sure." Veridian couldn't return. There was no going back from glorious death. She couldn't give back the blood. "I know it with as much certainty as I know that we will never make Yngarue her glorious marriage."

"No," Lyonene agreed, and Reed knew she was remembering the coldness in the princess's eyes. "The order will not be welcome in Cassor for generations. We have failed, Reed. We have made an enemy of a hero."

Hestion reclined in the storeroom on a sack of grain, watching Alsander pace a trench into the floor.

"We shouldn't have just let them take us," Alsander said. "The army of Cassor was with me. We should have fought."

"You'd have been overcome in the time it took to give the order," Hestion said, and Alsander glowered at him. Hestion reached for a sack of dried fruit and pointed to a jug on a shelf. "Is that water or wine?"

Alsander removed the stopper and sniffed. "Both. It's watered wine sweetened with honey."

"They know how to spoil a prisoner." He gestured for Alsander to bring it. The storeroom they'd been stuffed inside hadn't been cleared and they had their choice of things to eat. Alsander took a seat on another sack of grain and used his dagger to cut into a wheel of cheese. Both still had their daggers, and their swords. That was how little the guards thought of their threat.

Hestion watched the other prince from the corner of his eye. Alsander was handling their situation well, all things considered. He was a far cry from the boy who had visited them in Glaucia and wept during a hunt. And, Hestion supposed, even back then it had been unkind of him to laugh.

"You are right about the army," he said. "They would have followed you into a fight."

Alsander frowned. "Every army needs a commander to follow."

"But they could have looked to me. Instead they look to you. Even now the entire Cassan army would rise to your call."

"I don't know what I did to deserve it," Alsander said. But he seemed pleased. Hestion passed him the jug of wine and he sat with it between his knees. "What do you think they're going to do with us?"

"I don't know."

"This place is . . ." Alsander cast his eyes toward the ceiling, and to their small window, the only source of fading light. The look was wide and searching. When they'd been escorted through the city he'd barely blinked. At one point Hestion feared that both his eyes would simply pop out and roll down the stone street. Hestion had felt the same the first time he'd been brought here. With its fine buildings and elegant wares, and the eerily pervasive quiet, Atropa was like no other place he'd ever been. A place that few in the world would ever see.

But it wasn't a place he'd like to stay.

"The crossing of the Veil," Alsander went on. "The feeling that we're outside of time itself. It feels like here, anything could happen."

Hestion used his knife to carve yellow flesh from a fruit he had never tasted before. It was tart and sweet, and the juice turned his fingers sticky.

"These are violent women and we're at their mercy," Alsander said. "What an end for the princes of Cerille and Glaucia."

Hestion shrugged. "The gods would smile upon us for such a death."

"Your gods more than mine." Alsander leaned back against the wall and took a long drink from the jug of wine. "They won't kill us. Lyonene is always saying how the Aristene don't like to meddle. Where is the glory in killing two princes and starting two wars?"

It seemed to Hestion that there was much glory to be won in the wars that followed. But what Alsander said was true: in all the tales he'd heard from his father, and from Belden, that was not the way the Aristene operated. The heroes they guided were the ones to shape history, not the Aristene themselves. A small distinction, but an important one when it came to the safety of his and Alsander's necks.

"Alsander," Hestion said, "are you and Lyonene really . . ."

"Yes. She is my wife." He glanced at Hestion and nodded with a cocked eyebrow. "And you and Reed?"

"No. I asked, and was denied."

"Ha," Alsander scoffed with a curl of his lip.

"Though if your marriage to Lyonene is allowed to stand, I suppose Reed will have no reason to decline."

They laughed, and the sound of it echoed against the walls of their small storeroom prison.

"They're going to kill us." Alsander sighed.

Veridian watched as her former sisters drank before the flames of Mol's funeral pyre. Two more fires blazed on either side, built up high to cast light all the way to the stars. The emotions of the Aristene swung wildly from clothes-rending despair to the bubbling laughter of ecstasy, but Veridian felt none of it. Veridian felt nothing. And she should have. Mol had been an Aristene almost as long as she had been. Mol, who was fierce and quick and cranky. Who followed the goddess's laws and so loved Atropa that she rarely wandered far. There were few better Aristene than Mol. And yet Kleia Gloria had let her die, at the hands of a monster.

Aster sat at Veridian's side on the Citadel's steps and wept into her shoulder. This was the only thing that touched the apostate anymore. The love of this woman, and of their foundling. The love she felt for bratty Lyonene, and even the love she'd buried for her mentor, Tiern. But love was not enough.

The wildflowers draped over Mol's body burned and withered. The body itself was already mostly burnt, mostly ash. What remained of Mol would blow away upon the wind, through the square, past the tears of her sisters, to settle upon the fertile dirt.

"Veridian," Aster said as she cried, "please come home."

She wrapped her arms around Aster and stared into the fires. She couldn't come home. There was no home to come to. "Atropa isn't home," she whispered into Aster's soft shoulder. "There is nowhere that I can go."

FOUR

SAVIOR

46.

THE ELDERS' JUSTICE

In the morning, Reed and Lyonene were taken by acolytes to be fed, and allowed to bathe in a private pool of the communal bathhouse before they were taken to face Ferreh and Tiern, who would hear their explanations. There the elders would mete out their justice, for them and for their heroes.

Reed kept her ears sharp for Hestion's voice as she and Lyonene walked back toward the Citadel. The acolytes refused to answer questions about the princes. And since they'd been tossed into their storeroom cell, they'd seen no one but acolytes. Reed hadn't even seen Aster.

"I can't stop thinking of Yngarue," Lyonene said, her shoulders trembling slightly in the clean white tunic. "We just left her there, Reed. With the bodies of her family stacked at her feet. What if Denros changes his mind about sparing her and comes back?"

Reed had never seen what the prophet's bone had made of Prince Denros, but it took only a blink to imagine his massive shadow falling across Yngarue's face, his hands reaching for Wyrnnigrid. Reed squeezed her eyes shut and shook the images away. "We have our own troubles to face," she said. "And besides, Yngarue is a survivor. And now she's a queen."

"A queen with a monster on her trail."

"After this is over, that monster will be dead," Reed promised.

Their pace slowed as they reached the square. The fires were out, but smoke still rose from the remains of the great bonfires. The pale stones were smeared with coal and spilled ale and wine. It was mostly empty now, but a few mourners remained, lying upon the ground or seated upright in the shade cast by the walls of nearby buildings.

"Reed," Lyonene whispered. "It's Aethiel."

Aethiel had taken some of the ashes and marked her face, ash dragged in three lines across the black band of her Fennbirnian crown. She wore her armor, the shred of white cape dangling behind her shoulders.

"She has never looked smaller," Lyonene murmured.

The acolytes escorting them nudged them on, but not toward the Citadel steps. Instead they were ushered toward the stable. "Where are we going?" Reed asked, but received no answer. She supposed she didn't need one when they walked inside, and found their Areion.

And their mentors.

Reed put her arms around Silco's neck and he bit her, but very gently. Then she turned and nodded a greeting to Sabil, who she hadn't seen since departing for her Hero's Trial. Like the acolytes, their mentors offered no explanations, and Reed and Lyonene traded an uneasy glance. They'd had so many questions, left to themselves in the empty storeroom. But now Reed found she'd rather not know the answers. She was glad to see Silco and Aster, but a last moment with her Areion and her mentor suddenly felt like just that. Their last moments.

Aster crossed her arms. "I've never known you to be this quiet without a scowl upon your face."

"What is this?" Reed asked. "One last kindness? A chance to say goodbye?"

"Or a chance to escape," said Lyonene, with her fingers entwined in Strawberry's mane. "Are we supposed to overpower you and use them to flee?"

It was only a jest, but Aster looked at the girl with surprising coldness. She jerked her chin at Sabil, and the other mentor led Lyonene and her horse out of the stable and toward the pastures.

"Wait," said Reed.

"It'll be all right, Ox," Lyonene said. But as she left the stable, she looked at Aster one more time like she was hoping to be forgiven.

"Of course this isn't goodbye," Aster said once Lyonene and Sabil had gone. "You and Silco have done nothing wrong."

"But what about Lyonene? Where is Sabil taking her?"

"We'll rejoin them when we face the elders. You have nothing to fear, Reed. The elders will know that you haven't broken your oaths."

"You're not answering me. What's going to happen to Lyonene?"

"Lyonene spoke the oaths the same as you," Aster said, her face grave. "And she broke them."

Reed's fingers tightened around locks of Silco's mane. But Aster didn't want to be cold. She loved Lyonene. She was only steeling herself for what was to happen. "You don't know that she broke them," Reed started. "She might not have—"

"Don't lie to me, Reed. There's no point. Her deception would only have lasted until she next gave blood to the Outfitter. The

Outfitter would have known."

"You didn't tell us that," Reed said.

"We shouldn't have to."

"Aster, please. She made a mistake."

"She made a choice. And those choices have consequences."

"I won't let her be hurt," Reed said.

"It is the elders' decision. You will not interfere."

Reed stepped away from Silco and reached for her mentor's hand. "What would you do if it was me?"

"But it's not you," Aster said, and turned to lead Reed out.

"You probably wish you'd stayed with Aster," Sabil said as she and Lyonene walked back from the pasture after bidding farewell to Strawberry. "I think you always wished that she was your mentor instead of me. But I tried, Lyonene. I gave you my best."

"I'm sorry to disappoint you," Lyonene said dryly.

"No." Sabil smiled, close-lipped. "That's not what I meant." She touched Lyonene's chin and Lyonene looked at her in surprise. "Those years in the Summer Camp you were so fearless. So focused. You harbored no doubts about your destiny. But I didn't instill in you what I should have. I was too busy trying to keep up."

Lyonene didn't know what to say. Sabil was small, dark of hair, with an olive complexion. She wasn't as pretty as Aster was, nor as great a warrior. And Lyonene had never listened enough to her.

Sabil wore her armor of silver scales and leather that ended just above her knees, the white cape as clean and bright as Lyonene's tunic. When she lowered her head, her short black hair swept forward and obscured her face. "Whatever punishment the elders give should be mine to face as well."

"No," Lyonene said. "My choices were my own." She took a deep breath. "And they seem very stupid now." She smiled, and Sabil did, too, sadly. "I should have looked more to you. Learned everything you had to teach. I didn't make it easy." And now there was no more time. She turned back to Strawberry where the little roan mare watched from behind the wooden fence. "What will happen to her?"

"She'll be looked after. I promise."

"She barely had the chance to be an Areion," Lyonene said. She and the mare had just begun to understand each other. "Well. Let's go, then, mentor. The elders will not be put off." Sabil nodded and led Lyonene back toward the Citadel. It was hard not to look back at her horse one more time. Harder still to imagine her forever in the hills of Atropa, running free without her rider.

Reed thought they would face the elders' justice in the square before every Aristene in the city, with Mol's ashes still smoldering in silent judgment. Instead, Aster led her around the long, curving colonnade to the rear of the Citadel.

Reed's feet crunched upon the pathway of crushed white stone. She knew where they were going: to the walled courtyard that abutted the cliffs and the sea. It was peaceful, and the waves against the cliffs quieted her thoughts. Or at least, they usually did.

They walked inside. The sun was high and filled the garden with light, and the sweet fragrance of the large purple blossoms on the border shrubs was heavy in the air.

Aethiel was there, as were several acolytes. Ferreh and Tiern waited on the steps that led back inside. The elders' ancient armor shone upon their bodies, their white capes thrown back. Tiern had braided her many-colored hair tight to the sides of her head, leaving the back to flow loose in a warrior's mane.

Hestion and Alsander had been placed a few steps below the elders, their wrists bound. When Reed looked at Hestion, he smiled at her and winked.

It was clear that Alsander felt none of the same ease. His face was tense as he searched the grounds for Lyonene, and Reed felt pity; it was easy now to say that Lyonene had acted stupidly—done something none of them would have done. But the truth was that all could understand the urge to remain with a hero. Had Lyonene not crossed that final boundary and broken her oaths, she and Alsander might have been allowed to stay together.

Footsteps crunched on the stone path as Lyonene and Sabil entered. The resolute sadness on their faces made Reed's throat close with panic. It struck her suddenly that they had no plan. There was no way out of this.

"You beat me," Lyonene said.

Reed opened her mouth but found no words. It wasn't until Lyonene and Sabil had walked past that she realized what she should have said. "Like always," she quipped softly.

She and Aster followed Lyonene and Sabil as they went to stand before the elders. When Reed moved to stand beside them, Aster held her back by the arm.

"We are here only to witness. The elders will not question you."

"But," Reed began.

A change of wind brought a waft of wine.

Veridian had come.

"Am I too late for the farce?" The apostate crossed the grass, ambling off the groomed paths. She was so drunk that when she climbed the steps she stumbled and Aethiel had to reach out and catch her.

"We are here and not within the sacred dome so that you might attend," said Tiern. "Don't be ungrateful."

"Ungrateful." Veridian made a face. "Ungrateful, my balls and ass. With or without me, you couldn't have this in the dome." She waggled her fingers in the direction of Hestion and Alsander. "Those mortal princes aren't allowed there either."

"Veridian," Ferreh said. Her eyes shifted to Lyonene. "You disrespect your sister."

"No, please," Lyonene said. "I'd like for at least one of us to be having a good time."

Aster let out a small, exasperated breath, and Reed was inclined to agree. Already the elders were angry. Tiern's fingers hadn't left the hilts of her twin daggers.

"What are you doing?" Reed whispered. "Are you trying to force their hand?"

"That hand is as a blade that's already fallen," Lyonene replied. "This is all I have now, Ox. The choice in how I live to the last." She turned to the apostate. "And Veridian and I choose to laugh."

Ferreh frowned. Tiern showed her teeth. Perhaps this was why they'd chosen to handle the matter in private. They'd known how little control they would have over those in attendance.

"Will we be allowed to speak?" Alsander asked.

"No," Tiern said.

"What would you wish to say?" asked Ferreh.

Alsander looked at Lyonene. "Only to express my regrets. I did not understand the severity of the violation. Had I known, I never would have asked Lyonene to break her oaths." Reed thought he'd meant it as a kindness, but hearing it must have broken the last of Lyonene's heart. This was going to cost her dearly. And it hadn't even been worth the asking.

"Is that all?" Ferreh asked.

Alsander lowered his head.

"Then do you, Lyonene, have anything you wish to say?"

Lyonene looked at Tiern, whose hand had left her dagger and moved to her sword.

"No," Lyonene replied. Ferreh closed her eyes. She nodded, and Tiern drew her weapon.

"Wait!" Reed and Veridian cried together. Reed looked at the apostate with desperate hope. Suddenly, Veridian didn't seem so drunk. She would save them, like she always did. She and Aster would save Lyonene, like they had saved Reed since the day they found her in the wreck of her settlement.

"You can't do this," Veridian said. "She's the finest initiate this order has had in generations. And you would kill her for one bit of lovesick foolishness?"

"For one law broken," Tiern said. "For an oath betrayed."

"So change the laws." Veridian turned to Ferreh. "We both know that you can."

"If there are no laws, there are no oaths, and if there are no oaths, there is no order."

"There are no oaths!" Veridian shouted. She looked at Aethiel.

"Before you stands an Aristene with a black crown etched across her forehead, and yet." She pointed to Reed. "Before you stands an initiate who failed her Hero's Trial, and yet." She spread her arms wide. "Before you stands an apostate, still breathing. *And yet.*"

Ferreh looked at Lyonene for a long time. Reed grasped Aster's hand.

"All of these things are true," Ferreh said. "And perhaps that is why the order fails, why our numbers dwindle and our borders weaken. Because we, as her shepherds, have allowed it to go astray." Ferreh turned to Tiern. "Do it."

"No!" Veridian shoved Lyonene backward down the steps as Tiern came forward. Sabil moaned; there were tears on her cheeks. Reed saw Alsander bare his teeth and raise his bound hands, but he could do nothing. Nor could Hestion, who looked at Reed with fear in his eyes.

"Stop!"

Reed threw her arms around Lyonene, her back to Tiern to stop her blade. "I will take her punishment!"

"Reed," Lyonene cried. "Don't!"

"They won't hurt me," Reed whispered into her ear. "It's all right." She turned, and slowly knelt upon the steps.

"Reed," Aster said. "What are you doing . . . ?"

Reed stretched out low in supplication, her hands to the stone before Tiern's feet. "Whatever punishment you would give her I claim for myself."

Tiern lowered her sword. "Get up, Machianthe! This is not what you are meant for!"

"It is now," Reed cried. "So do it, or don't. Say her punishment is banishment instead and I will take it. Say she will be imprisoned for an age and I will take it. Say death, and I will take it." She raised her eyes to Ferreh. "I do this for my sister. And for all the Aristene."

"This is your fault," Tiern whispered to the other elder. "So fix it. Drag her away."

But Ferreh didn't reply. She simply stood before Reed's outstretched fingers.

"Aethiel, take hold of your sister Aster."

Reed heard Aethiel move to obey. She heard Aster begin to struggle.

"What is this? Ferreh," she gasped. "You mustn't . . . Veridian, do something!"

Reed heard the shifting of feet. No hands grasped her to help her up. No cries rang out as a fight began to save her. Ferreh drew her sword, the blade singing free in one long, slow motion.

"Reed," she said gravely. "Do you understand what it is that you ask for?"

"I do," Reed said, heart hammering. The scar on her chest began to burn. But they would not kill her. She knew that Ferreh would never kill her. "Whatever punishment was hers, I will take instead."

"Very well," Ferreh said. "Then rise."

Tentatively, she got to her feet. Lyonene stared at her in disbelief. Aster's fist was to her lips and Veridian had her arms around her. But it was going to be all right.

"It is a brave thing that you do," Ferreh said. And then the elder turned and plunged her sword into Hestion's chest.

"No!" Reed screamed. She ran up the steps to him as he fell

to his knees, and Alsander fell backward in shock to scramble backward still farther.

"Reed," Hestion said. Blood flew from his lips. He fell onto his side and she caught him in her arms.

His blood ran down the pale steps. Ferreh's sword had gone straight through. She looked wildly to Aster and Veridian, to Lyonene. "Help him!" But though their faces were slack with shock, none moved.

She kissed his face. "Hestion? What can I do?"

He raised his bound hands to touch her cheek. But "Reed" was the last word he said.

She felt him go still and heavy in her arms. She felt the last of his breath leave. He was dead. The hero she had waited for all her life. The young man whose fate Kleia Gloria had bound to hers. Was dead.

"Ferreh, what have you done?" Reed drew her sword from her back and turned to charge the elder, to cut Ferreh down where she stood. Hands held her back. Aethiel's and Sabil's. Acolytes. Her blade was twisted from her hand and fell to clatter against the stone steps.

"This is not what I meant," Reed screamed. "This is not what I offered!"

Through a haze of angry tears she saw the elder's face, and it was gentle. It was sorry. But not sorry enough.

"Take her to the dome," Ferreh ordered. "And chain her beside the sacred well."

47.

CONSEQUENCES

Lyonene stood numb, her ears full of Reed's fading cries as she was dragged away to be chained in the tower. *Ox*, she thought. *My sweet, foolish Ox*. Only Reed was no fool. She knew they would never harm their Glorious Death, their savior, their foundling. She just never imagined they would turn the blade on Hestion instead.

She glanced down at the steps, where Hestion's blood ran in dark rivulets. She stepped back to keep it from touching her toes and stumbled. The stumble jarred her back into the present.

Lyonene shoved her way past Sabil. "What have you done? She was your greatest defender! And he was a hero!"

"You will be silent!" Ferreh rounded on Lyonene and Lyonene stopped short. Ferreh's normally calm, clear eyes were wild and ringed with white. "You speak to us of fault? You speak to us of responsibility? Get her out, Sabil. Before I lose my temper and take back the gift her sister has given."

"Gift? You call this a gift?" Lyonene struggled as Sabil and Veridian pulled her down the stairs, the apostate's grip like iron.

"Don't press them now, Lyonene," Veridian murmured. "See to your own hero. And then we will see to Reed."

Lyonene looked to Alsander, who gazed back at her, terrified. They had escaped, again. And all it had cost was Hestion's life, and the heart of her very best friend.

Aster sat at the foot of the Citadel steps, listening to Reed scream and fight her chains high up in the dome. Veridian held out a handful of food.

"Aster. Take this. Eat."

She pushed it away. "They won't let me go to her. I have never heard her like this. Not even when she was small and the raiders would return in her nightmares." Back then she'd held Reed while she thrashed; she'd pressed her cheek against the top of the little girl's head and promised that things would be fine, and she was believed. "They won't even tell me how long they intend to keep her chained!"

"I'd say just until she no longer wants to kill them."

Aster looked at the food in her hand. It was meat stewed with vegetables and wrapped in a torn bit of flatbread. With the exception of pan-fried Orillian noblebird, it was her favorite, and she wondered how many taverns or food stalls Veridian had to go to before she found it. Veridian sat down on the steps.

"You wouldn't know it looking at this deserted square," Veridian said, filling the silence. "But there are more Aristene in this city than I've ever seen. The tavern was so crowded that I had to throw elbows to make it out with just this little bit of meat."

She picked at the flatbread and tossed a piece to a crow, one of many who scoured the remains of Mol's funeral feast for scraps.

"I know," Aster said. Over the past days, Atropa's eerie silence had been broken by screams and wailing and the burning of fires, but also by hoofbeats and nervous footsteps. "They return for Mol—but not only Mol." Some other worry drew the Aristene home, as if they could sense the threat to the order and the upheaval in its ranks.

Aster looked up at the dome, where Reed's cries had mostly stopped. The only sounds now were the sharp cracks of chains against stone.

"How could Ferreh do this? Has she been an elder so long that she's forgotten what it is we give up? Why would she break Reed's heart again?"

"Would it have broken her heart less to see Tiern's sword through Lyonene?" Veridian asked.

"Yes," Aster said. "Because there was cause. It would have hurt, but she would have understood. This, not even I understand. I cared for Hestion not at all, but this was wrong."

"Once you would have said that the elders have their reasons."

"Once. Now I am half an apostate, like you."

Veridian took her by the shoulders. "You must never say that. You're not like me. You're angry because you have all of this. You're hurt because you have Reed, and the Aristene, and your devotion to them. You are not empty, like I am."

"Veridian . . ." Aster touched her beloved's face, that wild woman whose shouts had always made her want to shout, too, whose green eyes danced with such vitality that one look could make her gasp. Only Veridian's eyes didn't dance anymore. They were tired, and dull as stones. "Whether I am an apostate or not, what the elders did today will sow doubt. Reed is a firebrand—you know that as many will cheer for her imprisonment as rail against it. When did we become so fractured?"

"I don't know," Veridian replied. "But you and I will not fracture. I'll stay here with you. For as long as it takes, until they let our girl go."

They had driven the anchors in deep when they chained Reed to the wall. Removing them would leave a scar upon the mural of ships at sea. Or perhaps the chains were there to stay. Perhaps the order would have many causes now, to chain one of their own to the wall of the dome.

Reed sat with a straight back, grinding her teeth until her jaw hurt. The skin of her cheeks was tight from the salt that had dried down them in streaks. Upon the ceiling, the eyes of the goddess gazed down upon her, but Reed ignored them. They had taken her weapons, but if she'd had a bow and arrow she'd have fired a shot directly between Kleia Gloria's eyes.

She lifted her arms, and the chains made a clinking, serpentine sound as she dragged them across the floor. Her wrists were already torn and bloody from her struggles to get free.

It had been Aethiel and Sabil who'd dragged her up here.

"Be still, little sister," Aethiel had pleaded. "Do not fight."

"Didn't you kill your sisters on Fennbirn?" Reed had said.

She shouldn't have said that. The big Aristene's eyes had begun to water like she'd been slapped. But Reed had been too full of wrath to take it back.

"Machianthe."

Reed turned toward the opening of the stairs as Tiern stepped into view. "What do you want?"

Tiern studied the blood on her wrists.

"I am sorry, initiate. I did not know what Ferreh intended to do."

"They say elders are always of one mind."

"Not this time. I swear to you."

"He did nothing!" Reed shouted. Her voice was hoarse, her throat raw. "He violated no laws! He did everything that was asked!" Fresh tears welled and fell. "He was—he was—"

"He was sacred," Tiern said.

Sacred. Reed nearly collapsed, hearing the word. Sacred and beloved. And gone now. Gone, because of her.

"Was Ferreh afraid to come herself?"

"Would you have wanted to see her?"

"I would have wanted to put a sword through her chest!" Reed shouted, and pulled against her chains so hard that Tiern glanced at the anchor in the wall. "All I've done here is imagine what I should have done differently. How much faster I should have moved. How we should have killed you both, before you said one word!"

Tiern looked away.

"We were going to have a life together," Reed said. "I was going to go to him, as soon as the priests were defeated. It would have been . . ."

"Your reward," Tiern finished. "And you would have deserved it."

Reed slumped against the wall. "Where is Aster?"

"Aster will come when she is ready."

"She must be angry," Reed said. "She must think I acted rashly."

"Her love has greater weight than her anger. She will come. Soon."

"What about Lyonene? What happened to her?"

"She and her hero are safe."

"Good," Reed said. "Good." Lyonene and her hero were safe. But Reed's was not, and though she didn't think she had any more tears left to cry, she lowered her head and cried them anyway.

The priests had been playing with the dead Aristene's hand all morning, and Denros was growing impatient. It had been a mistake to leave the battle at Erleven to instead go to Cassor in search of revenge. At the time the idea had appealed to him: Yngarue deserved it, for what she'd done. But breaking that feeble queen and that weak, pale princess under his hands had been too easy, and over too fast. It was only the Aristene, beautiful in her silver armor and white cape, who had offered him any satisfaction.

He could still hear her scream as she charged him, still feel the strength of her blows. He flexed his fingers, imagining the feeling of squeezing her neck in his massive fist. There had been no fear in her eyes, even then. She'd been magnificent.

The priests had been right after all. The Aristene were the only adversaries worth facing.

Denros sighed, and relaxed his hand. No matter how he tried to hold on to them, the memories of the sensations faded. But he would make fresh ones.

"Is it done?"

He looked down at the priest in his shabby robes, where he knelt upon the floor preparing the Aristene's hand. He'd been there since before dawn, chanting, and tottering back and forth from the heat of the forge, as he used his magics to preserve the hand, crafting it into a tool to pierce through the Aristene's spells of protection and open a way into their sacred, hidden city.

"It's done," the priest replied. He remained on his knees as he held it up, not looking Denros in the eye. Ever since he'd crushed the elder priest's head like a grape, they tended to fear him, the poor, delicate underlings.

Denros took the hand. It was slightly shriveled, and discolored by the magics the priests had cast upon it, but it was still her hand. He touched the smallest finger, shortened by a blade sometime before they'd met. He traced over the symbols they'd sliced into her palm.

"This will take us to them?"

The priest's eyes remained on the relic into which he'd invoked his god's favor. He extended a finger as if to touch it, and Denros lifted it out of reach.

"With this," the priest said, "the uniter will cut through the darkness that protects the abominations. It will be as a blade cleaving the blackness in two. The opening will stretch wide to let our armies pass."

Denros looked down at the dead Aristene's shriveled hand. The priests had bored a hole into it near the wrist and strung it through with a golden chain, and Denros placed it around his neck. The hand rested lightly against his chest, a macabre, purplish bauble.

"Gather the men."

"We need to replenish our numbers, King Denros. There will

be many more abominations in their own city, and we have suffered heavy losses—"

Denros left the throne room. He moved with speed, and with surprising grace considering his bulk. He walked out of the castle and into the keep, where the army waited. Soldiers sat hunched in the shade, elongated hands hanging between their knees. Many rested together in piles, like packs of sleeping dogs. There were fewer of them than there were before but still more than enough.

He looked over the army. They would need no horses, but his eye caught on an enormous white stallion, tied near the stable. Denros took hold of its rope and the beast pulled back and rolled its eyes, its ears pinned flat to its head. It was a fine stallion, flawless in conformation, with a long, straight back and muscular hindquarters. It stomped its hooves, and the feathering around its legs waved in the wind.

"Saddle this one," Denros ordered.

"My lord," the priest said as two grooms hurried to obey. "We need more time; there are so few new recruits to be found—we've already taken the men and boys from the nearby towns and villages." The priest drew the jawbone blade from his belt and worried at it, thumbing the remaining molars.

"I see plenty of new recruits," Denros said.

"My lord?"

Denros reached out and took the jaw, easy as stripping a doll from a child. He grabbed the priest by the robes.

"What—what are you doing?" He squirmed and kicked as Denros lowered the blade toward his face. This one was such a worrier. He would carve him a new smile, and then he would feel better. "You mustn't! Adonumrian—the shadow god will not—"

"Your god has more need of soldiers now than priests," Denros said. "And besides, in a very few moments, I will be your god."

48.
UNREST

"Let me pass."

Reed lifted her head when she heard Lyonene's voice. She'd been chained in the dome of the Citadel for three days, and had seen no one. They had allowed her to leave only under guard in the dark of night, to wash or answer calls of nature.

"I've never spoken a harsh word to an acolyte," she heard Lyonene say. "Nor treated them with a harsh hand. Don't make me start now."

Moments later, Lyonene's golden head came into view as she rose up the staircase.

"You look terrible," Lyonene said. Reed wiped at her face. She'd washed the salt stains from her cheeks every time she was allowed, but she kept crying fresh ones. She glanced at her wrists; the abrasions from the manacles had formed thick, dark scabs.

Lyonene held up some food—hollowed-out bread stuffed with goat meat and soaked with savory juices. Reed grabbed it and tore into it as Lyonene slid down beside her.

"Aren't they feeding you?" Lyonene asked.

"Where have you been?"

"They wouldn't let me come sooner."

"They didn't let you come now," said Reed. "You could have forced your way in anytime you wanted."

"I wasn't sure you'd want to see me."

Reed wiped her mouth with the back of her hand, and her chains shifted loudly against the floor. "Didn't you think I'd want to know that you were safe? That what I'd done hadn't been for nothing?"

Lyonene frowned. She looked around the dome. "Such a beautiful, sacred space. So quiet, and vibrant with the colors of the paints." She reached over and stole a piece of meat.

"I didn't know what to say to you, Ox. Should I tell you that you shouldn't have done it? That it should have been Alsander they killed and not Hestion?" She looked at Reed quietly. "You shouldn't have done it. But I will always love you for it."

"Alsander," Reed said, "is he safe?"

"He's locked in the storeroom. I'm taking him out of the city tonight." She tore off another piece of Reed's supper but didn't eat it. "Do you want us to take Hestion's ashes back to Glaucia?"

Reed's chest tightened. So it was done, then. He'd been burned. And she hadn't even been there, to stand beside his pyre. To weep for him properly. To rend her clothes and slash through her white cape with a knife.

"I'll do it," Reed said. "I owe him that."

"A hero burned in the Aristene city," Lyonene murmured. "What an honor."

Reed clenched her teeth. She felt the bread crushed inside her hand. "What an honor."

Lyonene stared at the ruined food. "Will you ever forgive me for this, Reed? It seems I am always asking for your forgiveness. After I hurt Silco. And now—"

"Silco is fine."

"But I did this," Lyonene said, with a sad sound. "I deserved the punishment. And you took it onto yourself. When I never asked you to!"

"Are you angry with me for saving your life?"

"No!" Lyonene shoved her with her shoulder. "But I will be angry with you when you hate me for it. And you will, someday, Ox. I know that as surely as if I'd seen it in that well." She looked at it, where it sat mute and uneven, its stones sparkling and full of shadows. She reached over Reed's arm and took another piece of meat.

"Stop eating my food."

"I brought you this food."

"And you can leave and get yourself some anytime you want."

Lyonene grabbed Reed's wrist and tried to bite directly from the bread. Reed shoved her face away and for a moment they might have been back in the Summer Camp, pushing each other down hills. Reed leaned against her.

"Aster and Veridian say they'll let you go as soon as you won't try to kill them. But if you want to convince anyone you'll have to put on a better face than that—anyone can see that you're still angry."

But Reed would always be angry. She had always been angry, ever since the night of the raid on her settlement.

"You know he really loved you," Lyonene said quietly. "When I first saw Hestion I thought he was as beautiful as those stone statues in that hall down there, and with a stone heart to match. I didn't think he was worthy of you. But I was wrong."

Reed lowered her head and Lyonene leaned over and kissed it.

She held Reed's face in her hands and rubbed the salt stains from her cheeks.

"You know you're a very pretty ox, Reed," she whispered. "Are you going to be all right?"

"I'm going to be fine. Get out of here."

Lyonene stood.

"I will be back as soon as I can," she promised. "If they haven't let you out by then, we'll try together to pull these out of the wall." She toed Reed's chains.

"Don't worry about me," Reed said. "They'll let me out of here soon."

Lyonene smiled quickly to cover her worry. "They'll have to. This dome is large, Ox, but you're still making it stink."

"The acolytes took me to the bathhouse this morning," Reed said, but she snorted a laugh as Lyonene disappeared down the steps.

Lyonene kept her head down as she moved through the Citadel to the storeroom where Alsander was being held. Reed's sacrifice may have saved Lyonene from the elders' justice, but the fact that she had betrayed her oaths was no longer a secret. Many of the other Aristene would have loved to punish her themselves, and most of the acolytes besides. When she reached Alsander's cell, the girl guarding him acknowledged Lyonene with the barest incline of her head.

"I've come to take him."

The acolyte got up from the stack of grain sacks she rested upon and stalked off without a word. Lyonene opened the door. It was neither locked nor barricaded. Was that how little they thought of mortal heroes? The acolytes guarding him were mortal also, so perhaps it was meant to be a temptation. If he'd tried to escape they would have had an excuse to kill him, too.

She opened the door and Alsander stood. He came to wrap her in his arms. "Do we go, then?"

"We go."

He nodded, his eyes a steely blue. "Glaucia and the Docritae should burn this place to the ground."

Lyonene put her fingers to his lips. He shouldn't speak so here. Not even when it was such a hollow threat. The Docritae could no more sail here than they could sail past the edge of the world. "Where do you wish to go?" she asked. "The Veil may take us anywhere we like."

"I must return to Cassor," said Alsander. "There is much to salvage there, and the Cassan army craves a leader. I can strengthen my ties to the Docritae through our mutual suffering."

"You speak of it so coldly. Was Hestion not your friend?"

"I speak of it as a prince. Hestion was my friend, and the finest of the Glaucans. But he is gone now, and that was not my doing."

Lyonene searched his eyes. Suddenly the path that he walked was startlingly clear: back to Cassor and into Yngarue's arms. He would claim her army and use it to wage war on his father and retake Cerille. It was all he'd ever really wanted.

Let that be the way of it, then, after all they had done and all they had been through. The ties of destiny could not be severed, and she was surprised to find that she didn't care. Her heart would ache when he left her, but she couldn't deny who he was. Reed had lost so much, and Alsander had not been worth it.

She lifted her hand and touched his head tenderly.

"Lyonene? What is wrong?"

Will he call to me for help in dark times? Lyonene wondered. *Will I go?*

"Nothing, my love."

As they walked out of the cool shadows to the steps of the Citadel, voices carried up from the square. Raised voices. She put her hand to Alsander's chest.

"Machianthe should be released! She's not responsible!"

"She took responsibility. She must take the punishment."

Lyonene looked down. The Aristene and many of the acolytes had gathered below. Aster and Veridian were there, as were Sabil and Jana. Aethiel stood in the crowd, her tall black head of hair towering above them all. Ellora, Mol's best friend, stood opposite Aster, her normally bright brown hair hanging in strings. Mia, the quiet healer with the dark, pretty eyes, stood near the bottom with her arms hugged around herself.

"The elders have decided," Aster said. "They will hold her. But they won't hold her forever. And you must accept that." Good Aster, always walking the middle of the road. But that pleased no one. There was grumbling, and shoving, and when the crowd came too close, Veridian drew her sword.

"No, Veridian!" Caution forgotten, Lyonene led Alsander down the steps and plunged into the fray.

"What are you doing here?" Veridian asked. "You'll only make things worse."

"What do they want?" Lyonene asked. She could feel the hostility rising as smoke into the air, acrid and bitter. All around them voices shouted that it should have been her, as if she didn't already know. Sabil came to her side.

"They don't know what they want," Sabil said. "They are hurting. They're afraid."

"This all started with them." Ellora jabbed a finger into Lyonene's face. "All was well until these initiates took their oaths."

"All was well, was it, Ellora?" Veridian asked. "Then what am I?"

"You're an apostate whose words mean nothing," replied someone within the crowd. Lyonene knocked up against Sabil as the crowd began to push. There were too many people. Lyonene pulled Alsander close, but it was as if the hero was invisible. The business of Atropa was with Atropa, outsiders shoved aside and forgotten.

"Where are the elders?" Lyonene asked. She had no wish to see them, but only they could calm this storm. Even Aethiel was knocked about within the crowd as she tried to keep the peace.

"Machianthe should never have undergone the Joining! She failed her Hero's Trial!"

"That, too, was the decision of the elders," Aster shouted. "Do you disagree with their wisdom?"

"They have long departed from the path," Ellora said, and many of the sisters quieted. "Long before they allowed the apostate to live." She turned red, swollen eyes upon Aethiel. "You were the first mistake. You also should never have been granted a Joining, *Fennbirn Queen.*"

It was not so great an insult, by Lyonene's measuring, but Aethiel seemed to disagree. The black-haired Aristene drew herself up tall and bellowed, "I have killed sisters for less!"

"Oh, goddess," Lyonene whispered as Aethiel and Ellora lunged for each other. She looked to Aster, who watched with an open mouth. "Where are the elders?"

Tiern found Ferreh inside the half-circle room that looked down upon the square. She was seated with a pillow upon her lap, and her knees tucked underneath her. She'd banished her armor in favor of a bright yellow gown with gold pins at the shoulders, and a deep orange sash that ran from her right shoulder to her waist. Tiern felt a pain in her chest. Seated like that, with her short brown curls framed by sun, Ferreh could have been any young and beautiful girl.

"Do you hear them?" Ferreh asked. Tiern walked to the balcony. She heard them, and she saw them, shouting their grievances and their fears. They would wear themselves out with shouting and shoving. And then they would return to their homes, to their lives and duties.

"Of course I heard them," Tiern replied. She held up a jug. "That's why I brought wine."

Ferreh said nothing, only watched her coolly as Tiern poured. But Ferreh could never remain angry with her for long. "Do you want me to say I'm sorry?" She handed Ferreh a cup.

"That depends," Ferreh said, and took it, "on what you are sorry for."

"I am sorry for having a different vision for the future of this order." She raised her cup, touched it to the other elder's. But Ferreh set hers aside.

"It was not a different vision that we had, Tiern. It was the same. And I do not understand how you can desire it to happen."

Tiern placed Ferreh's cup back in her hand. "My desires do not matter. We are elders, but we are her servants, just like any Aristene. Our duty is to Kleia Gloria. To the order. It is not only to that girl."

"That girl is part of the order. And if that is what must be done to preserve it—if that is what is required—" Ferreh dropped her gaze to the pouch tied to Tiern's belt, where the sharp fragment of bone remained hidden. "To make of her a monster?"

"It is our duty. Her duty. In order to save—"

"But what is it that we are saving? If we do this to her, what do we become?" Ferreh's long-fingered hands squeezed the cup, and Tiern feared for a moment that it would shatter. But then she sighed, and took a long drink. "You must stay away from her, Tiern. Until we have decided, I do not want you anywhere near her."

Tiern set down her wine. "I told you before, Ferreh. You do not give me orders."

"Stop this! Stop!" Lyonene shoved Aristene and acolytes apart. She ducked punches and thrown elbows, and tried to keep Alsander from doing anything foolish, like stealing a sword to join the fight. She heard Aster shouting, and Aethiel bellowing, and Veridian snapping at Ellora. It was only pain that drove them to this. They stood in the same square where not three nights ago they burned the remains of their sister. But someone had to put an end to it, before elbows and fists escalated to daggers and shields.

Lyonene was about to go back up the Citadel steps to drag the elders out herself when she felt the familiar sensation of the Veil opening in the hills. Only this time the sensation was not a gentle click. It was searing pain, a hot brand pressed to the cool darkness of her mind.

Every Aristene warrior in the square doubled over, clutching their heads. Lyonene turned, wincing, and searched the hillsides. And there she saw the mouth of the Veil stretched wide as the first of the corrupted soldiers of Erleven stepped through into the sun.

"What was that?" Ferreh asked. "Did you feel it?"

Tiern had. It had felt like a knife shoved into her ear. The elders rose and rushed out. The Veil had opened. It stretched and tore as abominations scrabbled through to stomp upon the tall green grass and gnash their teeth against the daylight.

Ferreh reached out and covered Tiern's hand with her own. She squeezed hard as the screams of the Veil carried through their blood.

"They are here," Ferreh said.

"How?"

"It does not matter how." Ferreh's voice had taken on an eerie excitement. Her eyes were bright, almost glassy. "It has come to us, Tiern. The elders of the Aristene will ride out once more together, and if it is our end, then so be it. The order of glory will perish in glory."

Tiern hadn't heard such a tone in Ferreh's voice for more than an age. And she longed to do it, to ride beside her again, to lead her sisters into bloody battle, to prove to the goddess once more that they were deserving of her protection. She looked out at the army of the corrupted spilling out across their hills. "I am so sorry, Ferreh," she said. "They come too late."

Ferreh turned to her, confused by the wobble in her step. She put an arm out to steady herself and knocked over the wine.

"Tiern?" Ferreh's brown eyes met hers, and Tiern looked away from the betrayal she saw in them.

"It's only for now," she said as Ferreh fell. She caught her and lowered her gently to the floor. "Only this one thing, this one battle they will have to fight without you."

Tiern caressed the other elder's face. "I will see you when you wake, old friend. And you will understand."

Then she backed out of the room and turned to find the winding stairs that led up into the dome, and to Reed.

49.

FROM THE VEIL

The Veil had never been breached. Atropa had never been attacked, not since Kleia Gloria had set the barrier, had swept it out of the worlds of men. Lyonene watched in disbelief beside Sabil and Aster as the army of Erleven poured onto the hills, every soldier malformed by the influence of the bones of the prophet. Even their battle cries no longer sounded like they came from a man's throat.

"How is this possible?" Aster whispered. But none of them knew. Only Aristene were able to open the Veil.

There was a collective gasp as Prince Denros emerged from the darkness on the back of a large white horse. The monster the prince had become was enormous, larger than when Lyonene had glimpsed him during his transformation. It was a wonder the horse he rode was still upright.

Below, in the square, the acolytes and some of the Aristene turned about in confusion, unable to see what those on the steps with unobstructed views of the hills could see.

"We are attacked!" someone cried, and in a rush Lyonene and the others found themselves within a tide of pale blue cloth and sandals as the acolytes rushed up the stairs for the safety of the Citadel. Aethiel snatched up those who passed close to her, shaking them and saying, "Slowly, slowly, do not panic." But being shaken by an Aristene didn't help. They ran, trampling over each other, and Lyonene wondered what they thought they were running to. The Citadel was a fortress now in name only. As ages passed, it had been opened up, its windows widened and its doors removed, secure in Atropa's promise of peace.

"Sisters!" Veridian cried. Lyonene turned to look at her and her lips parted in wonder. The apostate had called her armor. The legendary archer stood upon the steps, her white cape thrown back, her rags banished for laced leather boots and leggings, a dark leather cuirass with buckles of bright silver. The guards upon her wrists were laid with silver filigree, patterned in vines.

"Veridian," Aster said softly, and backed down a step.

"We stand in the ashes of Mol's funeral pyre!" Veridian shouted. "As the ones who took her from us spill out across our hills! So do we stand here and wait for them to come? Or do we meet them in the fields and show them what a mistake they've made?"

Veridian jumped down the steps as the Aristene charged from the square. There were so many pounding feet that the air around Lyonene seemed to vibrate. She heard the sound of wood cracking and saw the Areion breaking free from their stalls and pastures to join their riders. Their Aristene jumped onto their backs, and armor was called from the aether to settle gloriously onto shoulders and chests, and onto the faces of horses. In the hills were glimpsed still more, horses from the valley racing for the battlefield in shades of brown and white and gray.

"They are the riderless ones," Lyonene said to Alsander. Those Areion whose riders had died. They would fight as well.

"Me!" Aethiel gestured to herself as a black mare galloped toward them. "Nightfly! Me!" The horse snorted and slowed so the big Aristene could swing on, and the two took off, Aethiel bouncing and ungainly as she clung to the mare's mane.

Lyonene grasped Alsander's shoulder. "Find a sword. Get to Phaeton, and rally as many of the acolytes to fight as you can."

"Where are you going?" He tried to take her wrist, but she pulled free.

"You know where," she said. "I'm going to kill myself a prince."

Lyonene ran to Strawberry and heaved herself up onto the roan mare's back. The little horse looked tough in her armor, a full silver face mask that covered her ears. They were about to gallop away when they heard a familiar neigh, and turned to see a black colt with a bad foot come plunging into the square.

"No, Silco! You have to stay! Stay here and protect Reed!"

He squealed and stomped angrily. But he did as he was told.

"Even riderless and with a lame hoof he could still fight," Sabil said, turning beside them on her dark brown horse, Wonder. Lyonene smiled. Her mentor had waited for her.

"Yes," Lyonene said. "But if we survive we would have to fight Reed, for allowing him to."

"Yah!" she cried, and she and Sabil rode hard through the city, their Areion's necks stretched and long, their ears pinned against the wind.

"Veridian," Aster said as the Aristene flowed from the square, charging for battle all round them. "Your armor . . ."

Veridian held up her arms; the silver of her wrist guards dazzled in the light. "Not bad, eh? After all this time I thought they might be tarnished through."

"Does this mean—?"

"It means that today I'm no apostate. But as for tomorrow, we will have to see how today goes. Now ride! Lead our sisters like I know you can." She pushed Aster gently until she bounced up onto Rabbit's back. Then she grasped Everfall by the bridle and removed it to fall upon the ground. She pressed her forehead to the tall gelding's nose. "And take him with you."

"What about you?" Aster asked.

"I will catch up."

Aster looked at her doubtfully, and Veridian flapped her arms to shoo them off. "Go! Fight! I will join you soon!"

She watched as Aster and the horses raced out of the square, on the heels of the Aristene army, then allowed herself a moment to look at her armor.

She hadn't known if she would be able to do it, to call it one last time. It felt at home upon her skin, and the elm and horn bow, embellished with silver, was a comforting weight upon her back. Yet in the pit of her stomach she sensed that something was wrong. And it had nothing to do with the corrupted soldiers who came through the Veil.

She turned and walked up the Citadel's steps. Below in the square, a horse neighed, and she looked, expecting to see Silco. Silco was there, stomping and pitching a general fit—but he wasn't the one who called to her. Ferreh's Areion, Amondal, came up after her, his hooves loud against the stones. Together they ran into the hall of the Aristene.

When he stopped and would go no farther, she asked, "Where?" and he raised his nose toward the ceiling. Veridian climbed the winding staircase that led to the large half-circle room where the elders often passed their time.

The large, dark-wood doors hung slightly ajar. She drew her sword, small and sharp, and saw Ferreh lying upon the floor.

Veridian knelt beside her. The elder wasn't dead, but nor would she wake. Veridian closed her eyes. She drew on her magic and when she opened them, the beats of battle were revealed to her in footprints and swirls of gold.

It was not much of a fight. It was treachery, and stemmed from an upturned jug of wine spilled across the rug. She didn't need her magic to show her the glimmering silhouette of the person who'd poured it to know who it was. Nor did she need it to show her in prints where she'd fled to.

"Tiern," Veridian breathed as she turned and raced for the dome.

When Lyonene and Sabil charged onto the battlefield, what they found was chaos. There were no lines, no flanking positions. The Aristene weren't used to fighting as a unit, and every Aristene warrior fought on her own, a small battalion's worth of damage, attacking from whatever sides or angles she chose. Lyonene turned at approaching hoofbeats: Aster and Rabbit, and Veridian's red gelding. But no Veridian.

"What is the plan?" Lyonene asked as they looked over the fighting. "Is there one?" They watched as Jana rode before them, plowing through soldiers. The spear that she threw pierced the chests of three and she cackled with joy.

"What is wrong with these soldiers?" Sabil asked. "Their faces . . . their limbs . . ."

"Twisted," Lyonene replied. "Altered, by the bones of the prophet." She looked at Sabil's doubtful face. "We can still fight them. Though perhaps not that one." She nodded to the monstrous Prince Denros astride his white battle stallion and noted the talisman that hung around his neck on a golden chain. A shriveled, purplish hand, missing most of its smallest finger. "That's Mol's hand he's wearing," she said, and turned to Aster. But instead of being enraged, Aster smiled.

"Yes," she said. "But that is not all that was Mol's. Does that mount not look familiar to you?"

Lyonene looked again. "Verger!" She gasped. Denros was riding Mol's Areion. "Denros doesn't know."

"Of course he doesn't," Aster said as Rabbit tossed her pretty gray head. "Our Areion know how to put on an act."

"So what do we do?" Lyonene asked.

Aster gathered her reins as Rabbit danced upon the grass. "We get him to charge us. Yah!"

The Aristene sprang together, galloping toward Denros with weapons and voices raised. And like they hoped, seeing them come straight for him was a temptation he couldn't resist. He put heels to Verger and charged them back.

As the two forces neared each other, Denros dropped the reins, raising a sword in one hand and a dagger in the other—having no need for a shield, Lyonene realized. The hoofbeats were loud in her ears as their speed carried them ever closer, his horrible face and his terrible grin coming into sharp focus so she could see the strange lengthening of his teeth.

"What was the plan after the charge, Aster?" she cried, but just as she did, Verger drew up hard and threw his body in a circle. The motion sent Denros flying and the Areion screamed as he twisted and kicked—Lyonene swore she could hear the curses in the horse's voice as Denros struck the ground and tumbled. She felt Strawberry take aim beneath her, and angled her sword down to stab as she and the others ran over the top of him.

"Again!" Aster cried, and they wheeled around. Together the warriors and horses trampled and stabbed, stomped and cut, sending blood flying into the air. Verger joined them to stomp and tear at Denros with his teeth. Lyonene grimaced as she stabbed, feeling the sickening drain of the prophet's corruption weaken her magic. But still they hacked and sliced—there would be nothing left of Denros but a pile of meat by the time they were through. Or so she thought, until she heard Sabil scream as Denros grabbed Wonder's leg and threw them away, as easily as throwing a stone.

With a roar, the monstrous prince exploded off the ground. His arms swung and sent horses rolling and riders flying. Lyonene heard Strawberry squeal as he hit her in the chest, and felt them both fall through the air. She landed hard, and the mare landed on top of her, and then there was darkness.

Reed pulled to the ends of her chains. She had heard the cries rising from the square, and felt the searing pain as the others did when the Veil was breached. Now she heard the screams of battle, and the familiar sounds of blade meeting blade brought her armor crashing through the aether onto her body.

"Guards," she shouted with a throat still raw from days of scream-ing. When they came, they each had frightened tears streaking down their cheeks.

"What's happening?"

"We've been attacked," the taller of the two girls said. Her sash of light blue linen had been pulled askew; she looked like she'd been in a fight.

"Attacked? Here?" It was unthinkable. Impossible. "Have they reached the Citadel?"

"No. There is panic below. Citizens, acolytes, crowding into the strongholds."

"Get me out of these chains." Reed held out her wrists. The acolytes twitched toward her. Reed heard Silco, neighing to her from the square. "Now!" She lifted her arms and slammed the chains against the floor. The acolytes cried out and ran. Reed cursed her temper, and wrapped the chains around her wrists to lean back and pull.

"Machianthe."

Reed stopped as Tiern emerged from the staircase.

"Tiern—elder—what's happening?"

"The monster prince of Erleven has brought his corrupted army through the Veil."

"But that's impossible."

"Isn't it. We disparaged the priests as weak and as fools, but whatever magic is given to them by their god is real enough." She turned as screams from the hills carried through the open window.

"Tiern, let me fight! That's why you've come, isn't it?" But Tiern didn't raise her blade and strike through the chains. She didn't produce a key and unlock the manacles around Reed's torn and bleeding wrists. Instead she reached into her belt and withdrew the fragment of the prophet's skull.

"I've taken to carrying this like some kind of charm," Tiern said. "I think I always hoped, like she hoped, that I would never have to use it."

Reed eyed the shard of bone. It was small and sharp. It had blackened, like all the prophet's bones had blackened, but it still glistened with a curious, almost iridescent sheen.

"Glorious Death," Tiern said. "This is what we saw in the waters of the deep well. What Ferreh saw, when she looked into your eyes that night when you came to us, a little colt who was angry and broken.

"We built you back. We raised you up. So that you could become this and save us."

She looked up at Reed, and suddenly the fragment in her hand looked like a weapon. Reed crept back, nearer the wall. She wrapped the weight of her chains around her fists. "Stay away from me, Tiern. Do not come any closer."

"Are you afraid?"

"I am afraid of nothing. I just have no wish to become a monster."

"But it will not make you a monster!" Tiern darted toward her, and Reed jumped back. The elder's eyes were wild. "It will make you more of what you are. More glorious death. More of a warrior. It will make you the greatest Aristene the order has ever seen, greater even than Ferreh or myself."

Tiern opened her hand so Reed could look upon the piece of bone. She knew it would burn when it carved into her flesh. It might burn through her, until there was nothing left.

"Don't listen to her, Reed!"

Veridian leaped up from the stairway entrance, so dazzling in leather and silver and white that Reed almost didn't recognize her. She looked radiant. She looked like an Aristene. She looked like another Glorious Death.

"They're trying to make you believe that this is your responsibility—that it has always been your task to save them, but it isn't true! They were supposed to save you, little foundling." Veridian hefted her sword. "And I wish to the goddess they had."

"Apostate." Tiern drew one of her twin daggers. "You are not allowed inside this sacred space."

"I am not an apostate today." She sidestepped between Tiern and Reed, and Tiern's expression twisted with rage.

"A long time ago, I gave her the same choice," Tiern said, speaking to Reed. "And she accepted. But she could not take it! All those dead heroes. All that pain. She is weaker than you! You, Machianthe, are strong enough!"

"Strong enough to be a monster?" Veridian asked.

"Strong enough to bear this magic," Tiern replied. She held up the piece of bone. It was such a small thing, to Reed's eyes. How could something so small imbue her with so much power that she could save the entire order?

"How do you know?" Reed asked loudly. "How do you know that I can survive without being corrupted?"

"Because we have seen it," Tiern said. "Ferreh and I—we have both seen it. Kleia Gloria sent us the same vision. Of you. Of what you will become."

Reed looked at the shard, held tightly between the elder's fingers.

"Don't," Veridian said, her voice high with disbelief. "She's lying to you, Reed. Right now, Ferreh lies beneath us on the floor, put there by Tiern's hand. Reed—"

But that couldn't be true. Ferreh and Tiern would never cross swords. And if they did, Ferreh would not be put down so easily. . . . She turned to the window and listened to the cries coming from the battlefield. Aster was out there. Aster and Lyonene. And she could save them, if she was brave enough. If she was great enough.

She looked at Veridian. The apostate. The legendary archer. But it was Reed's time to be a legend now. She was the Glorious Death of this age. And this was her story.

"Reed," Veridian moaned. "All men desire to be legends. But those wants are beneath us. An Aristene desires only to serve. To live here and thrive in this place of peace."

"That might be enough," Reed said. "For some. Tiern. Do it."

Tiern smiled. With the speed of an elder she drew back her arm and struck Veridian aside, the blow heavy enough to send the apostate sliding across the floor of the dome. She tumbled across the vast silver disk of the World's Gate and lay in a heap.

But Reed wasn't thinking about Veridian. Her mind was on Tiern, and the fragment of the prophet's bone. The elder's eyes had taken on a mad glint as she held the shard between two fingers to carve it into Reed's chest. Reed held very still and waited for the sting. Her pulse raced, in fear and in exhilaration. Neither she nor Tiern noticed Veridian pulling the bow from her back and nocking an arrow as she lay on her side. It was only when the arrowhead flashed in the light that they looked to her and saw her taking aim at the prophet's bone.

"No!" Reed cried, or perhaps it was Tiern. They had only an eye's blink of time to react as the legendary archer took her shot.

And missed.

The arrow flew just wide, and Tiern thrust the sharpened fragment into Reed's skin, to nestle deep inside her heart scar and turn it black.

Lyonene came to upon the grass, nudged by Strawberry's armored nose. Every bit of her felt bruised, and her rib cage felt like a full cup that had been picked up and shaken. Sabil and Aster had dragged her to a safe distance from Denros, who stood, bleeding profusely in the middle of the field. Somehow he hadn't killed any of them, but Sabil's arm had been snapped; it hung limply below the elbow at an odd angle.

"Why is he not dead?" Lyonene asked. Denros must have seen her speak because across the distance she saw his eyes darken as he recognized her.

"You come straight for me as if killing me will stop this," he yelled.

"This will be stopped one way or another," Aster yelled back. "Look around you; our sisters harvest your men like wheat!"

Denros wiped slicks of blood from his arms and cast them away, flying from his fingertips to spray the grass. "But will they fight on if I put your head on the end of my sword?" He strode toward them, three women and a huddle of horses.

"Well," said Sabil. "What do we do now?"

"I have a plan," Lyonene said. "Sabil, I need you to go and find Aethiel. Send her to us. The magic of Fennbirn will fare better against him should the battle go on for too long." Sabil frowned, but then she nodded and pulled herself onto Wonder's back.

"I hope you know what you're doing," she said, and turned to ride into the carnage.

"I think I do," Lyonene muttered. Because she knew men. And she knew men like Denros would make mistakes if she wounded their pride. "Strawberry, can you still run?" The little mare snorted and tossed her head. Lyonene got into the saddle. She glanced at Aster, and at Verger and Everfall. "Follow my lead."

With a great whoop she and Strawberry charged. Trick shots and trick attacks from horseback were a game that she and Reed and Gretchen had often played in the Summer Camp, but that was only for fun. She had no idea whether it would work on Denros. When they passed by the monstrous prince, Lyonene hung low from one side of Strawberry's saddle and dragged her sword across the backs of his legs.

He roared and Lyonene yanked herself upright as he swung around. Kleia Gloria, he was strong. Had she done the same to any other mortal man she would have removed his feet. But his skin had thickened over his bones, forming a callous-like armor, so hard that Lyonene's hand rang from the impact. She'd also felt her strength drop out from underneath her when she'd cut him, like a pulled rug.

It was Aster's turn to make her charge, and she and Rabbit stayed far from Denros's grasp, instead throwing daggers to sink into his shoulder and arm. They stuck shallowly from his thickened flesh, a mere annoyance, like needles or insect bites.

"Prince Denros!" Lyonene called. "What a horrid creature our Yngarue has made of you!"

"She? She has not made me!"

Lyonene rested her hands on her saddle. "You speak as if I wasn't there. If it weren't for the magic of those priests you would be in the ground beside your father. Felled by poison inflicted by the girl you thought to make your wife." She barked a laugh. "You know she only had a few months of training with a blade. Yet she still made you into worm's meat."

She charged him again, veering out this time and slicing through the air, carving a red line through his hand as he tried to grab her. Aster followed with more daggers. Aethiel soon joined them on Nightfly, and together the three took turns antagonizing Denros, baiting him and attacking him. Verger and Everfall ran past him and lashed out with their hooves. But while it was amusing to see him angry, stomping the ground like a child over a broken toy, they weren't making any headway. He bled, but not enough. The cuts they'd made in their initial assault seemed to have closed over, and each new cut they made seemed shallower than the last.

"We need another plan," Aster said as they took a moment to breathe.

"If we keep him busy long enough for our sisters to kill all the corrupted soldiers, then we can swarm him en masse." Lyonene leaned in her saddle. The prophet's bones sapped her strength. Even Strawberry and the other Areion were breathing hard; sweat darkened their coats and foam flecked their lips and flanks.

"That's not a plan," said Aster. "That's a stall." And nowhere were the Aristene making much progress. In the hills beyond them the Aristene razed the ground of every corrupted soldier in their paths, only for the cleared ground to be swarmed by a dozen others. The screams of Areion made her sick to her stomach, and across the fields, bodies lay still in the grass in shining silver armor.

"We are losing," Aster said.

Lyonene spat blood upon the ground. Aster was right. Their fury at the invasion of their sacred city could only carry them so far. They needed reinforcements. They needed the elders, and Alsander to find and lead the acolytes. They needed—

They heard a terrible crash and looked toward the Citadel, just as the wall of the dome exploded and the hulking, dark Aristene burst forth.

50.

MACHIANTHE

Lyonene stared at the dome. Where there once had been a window there was now a gaping hole. The warrior who came through it seemed larger than even Aethiel, and she'd jumped and fallen all the way down to the lower steps before the square. The glimpse she'd caught, of long, dark brown hair—but it couldn't be.

"Reed," Aster breathed as horse and rider appeared. It was Reed, and upon Silco's back. But both horse and rider had changed. The Aristene who rode Silco had grown greater in size, her arms and legs ropy with muscle. The armor upon her chest and the greaves upon her legs were still leather and silver, but the silver was blackened in places, as if tarnished or burned. When she reached the battlefield she leaped from Silco's back and swung her arms. The chains that had once kept her imprisoned in the Citadel now sliced through the army of corrupted soldiers, so fast that the top halves of the soldiers continued to fight as they dropped to the ground.

"What has happened to her?" Aster wailed. "What has done this?" She turned to stare at the cracked-open wall where Reed had emerged. The shapes of two Aristene were inside. The elders? They were too far away to tell. "Rabbit!" Aster called her Areion and swung on to the gray mare's back.

"You're leaving me?" Lyonene shrieked. She'd never heard her own voice go so high. "You can't leave me! We can't face Denros without you!"

But Aster was already gone, cutting through the corrupted on her way to the Citadel to find her answers, and Veridian's big red gelding went with her.

"It's all right, little sister," Aethiel panted. "We are not alone."

Lyonene turned. Reed stood behind her, her body monstrous and stretched in strange ways. Veins stood out against her skin and she dragged the chains of her incarceration behind her in the dirt.

"Reed?"

Reed's eyes were ringed red with blood. She drew back her lips to show sharpened teeth.

"Ox?"

"Lyonene." The blood-ringed eyes shifted to Strawberry, who snorted a cautious greeting to Silco. The black colt was enormous; muscles bulged in his neck and shoulders. He pawed with his bad hoof.

"What's happened to you?" Lyonene asked.

"Only what needed to happen." She clawed at the manacles on her wrists and they broke off and fell to the grass. "I will handle this prince for you."

"Lyonene!" Lyonene turned and saw Alsander on his golden stallion, leading what looked to be a small army of acolytes. They had armed themselves with knives and tools. A few had wooden clubs. She turned back to Reed.

"We'll handle this prince together," she said. "And then we'll finish this war."

Reed didn't respond. She looked dispassionately across the hills at the rest of the battle still being waged. Aethiel edged away from her uneasily.

"Well," Aethiel said, no longer the largest Aristene on the field, "if you have Denros, I will go help the acolytes."

Lyonene and Reed faced Denros from the ground. Strawberry, Silco, and Mol's white stallion stood behind them.

"Go," Reed said to Silco. "We don't need your help." The black colt went, to fight on elsewhere. Strawberry looked at Lyonene, and not knowing what else to do, Lyonene shrugged and nodded for the little mare to join him. Only Verger remained. Mol's horse would see an end to his rider's murderer.

"Who," Denros bellowed, staring at Reed, "are you?"

"Mmmph," Reed grunted, as if he wasn't worth replying to.

"She's like you," Lyonene called. "Only better."

Denros lowered his great, misshapen head. His piggish eyes moved up and down Reed's new form. "You are of the serpent goddess! How can you contain the bones of the prophet?"

"Maybe the prophet never took your side," Reed replied. "Maybe you used him as you saw fit. Maybe he did not like it."

The prince clenched his fists and the muscles of his shoulders swelled grotesquely. Lyonene would hate to die after all Reed had done to save her. She would hate to die at all. But she supposed there were worse ways to do it.

Lyonene dug her heel into the trampled grass. Her arms felt weak and so very mortal. Fighting Denros had leached her magic until there was almost nothing left. Her armor no longer shone, and she could no longer see the glittering trails of glory won by her sisters upon the battlefield. She raised her blade.

"You do not have to fight. I can just—" Reed mimed a tearing motion with her hands, as if she could simply rip him in two and toss the halves away. Lyonene snorted.

"Ox. Always trying to hoard the fun."

They ran at the prince as he ran at them, two young women and one white horse. It didn't take long for Verger's and Reed's strides to overtake her, but Lyonene did her best to keep up. Reed and Denros collided—they punched and pounded, each rocking the other's head back with blows. Once, Lyonene had seen a pair of great brown bears fighting on their hind legs. They had bloodied each other with claws, ripped at each other with teeth. Watching that was like watching this. Only these bears could also speak.

"Weak little princeling," Reed growled. "Did it please you to murder Princess Wyrnnigrid and the queen? Did it make you feel strong?"

"The only pleasure I felt was when I squeezed the life from the Aristene," Denros growled back, and both Reed and Lyonene roared.

Lyonene joined the fight, darting in and out to pierce and cut with her sword, dodging Denros's attempts to swat her away. Reed had his head gripped in both of her hands; she appeared to be trying to twist it off.

"I want his head!" she cried.

"So kill him first and we'll cut it off after!" Lyonene shouted.

Denros grabbed Reed's arms and wrenched them loose. Then he spun her in a great arc and tossed her, end over end across the field. When she landed and didn't immediately roll back up, Lyonene backed off.

"Alone at last," she said as Denros began to circle her.

"Yes," he replied. "That is how I would want it, too. My priest said that the Aristene would be weakened by being near the prophet's bones. I wish it wasn't so. I would like to face you at the fullness of your potential."

"Your priests. Just where are your priests?" Lyonene asked.

Denros looked out at his soldiers and Lyonene followed his gaze, noting that a few of the corrupted wore robes of gray and golden medallions around their necks.

Well. That took care of one thing.

Denros attacked, and Lyonene braced, the last of her magic threading through the air in sparkling gold. But before he reached her, the horse that once was Mol's collided with him. Lyonene froze in awe of Verger as the white stallion battered Denros with his hooves, his ears pinned and full of wrath for the rider he would never get back. But brave and angry though he was, he was no match for a monster. Denros grabbed him by the mane and jerked him to the ground.

"Don't you hurt him!" Lyonene screamed. The same man who had killed Mol was not going to kill her Areion. Reed returned to her side and together they raced to the horse's aid. Lyonene gripped her sword. "Ox," she called. "A hand!" Without breaking stride, Reed scooped her up and threw her into the air. She turned her sword in her hands and landed upon Denros, driving the blade down between his shoulders.

Denros roared, and she felt her sword pull free. The shadow of his arm rose in her vision—but the strike never came. Silco had seen what was happening and came back to fight. He sank his teeth into the prince's arm and dragged him backward like a dog with a bone. It was good to see the colt was still a biter.

Strawberry soon joined him and the two horses stretched the shrieking prince out across the grass. Reed stepped on his legs. She drew her sword, for the first time during the battle, and the blade was as dark as the scar over her heart. Lyonene stood beside her, and the two angled their swords down over Denros's chest.

"For Yngarue and Mol," Lyonene said, and Reed nodded.

"And for Hestion."

51.

THE APOSTATE AND HER MENTOR

Veridian had missed. It was impossible to believe even as she stared at the broken wall that Reed had jumped through. Even as she heard the moment that she joined the battle: fresh screams and a roar that sounded not fully human.

"Do not blame yourself," Tiern said. "Even the legendary archer had to miss sometime." She turned and walked slowly around the interior of the dome, past the mural of the Areion, past the mural of the Aristene commanding the seas upon a fleet of ships. Part of the head of the legendary sea serpent was missing from where Reed had torn away chunks of it along with the anchors of her chains.

Except not Reed, Veridian realized as she listened to the tides of the battle turn outside.

Machianthe.

"I don't blame myself," Veridian said. "I blame you."

"I did what I had to do, Veridian."

"You made a monster of her."

"Only because there was a monster inside her to be made." Tiern touched a crack that had spidered through the mural's paint. "All this time and Ferreh was right. I didn't see it the night Aster brought her to us, but she was everything we needed her to be. She will save the order."

"There is no order. Not after this." Veridian spread her arms wide. "If this is what was needed, why did you not ask me?"

Tiern laughed sadly. "You were my favorite initiate. But I never would have given you this responsibility. Apostate."

Light, fast footsteps sounded upon the steps and Aster burst up into the dome. Her sword was still drawn from battle and she was streaked with blood both fresh and drying.

"How did this happen?" Aster demanded. "What has happened to Reed?"

Tiern walked back to them. The elder's shoulders slumped; her feet dragged. She settled herself on the edge of the broken wall and half turned to listen to the battle. "Peace, Aster," she said. "She has become what she was always meant to."

"Shouldn't you go now to join the fight?" Veridian asked. "Shouldn't you help?"

"They will not need it," Tiern replied, and leaned back. Her hand cast about as if looking for a cup of wine at the end of a hard day.

"What are you saying?" Aster asked. "What is wrong with Reed?"

"She's been joined with the bones of the prophet," Veridian said before the elder could speak. But though Aster's eyes widened, she must have already known that. Seeing the changes to Reed's shape—the monstrous stretching, the increase in size—it was impossible to think it had been anything else.

"And you did this, elder?"

"I couldn't stop her, Aster," Veridian said. "I'm sorry."

"There is nothing to apologize for," Tiern said. "Machianthe knew what was needed. She welcomed this. You should be proud of her."

Aster pointed her sword toward Tiern's chest. "I don't believe you."

Tiern's eyes fixed upon the weapon. She stood and walked toward Aster until the tip of the blade was pressed to her chest.

"You brought us an ambitious, angry girl who yearned to be great. And now she is." Fast as a mountain cat, Tiern drew her own sword and knocked Aster's away, slashing so hard that Aster cried out and dropped her weapon to clatter and slide across the floor.

In the next moment, Veridian's sword had crossed with her old mentor's.

"Veridian, don't," she heard Aster call. Veridian looked into Tiern's eyes. She expected to see madness, rage. Instead she saw a deep and heavy weariness. The same weariness, perhaps, that she herself had carried for far too long.

"You have this coming," Veridian said.

She attacked. She didn't know why she did it. She was angry about Reed—furious—but even through that anger she knew she was no match for an elder. Tiern blocked every thrust of her sword. But winning didn't matter. She only wanted to see Tiern bleed. The teeth of the order, who bit when they needed biting, cut when they needed cutting, who never regretted the cost to anyone around her.

"I'm an elder and you were my initiate," Tiern said when she had Veridian pinned to the wall. "What do you think you can show me that I didn't teach you?"

"Did you teach me to undermine your authority to such a state that even your most devoted would rise against you?"

"What?" Tiern asked as Aster lowered her shoulder and bashed into her, sending her crashing to the floor.

"Are you all right?" Aster helped Veridian from the wall.

"I can't believe you did that." Veridian clucked her tongue. "She's an elder!"

"Oh, shut up, Veridian," Aster said fondly, as both women turned, weapons raised.

"I should have killed you when you left," Tiern said, getting to her feet. "I was too soft." She drew her second sword, the short sword of bronze she'd carried in her old days of mortality, and faced Veridian and Aster with one weapon for each. They had barely enough time to get their blades up before she attacked.

"Spin!" Veridian shouted, and she and Aster spun away, separating themselves and forcing Tiern to fight them one ahead and one behind. But fighting Tiern was like fighting a windstorm, and eventually Aster was struck and fell to the floor.

"Aster!" Veridian tried to reach her, and Tiern hit her with the hilt of her bronze sword so hard that her skull bounced off the wall of the dome.

She looked up into her old mentor's eyes. It had been this way many times when she was trained. Tiern above, and Veridian below, at the end of her sword. Disappointment in the elder's eyes would eventually change to respect, and then to affection that wrinkled them in the corners.

"I'll never come back," Veridian whispered. "You made me, Tiern. So unmake me."

"Don't!" Aster struggled up to her knees. "Elder, please! She will come back to us. She will come back someday."

"No, she will not," Tiern said. She lowered the bronze sword from Veridian's chest. "She cannot. For she is a Glorious Death.

A curse to any hero she touches. She is that forever. And that she cannot bear."

Veridian ground her teeth. From the corner of her eye she saw Aster's lips part.

"Is that true?" Aster asked. "You drank the blood?"

"Just one more way that Reed takes after me," Veridian replied.

"Machianthe is nothing like you." Tiern put her swords away. She leaned down and grasped Veridian by the throat. "With Machianthe the Aristene will flourish. We do not need to keep you, to wait for you. We do not need to be soft anymore."

"But what's the point?" Veridian asked. "If you kill your initiate, if you turn Reed into a monster—if this is what you make of the order, then what is the point?"

Holding her, Tiern's eyes lost focus. "There is no point," she murmured. "Immortality is long, Veridian. There is no point." She looked at Veridian once more, and the apostate again saw the familiar emptiness swirling in the dark depths of her pupils. They were so tired. Both had survived on stubbornness alone, for far too long. "And you, archer, know that you could have stopped me, had you truly wanted to."

Veridian screamed and exploded off the wall. The elder was caught off guard; she reeled backward and when she stumbled, the apostate tripped up her feet and shoved her to the floor.

"Veridian, stop! Stop!" Aster tried to grab her from behind, and Veridian shrugged her off harshly. She swung her sword down at Tiern, again and again, aiming for that darkness, that void that she saw in the elder and felt in herself. Each impact of the blade against the floor sent up chips from the marble.

The elder tried to scramble away, and Veridian stabbed through Tiern's calf. Tiern screamed. She rolled and kicked the apostate in the face, knocking her back as she dragged herself across the dome to the broad disk of the World's Gate.

"No!" Veridian shouted.

Tiern flattened her palm to the silver. The gate opened, and Tiern fell through.

Veridian ran to the edge. The solid shining silver was gone, the swirling depths open and bathing her face and chest in light. She could still see Tiern, the shape of her, falling and falling. Into oblivion? Into something else?

"Veridian."

She looked up and saw Aster, and felt her heart swell with love.

"You and I have no end," Veridian said. And then she looked down into the light, and dove through the World's Gate after her mentor.

52.

GUARDIAN OF THE ORDER

With Denros dead, the corrupted soldiers had no direction. They attacked what they came across. Lyonene saw several attacking each other, as if all they truly craved was freshly drawn blood regardless of the source.

Across the hills, Alsander and the army of acolytes defended the entrance to the city, fighting bravely against the corrupted with improvised weapons of rakes and axes. They swung at them with spades and hacked at them with kitchen knives. A man Lyonene recognized as one of the goat herds wielded what looked to be a long sack with a heavy stone inside; he swung it around and around and used it to bludgeon any Erleven soldier who came near.

The Aristene did not miss their show of bravery, and quickly formed ranks beside them. It was by the bravery of the acolytes that their army took on any semblance of form. But too many of the Aristene still fought alone. They needed Ferreh. They needed Tiern to command them.

Lyonene looked at the corrupted soldiers, enough of them still to constitute a swarm. They were beetles. Insects. They sounded like beetles; she could hear their jaws and teeth clicking, and the noises that came from their mouths were not words but short, low screeches. They'd been men before this had been done to them.

Some could have been heroes.

But now they were not and she wanted them gone.

On the hill to her right, Reed and Silco plowed a clean line through the corrupted like, well, like a pair of oxen. On the hills below, Aethiel extinguished life after life, with increasingly tired swings of her sword. Mia had found herself surrounded by a horde and Jana rushed to her rescue. They could keep on like this, Lyonene supposed, for as long as it took. More Aristene would fall, but eventually, it would be those in silver armor and white capes who were left standing.

Except Lyonene didn't want to lose anyone else.

"Mia! Jana!" She waved her arms, and the Aristene fought their way to her, Jana helping Mia along as the healer dragged a wounded leg.

"Initiate," Jana said, leaning on her spear. "I'm happy to see you alive."

"We have to end this," Lyonene said. "These creatures don't belong in Atropa."

"I agree." Jana sniffed. "Their blood smells spoiled. I fear the flowers upon these hills will wither and not return for generations. After they're all dead, we'll dig a pit. Burn them."

Lyonene shook her head. "That's not enough."

Mia leaned upon a borrowed spear. "What do you want to do, Lyonene? I can't do much to help you. I can't fight anymore."

"You can't fight, but you can open the Veil. Open it wide, and we'll push the last of the army back through."

Mia and Jana looked at the corrupted doubtfully.

"They won't want to go," Mia said.

Lyonene turned. "They don't want anything anymore," she said grimly. She called for her Areion and jumped onto Strawberry's back, then signaled for Alsander and he rode to her on his golden stallion. "Take the acolytes wide," she told him. "Keep them to the rear. We are going to push the creatures back into the Veil."

He nodded and rode off, rallying his acolytes behind him in a stream of pale blue linen and raised weapons. But though Lyonene's magic began to glow at the sight of him, she turned away.

She put her heels to Strawberry and rode around Reed and Silco, "Reed! Silco! Push!" Reed raised her head. There was blood around her lips, and Lyonene didn't want to think about why. But Reed understood. She and the Areion began to advance from the lower hills, forcing the soldiers backward and up.

"Aethiel!" Strawberry raced past her and Lyonene pointed with her sword. "Push!"

"What?" the big Aristene bellowed.

Lyonene pointed again, and in her mind she felt a click as upon the summit, Mia opened the Veil. After that the Aristene knew what to do—they saw the blackness yawning open, saw it stretching wide, and began to herd the warped soldiers toward it like sheep.

It was hard and messy work; the corrupted wanted to bite—they wanted to cut flesh and break bone. Lyonene dismounted and she and Strawberry faced them together, hooves and blades slashing. Those who broke through the line, she killed.

Reed and Silco's herd of soldiers reached the Veil first, and when they hissed and fought against going into the darkness, Reed simply started grabbing them and throwing them into it. As the mass of soldiers concentrated before the mouth, more of the Aristene lent their voices to Mia and Jana's chants and the darkness expanded; even behind the crush of corrupted, Lyonene could feel its familiar sensation: sucking and cold. She didn't blame the soldiers for being reluctant.

"They won't go!" one of the Aristene shouted.

"So make them!" replied another.

"That is easy for you to say," Ellora growled, and the chestnut-haired Aristene's gaze flickered to Reed. To Machianthe. Every Aristene saw what she had become. And all were wary of it.

"Here!" Aethiel called.

The corrupted stopped fighting and turned toward her. Aethiel stood before the Veil, holding Prince Denros's head.

"Look here," she said, shaking it, and when the soldiers began to charge, she drew her arm back and heaved it into the darkness of the void.

What remained of the army stampeded after it so fast that Aethiel had to tuck her arms before her face and lean forward to keep from being swept into the Veil alongside them.

"Is that the last?" Lyonene asked. She looked around. A few surely lingered in the streets, pockets of soldiers who'd made it into the city and were away from the bulk of the fighting. But they could be dealt with. "Let it close," she called, and the Aristene ended their chant. The Veil winked shut, and Atropa, sacred city of the Aristene, was once again silent.

Lyonene went to Aethiel, standing over Denros's headless corpse. The black-crowned warrior bent and picked up Mol's hand, cradling it gently. It had fallen onto the grass when she'd cut off his head. "Where do you think they will they go?" she asked.

"Lost inside the Veil to die." If they were lucky. They might be trapped there forever, an army locked in the darkness to go mad and sane and then mad again until past the end of time. Lyonene touched Aethiel's arm. The warrior was favoring it; not surprising, since it bore a wound so deep that Lyonene could glimpse bone. "Are you all right?"

Aethiel shrugged, a movement that caused her to leak more blood. But she would be fine. Many of the Aristene would bear scars from this battle. Their scholars would record it in their histories and give it some grave name like "The Battle of the Breach" or "The Besiegement of Atropa." But already their magic recovered. Lyonene felt it in the tingling sensation of her injuries beginning to knit together. She saw it above the reddened and trampled grass in glitters of gold, feeding that goddess who they loved and scorned by turns.

They had lost many. Many immortal lives, snuffed out. Later they would build the funeral pyres. They would grieve, with painful wails and tearing of their clothes. But they would also feast and rejoice. The battle had been won. Their enemy had been vanquished. The safety of their city had been restored.

"Aster went back toward the Citadel," Lyonene said. "But where—" Her eyes swept the hills and caught on Sabil's tiled armor of silver. Her mentor lay at the foot of the hills, half-covered by the body of her horse. "Sabil," Lyonene croaked. She and Strawberry raced across the grass, and Lyonene stumbled to her side. She hadn't seen when her mentor had fallen. She hadn't felt it, like she was certain Reed would have, had the same happened to Aster. Lyonene held Sabil's cooling hand.

Aethiel followed her, and squeezed her shoulder. Then she turned sharply at the sound of shouts.

"Lyonene. You must get up. They move against Machianthe."

Lyonene wiped her face and stood. The Aristene had surrounded Reed and Silco to ask questions in raised voices. Lyonene couldn't hear what they were, but Reed and Silco didn't like them.

"What is she?" Ellora asked. "She is like them!"

"She is like us," Lyonene snapped as she reached them and jumped down from Strawberry. "She is an Aristene!" But it was hard not to see their point. They'd just fought an army of stretched and corrupted soldiers. And there stood Reed, monstrous and reeking of the same prophet's magic.

None of her sisters had drawn their weapons, but Reed's red-ringed eyes grew more hostile with each step closer the Aristene took. Lyonene searched for Aster, who could have protected her. She looked for Ferreh.

"Take her to the elders," Ellora ordered. The Aristene darted forward and Reed flexed, ready to fight.

Lyonene jumped in between. "No!"

Her sisters stopped. They were injured. Tired. None of them wanted to tangle with Reed.

Lyonene turned to Reed and Silco. She held her hands up. "You're still Reed," she said, though the words came out as more of a question than she'd intended.

Reed was covered in blood and worse than blood. Ropy muscle and veins stood taut against her skin.

"You are still my Reed, my Ox, my sister," Lyonene said gently, and Strawberry whickered to Silco in a motherly way. Enough of that biting, naughty colt. Enough of those pinned ears.

Reed breathed hard. She sounded like a great beast, and Lyonene thought that she must be mad to approach her, hand outstretched like she meant to touch her on a dare. *Lay one hand upon Reed*, she imagined saying to Gretchen. *The last one to be crushed by her, wins.*

Reed's large hand shot out and grasped hers. The strength in the grip was terrifying. She wanted to pull away. Instead she curled her fingers around Reed's wrist.

Reed closed her red-rimmed eyes. She breathed in and out. When her body began to jerk, cries of alarm sounded from the Aristene. They circled closer, and drew their weapons.

"Cut our little sister free," Ellora shouted, and leveled her blade toward the place where Lyonene's and Reed's hands met.

"No!" Lyonene cried. "Wait!"

"She is a monster now, child," Jana said softly. "She saved us. But it is too late to save her."

"That's not true!"

"Look at her," Ellora said, not without sympathy. "Look what it has done to her! Put her down. Now. Her and the black horse."

"You have to cut it out of her," Aethiel said. "Find the bone, and carve it out."

When Aethiel spoke, Reed bared her teeth, sharp and elongated, tinged red with blood. Lyonene looked into her friend's red-ringed eyes. Slowly, she drew a small dagger from her belt.

She knew where the bone fragment was. The blackened flesh of Reed's heart scar left little doubt. The Aristene waited tensely as Lyonene moved toward Reed, cooing to her as one trying to calm a wild animal. She raised the knife.

Reed grasped her wrist and twisted it around.

"No, Reed!"

Reed pulled Lyonene close. Her sharp, elongated teeth were bared right next to Lyonene's face. Lyonene was sure that the next thing she felt would be those teeth, tearing out her throat, sinking into her cheek—but what she felt instead was Reed beginning to shudder.

She held Lyonene in her arms as she took breath after halting breath, as she fought against the influence of the prophet's bone. The sounds of her body regaining its shape were awful—joints popped and tendons snapped back to normal proportions. But eventually the hands holding on to her were once again Reed's.

"Reed?" Lyonene whispered.

"It's Ox to you," Reed replied, and Lyonene turned and threw her arms around Reed's neck.

She looked almost like herself again. The red of blood had left her eyes, and the veins had shrunk back down under her skin. Silco, too, looked mostly like the black colt she remembered. Only— "You're still taller," said Lyonene.

"I was always taller."

Lyonene glanced at the scar over her heart, still black. "How?" she asked.

"Because I control it. It does not control me," Reed replied. "Because it was I who was meant to have it, after all."

53.

ALL THAT WAS LOST

They would burn the funeral pyres upon the hillsides and the fields where the battle was fought. There were simply too many to be contained within the square. And though the forests of Atropa remained mostly unspoiled, the Aristene and acolytes went into them with saws and axes, to fell dead trees for wood.

Lyonene stood atop the Citadel steps and watched the construction—pyre upon pyre built and erected, so many that they completely obscured the green of the grass. Both Aristene and acolyte would burn together there; they'd fought as one, and so would burn the same. For Tiern and Veridian, they would burn effigies woven from vines and draped in white cloth, for there were no bodies to be recovered from the depths of the World's Gate.

A tall shadow fell across her and she didn't need to look to see who it was. She could feel the presence of the prophet's bone whenever Reed came near.

"You make a fine shade now, Ox," she said, and smiled. She had to twist her head up farther to look into Reed's face, and beyond her glimpsed movement in the dome—workers were assessing the crater Reed had made in the wall. Lyonene sighed. "Life goes on. Recovery will be swift, despite the scars that this will leave."

"They should leave it alone," Reed said.

"As a monument to your achievements?" Lyonene snorted.

"They should leave it alone," Reed said again.

After the battle with Denros and the corrupted soldiers had been won, Reed had gained control over the shard of the prophet and had returned to herself. Only not quite. When they'd found Aster on the floor beside the World's Gate, Reed had held her crying mentor in her arms, but she had wept no tears of her own. Instead, she seemed quiet. Almost numb. But perhaps that was to be expected, after all that had happened.

"Ox," she said, "you're losing your sense of humor."

Reed turned. Finally, she smiled, and placed a hand on Lyonene's shoulder. When she squeezed fondly, it hurt only a little.

Lyonene raised her fingers to the tip of Reed's blackened heart scar, barely visible above her armor. "What does it feel like?" she asked.

Reed brushed her fingers away. "Like anger. Like hate." She touched it herself, tentatively. "And like power. The goddess and the prophet are getting used to each other."

"You know, some of the acolytes are calling you 'the guardian of the order.'" Lyonene smiled wryly. "Is that what you are now? Our guardian?"

In response, Reed flexed her arms, and Lyonene gasped at the sight of her veins bulging beneath the skin.

"They could remove it," Lyonene said.

"They don't know what that might do."

"Ferreh says—"

"I don't care what Ferreh says," Reed growled, and Lyonene took a half step back.

"I'm bringing his ashes back to Glaucia today," Reed said. Down in the square, two horses stood ready, one black and one white: Silco and Hestion's stallion, Target. "Aster says I shouldn't go alone. She says they might try to kill me, in their grief."

Lyonene glanced at her. Even with the monster contained, she was still a fearsome thing. "I don't think you have to worry."

Lyonene looked out across the city. Atropa was safe. The threat of the prophet's skull had been vanquished. They had only their long immortalities now, stretched out before them in heroes and time.

"After you return from Glaucia, we should go and visit Gretchen. She might be a mother by now." Lyonene smiled. "I would like to see that. What do you think, Reed?"

Reed frowned. "Perhaps. We'll have to see what the sacred well holds." She started down the stairs, and Lyonene followed. When they reached the bottom, Lyonene went to pat Hestion's stallion.

"At first glance I thought this was Verger," she said. Target wasn't quite so large as Verger, and he didn't have the other stallion's feathered feet. But someone had groomed him to a high, almost Areion shine.

"I ordered the acolytes to bathe him and brush him until he glowed like the full moon," said Reed. She moved around Silco, checking his saddle and running her hands over his rump and legs. When he saw Lyonene, he raised his bad hoof to remind her that it was her fault, so at least the black colt was still behaving like himself.

Reed lifted the flap of one of her saddlebags. Tucked inside was a golden urn.

"What will you tell them, of how he died?" Lyonene asked. "Will you tell them the truth?"

Reed placed her hand upon the ashes. "I'll tell them as much of the truth as they can stand. And then I will give him a better story, to be remembered in their songs."

"I know you loved him, Reed. Though you may have loved the order more doesn't mean that you didn't."

"He," Reed said haltingly, "died because of me."

"He died *for* you," Lyonene corrected her. "He would have followed you past the ends of the world."

Reed's thumb brushed the urn gently, and then she slapped the saddlebag closed. "And what about the other hero of Rhonassus? What will you do now, with Alsander?"

"I'll return him through the Veil once the funerals are over. Back to Cassor." She felt the weight of Reed's eyes, but couldn't meet them. There was nothing left to do with Alsander besides let him go.

Over the backs of the horses Lyonene saw Aster coming through the square. "Your mentor comes," she said, and thought she heard Reed groan. But she greeted her with an embrace, and lowered her head to allow Aster to fuss with the long brown waves of her hair.

"All is prepared for the burnings," Aster said. "I thought we might lay flower garlands upon Veridian's effigy. Wildflowers, or something else she'd like."

"Pulled weeds," Reed said, and they smiled. "Everfall likes to eat honeysuckle. I will lay some of that before I go."

"You're leaving? Before the funerals?" Aster asked. Her face fell, but then she shook the emotion away. "I suppose it isn't really a funeral for her, anyway. She isn't dead."

Lyonene frowned. Veridian and Tiern were not dead, but they were gone. Once one traveled through the World's Gate, they were unlikely to return.

Lyonene watched Aster sadly. She thought of Everfall, wandering one of the pastures alone. She didn't understand what could have driven Veridian to leave them both here, waiting.

"Are you sure you can't stay?" Aster pressed.

Reed tied Target's reins to Silco's saddle. "He's waited long enough."

"It's only one more night. Would you wait, if I asked you, as your mentor?"

Reed paused.

"I have no need of a mentor anymore," she said.

Aster looked like she'd been struck in the face.

"Come now, Ox," Lyonene said. "You don't mean that. Everyone in the order knows that you will always run home to Aster—it's part of your charm—"

"Of course she doesn't mean it," Aster said quietly. "Those words come from the thing still lodged inside her chest. I can see it, feeding on your pain. Trying to spread through your heart until you become the same thing that it is."

"You don't know what you're talking about."

"Yes, I do." Aster grasped Reed by the arm. "And I will cut it out myself before I allow it to happen." Reed rounded on her, and Lyonene froze, but Reed simply plucked Aster's hand from her and pushed it away.

"You are welcome to try," she said. She took Silco's reins and led him and Hestion's white stallion away.

"Give her time," Lyonene said. But Aster couldn't wait. She pursued Reed through the square, shouting at her. As she caught up to them, Silco squealed and whipped his tail. Aster stopped short in shock as the black colt raised his back hoof and kicked.

"Veridian doesn't even deserve an effigy," Reed said loudly, without turning. "She was an apostate; she was not an Aristene. And she worked to unravel the order to her very last act."

"She was trying to save you!" Aster cried.

"I needed no saving."

Lyonene rushed to take Aster's arm before she could push Reed any further. She had no wish to hear what other cruel things might be said.

"Let her go, Aster; she doesn't mean it. Let her do what she has to do, and then she'll return to us."

Then she'll return to us. The words hung in the air as Reed and Silco walked away, and Lyonene shivered despite the warmth of the sun. Reed would return to them, she knew. Yet some small part of her couldn't help but try to think back, to the last time she had looked into Reed's eyes and seen her friend inside them.

Epilogue

Ferreh was watching from the shadows of the Citadel when Reed left. She saw the way that the girl's Areion struck out at their mentor. She watched as Aster and Lyonene returned slowly up the endless steps and into the hall of Aristene, where the statues of their order's legends would watch over them with eyes of stone.

Ferreh waited until Aster had gone and the initiate was alone before she stepped out of the shadows.

"Elder."

"You worry about Aster," Ferreh said, and the girl's gaze followed where the mentor had gone. "But you need not. Aster's heart has been broken many times, into many pieces, but it has never hardened. It will remain soft, and it will be there for Reed when she is ready."

"Will she ever be ready?" Lyonene asked. She looked at Ferreh with eyes that were childlike with hope, and when Ferreh didn't reply, she sighed and walked away, back down the Citadel's steps. But she would be all right. Lyonene and Aster would cleave together around the things they had lost. Yet Ferreh wondered at the fairness of it, that two of their finest Aristene should have to suffer so. Would she be wrong this time, and in the years to come, would Aster turn bitter and cruel; would she become known as Aster Ironheart? Would Lyonene give in to her disgrace and become

Lyonene the Broken? Why should two so good as them be subject to so much loss and pain?

Because they can bear it, the elder thought. *Kleia Gloria is a hard goddess but she is not cruel. She gives us only what load we can bear to carry.*

Ferreh walked down the darkened hall and through the slim stone door, down and down to the chamber of the Outfitter. Her steps were hurried in the dark, as if she were late for something. But the elder had nothing but time, and slowed her feet, lest she take a wrong step in the blackness.

The straw scattered outside the Outfitter's door was illuminated by torchlight cast through the crack beneath it, and she opened the chamber to find Gria, the ageless servant of the order who wove skills into their hands and conjured costumes onto their backs. Who cast their many illusions. She stood beside Aethiel, who bowed her head in respect at the elder's approach.

"Machianthe has gone," Gria said, her voice conveying both statement and question.

"She has," said Ferreh.

"And what will happen to her?" asked Aethiel. "Will she remain our little sister? Will she be able to control the darkness of the fragment inside her?"

"No," Ferreh replied. "Though she thinks she can, the bone of the prophet will make of her a monster that none of us can control." She walked farther inside the chamber, to the table where the body of the fallen hero lay.

She looked down upon Hestion's face. He lay on his side as her sword, the blade that was as a wordless song, was still struck straight through his chest.

"You told her he'd been burned," Aethiel said. "And she believed?"

"There was no reason for her not to. She saw him die. We gave her the ashes." But of course, Hestion hadn't been burned. The ashes Reed carried with her to Glaucia had been collected from a hearth.

Ferreh gently brushed the gold hair back from his temple. His expression had softened in death. Only one small crease remained, between his brows, one last remnant of his will, as if not even dying could keep him from giving voice to his displeasure, from being a thorn in an Aristene side. Reed had said he was headstrong and he was. He was headstrong in the way that he loved that girl, so headstrong and true of heart that Ferreh knew she could trust him with the greatest task she had ever given.

Looking at him lying there, Ferreh couldn't help but smile. He must have been unable to believe it when her sword had pierced his chest. His heart had pumped until not a drop of blood remained, refusing to acknowledge that he'd met his end. And he was right. For Hestion was a hero, and his story was only just beginning.

"I don't understand," Aethiel said. "What use is he now, dead?"

Gria cocked her head, her hands hidden in the folds of her robe. "But he is not dead."

Aethiel grunted. "He looks pretty dead to me," she said, and Ferreh smiled wider.

"I swore to Tiern that I would find a way to save Reed, and I have." She nodded to Gria. "Weave your magic, Outfitter, so that this hero may sleep."

Aethiel looked on as the Outfitter pulled her golden thread, dipping her needle again and again into Hestion's flesh. It had been Aethiel who brought the boy here in secret, and she didn't like keeping secrets from her sisters. Her lips twitched.

"Will Gria need to run that thread over your mouth?" Ferreh asked, but her tone was kind.

"I do not like to think of her suffering," Aethiel replied, which was not really an answer.

"Nor do I," said Ferreh. "But she must, for a time." She looked at the big Aristene, at her eyes of black and the black crown etched into her forehead. The crown of Fennbirn Island, which no one could remove. Strange how Kleia Gloria wove her wiles as deftly as the Outfitter with her thread. Ferreh hadn't known what purpose Aethiel would serve when she broke the rules and accepted her into the order. She had seen only a warrior queen, brightly marked by the hand of the goddess.

"I still do not understand what good this dead boy will do," Aethiel muttered.

"The shard of bone that has darkened Reed's scar will dig itself deeper to darken her heart," Ferreh said. "Machianthe will become our great protector, and our great oppressor. Our savior and our monster. And if we are to have any hope of seeing our Reed again, we will need this boy's help to bring her back."

"It is finished." Gria moved away. The air above Hestion's body glittered with gold, a shroud that covered him from head to foot, over the sword and the bloodied blade that protruded. Slowly, the gold faded and disappeared, but the Outfitter's magic had been cast. Nothing would wake the sleeping hero now. Only when the sword was pulled from his chest would Hestion again stir.

"He must be kept safe," Ferreh said. She raised her head.

"Somewhere he can be forgotten, a place outside the world of men and Aristene, so that he is beyond the reach of both. He must go someplace that time does not touch."

Aethiel looked at Hestion and nodded, like Ferreh had known she would.

"I know of a place."

Acknowledgments

Well, there you go. When I started this series I didn't know how entwined the worlds of *Champion of Fate* and *Three Dark Crowns* would get, but ooo-ee! Ferreh notes the strange ways that Kleia Gloria weaves her wiles, but I find that stories do the same thing, and that's what I love about them. They go to unexpected places. They always wind up precisely where they're meant to.

Thank you so much to all the readers who have come along into the world of the Aristene, and huge thanks to the people who have helped me bring it to life: Alexandra Cooper, hello there, editor of editors. There is no one I trust more with Fennbirn and Atropa than you. You see down to what it could be. And then you make me get it there. My former agent, Adriann Ranta Zurhellen—I suppose this is the last time I will mention you in an acknowledgments page, but I should mention you always, because your influence remains.

Thank you to the team at Quill Tree and Epic Reads: Rosemary Brosnan, Jon Howard, Allison Weintraub (hi, Allison! Congrats again on that promotion!), Michael D'Angelo (I don't even know if he's working on this one but he's awesome so who cares. Updated to add that he IS working on this one, and I am SO HAPPY), Patti Rosati, Mimi Rankin, Anna Ravenelle in publicity, David Curtis in design, and the talented artist Tomasz Majewski (another gorgeous cover; isn't she PRETTY).

Thank you to all of the wonderful folks at Folio Literary and especially my new agent, Emily van Beek, her excellent former assistant Sydney Meve, and her colleague Estelle Laure.

Shout-outs to the Seattle-Tacoma crew: Marissa Meyer, Lish McBride, Arnée Flores, Rori Shay, Margaret Owen, Nova McBee, Martha Brockenbrough, and Allison Kimble. Tara Goedjen, we miss you; come back soon.

Thank you to my pet children: Tyrion Cattister, Agent Scully, Armpit McGee, and Tom Bezos-Daytona. Absolutely zero thanks to my new baby, Wesley Wyndam-Paws, who gave me no time to work while revising. But it's okay, you're a baby. Thank you to my friend Susan Murray for making sure I eat lunch every Friday.

Thank you also to *Xena: Warrior Princess* and the Jedi Order, without whom this book may never have been born.

And thanks as usual to Dylan Zoerb, for luck.